THE SECOND *MILAGRO*

THE SECOND *MILAGRO*

Linda Rainwater

Copyright © 2006 by Linda Rainwater.

Library of Congress Number: 2005906894
ISBN :   Hardcover   1-59926-255-X
                Softcover   1-59926-254-1

All rights reserved. No part of this book may be reproduced or transmitted in any form or by any means, electronic or mechanical, including photocopying, recording, or by any information storage and retrieval system, without permission in writing from the copyright owner.

This is a work of fiction. Names, characters, places and incidents either are the product of the author's imagination or are used fictitiously, and any resemblance to any actual persons, living or dead, events, or locales is entirely coincidental.

This book was printed in the United States of America.

To order additional copies of this book, contact:
Xlibris Corporation
1-888-795-4274
www.Xlibris.com
Orders@Xlibris.com
29843

DEDICATION

To my wonderful husband, Ray,
Who has made so many things possible.

"The Second Milagro took me into the heart of Mexico and the soul of a woman on a quest for life and love. Miraculous!"

Jeanne VanDusen-Smith, author, *Sindrome*

"The plot of Linda Rainwater's novel plunges forward at breakneck speed and is matched only by the urgency and desire of her characters. A great read!"

Sue William Silverman, author, *Because I Remember Terror, Father*, *I Remember You*

"With a fresh new voice, Rainwater weaves past and present into an absorbing tale of secrets, treachery and love."

Diane Chamberlain, author, *The Bay at Midnight*.

**Out of difficulties
grow miracles.**

Jean De La Bruyere
17th C. French Philosopher

ACKNOWLEDGMENTS

Those who play with words speak of their inadequacy, but no one can deny the wonder of praise. Kudos and appreciation go to my sweet husband, Ray, my wonderful sons, Jason and Joey Thrower and their families, April, Mark and Luke, and Alicia, Benjamin and Cason, and my Rainwater family, Steve, Karen, Robin and Mark, Linda and Nelson, and Matthew.

Unequaled thanks to writer friends Ann Allman, Diane Chamberlain, Jane Drewry, Sue Silverman, and a very special Jeanne Van Dusen Smith. God's blessings on Martha Cortez and her family who taught me to love Mexico. And, a merited tribute to friends Cynthia Denham and Donna Crouch for their longtime support, and to Carolyn Walker Crowe for being my blessing.

Those who love Mexico, and especially Real de Catorce, will recognize some author's license of creating fantasy in a truly fanciful place. The story and characters are entirely of my own making, and I take responsibility for any and all mistakes of judgment.

PROLOGUE

Darkness circled Max, thicker here than there. Walls of the mine were near, he guessed. He stretched out to find them. As he moved, his head throbbed. Fighting against his sluggish, aching body, he crawled until he found the rough hewn, cold, damp rock. He slumped against it.

Tears pricked at his nose and eyes like cactus needles. He breathed deeply the rank, slick air, whispering the words he had shouted at his mother, "I'm seventeen. I'm a man, I can do this."

Thoughts of her and how he had failed unleashed the tide, and he cried in sobs and pain. As he shook off the memory of his mother and how he had left home, the image of his father filled the black void around him. Even though Tomas had been dead for a year, Max could feel the man's disapproval like a heavy arm resting on his shoulder.

Not that Tomas would have said Max was wrong to come to the mines. No, he would have told his son to go, but for a very different reason.

His father, a dark force of determination, would have stormed into the little town with an army of workers, pushing aside the wounded, the dead, and clearing the scene of the miners unfit to work. In a day's time, silver would have again flowed from the mountain, and the cave-in would be unmentionable.

Max had just wanted to help the people whose lives had been crushed by the mountain.

His father was ruthless, but saw himself as strong; his son, weak. Max wiped tears from his cheeks and his scruff of a beard with the torn sleeve of his shirt. He wasn't as soft as his dad thought. So why had he not been able to show his mother that he could handle himself? He picked up a loose stone and threw it into the hollow space that stretched out in front of him.

Voices. Low, then louder. He stood slowly, sliding his back along the jagged wall. Light blinded him, and he jerked his head to one side. The sudden movement made him dizzy.

A flash of black, thin and lightning quick, cut across the thick, shadowy air. Max thought "snake" for a moment. Then he heard a piercing snap.

The whip.

CHAPTER ONE

WASHINGTON, D.C.
September 24, 1989

It had been a Tuesday, and she was preparing dinner, the last time Patricia Morelos saw Max, her son, her only child.

Circling the butcher block island, he sneaked pepperoni slices as he questioned her about the mine that had collapsed in Mexico. For two hours they turned over the few details they knew of the cave-in.

While their words blurred in her mind, the image of Max that night was sharp, painful. At seventeen, he was slowly metamorphosing into manhood. His face was shadowed and shaped by a day-old beard which partially camouflaged a new crop of pimples. His gait was unfinished. One minute he glided on skateboard feet; the next, he stalked with the assurance of a senator. He seemed all legs and arms as he folded and tucked himself into the breakfast nook.

She picked at a salad while he dove into pizza.

"Sure you don't want any?" he mumbled, mouth half-full. A moment's lull in his interrogation of her. "So, what do you think we can do? We are going down there, aren't we, Mom?"

Like the pepperoni he was eating nonstop, Max devoured every fact, savoring it, living it. His eyes seemed to reflect the falling rocks, the crushed bodies, the anguished faces. "Well, aren't we going?" he demanded.

"Max, honey. I've told you we're sending supplies and men down. People who know how to handle these situations. Professionals."

"But they're not Moreloses! *We're* the owners. We should be the ones to go!"

"Jim is going," she half-whispered, regretting that she sounded afraid. It wasn't that. She just knew the mention of Jim Mainland's name would trigger another argument, and she was tired. Tired of Max's efforts to wear her down.

The next hour repeated the two before. The salad was wilted and warm; the pizza, cold concrete.

Max stalked the length of the kitchen, with her captive in the little nook, arguing on and on that he was a Morelos and mature for his age. He was well-traveled, fluent in Spanish. He had friends in Mexico and had been there many times.

She had laughed at his bravado, making him angry, but she had feared his foolishness, his bravery.

Finally, she cleared the table. "I'm going to bed, son. I know you feel sorry for these people and so do I. We're doing everything we can, I promise. But you're not going anywhere, and that's final."

That's all a mother needed to say. Especially to a son who was usually obedient. She didn't know when her final word had stopped being the last word, but it had.

She took her motherly stance, and he stood his ground. They fought. The next morning, he was gone. He left a note saying she was not to worry.

She had almost gone crazy with it. A week and a half and two phone calls. Then nothing.

And, now, she knew why. He had been kidnapped.

She pushed the thought away as she slipped into the chair at the head of a burl oak conference table and looked beyond the three men who flanked her. The oblong stretch of wood gave her the sensation of being on a boat where all the people had slipped to one end. It was surely sinking.

She vaguely heard a murmur of greetings and felt the questioning looks. For the moment, she let them continue with their reports.

"Eight dead, thirty-two injured. That's the last count we have in both mines. Some miners are still missing in R-5. They haven't reached that cave-in yet, but the other one's cleared. Three rescue units are still in place. They'll stay until it's over." Marco Cortina, the Director of Mining Operations for Morelos Industries, reported the latest grim news from Mexico. His voice droned on in Patricia's head like a tape played at the wrong speed.

"We'll keep doing whatever is necessary to clear those sites and help the workers," Marco continued, "but we also have the problem of a strike. All the mines are shut down now. The rest of the men walked off Friday and probably won't come back to work tomorrow." Marco rubbed the back of his neck hard as if to dislodge the burden of his rounded shoulders, slumped as if in image of the miners.

"The worst thing is that production has stopped, and, as we all know, our contracts will be in jeopardy if these crazy miners hold out. How far are you willing to go to get the Mexican mines working, Patricia?" Luis Hernandez, Director of Finances, stared at her, waiting for an answer. He tugged at his expensive jacket, beefy arms ready for a fight. He would not have had to ask her husband that question.

She looked up at the sound of her name. Everyone was staring at her. Her hand slid over the silver pendant that lay against her gray silk blouse, fingers hugging the cold metal of an intricately carved Mayan god mask. Its edges ridged her skin.

Sole owner of Morelos Enterprises since her husband Tomas's death the year before, Patricia had worked hard to gain the respect of the upper ranks of her husband's empire. It had not been easy. They saw her simply as an attractive woman, good at hosting cocktail parties and arranging displays at the Morelos Galleries. To them she was the quintessential trophy wife. At thirty-nine, eighteen years younger than Tomas, they questioned her ability to run the company.

The truth was that she had worked in the various departments of Tomas's silver business since she was a teenager and long before she became his wife. Tomas had groomed her, molded her for what he knew was her future. If only he had thought to reassure his directors along the way, her move to the helm might not have been met with so much opposition. The Mexican machismo had been especially hard to fight. Now, after resisting her lead for so many months, they were expecting her to solve all their problems single-handedly. And as effectively as Tomas.

"Patricia doesn't have to make that kind of decision this minute, Luis." Jim Mainland, Director of Operations for all of Morelos, jumped to Patricia's defense. It wasn't the first time. Jim was always there for her. He paused and looked at her, as if to see if she would say something, then went on, "Tomas told us many times that we ought to think ahead to the possibility of a cave-in. These mines are old and we haven't had time to bring them up to code."

"Tomas would not have expected us to fall all over ourselves about these lazy workers," Luis said. "He would have taken care of this in a day. And if not, he knew how to ride out downturns and profit loss. We don't have his expertise anymore, now do we? And calling us out to meet on a Sunday night in the middle of a hurricane isn't going to help either." Luis held Jim's stare, defying him to deny that truth. Muscled, rigid, all square and on edge, the hardness in Luis went bone deep. His dark, harsh face mirrored his soul.

"We are talking about men's lives, not just the bottom dollar. All you think about is money, Luis, and it is not even yours!" Marco reared off his chair as if he might lunge at the taller, heavier man. "Three weeks ago these people had a major catastrophe in their lives. It happened in the Morelos mines. We are responsible."

Patricia listened as Marco reiterated in more human terms the disaster that had befallen the little town of Real de Catorce, a mountain village north of Mexico City. News was sketchy. The number wounded and dead still not firm. Rescue efforts were hampered by the inaccessibility of the site and by the lack of communication. Now the strike jeopardized the livelihoods of the impoverished families.

It was all so horrible to think about, but as catastrophic as the cave-in was, to Patricia, it was only the beginning.

"I have worse news," she said, her voice a whisper. "That's why you're here." She had to say it twice before the others heard her words. Her hands shook as she took something from a folder. A sheet of coarse unbleached paper with wide spaces between thin blue lines torn from a child's notebook.

"This was in my mail Friday." She cleared her throat. The words came without rhythm, her eyes not on what she read. "*Su hijo es raptur. No policia. Espara para instrucciones.*"

"*Mi Dios*! Max? Max has been kidnapped?" Marco cried.

"Your son? In Mexico? What the hell was he doing down there?" Luis had no love for Tomas's "spoiled brat."

"Why didn't you tell us?" Marco asked gently.

The questions came at her like buckshot. She retreated behind the wall of her thoughts. In the distance, Jim Mainland intercepted, answering for her.

She let him.

She didn't give a damn what any of them thought about Jim taking over. Right now she needed him, and he was there. She didn't give a damn about Morelos Enterprises or the silver, or the contracts. She cared about the people, hurt and dying. But now, at this moment, all she could concentrate on was Max. She had lived a lifetime in the past three days. Fifty-five hours had dragged by since the news first came.

Su hijo es raptur.

YOUR SON HAS BEEN KIDNAPPED.

The spinning roar of those words had hollowed out her mind, her body and soul, until she was no more than a rigid shell.

"Have you called the police? The FBI?" Marco asked.

"We talked to the police and the FBI Friday and again yesterday," Jim said. "They—," he glanced at Patricia, "They'll do what they can. Bad timing, one of them said."

Hurricane Hugo had just slammed into the coast of South Carolina three days earlier and the death toll was still rising. No one wanted any more problems to deal with.

"Anyway, we'll probably get Max out of there before they can write a memo." He smiled. When no one commented, he went on. "We don't want the press in on this. Max's life could be in more trouble if these people get ticked off. It has to be handled carefully. We've received no ransom demand or instructions, but we know the note came from Real. It's got to be about the mines. If we can get this strike settled, Max'll be okay. In the meantime, I've hired some of the best men in Mexico to comb the mountains and get to Max whatever way they can. Pronto. I don't care if that little mountain town's closed up like a tamale. There's no way anyone would dare hurt Tomas's kid," Jim nodded, as if at an unarguable fact. "Too many people down there owe their lives or at least their living to Morelos Enterprises. And frankly, some of them already lived to regret going against Tomas. They remember. Max'll be okay. Trust me. Nothing else to do at this point. Until we hear something, it's a Mexican standoff. I'll be going down tomorrow if the plane's okay. The winds are finally dying down."

So, Patricia thought, she would wait again. On the far wall a clock made of silver coin-sized ovals encased in dark wood marked the hours. One of two silver lines jerked forward. Then jerked again. Almost nine o'clock, three hours until tomorrow. The torments increased with each tick of the clock, but the stretch of time was perhaps the least painful. Relentless though it was, time had an order to it. No surprises. Just sixty more minutes. Twenty-four more hours. Another day.

Words were a far worse torture, and that's all she'd had. Simpering, condescending words from bureaucrats and high paid lawyers. She didn't want to hear anymore. She wanted results. Wanted to wrap her arms around her son. Listen to his loud music until her ears hurt. Tousle his hair the way he hated for her to do. Hear him say, "Aw, Mom."

The sound of his voice echoed in her mind, and she shuddered.

She tried to focus on what she should do. There had to be something. She had called the police when the note came from the kidnappers. When she finally got to talk to someone, he had called Max a runaway. Maybe he sent the note himself, he suggested. The kid was probably bumming on some Mexican beach and going to hit her up for a few bucks in a day or two. Right then, he had to go take some more calls. The hurricane, you know. The man from the FBI was all bureaucracy and no compassion. He'd not returned her calls.

Her teeth clinched until her jaw ached. Her pulse at her temples seemed to beat out the words: To hell with all of them!

She stretched her legs and arms. Something inside her stirred, wanting to move, to act. To do what? She was not Tomas. She knew it was not possible for her ever to be the powerful person he was. She wouldn't want to be. Flashes of what she had thought of as cruelties committed by Tomas made her sick. No way she could fire people for petty reasons, or manipulate land purchases, or break promises for personal gain. She had learned more than she wanted to over the years of Tomas's "powerful" ways.

She was weak in comparison to her husband, but this was her son. Max. Her precious child. Her sweet seventeen year old. Her hard-headed brat who had disobeyed her. Her independent, caring, almost man, child who thought he could do anything. She had to do something.

Then she knew.

She should be in Mexico looking for Max, not sitting in the Morelos Silver Enterprises board room, hashing out the effect of Max's kidnapping on the strike. She cared about the people who were hurt and the business, but not while the fate of her son hung in the balance.

Her fingers curled around the necklace. A present from Max. His first attempt at silver designing, something Tomas had taught him. She thought of her child's long slender fingers preparing the silver mold and rubbed the god mask again. Her finger traced the face. A nail ringed the wide, hollow eyes. Were they bulging to take in the horror of a human sacrifice? She lingered on the gaping mouth. Open as if in a silent scream.

CHAPTER TWO

"Besides getting your son out of trouble, we still have this problem about our contracts, Patricia. What are you going to do about them?" Luis Hernandez spoke without taking his eyes off the silver pendant, admiring it with open, greedy eyes.

"Luis, you insensitive bastard. Can't you forget the bottom line for once?" Jim hit his fist against the hard oak table. "Sorry, Patricia," he added, his face red below thick sandy hair. His eyes blazed like blue flame as he reached for the phone.

Jim, her staunchest supporter. He had moved easily from Tomas's right-hand man to her advisor. The token Caucasian on the Board, he liked to say, since all the other members had Hispanic ties. Patricia had been accused of promoting him to a director's position for this reason. Some even speculated, not too discretely, that his youth and blond good looks were a welcome change for her after Tomas. For that reason or some other one, Jim was not well liked by the others. He was a little rough, but he was faithful to the Moreloses.

Luis squinted his coal dark eyes. "I'll bet if we melted that gaudy necklace down, we could have several day's worth of silver to buy us time on our contracts. I think it's in the best interests of the company—"

"A week of mining is not the problem, Señor Luis." Cortina nodded toward Patricia.

"How much should I put in the debit column to cover that thing, Patricia?" Luis made a circle with his index finger and thumb and peered through them as if assessing a diamond through a loop. "Five thousand, ten, fifteen?"

She clutched the pendant tighter, as if to hide it. *Damn you, Luis,* Patricia thought. She wanted to tell him to get out, to fire him. Before she could say anything, Jim slammed down the telephone and told Luis to shut up.

"We are not here to discuss a piece of jewelry," Jim said and pinned Hernandez and Cortina in their chairs with his stare. "You're in charge of those damn miners in Catorce, Marco. Do you think they're in on the kidnapping? What do they want?"

"They will have many demands. It is always hard to get to the leaders in a strike." Cortina tilted his head. "Señora, you know how it is. I am sorry about Max. Maybe tomorrow—"

"It's always *mañana* to you, 'Marco Polo', ain't it?" Jim shouted.

"You go there, Señor," Marco's voice rose steadily as he spoke. "You will accomplish nothing. Maybe you spend your time with the señoritas again? Or maybe you will not see the miners because you would be scared they eat you alive. Maybe you taste like iguana, or *pollo*." He threw his head back and laughed.

Patricia jumped at the sound. Jim was glaring at Marco, as if ready to pounce on prey. She was letting Jim fight her battle alone.

Struggling against the deep hole that was swallowing her, she threw words out like lifelines. "The mines. The workers. We have to settle with them." She stared at Luis, then, Marco. Didn't they know that the only important thing was Max? If they made the miners happy, Max would be released. She was sure of it. Who else would have taken him? She shoved her chair away from the table, braced her arms against it, and pushed herself up. "Don't any of you understand? We have to give those people whatever they want. I don't care what. The silver! The sun! The mines themselves! Just give it to them! Now!"

The sound of her words bounced off the walls. She tried to compose herself. Strands of chestnut hair had slipped from the silver clasp at the nape of her neck. She brushed them back.

"I'm going to Mexico myself." She straightened her shoulders and looked around the room, daring anyone to argue.

No one said anything. Jim stood and walked around the table to her. "We have to talk," he said. She turned her back on him, ignored the voices behind her and stared out the window down the lights of a wet and blustery Pennsylvania Avenue toward the nation's Capitol, glowing in the distance.

The small statue of Liberty atop the dome was barely visible. Something prophetic, she thought, about a woman over-looking the country's lawmakers. Something ironic about Liberty being a woman. With all the wealth and power she had, she was far from being free. Her husband's death had fettered her with responsibility, obligation, and now, danger for their child.

Jim gripped her elbow. He steered her toward the door. "We may as well go home. All of us. Get some sleep. We'll meet again tomorrow when we have some news."

She tried to pull away. "I wasn't ready to close the meeting, Jim. I had—"

"It's late and you need rest." He put his arm around her shoulder, and she let him lead her to the elevator.

She hardly noticed as they moved through the garage and into his limo. For three days she had been locked in a dark hell that had caved in around her. Now she wanted to claw her way out and didn't know where to begin. She might bury herself deeper, but she'd have to take that chance. She didn't resist when Jim took her into his arms, but settled into their warm familiarity. When he shifted her away, she thought they were still in front of the office until she looked past him and saw her house. She had missed the drive down Massachusetts and out to Spring Hill.

"You can go, Jim. I'll be okay," she said at the door. He pushed past her into the living room. She followed him.

He told her she wasn't going to Mexico. It was dangerous, he said. The miners had no love for a Morelos. She wouldn't be safe. He promised that he would leave that night, if possible, and fly to Mexico City to see what else he could learn. He would see her as soon as he returned. She heard only the sounds of his words as she gazed out the window. The rain darkened the shadows outside.

She didn't hear the door open and close. Feeling a presence in the room, she turned to say something to Jim, but standing quietly in the doorway was Rachel Davis, her longtime friend, come to stay for the duration.

Before Patricia could move, Rachel had joined her in front of the window.

"Watching it rain?" Rachel asked.

"Yeh, seems to be letting up," Patricia replied. Her shoulders relaxed a little, making her realize how tense she was.

"Did I miss anything?" Rachel was all ready for bed, dressed in soft, comfy gown and housecoat, her hair pulled back with a headband. Obviously, she had been at her nightly regime of face cleansing.

"Just bossy Jim seeing me home," Patricia answered.

"That man's out for more than he deserves. We need to watch him like a hawk."

"I know. You tell me that every day," Patricia retorted, and smiled, easing more tension. How good it felt to spar with her old friend. Rachel's watching Jim was a two sided joke. A car accident when she was fourteen had left Rachel blind, but she "saw" more than Patricia knew.

"Want some tea?" Patricia asked, and pushed an intercom button. After she had asked Josephina, her housekeeper, to bring them some tea and some kind of sandwiches, she went upstairs to put on her own nightclothes. When she returned, she and Rachel settled onto the sofa. The two looked like opposites, from Rachel's homey outfit to Patricia's silk peignoir, Rachel's pale hair and eyes to Patricia's darker features.

"How's Annie?" Patricia asked.

"The university's making them stay put until the storm's over. Works for me. She's safe and I don't have to tell her about Max. She'll go berserk, you know."

"No, she's pretty level-headed."

"Are we talking about the same girl? My Annie? She loves Max almost as much as I do. All she'll be is talk though. She's not one for action."

"Guess we better keep it to ourselves, for now then," Patricia said softly.

Quiet settled around the two women. Rachel patted Patricia's hand in a grandmotherly way. Patricia let herself be silently consoled by years of friendship. The two of them had met when they were just fifteen and had bonded immediately. Except for a brief period in their teens they had been inseparable companions. Patricia felt that the best thing life had given her, other than Max, was her devoted friend. A pain in the butt sometimes, Rachel was always there for her. She had tried to be there for Rachel, but despite her blindness, Rachel usually seemed to need less help than Patricia.

Rachel had never liked Tomas, didn't like Jim, either. Patricia was always making bad choices to hear Rachel tell it. Besides Patricia herself, the one thing in Patricia's life that Rachel did love was Max. She felt as devastated by his disappearance as a mother would. Her own daughter Annie and her husband, Roger, were more than Rachel had ever asked for, but she had a special soft spot for Max.

When Josephina had brought tea and sandwiches and quietly left, Rachel broke the silence. "He's okay. You'll see. The kid's always been able to take pretty damn good care of himself."

When Patricia said nothing, Rachel laughed. "Hey, did you show Luis the pendant yet? I'd like to see the look on his face when you tell him Max made it, not Raul. Nothing like messing up ole Luis's mind with a new Morelos designer." Her short laugh fell silent.

Patricia's fingers closed around the pendant hanging from her neck as if protecting it from scrutiny. She had not been able to take it off in days.

After a few minutes of listening to the rain beat against the windows, Rachel tried again. "No word from the police?"

Finally, Patricia began to talk. "Jim has been calling them regularly, but they still think Max is just a runaway. They're not going to do anything. Too much else on their minds, I guess. They won't even listen to me. And who could blame them?" Patricia practically jumped from the couch and strode across the room. "He IS a runaway. A delinquent. A smart-assed brat who's gotten himself in trouble!" She turned her head away and her shoulders shook as if she were throwing off some coat or sweater that had grown heavy.

Rachel stood, zeroed in on Patricia, then embraced her. "He's also ungrateful and inconsiderate," she said. "And when he comes trudging home, dirty, spent and apologetic, you can ground him until he starts drawing Social Security."

Patricia's tears were too close to the surface. She slumped back onto the couch, pressing her fists into her stomach. "Crazy kid. Why couldn't he listen to me? What did he think he could do down there? He's just a child." Her voice broke, her eyes ached. "Surely they won't hurt him."

Through her sobs she heard Rachel sit back down. Her friend would wait until the tears were gone. Longer ago than either remembered they had made a pact never to encourage bouts of self-pity. Rachel's blindness was like some secret power that she protected, and Patricia guarded every sorrow in her life with the same fierceness.

When all the sobs were quieted, Patricia laid her head in Rachel's lap and fell asleep.

CHAPTER THREE

September 25

Patricia wandered through her empty house. Josephina had taken Rachel home. She only lived a mile away and would be back before she was needed. The telephone sat as a silent effigy to Patricia's misery.

She watched television for a while, but the miseries caused by the hurricane increased her own.

In the late afternoon rain shadowed the windows like a veil. The air smelled musty. She refused all calls unless it was Jim. He had not called. The clock on the mantle ticked.

She balanced on the edge of a Queen Anne chair and leaned toward the cold grates of her library fireplace. She had forced herself to dress in simple slacks and blouse, her long hair pulled up and clamped high on her head. She drew the line at makeup. What did she care.

She studied the deeply carved black marble surrounding soot covered firebricks and brass andirons. When she searched the shadows, a dark hole stretched before her. She could see Max's face in the blackness. A sudden draft forced acrid fumes down the chimney. She clutched her shaking arms and shivered.

Was Max shackled to some chain in the depths of a Mexican mountain, hungry and thirsty? Why had they taken him? She should be the one imprisoned. If anyone was responsible, she was. Certainly not Max.

Tears blurred the fire-charred bricks. Her shoulders sagged as if they were holding up the beams of the darkened hole where she envisioned Max. Her body buckled and trembled in a rush of sobs.

Her pain seemed more acute as the day wore on, and she waited impatiently for news.

Eventually, Josephina returned with stories of trees down and damaged roofs. She babbled on about how lucky they were. Patricia tried to agree. Josephina prepared a dinner Patricia couldn't eat. Rachel called and Annie was home for the evening, so she would see her tomorrow. Patricia was glad to be alone. She had to figure out what she would do if Jim wasn't successful.

Late in the night, a bell chimed, then the front door opened with a blast of wind against the wall.

Jim was back. Patricia had been lying on the couch, but she met him halfway across the room.

"What did you learn?" she asked, her fingers against her lips. She tried to read his thoughts.

He shook rain from his hair, like an overgrown puppy, then put a hand to his scruffy, sandy beard as if extracting an answer from it.

"That's the craziest damn bunch of locos down there. Nobody knows nothing." He stood with his back to the cold fireplace, hands behind him.

"What do you mean? Max?" She whispered his name.

Jim moved to face her and then put his arms around her tightly. She held her breath, afraid of his words. He whispered in her ear, "As far as I could learn, the little shit's alive."

She pushed him back and smiled. "You're sure?"

"That's what they say."

She threw her arms around him and held on. "Oh, Max," she cried against Jim's shoulder. When she finally released him, Jim turned and struck the mantle, shaking Chinese vases and picture frames.

"I can't wait to get ahold of that kid. I'll dust his britches, if it's the last thing I do." Jim's face had become stern and hard. He paced the room.

"Worry you like this. He deserves a beating, you ask me." He stopped midstep, his words hanging in the air as his face reddened from his thin blond hair through to his beard. "Aw, shit. You know what I mean. He's okay. Sure he is. Those people got better sense than to hurt him. Why, you know how he always falls on his feet. Remember when—" He was reaching for her, but she walked away.

"Who were you able to see?" Her voice was stronger. Suddenly, Jim's irreverence for Max's plight unnerved her. She crossed her arms, as if they could prop her up. Just hearing Max was alive gave her strength, but she wasn't sure she could stand to hear what else Jim might say. She stopped in front of a collection of crystal decanters and half made a motion to Jim to help himself.

"Everybody. Nobody. Seems the miners that escaped the cave-in were the first ones causing the ruckus. With eight of their buddies buried in the mine, they refused to go back in. They're the ones called the strike. I talked to some of them and they swore they had nothing to do with Max's disappearance. Claim it was a bunch of renegades that's always causing trouble. No accounts that want to take back the mines for themselves. They think the silver in it belongs to them, not to the *crillos* or *gringos*. Never mind not one of them has a peso to his name to operate the mines. That don't seem to occur to them."

He poured himself a tall drink and asked if she wanted one. She shook her head.

"Did you get to talk to any of the, the renegades?"

"Hell, no. They don't talk to nobody. I don't think they even know what they want, or they'd be talking their heads off. I couldn't get near Real. They got the place cut off."

"Who did you see in Mexico City?"

"Officials, unofficials. You know how they are. Always putting on a front. But with the peso taking a dive like a crooked boxer, all they're really interested in is the dollar and getting bailed out. Now if you want to spend a couple zillion dollars to fatten some pockets, they'll have the kid out of those hills in a limo before you can say corruption. That's my take on it." Shaking his head, he rummaged through his beard.

"That would be fine if I knew who to give the money to," she countered. "And to find that out, I'm going to Mexico myself."

Jim shot up from the couch. He had looked tired a moment before, but now determination stiffened every muscle. "Patricia, be reasonable. There's no one you can get to that I haven't already seen. It's not safe. You know it."

She stared at him defiantly. "Tomorrow, Jim. I want to go tomorrow. I won't wait any longer. You understand?"

He paced the room, refilled his drink and argued each point over and over again. She stood her ground.

Finally, he asked with resignation, "Is there something you have in mind that I haven't thought of?"

He handed her a small glass of brandy as if a peace offering. She downed half of it, then said hesitantly, "There is one possibility. What about Miguel Ramirez?"

"Ramirez? You mean Tomas's brother?" He drew his lips in, making beard and moustache one, a face he often made.

"Step-brother. Doesn't he have something to do with the Labor Department?" She concentrated her thoughts on sipping the brandy slowly, trying to quiet her heart that had begun a marathon at the sound of Miguel's name.

"Well, the answer to that is yes and no. I gather he's kind of a renegade. Always out for the poor and against the wealthy. His title is Deputy Interior Minister. But who the hell knows what that means in Mexico? I gather he makes whatever he wants to his business. The government has to deal with him when there's a strike, but they'd rather not. Probably cause most of them are rich. He's a Mexican Robin Hood. Probably the reason Tomas hated him so much."

"You didn't try to contact him when you were in Mexico?"

"No. I recall someone said he was in Real. Don't know what help he'd be, anyway. Considering how he and Tomas wasn't on the best of terms, I don't figure he'd care one way or the other about his nephew. Besides, he'd be on the miners side for sure. He's been working for labor in one way or another since Echeverria was President."

So Miguel hadn't changed. When she had met him eighteen years ago, he'd been kicked out of the University of Mexico for taking part in student demonstrations. He and Tomas were at opposite extremes in their ideologies. Miguel idealized the populist President Lopez Mateos because Mateos had put his father in charge of the land distribution to the poor. Tomas was a friend of his successor Diaz Ordaz who sent troops against the poor, the middle class, intellectuals and students. The two argued long hours over politics. But Jim was wrong about that being why they hated each other.

"I don't think it would be a good idea to involve Tomas's brother. Right?" Jim asked. "I don't like working with someone that's already fighting for the other side. Cuts your odds that way."

Patricia picked up a silver frame from the mantle and rubbed her finger across a picture of Max and her. Graduation Day. He was in his cap and gown, trying to look serious, but laughter rode in the dimple creasing his right cheek, giving away the little boy in costume. His arm draped down over her shoulder. His height he inherited from her family, but his black hair and eyes contrasted to her auburn hair and green-brown eyes. How could he look so little like her and be part of her soul?

She looked back at the fireplace, into the long mysterious tunnel that seemed to begin there. Not the one Max might be in, but one for her. If she took one step in the direction her mind was running, her world could change forever. What if it was the only way to get Max back? Without him, nothing else mattered.

She took a deep breath, turned and went to an antique secretary against a far wall. She took some paper from a drawer and handed it to Jim over his shoulder.

"Thanks for going down there. Now, if you don't mind, I want a list. Everybody you talked to and anyone else that needs to be questioned."

"Got it right here. Figured you might want to know." He took a folded paper from his coat pocket and handed it to her. A nod was all she could manage.

Jim pulled her down on the sofa beside him. The liquor had relaxed and warmed her. She smelled his cologne.

His fingers touched her cheek. She jumped. Had she almost been asleep?

"Come on," he whispered. "Finish your drink, then off to bed."

Yes, she needed to rest, for her trip. She needed her strength to find Max. After she slept, she'd go and bring him home. Jim led her up the stairs. She felt weighted, as if her clothes were soaked, her feet too heavy to lift from one stair to the next. In her room, Jim unbuttoned her blouse and unzipped her skirt. She sat on the bed in her slip and bra, and slid her feet beneath the sheets. She felt his hand brush against her breast and heard the plastic catch of her bra snap loose.

"You'll be more comfortable without this," he said as he slid her bra free. He kissed her neck, unclasped her hair and fanned it across the pillow.

His voice came from the rain. The sound and his touch soothed her. She didn't want him to leave. Clinging to him, her arms locked, she buried her head in his chest.

"Shh," he shushed her silence, pushed her down on the pillow, saying, "Sleep."

She thought she heard the door close, then nothing. The silence shifted and she heard Max call her.

A damp, black wall enshrouded her. She could not move, could not reach out for her son. She was blind. Or was she only blindfolded?

Sound existed. Inside her tomb, life emerged at all levels. Tiny inching feelers swished, testing the air. Bold, tougher appendages scraped, scratched. Whispers floated in and out. Or were they loud voices flowing through a long tube?

"Max?" she called.

Behind the dark, inside her imagination, she saw Tomas carrying Max. His lanky legs draped over her husband's arms, almost dragging the floor. What was he now? At least three inches taller than she? They had stopped marking his height when he turned fifteen.

"Come here, son," Tomas had said, a thick pen held high between his fingers. He pointed at the inside of the hall closet door. Lines and dates recorded the years in a rainbow of colors. So, too, did the handwriting. Block letters, shaky cursive, bold, firm inscriptions. Hieroglyphic history of Max's changing personality as well as his stature.

Max focused on the line that marked his fourteenth year.

"That's for kids," he had said and turned to walk away.

Tomas caught him by the arm and shoved him against the door, held his head still, and sliced the marker across the wood just above the thick black hair.

Max had said nothing. The next day, he painted the door.

Tomas was not angry. He had really hoped for more. He wanted tenacity, ruthlessness, defiance from his son. What he called, "backbone." Max had just wanted to be taller and didn't want to be reminded that he wasn't getting there.

Now he is seventeen, she thought. Much taller and time to grow more. Maybe.

She drifted in and out of dreams and sleep. Someone else was carrying Max, then two men were dragging him. His legs were broken, bloody, useless. A metallic smell seeped through her nostrils. The taste of blood was on her lips. She cried and cried. No tears wet her cheeks.

Max had wanted to stand on his own two feet. He had said that. He wanted her to let him grow up. But she had let him. Hadn't she been the one to help him take his first steps? *Come on, Maxie, you can do it. Hold on. Mommy's got you.*

She had not meant to hold him back.

She struggled against her shroud. Slowly it unwound. She tossed the bedcovers aside and opened her eyes to the dark of her bedroom. Jim was gone. She stood up, reeling. Like a drunk. Like someone drugged.

She stumbled to the bathroom and threw up.

CHAPTER FOUR

September 26

Patricia was up and dressed in her most comfortable traveling suit before dawn. The effects of the sleeping pill Jim had slipped into her brandy had been drowned in a pot of coffee.

"Damn him," she muttered. "Damn him." Her hand struck the mantle. How typically "male," she thought. Just because he'd been Tomas's best friend didn't give Jim the right to boss her around. Of course, he'd argue that he was just trying to keep her home and safe, but he was taking over her life. Last night he had gone one step too far.

She'd given him the proverbial inch, so she guessed it was her fault that he wanted it all. She *had* needed him to go to Mexico. And it had felt good to let him hold her. For a moment. Her anger began to fade. She was to blame, not Jim. She knew he cared and was probably trying to protect her as usual, but she was letting him manipulate her. That had to stop. She had made her own decisions for many years. Before Tomas. And after.

Since Max had been gone, she had wallowed in grief. She had to snap out of it. Time for control, over the others, over herself. She was all Max had.

When dawn highlighted the windows, she made some calls, packed a suitcase and drove through empty streets to her office. The soft glow of morning promised sunshine.

A guard let her into the building. Several fortunes in silver were displayed in the Morelos Galleries on the main floor of their headquarters. A number of guards were on duty around the clock.

How useless they are, she thought. Why couldn't they have been protecting Max instead of some pieces of shiny metal? She stared so hard at the man as she waited for the elevator that he turned away.

When she reached the ninth floor where her office was, she combed every secretary's desk and opened every office door just in case someone had left a ransom note. It didn't necessarily have to come in the mail, did it?

Finally, in her own office, when she was sure there was nothing to find, she put coffee on and paced the floor while it brewed. Overflowing a mug, she ignored the spill and slumped into the chair behind her desk. The old green leather swivel groaned even under her slight weight. She propped her elbows on the silver edged, tooled leather desk, and studied her surroundings as if she had never seen them.

Everything in the room was massive, masculine, trimmed and bought with the ore that had made Tomas Morelos rich. She had no intentions of remodeling it. She liked the power and wealth that exuded throughout the room from the silver doorknob to the jade Olmec gods in the glass case. It was where Tomas had run his empire and where she had tried to carry on his wishes. The strength of the room invaded her, steeled her. From now on, it had to be her wishes.

As she drained the cup of coffee, she picked up an oval frame from the desk and gazed at a photograph of herself and Tomas. She felt the silkiness of the Dior gown and the weight of the jade necklace she'd worn that evening of her thirty-sixth birthday three years ago. With her dark hair swept high, she looked taller than her five-five height. She stared at her late husband. Tomas had not been a handsome man. Swarthy skin, insignificant moustache, dark, boring eyes. She had not married him for his looks or for love. And not even, as most thought, for his money. He had known the real reason, and somehow, she didn't think he had ever regretted his decision.

The figures blurred as her eyes filled. She had never loved him. Even after all the years. Maybe if she'd given him more, he'd have been happier and lived longer. A deep breath trembled in her throat. She brushed the back of her hand hard against her cheek. God, she *needed* him. Max needed him. Damn him for leaving them! Nothing was right. All the years amounted to nothing. She slammed the photograph face down onto the leather.

Another picture remained on the desk. A face etched into her heart. Dark haired man-child, cocky-tilted head, saucy mouth, twinkling eyes. Max. She lifted the frame and pressed it to her chest. Her sobs heaved against the cold silver weight as if it were a mountain of stone.

She would go to Real de Catorce. Wherever the hell the place is, she thought. Somewhere in the Sierra Madres. Couldn't be too hard to find. Not if Max had found it. Not with his sense of direction. Or lack of it. A crooked smile let in the taste of tears.

First, she had to go to Mexico City. People there owed Tomas. Officials. Businessmen. She knew better than Jim how business was done in Mexico. The network of childhood friends who pulled, pushed and tagged along through school and life until the one chosen leader carried the rest with him to the top. Tomas had friends among these. They would help her.

Jim had met with some of them. She picked up the list he had given her. She would start there. Where Jim had struck out, she would make them listen. After all, she owned the mines. The miners worked for her. And Max. If she had to give up everything, she would. No one else could make that decision.

If Tomas's friends didn't help, she would do what would have been unthinkable before Max was kidnapped. She had thought about it for days. Agonized over her decision. She knew her world, Max's world, could change forever. It might be the only way to get her son back. Without him, nothing else mattered.

For the first time since Max left, she felt light, mobile, alive, as if she had lifted the heavy stone that crushed her. She would find her son. And she would bring him home.

No matter the cost. No matter what she had to do. Who she had to bargain with. Even if it meant dealing with the devil himself.

Still clutching the frame with one hand, she picked up Jim's list of names. In bold black letters she added MIGUEL RAMIREZ.

Yes. Even if it meant the devil himself.

CHAPTER FIVE

Patricia heard a rap on the private door to her office. She ran to it, jerking it open. "What? Oh, it's you," she sighed and waited for Rachel to walk past her into the room.

"I'd be offended, except you have reason to be disappointed. It is only me, and I have no news. Except that it has finally quit raining, but I guess you knew that."

With her usual casualness Rachel went straight to a hand carved mahogany chair, fit for an Aztec princess. Her tall slight figure, frosted hair and green eyes belied the part. She was impeccably dressed as always—from her silk blouse tucked into the slim Halston skirt to her hair neatly combed in a cap of soft curls. Picture perfect in her dark imperfect world.

Patricia didn't trust herself to speak. She sat down and placed the frame with Max's picture on her desk.

As silver settled against leather, Rachel turned toward the sound. "He's okay, Patricia. Didn't Jim tell you he was?"

"Like you believe anything Jim says," Patricia reminded her. "Want some tea?" She stepped quickly to the kitchen alcove where she tried to compose herself amid the sounds of clattering china and silver tea cozy. When she was ready, she placed a half-filled cup in Rachel's hands.

"Thanks. Now I can be civil," Rachel said, sipping the hot tea. She smiled and a dimple scooped her left cheek.

"How did you know I was here?" Patricia sat behind her desk and watched her friend. She knew Rachel was up to something.

"Where else would you be if you're not home? I went to the house and Josephina said you left before she got up. When I called here, the receptionist said you weren't coming in today. Seems that's what Jim told her. Naturally, like you said, I didn't believe it. So, I got Stevens to bring me to your private door. Want to tell me what's going on?"

Rachel's delicate eyebrows raised. As often was the case, Patricia felt a probing look emanate from those lifeless eyes even before the question came.

"Let's just say, Jim made a shot at keeping me from going to Mexico."

Rachel shifted to the edge of her chair as if to challenge Patricia.

"Don't look at me like that. I am going. And let's forget about Jim's little tricks and find out what you have working up *your* sleeve. If you're here to talk me out of it, you don't have long, and you're just going to waste your energy." Pulling papers from a drawer, she organized them into her briefcase.

"So, you're going to Mexico."

"What else can we do, Rache?" Patricia's voice cracked. "Oh, I'd just like to shake him," she said, trying to compose herself.

"Oh, it's 'we' now. Since when are you going to let me have a say in bringing up Max? I've been wanting to turn that kid over my knee and spank the goodness out of him for years. And I do mean 'goodness'. Patricia, Max is a saint compared to most kids. Annie, for instance. I couldn't love my kid more, but I just wish she cared a fifth what Max does about people. It's not his fault. He didn't run away. He told you where he was going. He just wanted to help those people."

"And look how they thanked him. This is the fifth day, Rache. I have to do something. If the law can't do anything, I can, me and the almighty U. S. dollar. I have a list of people to see and if I have to camp on every doorstep and grease the palm of every official in the Mexican government, then I'll do it." She fingered several stacks of $100 bills. "And you may as well save your breath about *whom* I see." The unspoken name of Miguel Ramirez hung in the air like a spider on a thread. She snapped the briefcase shut. "Well?"

Rachel uncrossed her long slim legs and stood up. Her eyes seemed to look through Patricia and out the window. The two women leaned across the desk and sparred silently.

"Well, what time do we leave?" Rachel asked, cheeks soft, undimpled, no hint of a smile.

"Thanks for the offer, Rache, but you have a daughter who needs you at home." She picked up her briefcase, walked around the desk and put a hand on her friend's shoulder.

Rachel shrugged it off. "And you have a son in Mexico who might need us both. I speak better Spanish than you, remember? Besides," Rachel bit at her lower lip, "Annie went back to the university today. State of emergency is over."

"And she'll be calling you about some other crisis before the week's out."

"She can call Roger this time. It won't hurt him to take on a crisis for a change.

Patricia turned away. "I have everything ready. I'm packed. I don't have time to wait for you, Rache. I'm sorry."

Rachel came around the chair and walked to the door she had come through shortly before. She opened it, picked up a tapestry bag which sat against the wall, and held the door for Patricia. She smiled. "I'm ready, too."

*   *   *

Jim Mainland opened the door to Patricia's office, stepped inside and shut the door. It was already nine o'clock. There had been no reason to hurry in this morning. Patricia would sleep most of the day. His eyes scanned the room, lingered just a second longer than usual on the best pieces of jade, the shiniest gold. He strolled the length of the room to the desk, trailed his fingers along the cool silver edges, and eased into the cracked leather chair. The desk and chair, the room, were built for a man, not a woman. Even down to the ornate eighteenth century silver tea service which needed a man's strength to lift. He leaned back in the chair, his six-four frame feeling uncomfortable in the deep impressions left over the years by Tomas's short, stocky body.

When everything is over, the chair is the only thing I'll get rid of, he thought. Everything else he would keep just as Tomas left it. His gaze fell on the picture of Tomas and Patricia. What an odd mix. A little ugly old man and his beautiful young wife. Her green dress curved at all the right places. That face would turn any man on—high cheek bones, slender nose, dark eyes, full red lips. The shiny hair was pinned up, sexy and proper at the same time. He remembered the feel of the soft strands he had spread out onto the pillow the night before. Yes, his old friend had had good taste. Soon he would take Tomas's place as Patricia's husband. They would be good together. He smiled, then frowned at the photo of Max.

He reached for the phone, punched some buttons and asked his secretary if there had been any calls from Mexico. None. Maybe that was good. No news, good news. Of course, no one really believed that. The boy wouldn't be hurt, he would see to that. And when he got Max home, Patricia would be one grateful mom. She would know by then how much he wanted her.

In the meantime, he needed to keep Patricia safe and out of the way. He'd convinced her to let him deal with the police and FBI. The hurricane had been a help in getting a slow response from the authorities. As long as he had them listening to him, things would be okay. He couldn't take a chance on her raising enough hell that the Feds changed their view and got involved. Heaven forbid she talked to the press. Or went off half-cocked to Mexico. He just needed time and everything would be all right.

The door opened with a pop.

"Well, while the cat's away . . ." Luis Hernandez stood in the doorway, a crooked grin shifting his trim beard to one side.

"What do *you* want?"

"Relax, Mainland. Your secret's safe with me."

A shot of freon coursed through Jim's veins. He smiled, waited.

Luis pirouetted a tight turn taking in the room. "Can't blame you. It's quite a showplace. Of course, I'd be more interested if the catch of the day was young Max, not his bitch mother." He laughed, sat down in the high-back mahogany chair.

Jim felt a mixture of relief and disgust. Correction, he thought, Tomas's chair wouldn't be the first thing to go.

"And, I guess I might need to spank the kid a little for causing us so much trouble. I guess when you get to be step-pa you'll take care of that, won't you, Señor Mainland?"

"Luis, you're a disgusting little prick."

"And you're a disgusting grande one? Is that what the Señora likes?"

Jim slammed the chair back against the wall, shaking the windows. Before he breathed again he was on the other side of the desk hauling Luis out of the chair like a fork lift.

"If you have anything to say about the profit and loss of this company, spit it out, Luis. Otherwise, don't open your fuckin' mouth again."

Luis struggled to free himself from the fist that gathered his tie and shirt into a noose. All his pumped up muscles didn't make him a match for Jim. "Loss. Your loss. Thought you'd—want to know—Patricia's gone."

Jim relaxed his hand. "What do you mean, gone?"

Luis shook himself out of Jim's grasp, straightened his tie and grinned. "Up, up and away. The Señora is on her way to Mexico via the company plane."

Jim stomped his foot as if squashing the bug he'd been toying with. "Get out of here Luis, before I throw you out."

* * *

The door to the Lear opened as quickly as it had shut. Jim stormed through, bringing a blast of damp air with him. "What th' hell are you two doing?"

Patricia knew now it had not been the weather keeping them from departing. Jim must have telephoned the pilot. "I told you I was going to Mexico. Don't act so surprised. But, of course, you are. Too bad your sleeping pill made me throw up." Patricia folded her arms as he put out his hands.

"I was just trying to keep you from being as crazy as Max. What do you think you can do?"

"Well, Jim," Rachel spoke up, "I don't know whether to be impressed with your opinion of Max or your faith in Patricia."

Jim narrowed his eyes at her. "This has nothing to do with either, Rachel. I don't want Patricia getting herself *hurt*." His lips squeezed together, clamping down on the word.

"I'm a big girl, Jim," Patricia said. "I think it's time you recognized that I can take care of myself." She wanted to say more, but Rachel was baring her teeth. She didn't want the two of them to get into one of their fights. She needed all of them concentrating on Max.

"Now if you'll be kind enough to tell the pilot you're leaving, we can get underway."

Jim stared at her for what seemed like minutes. Finally, he turned on his heel and went to the cockpit. Patricia was afraid he might be arguing with the pilots, but he reappeared in a moment and left.

"Did I hear right? He tried to drug you?" Rachel asked.

"It was just a sleeping pill. And it didn't work. Let's forget it."

"That son-of-a-bitch!"

"Don't be so hard on him, Rache. He's under pressure, too. There's a lot at stake for him."

"I'll bet on that," Rachel said.

Patricia thought about her words. Jim's future depended on Morelos Enterprises. No doubt he would protect his interests, but she also knew he cared. "Rache, I'm sure he *is* concerned about my safety."

"Sure, St. Pat, think the best of the lout. I won't argue."

Once the jet reached its cruising altitude, Patricia unfastened her seat belt and moved to a lounging chair. She still felt sleepy. There was a bed in the rear of the plane where Tomas had often slept on flights, but she wanted to stay in the cabin. She was glad now that Rachel had come along. She enjoyed the nearness of her best friend. Rachel had left the subject of Jim and was doing what she did best, talk about her daughter. She had managed not to tell Annie about Max and had come up with a good story about the short trip she and Patricia were making to Acapulco.

"I know being a girl makes a difference, but can you imagine my Annie running off to Mexico alone?" Rachel laughed. "She needs at least three friends with her to go to the Seven-Eleven."

"I don't think Max has ever *needed* anyone. Not even me."

"Yes, I know. That's because he's just like you. Independent, resourceful. Know-it-all."

"Well, I didn't grow up in the lap of luxury you did. You learn, when you have to."

"Strange, isn't it? Max did. He had the best handed to him, yet, he's more independent than you. Tomas sure tried to spoil him. He must be turning in his grave to know his son went to Mexico to 'champion the poor'."

"And what about me? Here I've lied to Max all these years, telling him about a fairytale childhood I had, thinking I was protecting him from my 'tobacco road' experience. If I'd known he was going to become so enamored with the poor, I could've bragged my heart out."

"First time I've heard you mention that in a long time."

"Well, I try to forget."

In the silence that fell between them, Patricia's words circled in her mind, closing in on her memories like a descending spotlight. As they came into focus, she could smell wet pine, a pigpen, an outhouse. She could feel rough cotton ticking stiff with dry urine, hear a screen door slam, taste dust. She saw herself, a little girl with dirt-curled ringlets in a hand-me-down dress with tattered lace, eyes the color of acorns, face still baby-round. Her name was Dorothy Tucker.

CHAPTER SIX

ALABAMA 1954

Dorothy peered around the side of the wellhouse at a woman and man she'd never seen. Her look went past them to the car.

"We come for the girl," the woman said to Preacher Johnny.

Dorothy had planned to run away before the people came. Now she was glad she'd forgot to. She wouldn't walk to her new home like her brothers would. They were just going to the next farm. She was going a long way off. All the way to Talladega. And she'd get to ride in a car.

"Does she have a clean dress?" the woman asked.

"Nope, ain't had time for no washin'. Only laid their ma to rest yesterday," Preacher Johnny said. "My wife's been takin' care of the new one and the twins. That there's a handful. But Dorothy Mae here, she's a big help. You'll see she's no trouble. Go inside, girl, and git your things. These folks'll be wantin' to git on their way."

"You want some help, honey?" The woman blocked out the sun. "You poor thing," she said. Her big arms squeezed Dorothy's shoulders tighter than Billy did when he was being mean. She ducked down and slid from the woman's grasp. Jackson and Hank had taught her how to do that. As if summoned, her brothers tore around the side of the house. Billy chasing the others, throwing dirt at them. He missed, splattering the man's trouser legs.

"Weeohh! Look at that!" Hank shouted and hit the car, making thumping sounds.

"How 'bout a ride, mister?" Billy rubbed his hands down the back fender.

"You boys, just get on back, now, you hear. Just get on back."

Pa would've thrashed them, but the man just walked around, flinging his arms like he was shooing chickens. The boys jumped into the car. Billy banged the horn, twisted the steering wheel.

Dorothy grabbed his leg and screamed. "Ya'll git outta there or I'll tell Ma!"

Billy pushed her backward. "Ma's dead, you idiot," he screamed. She landed on the ground, got up and started for him again.

Preacher Johnny grabbed her, pulled her around. "Look at me, girl. You behave yourself or these folks won't take you home with them." He pushed her toward the house. "Now, git."

She ran to her room. Butterflies in her stomach outran her, and she pressed her hand against them, whispering, "I'm gonna go on a trip. In a car."

She knew what she would take with her. Her china doll Ma had given her. She spotted it between the sleeping twins, all three tucked together like spoons. She pulled the doll out and the twins wiggled, filling the vacant place. Preacher Johnny was hollering for her. She tiptoed out of the room.

"Why does she get to ride and we don't?" Jackson whined.

"Yeah, she didn't even go in the creek this mornin', like you said to, Johnny." Billy said.

She stuck her tongue out.

"Dorothy, you said you took a bath. You better not be lyin'. The devil's goin' take you to hell for your lyin'."

He grabbed at her, but she was already in the back seat of the car. It smelled beautiful. As they drove off, she heard Billy call her name. She didn't look back.

They headed out Dry Valley road in a direction she'd never been. The man and woman talked about how hot it was and asked her questions about school and what she liked to eat. She mostly nodded her head. Arms propped on the back of the front seat, she looked down the long hood at the silver angel riding on the front of the car. She pushed her feet back and forth when the man did.

When her legs tired, she leaned back and watched the fields go by. Miles and miles of cotton. Ma used to tell her that's what snow looked like. Someone had once sent them a Christmas card picture of snow-topped mountains. Cotton didn't really look like snow like Ma said. Ma lied, too, sometime. She wiped her eyes hard with the back of her hand and thought how glad she was to be away from Billy and Preacher Johnny.

The car stopped and she opened her eyes. It was dark outside. The woman was talking.

"She's asleep, poor thing. I'll put her to bed. Take the car back to Mr. Granger's. Maybe he'll give you a lift home."

"Better give her a bath before you tuck her in. May need to take the hose to her."

"Jeff McFall, behave yourself. That child's been through enough. Her ma dead and her pa in jail. She needs a lot of lovin' and we're going to give it to her."

"You know I's just pullin' your leg, Elsie. Be back soon. Sure you can pick her up?"

The woman pulled Dorothy across the seat and lifted her out of the car. Dorothy stayed curled around her doll, faking sleep. She sneaked a look around as the woman carried her past a beat up truck into a house with a porch across the front. Inside, the woman placed her on a couch and turned on a lamp.

"Well, Miss Sleepy-head, how about a bath before we go to bed?"

Dorothy stretched, taking her time "waking up." "I already had me a bath today."

"Sure you did. But we're going to take a special one. A bubble bath."

She sat up and stared at the woman. "A what?"

She'd never been in a real bathtub. In winter they bathed in a washpail in the kitchen, the rest of the year they went in the creek. She didn't like it. The water was cold and Billy said there were snakes in it.

All this bath had, as far as she could see, was bubbles.

The woman was washing her back. "I'll try to be careful. Don't want to pull the scab away. How in th' world did you get such a bad scrape? Did you fall?"

Dorothy slapped her back, sending tiny balloons of soap into the air. She scratched a piece of the "scab" away. "Oh, that'll come off. I ain't hurt. It was Billy. He throwed somethin' at me down in the pasture. I guess it didn't come off when I bathed."

The woman looked sick. She walked over to the sink, ducked her head under the spigot for some water then spit it out. When she came back, Dorothy thought her hide was going to be scrubbed away. That was what she got for telling the truth. The devil might take her to hell for lying, but telling the truth hurt more.

They put her to bed in a room all by herself. She cuddled up with her doll, but couldn't sleep. She played with the lace on the pillow. Everything smelled like flowers. The bed was so big, there would have been room for the twins, too.

She thought of Billy and her bath. It was all his fault. She hated him. Should just have told the woman she didn't know what was on her back. What difference would it have been if she'd lied? After all, they'd just as much as lied about the car, hadn't they? It wasn't even theirs.

Looked like everybody she knew lied. Ma lied about the snow. Pa said he was coming back and taking care of them, but the sheriff took him away. Billy said Pa was doing five years for moonshining. Billy lied all the time.

And even Preacher Johnny. Hadn't he lied when he told them they'd all stay together when Ma died? Didn't seem to her that telling the truth got you anywhere. She doubled her hand into a fist, curled around her mother's china doll, and fell asleep.

CHAPTER SEVEN

MEXICO
September 26

Patricia unclenched her hands and stretched. For a minute she wasn't sure if she had been dreaming or remembering. The image of tiny cracks on the china doll's face was too vivid for a dream. That doll still existed. Not that Patricia ever thought of it, or looked at it, locked away in a chest as it was.

"You take a nap?" Rachel asked.

"No. Just resting," Patricia answered. "Thinking about Max."

"Happy thoughts, I hope."

"Very," she murmured. She had to do something to shake loose the memories that haunted her. "We have enough time for a cup of tea before landing. Want one?"

Sipping her tea moments later Rachel asked, "Can you see Popocatépetl or Ixtaccíhuatl?"

"Not yet." No need to look. Patricia knew they were not where they could see the snow-topped volcanoes. She knew every landmark on this flight. During her marriage to Tomas, they had flown to Mexico regularly. However, she seldom got off in Mexico City, choosing to spend the time at their villa in Acapulco. That's what she intended for Rachel to do now. Too many hazards in the crowded city. Watching after Rachel would slow her down. At least that was excuse enough.

"Look, Rache, I want you to stay on the plane. Robert will fly you onto Acapulco and you can wait there for me. I'll give him a call when I'm ready to join you."

"Well, don't beat around the bush, Patricia. Just tell me you don't want me along."

"Funny, Rache. Now don't give me a hard time. You know there are good reasons. I'm just—"

"Lighten up, sweetie." Rachel cupped her chin with her hand and leaned forward on one knee. "I know life is serious and terrible things are happening, but you're going to fray if you stretch your strings much more." She reached out, found Patricia's hand and patted it. "I'll go on to Acapulco without a fight. On one condition."

"What?"

"That you don't leave Mexico City or do anything rash without talking to me first."

Patricia considered the request. Finally, she said, "I don't intend to do anything rash, but I promise to tell you if I change my mind. How's that?"

Rachel sighed. "Well, I guess it'll have to do. And while I'm waiting, I'll have Marta cook *quesadillos* three times a day and be fat by the time you and Max get there."

"You fat? Never." Patricia laughed, but her humor found no hold and faded quickly. She got up and walked toward the back of the plane. "I think I'll call Washington before we land," she said in a hollow voice.

Jim answered on the first ring. He hadn't expected it to be Patricia. Actually, it surprised him how far away she was from his thoughts at the moment.

"I hope you're calling to say you've come to your senses and you're on the way home. I'll meet you at the airport."

"No, Jim. We're landing in Mexico any minute. Any news?"

Her voice quivered, and he pictured her biting her lower lip as she did when she was under stress. The thought of her bruising that luscious mouth gave him a sudden rush of heat. He lowered his voice. "You know I would have called."

"Well, I'll be at the office or the hotel."

He heard her sigh. "I'll call you tonight. Be careful, Patricia."

When she hung up, he lowered the phone slowly, reluctant to give up the too short moment of levity. His shoulders slumped and he felt the muscles in his face droop as if gravity had increased its pull. Scattered across his desk were telexes, brokerage reports, phone messages from people demanding money.

He picked up one and stared at the number he was supposed to call in Mexico, 56-79565. If he put a dollar sign in front, it would just about represent what he stood to lose. He let that thought go in a hurry. If everything went as he planned, he'd have twice that. And he was not going to let anything stop him.

A knock on the door and his secretary, Peggy Wright, stomped into the room, gray hair framing her flushed cheeks. She shook her head. "You can't keep that Mr. Smith, if that's his name and I doubt it, waiting all day. He's just sitting there aiming those BB eyes at me. Gives me the creeps. If you want to stall him again, you'll have to do it yourself."

"Show him in, Peg." He groaned and quickly gathered the papers on his desk, stuffing them into a drawer.

She straightened her back and opened the door. "Mr. Mainland will see you now, *Mr. Smith*." She exaggerated the name.

Nothing about Mr. Smith looked threatening to Jim. Small frame, pinched face, narrow eyes. Only a slight bulge under his left arm said something different. His name was Willie Bates and he and Jim went back a long way.

"Wasting my time, Mainland. You're lucky I'm a patient man." He stretched his hand out as if checking his nails. The voice, knife-edged and cold, carried the threat the body hid. He didn't wait to be asked to sit.

"I thought we had a deal. Why'd you come here? I don't like it," Jim said, his jaw set, his spine a steel rod.

"Hey, Jim-boy, is that a way to treat an old friend?" Willie leaned forward and took a silver paper weight in the shape of a dollar sign from the front of Jim's desk. "Man, you've done okay. Yes sir, must be a lot of this stuff coming your way."

Jim suppressed an urge to grab the paper weight from Willie's hands. "I asked you what you're doing here, Bates. Our agreement was—"

"Well, you know how things change. Word is, you might have a problem delivering. There's a lot riding on you, Mainland, so, I'm just making a friendly call. Don't get so uptight." A loud laugh shook the man's small body like an electric shock.

Jim didn't even smile.

"Okay," Willie said, putting the silver dollar sign back on the desk, "Business it is. So, let's talk some Mexican shit. What's going on south of the border?"

Jim shifted in his chair and felt his spine ease. So they didn't know about Max, or Willie wouldn't be asking. "No problema, amigo. No problema," he laughed.

"Well, the boys need some assurance. You see, there's this man that deals in trash. Cat-something. He's nosing around and that makes people nervous. Why is that, Jim? What's a garbage man have to make people afraid?" His thin lip rose on one side.

"I can't imagine." Jim sat motionless.

"Don't understand it myself, either. Only thing I know about garbage dumps is they got lots of rats. But, you know, rats kill easy."

Willie fixed his dark eyes on Jim as his right hand moved inside his coat. Jim froze. The little man withdrew a package of Camels, tapped one an inch above the others, took it in his mouth and put the pack away. He didn't light it, just passed it from side to side with his lips as he talked.

"You and me been along the same road, Jim-boy. We both killed us a few rats, that's for sure. Why, hell, we grew up *on* the tracks," he laughed, then spoke in a more serious tone. "Had drunks for dads and sluts for mamas."

Jim rose up in his chair.

"Well, some were better than others." Willie grinned. "Whatever they were, they gave us two things, a hard-on for what our birth fucked us out of and the balls to go after it."

He glanced at the silver paperweight, then gave Jim a hard stare. "Now that's where the similarity ends. It's for sure you don't know no garbage man. Why, look at that fine suit." He looked Jim over as if he were a tailor. "Problem is, my boy, you went out and got all the trappings before you got the means. Me, well, as you can see," he held out the lapel of his cheap coat, "I'm waiting until I can afford to go shopping at Brooks Brothers."

Jim stood up, locking his knees to hold them steady. "If that's all you wanted—"

"Sure, sure. Busy, important man like you doesn't have no time for reminiscing. I understand. Sorry to bother you. Guess our information must have been wrong. We'd got the idea that you and this Cat-person had something in common, some deal you were working on. Glad to hear you don't know nothing about him. It'd be mighty upsetting to the boys to find out you did." His hand was on the doorknob before he turned to Jim.

"By the way, almost forgot to tell you, they said they needed a 'good faith remittance', I think they called it. A hundred grand by tomorrow midnight. If not, well, you know the consequences. See ya, old friend."

A malachite figurine rocked and fell over with the vibration of the door slamming. Jim made no move towards it. He could not have been more still if he'd been dead. Willie's words wormed through his motionless body.

Tomas had first introduced Jim to Juan Catera at a meeting in Tlantaloc. A tall, light-haired Mexican dressed like one of Al Capone's sidekicks, Catera was too slick to look like what he was, a slum lord who controlled the *pepenadores*, the swarms of garbage pickers who gleaned trash heaps. He was one of the most hated men in Mexico. And one of the most powerful. He was never seen out in the open. That was because he didn't want to go to jail. Which was where he would be except he was a personal friend of Carlos Gutierez, Mexico City's Chief of Police. To be compared to Catera by anybody made Jim sweat.

It was obvious that Willie hadn't believed he didn't know Catera, but he didn't think that was what Willie would report. A warning. That was what Willie was giving him. Maybe it was because of old times.

Just like Willie said, they had been born on the back edges of life, but Jim thought himself luckier than most. At least where his old man was concerned. A hard worker, he had called himself a gardener. What he did was haul horse manure in an old pickup from Middleburg farms to ritzy D.C. homes, spreading it by the shovelful onto grass carpets and into flower beds. Jim could still smell the odor that permeated his young life. Willie was dead-on about the mother. When she came home, which was seldom, she smelled worse than the stuff his father hauled. Jim had hated her, wished her dead, until one day she was. His old man cried and carried on like the Virgin Mary had passed away. That night Jim found his father hanging from a rope in the garage.

With no one to care, Jim, at sixteen, made a life on the streets of D.C. It didn't take long for him to get into trouble with the law. He had been in and out of jail for a year when he was caught stealing from the silver shop owned by Tomas Morelos. Tomas pressed charges. Jim was tried as an adult, and when the eighteen-month sentence at Lorton Correctional Institution ended, Morelos was there to pick Jim up, in a limousine.

At first, Jim used his tough guy attitude that he had perfected in prison, threatening to wait for the right time and place to get back at the man who had sent him there. Morelos let the boy wail and fume, curse and threaten him. He just smiled. When they reached the Morelos house, Jim was stunned into silence. He never knew such beautiful things existed that he was now being allowed to see and touch. He ran his fingers through thick rugs, caressed a silver candelabra, smoothed the delicate fabric of the sofa.

"You have an appreciation for fine things," Tomas said.

Wary, Jim eyed the door, half expecting a policeman to enter and accuse him of some trumped up charge. He moved to a window and looked out at the street, ready to bolt.

"Relax. I have invited you to my home for a purpose. Sit down. We will have a drink."

A black man entered carrying two bottles of beer and two glasses of wine on a silver tray. Jim reached for the beer, changed his mind, took the cut crystal with the pale yellow liquid. He had tasted wine before. Sweet, cheap stuff his mother brought home. Somehow he knew this would taste different. The smile on Tomas' face said he had made the right choice.

The game of choices went on through an evening meal that Jim would savor in his mind for weeks. He was being tested. For what, he didn't know, or care. At the moment, he only wanted to win, whatever it meant.

Later, Tomas directed him to his office. Around the room in glass cases were strange statues, some of silver, others of gold.

"Let me ask you, Jim Mainland, if you could have any object in any case in this room, which would it be?" Tomas smiled and motioned for the young man to look more closely. Somehow Jim knew this was the final test. The important one. After looking over all the pieces, he stood in front of one that was green and gold, ugly, but old, not shiny or decorative like the others. He lingered just long enough.

"Good," Tomas said. "A pre-Columbian worth $800,000 at auction." He took a key from his pocket and opened the case. He held the ancient art work for a moment, then handed it to Jim.

Prison-hardened hands shook as Jim caressed the clay form. His heart beat was a jungle drum as he listened to Tomas's tale of how and when the article was found, unearthed and added to the Morelos's collection. Gently, Jim replaced the artifact in the glass case. Tomas locked it. Jim stared at the object, so near, yet now, so untouchable. His gaze roamed the room at all the finery of a life he'd never have. Anger rose inside him. At the fates for giving him so little. At this man for showing him what he'd missed.

"What th' hell you want from me, Morelos?"

"I am offering you a job. Two years ago, you stole from me, but you did not take something easily melted down. You took one of the most exclusive pieces. I knew then I could teach you someday to understand why you took what you did."

"If you knew that, why'd you let me rot in that hellhole for almost two years?" Jim clenched his fists.

"Think of it as education," Tomas said. "You had to grow up. Learn how not to get caught. I trust your 'classmates' taught you a few things?" He smiled, "You want the job or not?"

"I could knock you in the head, man, take what I want and you'd never find me. And you talking jobs. Doing what? Shining your shoes?"

"That and anything else I tell you to do. In return you'll learn everything you need to know to possess your own collection someday." He held out his hand in the direction of the glass cases.

Jim wanted to kill him. He thought of all the abuse he had suffered in prison. A "new piece of meat," they had called him. This man standing in front of him, offering him a job, was responsible for that.

Then Jim made a decision that would take him into a world as tough and ruthless as any prison. Over the years he had done anything and everything Tomas had asked, and the man had taught him a great deal.

Now, the promises Tomas had made were within his reach. All the years of doing Morelos's dirty work was about to pay off. If he could just get everything to fall into place.

He left his office and went straight to Patricia's. With a key hidden beneath a false drawer in the desk, he unlocked one of the cabinets and took a small gold ceremonial necklace. He admired it for a moment, sighed and dropped it into his pocket. It should bring about a hundred grand, from the right buyer.

CHAPTER EIGHT

In the Benito Juarez Airport, Patricia hardly noticed the officials who smiled at her and stamped her passport. One of the airport workers collected her suitcase and headed for a side door in the terminal. She followed, ignoring the offers of *ayuda* from the boys who dogged the tourists. A dark gray Fleetwood limousine was parked in a special area near the building. A young man in a gray uniform was putting her bag in the trunk.

"Señora Morelos." He hurried to meet her. "*¿Como esta?*"

"Very well, Jaime. And yourself?"

"Very good, Señora. Do you go to the office or the hotel?"

"The office."

Patricia watched arriving and departing passengers exchange taxis as Jaime drove away from the airport through *zona rosa*. They drove past museums, palaces, and Alameda Park where she and Max had spent many afternoons while Tomas worked. The monument to the Aztec Chiefs came into view, and she thought her heart would break as she remembered the stories Max used to make up about a chief named Maxatec. When she cleared her eyes, Chapultepec Park lay just ahead. She could see Max at five scurrying from statue to statue in the Anthropology Museum, asking if he looked like this Mayan or that one, fascinated with the history of his father's people.

She pushed her fist against the empty feeling in her stomach. She was closer to Max, now. Could almost feel his presence. She tried to concentrate on why she was here and not let herself succumb to the endless visions of her son that could play through her head for hours like a video. Every night instead of sleep, reel after reel of a little boy, bright-eyed at Christmas, sand-covered at the beach, cuddled between stuffed bears, filled her head. She tried to make him grow in her thoughts, to see him as a young man, as he now was. Only the little boy possessed the screen. She had to think of him as a man. Capable. Strong. Able to survive hardships.

She needed it for herself, too. Seeing Max as a teenager made her see herself as she was, a thirty-nine year old woman. A successful, powerful business owner. Not a poor, dirty little girl waiting for handouts. Not someone afraid to stand up for herself or for her child. She would need all the self-assurance she could scrape together to face the officials she would meet. And if it became necessary for her to see Miguel Ramirez, she would do it, despite what that encounter might cost her.

At the Diana Monument Circle, traffic was snarled, people streaming into the street stared, trying to penetrate the limo's smoky windows. A young man walked up to the glass nearest her and cupped his eyes with his hands. His face only inches away was mesmerizing. The dark curly hair, the eyes set slightly too far apart. The soft moustache framing his full lips. The light shaded by his hand gave him a brooding, familiar look. Not that he was anyone she knew. It was just the nearness of his face. The similar features. Her thoughts of Miguel.

As the car pulled away, she tried to shake the image. The face seemed to filter through the window into the car, changing as it emerged. The hair shorter. The chin more prominent. The eyes darker, more provoking. The features of another young man from another time. In her imagination he sat beside her; the metamorphosis complete.

She felt the heat of a hand placed long ago on her thigh. Like a branding iron burning her skin. She rubbed her palm across the leg of her pants pushing at a phantom pain. Fighting the rush of warmth and memory, she looked out the windows. The quick succession of shop fronts, pedestrians and passing cars could not hold her attention. They blurred until what she saw through the window changed to trees and shifting moonlight along the Potomac River.

The past became the present. Miguel was twenty-one and she was twenty.

A cool June night in Virginia. A welcome breeze blowing through open car windows. Miguel smiling at her. Touching her hair, her lips, her cheeks, her eyes with a piercing, seeking gaze. He, leaning against the door of the back seat. She, curled in his arms. They had been there together before, groping, doing little, wanting more. This night, an unnamed, unmarked threshold had been crossed, and she had been afraid.

His kisses stroked the contours of her face, neck and shoulders. She loved him. That would overcome her fear, she told herself. His hand moved along her thigh until it touched the lace of her panties. She stiffened her legs. "I love you," he whispered. She looked away from the dark eyes that searched the meaning of her hesitation.

Slowly, his hand retreated to the buttons of her blouse. This she had allowed before. The blouse, the bra. His fingers slid along the band of her skirt. The button. The zipper. She was naked except for a half-slip and panties. She was cold. He tried to separate her legs. She held herself rigid above the stiff, ribbed seat beneath her. He rubbed her thighs through the silky material until they parted. Again he whispered, "I love you." She tasted the salt of her tears.

When she was fully undressed, she tried to slow his eagerness to explore her body. Tried to stall the moment. As she felt her resistance dissolve, as the moment they had waited for happened, she was truly convinced that her love would overcome everything. That his love would make him understand. That he wouldn't question. That he wouldn't care that she wasn't a virgin.

Feather touches, kneading hands, hungry kisses, probing tongues. Fireflies of memories filled the air in the limousine. Hiding in the dark was the truth. Love had not been enough, if it had been love. Miguel had questioned her lack of innocence, as if she had betrayed him. In time, betrayal became less important. His torture and her torment became the question, "Who?" Angry voices, accusations, denials chased away the fireflies.

The image of the young man was gone.

"Señora, you want I should wait?" Jaime was standing by the open back door. Behind him was the gleaming steel and glass Morelos Building. The eight story structure designed by Paolo Munez looked like a giant bar of silver.

Patricia gathered her purse and briefcase with shaking hands and got out of the limo. "No, Jaime. Just drop my suitcase off at the Nikko and I'll walk over later."

A gray-haired man in a silver uniform rushed through the main lobby door. "Señora, Señora, *mucho gusto deverte.*" He took her hand and pumped it as he grinned and jabbered in Spanish.

"It's good to see you, too, Enrique. And your *espousa*?"

"Beatrice is good, much good, Señora." He straightened his shoulders and stretched his frame. "*Mi hija*, Elena, *te esparar en su oficina*." He looked upward toward her office, then opened the massive glass door to the lobby. The sea green terrazzo floor gleamed like a mirror. Near the entrance sat a huge, deeply carved concierge desk. The dark massive wood sank into the cool colors of an Aubusson rug, like a ship riding the sea. She stood near a three-story palm in the Atrium and waited for the elevator.

She confronted her image on all sides in the small mirrored enclosure. Not one, but hundreds of her stared back, lined up in the silver backed glass. She looked less haggard than she had before deciding to come to Mexico. Dressed in sky blue pants, jacket and white silk blouse, she actually looked cool and calm despite how she felt. Makeup hid the circles ringing her eyes and her dark hair was shiny, if severe in its bun. Max liked her hair free, flowing. When she found him, she'd never wear her hair in a bun again.

As the elevator ascended and each button on the panel lit, she could picture what was on that floor. The latest equipment, research departments, silver design shops, elegant offices. She had studied every aspect of the Morelos silver business for almost twenty years. There was no part of it she wasn't familiar with, except one. The mines. Why had she never been there? To Real de Catorce. Others had the responsibility of the raw ore, but that was no excuse. If she had visited there, knew the people . . .

"God, please don't let Max pay for my ignorance," she whispered as the doors opened.

"*Buenos tardes*, Señora." Elena was waiting as her father had said, a cup of coffee in one hand, pad and pen in the other.

"My goodness, Elena. Your father must have buzzed you. Or have you been holding this all day?" She smiled at Elena's glowing face, took the coffee, sipped it. "No, hot as always. *Gracias*."

She quickened her pace past Tomas's hodgepodge collection of nineteenth century silver mirrors lining the corridor to her office. She had kept this room and the five room penthouse on the floor above just as Tomas had left them. Unlike the office in Washington, she felt uncomfortable here. And she never stayed in the penthouse. It had always been used by the men in Tomas's inner circle and she never liked how they appeared without being invited. Even now, she preferred a hotel.

Patricia read her messages with quick glances. Her shoulders sagged as she saw no news of Max. She took the list of names from the briefcase and gave it to Elena.

"I want to meet with all of these people tomorrow, if possible. If not, I want to know why. Be persistent. Just tell them a member of the Morelos Company wants to meet. Don't mention my name. Don't let them wiggle into a lunch date. I don't have time for a three-margarita lunch."

Elena smiled and nodded. She scanned the list. A frown drew her face downward. "Miguel Ramirez? Señora, are you sure? Señor Tomas would not want his brother to come here."

"If I get what I want from these people who should have some say with the miners, I won't need to see the wicked step-brother, now or ever. However, just in case, I don't want to waste time. I'll have to see him, even if he does bite."

"I think he does, Señora. I have heard Señor Tomas scream loudly many times when he talk to his brother."

"Well, I'm not afraid of him, so make the appointment. Just don't tell him who's asking for the meeting. We wouldn't want him to have a chance to sharpen his teeth. Just in case, right?" She picked up her briefcase and hugged Elena with one arm. "You know you've made your father very proud. I wish I could mint the look on his face when he speaks of you."

"It is the same look you give to Maximilian. The one you will give him again soon."

Elena's smile was framed in sympathy. Before Patricia could turn away, tears filled her eyes.

"Thanks, Elena. Call me at the hotel, if there's word." She turned away into the elevator, begging its doors to close quickly.

* * *

Room service arrived with tortilla soup and fruit just as the phone rang. Even though she had eaten little during the day, she had no appetite and was glad for the interruption. As she said hello, her heart quickened with the ever present hope.

"I just had the biggest plate of *chile rellenos* and gained three kilos. Have you eaten?"

"Rache, you and your seventh sense. They just brought dinner." She stared at the cooling soup. "You get settled in okay? Marta looking after you?"

"That woman acts as if I can't hear or see. Either that or she's getting hard of hearing herself. But yes, she's seen to everything. What about you? No news at all?"

"None. Elena was waiting. She's making appointments with the people I need to see."

The telephone line crackled in the silence.

"Rache, you there?"

"I guess you're going to see *him*?"

"He has a name."

"Which one of them you want? Seems I remember Tomas using a number of them. None of which a lady would repeat."

"I don't care who or what he is, if he can help get Max out of those mountains."

"And what if he won't even listen to you? You going to get down on your knees and beg? I can just see that. Wouldn't he have a laugh."

"Maybe not. He can't be all that bad. There was a time—"

"Oh, you remember?" Rachel asked. "You going to tell him the truth?"

"Damn it, Rache."

"Just the truth, Patricia. You have a hard time with that sometimes, face it."

"It isn't always advisable, Rachel. Or necessary."

"It might just be this time."

"Okay. You've made your point. Tell you what. It'll be my ace in the hole, but I'll decide when I need to use it, understand?"

"Sure. Whatever. Talk to you tomorrow. Try to get some sleep. And eat your soup!"

Patricia lowered the phone and smiled. Rachel, always controlling, she thought. What would the world be like if that woman could see. Not that being blind had ever held her back, that was for sure. Rachel had been a driving force in Patricia's life since the day Rachel met Dorothy Tucker.

CHAPTER NINE

ALABAMA 1962

In time, life with Elsie and Jeff McFall in the little house on Coffee Street, a few blocks from the town square, became quite ordinary to Dorothy. She walked to a nearby school and did chores in the afternoon while Elsie worked at the Courthouse Diner. By the time Dorothy was eight, she was good at washing dishes, peeling potatoes and sweeping. She fell into the routine without fuss or feeling.

Jeff was a mechanic. He worked long hours and spoke little. He had one love—flowers. He tended his roses and left his wife to tend Dorothy. Elsie turned her sewing room into a bedroom, decorated it with frills and ruffles, and still made more little dresses than Dorothy could wear out. On her bed lay a collection of new dolls. The only one she cared about was the one she had brought from home. The tiny faced china doll.

By the time Dorothy was a teenager, she helped out at the diner on Saturdays and during school vacations. One hot August day when she was fifteen, she sat at the counter putting paper napkins into metal holders. Now and then she twirled round on the stool, stirring hot air. It cooled her more than the big fans swirling in the ceiling. She'd wanted to go to the pool, but Elsie's help didn't show, so she had to work.

The screen door opened. Customers. She hopped down, got some glasses and a pitcher of water. A man, woman, and a teenage girl were sitting in a booth when she returned. They looked like a family in *Saturday Evening Post*.

The man mopped his brow with a monogrammed handkerchief. His greying hair was damp. His seersucker suit was fresh and cool-looking. He was as handsome as a movie star. The woman, in a silky green dress, matching hat and gloves, whipped a fan back and forth. A sweet fragrance swirled around her. The girl was beautiful. Brown hair in soft curls, green eyes, deep dimples. A miniature of the woman. Down to the gloves.

"What ya'll want to drink?" Dorothy smiled at the girl.

"I'd like a cherry Coke, Father." The voice was as clear as the chimes on the Episcopal church. The green eyes didn't look her way.

"And what for ya'll?" She nodded to the man.

"I'll have some lemonade," the woman said.

"Same here, and two menus, please," the father added.

Looking back from the kitchen pass-through, Dorothy watched as the man and woman read from the day's fare. The girl stared toward the counter, nodding her head.

"Here. Take their orders." Elsie pushed a pad of paper into her hand.

"That girl's blind," Dorothy said.

"Shush, she'll hear you. And don't stare. Those folks sense when you're staring at 'em. I've *told* you that."

The girl didn't look like the ones from the Blind School, except for the blank stare. She didn't blink much. If she moved her eyes, they looked normal. They were see-through, like an empty green bottle.

The man and woman finished their ham sandwiches, but the girl hardly touched hers. Dorothy refilled their water glasses. The girl looked toward her, just to the side of her face. "Have you a restroom?"

The woman got up and took the daughter's arm. "If you'll tell me where, Miss, I'll—"

"Oh, I'll show her." Dorothy clasped the girl's hand and pulled her around tables and chairs. She kicked her own foot into a chair leg, almost tripping. When she giggled, the girl halted. She started to apologize, but something in the girl's face stopped her. A question on the brows, then a frown. The girl seemed to look through her. Suddenly, they squeezed hands and laughed, as if they'd just shared a secret.

"Ya'll on a vacation?"

"I'm coming to school here," the girl answered from behind the stall door.

Dorothy studied her pixie haircut in the mirror over the sink. She pulled at the short straight strands, curling them around her fingers. Then she shut her eyes and tried to imagine not being able to see herself. She stepped back from the sink in her self-imposed darkness and swayed against the wall. Her foot struck the trash can, overturning it with a loud clatter.

"You okay?" the girl called out.

Dorothy opened her eyes and picked up the trash quickly. "Sure, how about you? You need anything?"

"I'm fine." The door opened. "You can check and make sure things are in place, if you don't mind." Turning slowly, the girl touched the wall and sink as she moved, as if she knew right where they were. Her oxfords looked expensive; her hair neatly styled; the blue voile dress store bought. The skirt wasn't turned up. Dorothy brushed her hand against the fabric anyway.

"What's your name? Where're you from?"

"Rachel Wellington, from Alexandria, Virginia. Close to the capital, Washington. My parents brought me down to get me settled at the school. They fuss too much, since I became—"

"Well, that's what parents do, isn't it?" She didn't want to hear the girl say the word "blind." "They seem nice. Your mom's pretty."

Rachel held a damp towel in her hand. Dorothy took it. "And you? I don't know your name." She laughed and leaned against the sink. "And I'll bet your mom's pretty, too."

Dorothy stared into the bottomless eyes, reflecting the bright single bulb hanging from the ceiling. "I'm Dorothy, Dorothy—McFall. My—my mom and dad own this place." She hadn't expected to lie. It just came out. Everyone in town knew she was a Tucker, but this girl didn't have to know. It wasn't like she'd be seeing her anymore. She wouldn't go to her school or hang out with anyone she knew. She could tell her anything.

"Pleased to meet you." Rachel held out her hand. "Do you still go to school?"

Dorothy blew her nose to buy time. Lying good meant gathering stuff, throwing out the bad and piling up what was left. "Sure, I go to school. I'm here in the afternoons some time and on Saturdays for

Elsie—Mom." Drat, she thought, but recovered quickly. "Sometimes I call her Elsie. Makes her really mad." She laughed and rolled her eyes.

"Is your mom here now? I'd like to meet her."

Dorothy took her time opening the door. A swarm of hornets filled her head. Elsie could be a problem. "She's probably busy; usually is. Unless I need her," she added, trying to move her mouth the way Mrs. Butenschon made them do in choral so the vowels wouldn't sound flat.

Mrs. Wellington was frowning at them as they walked back to the table. "You all right, sweetheart?" Her soft, lilting accent was answered by a broad, coarse drawl.

"What ya'll been up to in there so long? Had this girl's ma worryin'." Elsie came from behind the counter, sloshing water from a pitcher. "Oops, gave myself a bath." She whooped a laugh, dabbed at her ample breasts. Dorothy looked back at Rachel's mom, so cool, slim and beautiful.

"Is this your mother?" Rachel asked.

"Yes." She shot Elsie a look. "Mom, this is Rachel Wellington from Virginia. She's gonna go to school here. Isn't that great?" Her smile stretched her jaws. Elsie had her "liar, liar, pants on fire" look that meant trouble later.

"What class are you in school, Dorothy?" Rachel was talking to her and the adults were shaking hands and all talking at once as if they were old friends.

"Sophomore." She strained to hear Elsie's words.

"That's what I am, too," Rachel said.

So they were in the same grade, but Rachel wouldn't attend Talladega High. Wouldn't be going to ball games and hanging around. They'd probably never see each other again. She looked at the three Wellingtons, as out of place in the diner as royalty.

"Won't you, Dorothy?" Elsie said.

"What?"

"I was telling Rachel's folks how you'd be delighted to show her around, look after her. I'm always telling this girl to go be with friends. She sits in here with me too much. Course, she is a help, but it'd do her good to have a friend."

Dorothy stared at Elsie. She was sorry she had called her Mom. She looked at Mr. and Mrs. Wellington and saw hope on their faces as clear as the Dr. Pepper sign over their heads. And Rachel's smile had scooped her dimples deeper. Well, she'd really done it now. Elsie would have to stay "Mom" or she'd be caught lying. "Sure. I was gonna ask if Rachel wanted to do something, some time." She grinned at Elsie. "Mom won't need me this afternoon, will you?"

Elsie shook her head slowly.

"It'll have to be another day, I'm afraid," Mrs. Wellington said, as she got up from the booth. Mr. Wellington handed Elsie money and the check. "We have an appointment at the school today. One of my college chums is the director. He assures us that Rachel will be in the best hands here. It's nice to see how friendly people are already. We'll be leaving tomorrow and I'm sure Rachel would love to see you again, young lady."

Dorothy followed them out the door, telling Mrs. Wellington that her hat was pretty. When she walked back in, Elsie was looking in the mirror above the glasses, patting her hair net. Dorothy thought she saw the letters MOM across Elsie's broad back like a football player's name.

Sunday morning she dressed early and left a note for Elsie that she was going for a walk before Sunday School. She would meet her and Jeff in church.

It was already hot and humid. Her slip stuck to her like an extra layer of skin. She headed up Coffee Street, then up by the "silk-stocking district" where the worn dirt path became concrete sidewalks lining manicured lawns, and the houses were mansions shaded by giant magnolias.

She liked to daydream about these places, about spiraling staircases with portraits sidestepping up the stairs. And grand pianos in parlors with Queen Anne chairs and fireplaces. She knew such things because she read about them. *Jane Eyre. Wuthering Heights. Gone With the Wind.* Whatever these houses held, it was as far away as Tara to her.

She crossed South Street onto the campus of the Talladega School for the Blind. The buildings looked empty. Sunday. The offices are closed, she thought. How would she possibly find Rachel? This was a stupid idea.

She tried doors on several buildings. All locked. She was getting hotter. Her skirt was limp, her blouse damp. So, what was a promise to a girl that probably didn't want to see her again anyway? Rachel had a ma and pa. She didn't need anyone else. She was rich enough to hire someone to show her around town, if she wanted to. She headed back across the campus toward Grace Baptist Church and familiar territory.

As she turned the corner of a building, she heard a tapping sound, above that of distant music and laughter. Rachel was coming down the walkway in front of one of the dormitories. She stopped several feet in front of Dorothy, her white cane silently poised in front of her.

"Hello?" Rachel called out. "Who's there?"

How did she know? Dorothy wondered. Forget leaving. She wished it wasn't necessary, though, to explain all the things that the girl would know if she could see.

"Hi. Remember me? Yesterday?"

"Dorothy. Of course I remember."

"You knew someone was here?"

"Oh, I—we, have all kinds of strange abilities. Do you want me to tell you what you're thinking?" Her eyebrows arched, as she leaned forward on her cane.

"Oh, sure, and I guess you can smell what I'm wearin'." Rachel frowned and Dorothy regretted her words. "I'm sorry. I didn't mean to—"

"Don't apologize. As a matter of fact, I can," Rachel interrupted and propped her hands on the head of her cane like a tap dancer. "You're not wearing anything," she whispered. Her dimples deepened.

"I'm what? I am—"

"You are not wearing any perfume, that is." Rachel giggled. "I smell Ivory soap. Um, and maybe a rose you picked. Not rose perfume though. They don't smell the same, you know."

Dorothy wanted to sit down. Her confusion and agitation exhausted her more than her long walk. She sighed, wishing she'd gone on to Sunday School. Why had she tried to find this girl anyway? Was she being a smart-aleck or what?

As if sensing Dorothy's questions, Rachel put a hand out. "Why don't I show you my room in the dorm? Wasn't that why you came over? To find me?"

Dorothy thought of the mansions on "silk-stocking" street. Rachel's room was probably like those houses. She imaged a carved bed with a heavy brocade canopy, lace curtains, a fireplace. She'd never want to bring Rachel home to Elsie and Jeff's. So, what difference did that make? Rachel couldn't see it anyway, so she could tell her whatever she wanted to. Besides, she'd like to find out why this girl's ma and pa would bring her so far from home and leave her. School hadn't even started. They acted like they loved her, but family that loved you didn't send you away.

"Well, I'm supposed to meet, uh, Mom in church. I guess I can miss today. Yeh, I'd like to see your room."

Rachel pointed her cane across the grassy courtyard. "This way." She slid her hand under Dorothy's elbow where it lay lightly on her arm.

Which way? Dorothy thought. There were three buildings straight across from them. How was she supposed to lead Rachel if she didn't know where they were going? Her feet simply wouldn't move. What if Rachel stumbled? How would she get her across the street?

They stood for what seemed like forever. A couple of mannequins. Suddenly, she was moving. She was being nudged along by a pressure from Rachel's arm and side. It was such a light touch, she could hardly tell that Rachel was in complete control.

CHAPTER TEN

MEXICO CITY
September 26

"Señor Ramirez? I leave now. My class, you know?"

Miguel looked up as his secretary, Gena, appeared around the door to his office. He ran his fingers through his hair, lifting damp strands from his forehead, and tried to wipe away the frown he felt across his brow.

"Señor?" she called again. "My English, you know."

She came closer. "You okay? I go now, you know, to school."

Miguel raised his eyes. Dark as anthracite, they softened as he smiled at the dark, round face carried forward by an arched Mayan nose. She was his project for the moment. His position as Mexico's Special Liaison to Labor made it easy to manipulate the system. Gena was the latest of many he had brought to the city from some rock and dirt farm. He had managed to save her from the back-bending work of a Chiapas *granja* while she was still unstooped, but not before her hands were calloused as iguana hide. She stood with her hands hidden behind her. However, she was gaining more poise everyday.

"*Esta bien*, Gena. *Vete. Adios.*" Miguel waved her away. His close trimmed moustache curved around his smile.

"Speak English, Señor. I practice, you know." Dark gaps showed several missing teeth when she spoke.

"Why are you not wearing your teeth, Gena?" Miguel asked in a fatherly tone.

"*El dentista me lastima mucho.* They hurt, you know." She clamped her lips shut.

Miguel leaned back in his chair, hands behind his head. "Tell me something, Gena. The English teacher, does he tell you to say 'you know' in every sentence?"

She arched her dark brows. "*No entiendo*. What you say?"

Miguel laughed, turning his hands up in resignation. "Go, you know. Learn English."

When she left, he sobered again. He was tired, but not in his body, though after days of long meetings and drives to Real de Catorce, he had a right to be. Emotionally drained. That's what he was. Part of it was the heat. Mostly, it was the cave-in. A new national disaster, even a small one, was too soon after the horrible earthquake that had hit a year ago.

He still had nightmares about that morning, September 19. A late night had made him lazy and he was still in bed in his small apartment near the *Zocalo*. He thought at first that someone was trying to shake him awake. Then, plaster, dirt and timbers fell around and on top of him, pinning him to the bed. He had tried to put his hands to his face, to shelter it from falling debris, but he could not move his arms. It seemed like hours that his face was assaulted. He opened his eyes to be warned of what was coming at him. When he did, dirt filled them. He was one of the lucky ones. The shell of his building stayed upright and rescuers soon dug him out. His physical injuries, including his eyes, healed. He imagined his heart was still broken from witnessing the devastation of his beloved city.

He stood and stretched, first one side then the other. His fingertips almost touched the ceiling. Before the mining disaster at Real, he had been volunteering his time, rebuilding some of the houses near Tlatelolco that still needed repairs before families could move back in. He had used muscles that had gone to sleep in his body, and now after several days of rest, they were wanting to be used again. He patted his lean abdomen, realizing the benefits of many months of physical labor.

Sticking his head out the window, he captured a small breeze and thought of sitting on the balcony of his house in Cuernavaca away from the hot city. It had been three weeks since he'd enjoyed the calm and cool of his home. He thought of the new rose cuttings. They would be suffering from last week's heat wave. Carmina would water them. They would make it. Flowers were even blooming in the city, amid the ruins and new construction.

Thoughts of Carmina, his cook and housekeeper, reminded him that he hadn't eaten since breakfast. It was getting late. Past six o'clock. Still he couldn't leave. Not until he figured out his next move.

He paced his small office, studying the cracks along the dirty cream walls, meticulously deciding which had been made by the newest earthquake, which were the legacy of age. Some were as old as his Revolution vintage desk. The metal shelves filled with books and papers were the newest acquisitions of his office. He paused in front of a yellowed print of the Mexican flag, then before an ornately framed portrait of an attractive middle-aged woman, his mother. With a sigh, he returned to his desk and picked up a pile of news releases about the Real silver strike. It was the latest bad news and the one that needed his wandering attention. Almost hidden in the pile was a blue folder filled with documents.

A knock on the door interrupted his thoughts.

"Ola, amigo." The American accented voice came from Rick Winn, a news reporter. Without being asked, he glided into the room like he was on skates. Dressed in jeans and white tee shirt, plump faced and rosy-cheeked, he could have been an innocent young man. Miguel knew he had a bloodhound's nose and the conscience of a vulture. He had been a cactus thorn in Miguel's side for years. Only that familiarity made him tolerable.

"Where's that pretty little secretary of yours? Gena?" He laughed. "I don't know where you find 'em, Ramirez."

"What do you want, Winn?" Miguel picked up a pencil and twirled it between the palms of his hands.

"Oh, just the latest. How did your meeting go today with the strikers?" He half sat on the edge of Miguel's desk, eyes wandering over the papers. "I know you met with them. Or their union lords, *caciques*, or whatever you call them. Just how many are into this, Miguel? All the miners or just the Morelos crew?"

"You seem to have enough information." He picked up the blue folder and tossed it into a drawer.

"Any of that have to do with Patricia Morelos?" Rick leaned over the edge of the desk.

Miguel slammed the drawer shut.

Winn shook his fingers, frowning as if they had been caught. "Got word her Lear filed a flight plan to Acapulco, via Mexico City. Think she's planning something?" Rick grinned. Cigarette stained teeth matched the color of his skin.

Miguel pressed his hands against his desk and levered himself out of his chair. He walked to the window. "The Morelos Silver Company knows we are doing everything possible to work things out with the miners. I see no reason why Señora Morelos would come to Mexico. If she chooses to come, well, it is a free country."

"Aw, what prose. Can I quote you on that?" Winn picked up a pencil and pretended to write on the palm of his hand.

Miguel knew the newsman's eyes were searching the papers on the desk with a renewed interest. Let him. All the ones concerning Patricia and her son were now safely tucked away. If the media learned about the kidnapping, the ante would go up. For everybody. The presses were usually controlled in Mexico with ease. After the earthquake, a leniency prevailed that was making the excesses difficult to curtail again. The story of the Morelos kidnapping had been checked. Miguel intended to keep it that way.

Rick picked up one of the news releases and read it. "Eight miners killed. Shit. Life's tough. 'Course that probably means twenty were really killed, if they're lying about the dead the way they did last year."

Miguel clenched his jaw. He did not rise to the bait. He knew what Rick was up to. He knew his temper sometimes caused him to spout off about things and he would have the embarrassment of reading about them later. Although, to give Winn credit, the source was always said to be "anonymous."

"Got to be a big problem for the Morelos people to have all their silver dry up. Understand they may lose some of their contracts. That so?"

Miguel watched a squat Indian woman cross the courtyard below. She had a metal pan with *dulce de tamarindos* piled high. Her *welpel* apron looked clean and fresh even though she had been out selling all day. He never ceased to be amazed at what these women did to earn the few pesos they got for their trouble. Some of them had husbands working the mines, saving and scraping and hoping to come home with enough money to quit living in the dark.

"'Life's tough', you say, Winn? How would you know?" Miguel stared into the boyish face. "You ever slip through the darkness of morning into the pitch black of a mine, leave the smell of fresh air for the putrid stench of gases, dirt and urine? Ever wonder where the miners piss during the day? Think they have some portable potties down there? You would not last two hours in one of those hell holes. Creaking timbers a century old holding millions of tons of earth above your head." He grabbed the newspaper out of Rick's hand and crumbled it in his fist. "Imagine what it would feel like to be buried alive with all that dirt crushing your arms and legs, filling your mouth, like pouring water in a jug. Think about it, amigo." He turned back to the window. He was shaking inside, remembering the dirt falling on his face, into his eyes. The feel of being buried alive. He tightened his fists and spoke through clenched teeth. "Yeah, life is tough for some, Winn, and it is hell for many."

"You know, you got a real way with words." Rick's face flushed. He recovered quickly. "Must be how you always manage to hang on to your job every time a new regime takes over." He slid off the desk and walked to one of the bookcases, ran his fingers along the spines of several volumes, chose one and read the title. "*Plata y Los Mercaderes de Esclavos* by Miguel Ramirez. *Silver and the Slave Traders*. Just like the rest of us pencil pushers, those words can make enemies. Tomas, for instance? Must have been hard to be all pro-labor with him for a brother, with all his silver mines."

"He was not my brother," Miguel growled. "And you know it."

"Well, step-brother. I'll keep the facts straight. Say, how come you didn't take to the rich life? I hear the great Maria Ramirez liked having loads of money." He turned from the bookcase to stare at the portrait on the wall.

The muscles in Miguel's cheeks hardened like steel. Ridges striped his neck and beads of sweat filled his moustache. His fist shot out into the room before he had completely turned to face Winn. The blow only clipped the newsman's jaw.

Stumbling backwards against the door, Rick rubbed where his skin was already turning red and smiled behind his hand. "That was some nerve I hit. You haven't punched me in quite awhile. What's going on?"

"Get out, Winn. Go crawl in the garbage with the other *pepenadores*." He stepped behind the desk, putting the newsman out of his reach.

Rick gave his head a slight shake, tossing off the pain of the blow. "Okay, I guess I've overstayed my welcome. I came by to warn you, word is some of the Morelos people think you're knee deep in this burro shit yourself. Must be your reputation for being the original Cisco Kid. They know you're usually in the middle of every Indian uprising, *ejito* squabble, or strike. Tell me before I go, off the record, is this your idea?"

"Out, Winn, before I really lose my temper."

"You sure don't give a working fellow much help. Sure hope you're more gracious to your sister-in-law. I got a feeling Señora Morelos is going to be looking to you for more than you gave me." He rubbed his jaw. "Information, I mean." The sound of laughter followed him out.

Miguel reached for the phone as soon as the newsman's footsteps faded. "We have problems," he said almost immediately. "Rick Winn was just in here. He is being very inquisitive. How about putting him in jail for a few days. And, tell the Secretary I will meet him in the usual place at nine tonight."

The room fell quiet and the last light of day faded from the window. Patricia. She had not been to Mexico since Tomas' death. She will come though to see about their son, he thought. What mother would not go to the ends of the earth for her child?

He stared at the picture on the wall, shadowed in black and gray by a streetlight below. He could not see the painting, but knew every brush stroke by heart. *The great Maria Ramirez liked having money.* Winn's words cut at him. His mother had been dead now for ten years. The decade before that had been one of dying.

It was not the image on the canvas that filled his mind, but one of Maria Ramirez as a young woman. Her hands had fascinated him. Always moving. Patting maize into tortillas, rolling tamales inside corn husks, grinding spices with a pestle, smoothing the pages of a book. Books. She had given him a love for them. When he was not out looking for charcoal, he spent his days in the corner of an adobe school where she taught in the village of Ixtaban de la Sal. His father was a sheep farmer until he got caught up in the changes of Miguel Aleman's politics in the forties. A new emphasis on industrialization made the farmer's plight worse under the newly reorganized PRM and Pepe Ramirez became one of many civil servants. A born leader, he moved from mayor of their village, to federal official of the state.

They were in Mexico City for a political meeting when tragedy struck. His father was run down by a car, driven by a rival. Maria and Miguel were devastated. The incident drew attention to the family, and Maria began to speak as her husband had done, for the poor, the uneducated, for women's suffrage. The people loved her.

One day after they had moved to an apartment in Mexico City, Maria came home from a rally in a limousine. She was a heroine to her people. The women of Mexico had been given the vote. Miguel had watched the black car. Though he could not see beyond the murky windows, he knew his mother and a man were sitting in the back seat. Only ten years old, he had taken his father's place as head of the family and the limo symbolized a threat he did not know how to fight. After his mother got out, he ran in the streets throwing rocks at the car.

Maria Ramirez and Maximilian Morelos were married in 1958 when Miguel was twelve. And everything in his life changed. From two rooms they moved into one of the *Profirian* mansions just off the *Paseo de la Reforma*. He was enrolled in the prestigious National Preparatory School and was being groomed for the law school at UNAM, the Universidad Nacional Autonoma de Mexico.

Eventually, he met his new brother Tomas, eighteen years his senior. He was set to idolize Tomas. Stories of his brother's business success in the United States were the topic of every meal. Maximilian was proud of his only son. The first evening Tomas was home, Miguel overheard him and his father talking in the grand salon where Miguel was not allowed. He heard Tomas laughing at Maria and him. He melted into the shadows of the hall, staring up at the honored Morelos ancestors and heard Tomas call his Mother a peasant and Miguel *estupido*, mocking their speech and manners.

Miguel swelled and waited for Maximilian to slap his son as he'd done Miguel once for saying a cruel thing about a servant. His stepfather laughed. He heard the man remind Tomas about how he'd married Maria to gain the sympathy of the labor class. She had been getting much attention and he needed her to quiet the workers who were always demanding from him. Miguel ran away from the room when Maximilian began telling crude things about his wife in bed.

He'd sought his mother and tried to tell her what he'd heard, but he couldn't speak for crying. When he calmed down, she chastened him before he could begin his report, saying he should never eavesdrop. He must be respectful of his stepfather, to look around him and see how fortunate they were. She twirled her wedding band with its shiny, canary diamond and smiled at him with a happiness he did not understand.

He never told her what he had heard. He watched as she changed her dress, her hair, her manners, her speech, and eventually, her beliefs.

When he started at the university, he stayed with friends, hardly ever going home. He was happier than he had been in years. Then, during his second year Maximilian died. After the will was read, he had reason to hate his stepfather more. Tomas had been made sole heir with only a pittance for Miguel's mother as long as she lived on in the family home and stayed out of politics.

Miguel even had to ask Tomas for school funds. When he came home, his mother made a grand show of being the widow, even though she was only a shell of herself. Having filled her life with Maximilian, she had nothing of the great Maria Ramirez left.

When the student unrest of 1967 mushroomed, Miguel was a leader. It was because of his involvement that he was summoned to Washington to answer to Tomas. He had already heard of Tomas's American protégée, Patricia.

He had not expected to fall in love with her.

He stood up from his desk and walked to the painting. The dim light outlined his mother's face. He frowned, trying to equate the image of the beautiful, passionate Patricia with the mother of a seventeen-year old son. Now that Tomas was dead, would she marry again and forget her son? Hand clenched, he hit the wall, making the frame bounce against the thin partition.

"Enough of women," he muttered, as he gathered some papers before turning out the light and heading for the National Palace.

Miguel's office was in one of the yet-to-be restored century old buildings in the Zocalo's Historical Center that had survived the earthquake. He walked up the street past new-old Colonials, crossed Guatemala Street and past the excavated ruins of the ancient Aztec city of Tenochititla. Some archeologists were still digging by dim lights beneath wooden walkways. They were like miners in shallow shafts, retrieving earth's hidden riches. The robbing of the past. The cycle continued.

Arriving at the Palace, he slipped out of the glow of a street lamp through a side door into the deserted courtyard. His footsteps echoed as he climbed the stone steps to a brass-railed balcony. He was early, but better he wait than the Secretary. A top official in a government filled with corruption, the Secretary was forced to work behind the scenes to try to help the people. He was one of the strongest in a chain of goodness missing most of its links.

Miguel positioned himself in his usual place to watch for anyone coming. In his line of sight stretched the towering murals of Diego Rivera. Tourists trailed by these paintings every day without understanding what they saw. Miguel knew every figure. His mother had brought him here as a young boy and taught him the story of the Mexican people that Rivera had immortalized.

"Dreaming, my friend?" Soft Spanish words came from the shadows.

"No. Unless I am asleep and you are my nightmare." Miguel chuckled softly.

"Let's walk."

The two men moved silently into an inner courtyard away from the possibility of prying eyes. Miguel was too well known as a dissident, as a promoter of strikes and a people's rights' advocate. The Secretary could not afford to be seen with him.

Near the center of the manicured lawn was a stone Altar of Skulls. They stood in its shadow.

"Tell me about your visit from the journalist."

Miguel gave a short version of the encounter with Winn, leaving out the personal part. "I told Manuel to take care of him," he added.

"*Buena*. Now. Señora Morelos and her son."

Cold crept through Miguel as if the ancient stone he leaned against had extracted his blood. "I do not know if the Señora is coming here. Winn's information is not necessarily correct."

"It is."

"Well, she will not be a problem," Miguel answered quickly. "She will only want assurances that her son will be freed."

"And will he?"

"Yes. When the time is right, the miners will help us."

"I do not have to tell you what this would mean if things should get out of hand. Or if something should go wrong. As sure as the hearts sacrificed upon this stone beat no more, other lives will be lost." He placed his palm on the altar, caressing one of the skulls. "It is in your hands, my friend, more than in any other. We depend upon you."

Miguel stepped out of the shadows and stared into the face of the Secretary. He met him eye to eye, resolve to resolve. Then the two men shook hands and walked separately into the dark.

CHAPTER ELEVEN

SEPTEMBER 27

Patricia slept better that night than she had in weeks. After a breakfast of *huevos* Mexicana and toast, she dressed in a mint green cotton skirt, white blouse and sandals. Something cool and clean feeling for the hot, dirty city. She twisted her hair into its usual bun at the nape of her neck, then thought of Max. Brushing the curls out, she clipped them with a silver clasp high on the back of her head. Just the image maybe to present to these macho Mexican men. She had made the mistake of dressing in a suit, heels and hose on other occasions. The men she had dealt with were not impressed with the power look and the lack of adequate air conditioning in a lot of offices made it too uncomfortable.

The phone rang. She said "Hello" before she had lifted the receiver to her ear.

"*Buenos dias*, Señora."

"Elena. What do you have for me?"

"Representatives for the miners will meet you at 10:00 in your office. Is this okay?"

"What do you mean, 'representatives'? What about Mr. Carrera and Tomas's old school chum, the head man in the Foreign Ministry?"

"Mr. Lopez? I called each of the men on your list, Señora. They all returned my call and said the same thing. The representatives of—"

"Okay, Elena. I understand. They're presenting a united front. That's strange. These people are usually not good team players. I guess they don't want me to have a chance to call in my personal markers."

"Markers, Señora?"

"Never mind," she sighed. "So they're coming to see me. This way they can give me one sand-bagging speech and leave on their own terms. Well, we'll see about that." She tapped her fingernail against the window as she looked out over the smog-strangled city toward Chapultepec Park. "What about Ramirez?" She braced her hand against the window.

"Señor Ramirez will see the representative of Morelos Enterprises in his office at 11:30 this morning. No later, no earlier." She announced, accenting each word.

Patricia leaned against the back of her hand. "Well, bless him," she said, a little too loudly. After giving Elena some instructions for other correspondence, she called for Jaime to pick her up.

The conference room next to her office had been set up for the meeting. A silver urn of cooling coffee and sugar frosted *galletas* waited on a credenza near the windows. Six empty chairs circled a marble-topped table. Patricia paced the floor between the two rooms. It was already 10:30. Her appointment with Miguel was an hour away. He had said he wouldn't wait. As unlikely as that was, she didn't want to take a chance.

"Guess you'd better reheat the coffee, Elena. But wait 'til they show. Of course, that could be *mañana*. If they're not here by 11:00, we'll have to reschedule."

"I am sorry, Señora." Elena took the coffee urn back to the kitchen.

Patricia dropped into the chair behind her desk. She had spent almost eighteen years married to a Mexican and she still didn't understand their Latin attitude toward time. She couldn't say it made them less successful, though. Tomas certainly got things done, and he was as bad as the next about being late. He had his own philosophy of time: The past is hallow, the present malleable and the future illimitable. After years of complaining, she had stopped trying to change him. Today the old frustration had come back in volumes. Damn them. Didn't they realize how precious time was for her son? She tried to make herself read some reports and be patient. It was 10:45 when she heard voices in the hall. She waited until they had time to sit down.

When she opened the door, four men waited for her. An exchange of looks told her wagers had been made as to whether she was meeting them personally, and someone had won.

"Good morning." She went straight to the chair at the head of the table and sat down, giving no one the chance to rise or greet her with an outstretched hand. She leaned forward, arms on the table, hands folded. She held them tightly to stop their shaking.

"Buenos Dias, Señora Morelos," each said in turn. Dressed in various hues of native *guayabara* shirts, sporting various size moustaches, smiling and nodding their heads, they looked like caricatures, sent to mock her. She knew from Tomas about *equipos*, groups of followers sometimes attached to a man of position since his childhood. This bunch took the concept to a new level.

"I am Juan Sanchez," the oldest of the men spoke up. He had salt and pepper hair, kind eyes, and a too quick smile. "I speak for the unfortunate miners of Real de Catorce. We welcome you back to Mexico. We still mourn the loss of our friend, Tomas Morelos; however, it is a pleasure to see his widow looking well."

Lingering odors of tobacco smoke, bacon grease and musk cologne filled the air. Patricia pushed against her stomach and took a deep breath.

"I have come here, Señor, for my son," she said to Sanchez. His reference to the "unfortunate miners" had caught her by surprise and taken the strength from her voice. It was clear who owned his sympathy. They would not get to her. She would learn what she could from them and throw them out.

"Si, si. Of course. We regret the problems at your mines, Señora. And surely you know the safety of the son of Tomas Morelos means much to us. Morelos Silver is an important industry of Mexico and in these troubled times for the peso, well, we need our industries to be prosperous." He glanced around the table and the men nodded again.

"Señor Sanchez, Max is *my* son and he is being held against his will by *your* people."

"Yes, it would seem the boy has trouble for himself. A boy so young. He should still be in his home. Why did he come to Real?" He kept smiling through the obvious rebuke.

"He came to help the miners after the cave-in," Patricia said. She would like to have wiped that smile away with some lye soap. "That's not important. Getting him freed is. My negotiators have reached an impasse. What are you doing to free my son?"

All the strength she drew together not to shout the question pooled in her hands and twisted her fingers until they hurt. Tired of talk, she felt guilty sitting around drinking coffee and having cookies while her son was a few hundred miles away probably hungry and thirsty. She had felt the same guilt for weeks with every bite she ate. These men gave no indication they felt anything. She wanted them to tell her the lies they were given to deliver and leave. Then she could go to Miguel. He was the only one, she was sure, who might give a damn. And if she couldn't make him care, what then?

Sanchez cleared his throat and reached across the table to pat her hands. She drew them back into her lap. He rubbed his hand across the cold marble instead, as if polishing it. A large silver ring on his little finger scraped the surface, making the sound of a fingernail on a blackboard.

"Surely the Señora knows we are doing everything that can be done. Everything. The miners of Real de Catorce have much sadness. They have lost loved ones in the cave-in. They would not hurt another. They know too much of suffering."

"I am very sympathetic to the miners, too, Señor Sanchez. I have offered to go to any measures to make the mines safe before they're reopened and to take care of the families of those who died or were injured. As unfortunate as the cave-in was, holding my son will not give the miners more. I don't understand what they hope to gain by kidnapping Max."

"Kidnapping is a very harsh word, Señora. We understand the young man came there to help and wants to stay. Perhaps the men only agree that he stay with them until they are sure of what is to be done."

"That is preposterous. And you all know it." Anger roiled inside Patricia like water in a hot kettle. She swallowed hard and leaned closer to Sanchez. "If Max were allowed to leave, he would have been home. I won't even discuss that fact with you."

The man continued to scrap his ring across the marble. "Whatever is the case, these miners are good persons, Señora. I assure you that we can work something out with them."

"I am glad to hear you are so certain. You can assure me then of getting my son back? Unharmed? And if so, when? Tomorrow? That wouldn't be a moment too soon. Where? Here? I'll be waiting." She stood up and looked at her watch. She felt like a hundred flying insects were trying to get out through her skin. She couldn't possibly sit still another minute, couldn't say another civil word to these men who did not care if she ever saw Max again.

Standing quickly, Juan Sanchez's hand captured hers and squeezed. His thumb rubbed across her palm. "Señora, as much as I would like to make this promise, I can not. Tomorrow may not be possible. As I said, these people have so little. The silver goes through their hands and they have nothing. Perhaps—"

"How much, Juan?" She jerked her hand free, wiped it on her skirt, and stepped away from the table. "I'll get a check."

"Señora, Señora. Not now." His moustache twitched as he looked down at his hand. "You go to your home in Acapulco. Or maybe better, back to Washington. We will negotiate with the workers for you. We have been talking with your Mr. Mainland already. Your son will be safe. I am sure Morelos Silver will be willing to give some little thing to the miners. We will let Mr. Mainland know what you can do to help the people."

Patricia looked into each of the men's faces as if memorizing them. Then she spoke to Juan in a soft voice. "If one hair on my son's head is harmed, I'll use every dollar of Morelos money to bring—"

"Oh, Señora." Sanchez raised his hands as if to ward off evil. "There is no need for threats. The money of Señor Morelos will only be needed to pay for the suffering of the miners. I assure you." He grinned, his thin moustache, a shaded line, stretched across his face.

"You'll get your money. All of you." She swept them with her eyes like dust before a broom. "Only after I get Max, unharmed." She stared at Juan until she was sure her words had left their mark, then turned and walked away. She shut her office door behind her, leaving them to find their own way out.

"Greedy bastards," she said to Rachel when she got her on the phone. She had washed her hands until they were red. Still shaking, they vibrated the receiver against her ear. "They made no bones about what they wanted. I would give them every cent I have, but I know they can't get to Max. If they could, they would not be negotiating."

"What next, then?"

"What choice do I have? Miguel is my only hope."

CHAPTER TWELVE

Gena pecked at the old, manual typewriter sending staccato notes like a telegraph key through the open door to Miguel's office. Sitting at his desk making notes, he tapped his pencil in sync with her rhythm.

He looked at his watch. Ever since Elena called this morning about a meeting with a Morelos representative, a war had waged inside him. He refused to believe Patricia would be the one to show up despite the Secretary's confirmation that she was in the city. Coming to his office would be the last thing he would expect of her. Coming to Mexico at all had put her in more danger than she could know. She would be able to do nothing to help her son. Not here. She should have stayed in Washington where she was safe.

He stopped tapping and hit the desk hard with his fist. Why should he care what happened to her? He rubbed his palms together. My God, they were sweaty. From the heat. Certainly, it had nothing to do with any feeling he had for Patricia Morelos. Not after eighteen years. Not after what had happened between them. Unbidden, images of the first time he had ever seen Patricia assaulted him, shoving aside all other senses and thoughts.

It was December 1967. Tomas had ordered him to Washington. Kicked out of UNAM for participating in student demonstrations, he had no money and, he thought, no choice but to go. He carried a chip on his shoulder the size of a Mayan temple.

Tomas' home, on a tree-lined boulevard not far from D.C.'s Embassy Row was a symbol of all Miguel had been protesting against in Mexico. The rich, the oppressors, the enslavers, the Moreloses of the world. He betrayed his conscience just walking in the front door.

Patricia Wellington was his enemy before he arrived. Miguel knew she was still going to the university, but listening to Tomas, he got the idea she ran Morelos Silver Enterprises single-handedly. Tomas bragged about her accomplishments in the same sentences that he condemned his young step-brother's failures. Miguel had envisioned a titan, a bespectacled automaton of unending energy and intelligence, a social climber with an eye on the Morelos fortune. His first meeting with her confirmed this image, but time changed everything. How disarming to find her helping the cook in the kitchen on her day off. Her slender figure, dark curls, soft chocolate eyes, and quiet voice haunted him every time they met. For all her business acumen and stamina that he came to know, she had a vulnerability, a softness under a hard crust. He set out to uncover her secrets and was shattered by them.

The upshot was she lied to him and he returned to Mexico.

There, social unrest drew him closer to the ideals of his parents. Poverty equaled purity, wealth equaled wickedness. Yet the poor wanted theirs. He marched and led and raged against the establishment. He and thousands of others tested the fiber of President Diaz Ordaz's regime that summer of 1968. The eyes of the world were on Mexico because of the upcoming Olympics. Dissidents thought the government would not want to be embarrassed and would cave-in to demands. They calculated wrong. On the second of October, ten days before the Olympic flame illuminated the Aztec Stadium, the final clash took place at the Plaza de Tlatelolco. Two hundred people lost their lives. Many were Miguel's friends. He could still hear their cries. See the blood streaming like banners as they ran. More clearly, he could hear the clanging of iron jail doors shutting on his freedom. He spent three years locked in hell.

Tomas could have had him freed, but then he might have come back for Patricia, and Tomas did not want that. Perhaps Patricia had never known where he was. Many people disappeared forever that terrible night. Had she cared? His teeth clenched, muscles constricted, as if warding off blows. That was all long ago. He had survived. He would not blame her. He would have to feel *something* even to hate her.

It was almost 11:30. If she or he or whoever did not arrive on the dot, he was leaving. He stepped to the office door and got Gena's attention. "No appointments for me tomorrow. Cancel what I have this afternoon. I'm going to Cuernavaca."

He shut the door to his office and clicked the fan control. It creaked as it whirred faster overhead, sending new found dust into the corners. *Mi Dios*, it was hot. He walked to the window, forcing himself to think about swinging in the balcony hammock at his house. The aroma of tortillas frying at a courtyard *tienda* made his stomach churn.

He saw the gray limo before it stopped and watched the chauffeur open the back door. Patricia. He knew before he saw her face. She crossed the courtyard below in swift steps. Her hair swung full and loose behind her, like a curried mane. She bounded up the steps and under the far archway. Either she was going to see someone else or didn't know where his office was. She stopped a man coming out a door. He pointed across the way. Shading her eyes with her hand, she looked straight at Miguel.

He stepped back into the shadows, cursing. At his desk he opened a drawer and pulled out the blue folder. It is all there. As much as she needed to see. The paper trail of what government agencies had supposedly done to free the Morelos boy. There really had been nothing anyone could do. The miners who took the *muchacho* had someone behind them. And the identity of that person was locked into that little mountain town as tightly as the kid was. Not that they did not have suspects. But what did you do when that included the chief of police?

The only thing everyone agreed on was that the last thing Mexico needed right now was to piss off the U.S. So far the little that had been in the papers was about the cave-in. If the truth got out about the kidnapping, it could fuel the fires of those who wanted to halt more loans to Mexico or demand repayment of some of their monstrous foreign debt. In just a few months the grace period for paying principal on $23 billion dollars in loans would end and renegotiations would begin. Mexico needed no bad publicity.

He wondered why Patricia had not gone to the press. Obviously she had not or the American media would be screaming in outrage. Anybody in the government would have given her the same information he had in the folder, yet she was coming to him. Was she expecting him to remember, or to forget?

The door opened. "Señor. Someone to see you. Señora Morelos?"

"Show her in, Gena."

Patricia stood four feet away for the first time in a lifetime. Neither of them spoke. She looked slowly around the room, stared at the painting of his mother. One just like it had hung in the gallery in Tomas's home. He wondered if she had kept it.

"Señora Morelos." He nodded. His voice seemed to come from somewhere outside the room. He started to put out his hand, but not wanting to feel her touch, he pointed to the chair instead. She hesitated, looking at the sagging cane bottom and he almost smiled. That chair would hold an elephant.

She did not look like the typical American business woman. The owner of a multimillion dollar corporation had no right to look like a young girl. Her flowing hair and rosy cheeks belonged too much to the one he had known so long ago.

He realized that was probably her plan.

"It is an honor to have so important a person visit my humble office."

She stared at him as if his words were an insult.

"Did you not expect it to be so?" he continued. "The offices of Morelos silver would have been much more comfortable for you. But I have never been welcome there." He made no attempt to withhold his sarcasm, but her silence turned the point of his knife-sharp words onto himself. He watched confusion etch her face, then something else. Hate? Disgust?

"I didn't come to compare interior designs," she said softly.

"Nor to discuss the advantages of wealth. I apologize."

She nodded, her gaze fixed on the wall above his head, as if caught up in a thought or memory. "Obviously, graft and corruption hasn't lined the hallways of your department," she said, smiling slightly. Her voice chilled him. It was as cold and hard as the terrazzo floor she continued to scrape with her sandals. He stared hard at her. They had fought this battle before and he had no desire to arm himself again.

Custom demanded that he offer her some refreshment and idle gossip before getting down to business. Obviously, she would say no to any such overtures and he was in no mood to make them. Instead, he picked up the blue folder and held it out to her.

"Everything I can tell you about your son is in here." Her hands shook as she took it from him. He watched her eyes scan each document quickly as she flipped the pages. She said nothing, but clutched the papers to her chest. He could hear her breath beneath the sounds of birds in the courtyard. Suddenly, she threw the folder onto the desk.

"I had hoped for more from you. I guess I shouldn't have. This is the same thing I heard this morning from the miner's henchmen." Her voice broke, then exploded. "Max is a head-strong teenager, but he came to Mexico with good intentions. What right have these workers who hold out their hands for Morelos money to take my son? Working in a mine is hard. I can appreciate that. I empathize with the families of the men who died in that cave-in. If it were not for the mine, how would any of these people survive?" She had come out of the chair and stood leaning almost into his face, but she looked back down at the papers, as if she would not let him hold her gaze.

Many arguments came to his mind about what better lives these people could have without the mines, but he said none of them. Anger rose inside him as he realized that she had always been rich and had no concept of what life offered that money could not buy. He said only the words she wanted to hear.

"Efforts are continuing to find your son. I do not know what the representatives told you this morning, but if you read these documents carefully, you will see the ones who hold your son are probably not the workers of the Morelos mine. There is another group of men who have been miners but now band together in hopes of reclaiming the mines for themselves. Perhaps they are responsible."

"I can read. That doesn't tell me why Max is still there. He's just a boy! Are you telling me no one has any power over these men? Can't the police go in there and just take him?" She struck her fist hard on the table.

He winced, feeling her pain, then struggled against the sentiment. Her attack was personal. As if this kid were his responsibility. His duty was to his people. Max was her son. Why had she not kept him at home? He should laugh in her face at Tomas's teenage runaway being kidnapped.

She had not moved. The fire that came from her eyes burned through him. Battle drums beat a double cadence inside his heart.

Images of her full red lips meeting his blurred his view of her. He shook his head more to clear it than to answer her. "No, they cannot storm the place where your son is. Have you ever been to Real de Catorce? No? I did not think so. It is in the mountains. There is only one way in, through a tunnel which they control. They know everyone."

He stood up and moved to the window while he talked. A little boy bounced a ball against a tree in the courtyard. Thump. Thump. Was it the ball he heard or his heart?

"What else can be done?" she asked quietly.

He looked back as she cleared her throat. He watched her bite her lip and blink back tears. Her fist pressed her stomach in a remembered gesture. She would not let him see her weak. She would not beg. He knew her that well.

He walked to the bookcase and drew down a map of Mexico. Please do not cry, he pleaded silently. He must tell her what he could quickly, and she would leave.

"Here is Real." He pointed with a pencil to a place north of Mexico City. "The Sierra Catorce mountains surround the city." His hand shook slightly and he dropped it by his side. "The fourth of October is the feast day of St. Francis at the church of *La Purisima Concepcion.* Many people from all over the country come to pray to the Saint for favors—riches, health, the return of a loved one. Or give thanks for miracles he has given them. They buy *milagros*, little silver medallions, to give him in offering. It is a beautiful cathedral. It was the old Spanish custom to permit miners to take each day out of the mine as large a piece of ore as one could carry in his hand. They gave it to the priest to build the church."

Mi Dios, I'm rattling like a tour guide, he thought. She had moved closer and stood only a step or two away. The scent of her perfume surrounded him with each turn of the fan.

He leaned toward her. "Preparation for the festival begins this week, the last week of September. Vendors are moving through the tunnel now. To set up stands to sell goods to the pilgrims. The miners let them pass, but they search the people and watch them carefully. After the festival measures can be taken to get to your son."

"That's another week! We can't wait. We have to get Max out now."

"It is not possible. Before the festival it is too dangerous for the people."

She stepped closer to the map. "How do you get to Real? Can you drive through the tunnel?" She drew a line with her finger from Mexico City to Queretaro, to Matehuala and Cedral, then up the winding mountain road to Real. She smiled for the first time.

His heart withdrew from the blow.

"The tunnel is closed to motor traffic until after the festival. The miners search any service vehicles and wagons for those who do not belong." He knew she was not listening. Knew where her thoughts were. He had to stop her.

"Patricia, you cannot think to go there yourself." It was the first time he had spoken her name. The sound was like a sweetness on his tongue. He wanted to taste it again.

"Patricia?"

"It's a free country, Miguel. I can go anywhere I please."

"Damn it, you cannot go there." He slapped the pencil down onto the bookcase. The map slipped, streaked upwards, flapped on its roller. His hands moved toward her, but he stopped them and skirted around her to his desk. He shook the blue folder at her. "I told you these men are not the miners of Morelos. They have no loyalty to you and do not respect you. You do not know them. Many people could be hurt besides your son. It is dangerous!" He drew his brows together so harshly the furrows felt like cuts.

"And you don't know me very well, Señor Ramirez, if you think I am going to sit still, wringing my hands, while nothing is being done to get my son back."

The creaking fan filled the silence.

"No. I have never truly known you, Patricia." His voice felt weak, vulnerable, but she jumped, as if he stabbed at her with his words. He recovered quickly, strengthening his resolve and his voice. "But that is not important, is it? As I said, you do not know these men."

"All the more reason I have to go and get Max myself. They don't know me either."

"What can you do alone?" he asked, a sliver of fear for her and her determination edged under his skin.

"Once you know exactly how things get done down here, you can accomplish anything by yourself. As long as you have money. I certainly got that message this morning. All I have to do is use some good old-fashioned dollars. Pay '*la mordida.*' The bribe." Her words came at him like machine gun fire, but her fingers trembled as she took her billfold from her purse and pitched it on the desk.

He stiffened as he watched it slide toward him as if it were a live grenade. "I guess I should not be surprised at such a statement from the wife of Tomas Morelos. So he taught you everything. Even how to buy your way through life."

"If that's what it takes, yes. And I'm sure he would not care if I spent every dime to find his son." She gave a little choking sound. Her last words came out muffled.

He could handle her anger, her spite, her hatred, but not her tears, or her mother's words of a son. He wanted her to rage again, so he shouted, "You will not go, Patricia."

Her stare, her silence said she was not listening, but contemplating how she could defy him. "I will see to it that you do not get to the tunnel, Señora. Do not try it." His words were even, firm, final.

She said nothing, picked up her purse, replaced the billfold, and walked to the door. With her hand on the knob, her back to him, she spoke softly. "I will get my son back, Miguel."

"Go to Acapulco. Stay there, Patricia. For your own good, stay there."

Miguel. Miguel. The name ricocheted about her in the hall outside his office. She struggled to put one foot in front of the other.

At the end of the hall she saw the faded letters DAMAS. She fell against the door, praying it was not locked. A hot blast of stale air pushed her back as it escaped the room, but she hurried to the grimy sink that hung precariously from the wall.

When her body had ceased its convulsions, she washed her face and rinsed her mouth with the water that dribbled from the faucet, inviting the germs lurking there to attack her. She didn't care.

A piece of broken mirror propped on a rusted shelf gave back the image of a tear stained face twisted in grief, anger, and shame. Tears begat tears and she mourned her son, loud and laboriously.

She also mourned her lost love. The passion. The innocence. It all ended so long ago. Admitting this, she also had to acknowledge that it was she who destroyed the love she and Miguel had known. Destroyed it by the very truth that she had not been innocent.

She washed her face as anger took over. She should have known Miguel would not help her. Widow of the man he had hated. She was a fool to come to him. He had not changed. That shabby, dingy office. The portrait of his mother. He still worshiped at the feet of poverty. He still hated money and those who had it. Max was just a spoiled rich kid to him. The son of a man who worshiped riches.

The son.

Shame washed over her anger. Rachel had counseled her to tell the truth. "And the truth shall set you free." The laugh she heard must have come from someone else, but she was alone.

She imagined herself going back to Miguel's office. She could feel the sagging chair beneath her. Hear the whirring fan. See Miguel's face, his angled jaw, dimpled chin, distinguished Mayan nose. The image changed to the memory of him at twenty. No. It was Max she saw. A young Miguel. An older Max. The images blurred.

The truth.

There was no need for her to tell Miguel anything. He would know soon enough. When he came face to face with Max, he would know that he, not Tomas, was the boy's father.

The truth would *not* set her free.

CHAPTER THIRTEEN

A broad-winged frigate soared in the blue sky over Acapulco Bay. Below, waves slapped and swirled in white foam. Rocks dunked, popped back. Between sea and sky jutted a pink house, a giant shell against the blue. Sitting on the balcony, Patricia watched as the bird's long black wings winked, then caught a draft and disappeared into the sunlight. Leaning forward, she rested her head and arm against the cool metal rail.

"Patricia? Are you there?" Rachel's voice drifted from the cavernous house.

"Yes." She stood and cleared her throat. "Any calls?" She wiped her eyes with her palms, and dried her hands on her shorts.

"No. You okay? Marta told me you were out here. Why didn't you let me know you were back?"

"You were asleep. Didn't want to disturb you."

"Siestas. They're habit forming." Rachel's hand drifted along a hammock, then reached across open air for the railing.

Patricia took her hand, squeezed it, then placed it beneath hers on the iron bar.

Cries of birds filled the air.

Rachel turned her face toward the breeze. "What are they?"

"Pelicans."

"They must be the ones I hear going toward *Pie la Questa* Lagoon every afternoon. How many?"

"Twelve, fifteen, maybe. They're flying in a "v" shape." She listened to what Rachel could hear. "I've been watching this frigate circling Roqueta Island. It's always alone." Just how she felt. She leaned into the breeze and wrapped her arms against her sides. "Have you talked to Annie?"

"No, she still doesn't answer. I hope Roger doesn't forget to check on her. He may not even remember where she is."

Patricia laughed. "Annie will remind him."

"Want to tell me what you found out today?"

"Nothing to tell. Zero. Nada. I told you about the thieves in *guayabara* shirts. And Miguel, well, I'm not sure about him. I think he may be worse." She had labored over their meeting, picking at each phrase he'd uttered. When she had scratched away the surface, the stark bones of what he'd said frightened her. *He knew the kidnappers.* She was sure of it.

"What did he have to say?" Rachel asked.

"Well, I'll start at the end. He yelled at me to stay in Acapulco and stay out of Real. And ever since I left his office, I've had doors slamming in my face. Can you believe the plane is grounded unless we're leaving the country?"

"Can he do that?"

"That and more. I called around to rent a plane, and there's not one to be had. For any price. I can't find a parrot to fly."

"I'd say you made him a little mad at you. What'd you do?"

Patricia looked at Rachel, willing her to feel the intensity of the stare. "I didn't 'do' anything." She sat down and got back up like a jack-in-the-box. "All I did was try to get some answers."

"And did you?"

"Well, he tried to tell me some renegade miners are holding Max. And since they don't like anyone named Morelos, I'd be in danger going there. If that's so, what about Max? Doesn't it make sense that we need to get in there and rescue him? Now?"

"Miguel refused to do that?"

"Oh no, he will. He says. On his own timetable. He's waiting for the festival to be over."

"The festival?"

Patricia was suddenly very tired. She gave Rachel's arm a little squeeze and said, "How about I tell you all about it at dinner? I need to make a couple of calls, and then maybe I'll try on one of those siestas. You mind?" She summoned up a smile because she knew Rachel could hear it in her voice.

"Course not. I'll give the hammock a ride. Let me know if you need me."

By dinner time, Patricia had not slept, nor had she found a way to get to Real. A car or jeep and a good map looked like her only hope. She had accomplished one thing, a stronger determination.

She spent the cocktail hour on the balcony telling Rachel about her meeting with Miguel.

Marta called them to dinner and they sat down to a table heavy with food: *ensalada, chile rellenos, arroz,* and *biftec tampico.* They ate in a small sitting room just off the garden. The night air carried the fragrance of flowers.

While Rachel ate, Patricia raved on about Miguel. "He may think he has me cornered, but he ought to know me better."

"What are you going to do?"

"I haven't a clue," Patricia muttered and absentmindedly chewed on a piece of cheese from one of the chiles.

"Well, I may have an idea." Rachel put her fork down. "While I was sitting around doing nothing, I talked to Roberto. It seems he has a cousin that knows these mountains near Catorce. You might could hire him to go there and look for Max."

"What?"

"If you'd like, you could ask Roberto about this cousin."

"Roberto?" Patricia said, picturing a mud-smeared Mexican boy running through the spray when his father, Mario, was watering the plants. Mario had been the Morelos's gardener even before she married Tomas. She had not seen the child in several years.

"Yes, I think he's around somewhere."

As if summoned by Rachel's quiet words, an equally quiet voice called from the garden, "Señora?"

"Come in," Rachel said.

Patricia saw that Roberto was still a child, probably eleven or twelve, and still unwashed. He was small boned, but wiry and muscled, a miniature of his father. His eyes watched her, but he moved closer to Rachel.

"Did they find him?" Rachel asked, her hand on his arm.

"Max? Someone found Max?" Patricia almost screamed, standing abruptly, Roberto pulled himself away from Rachel's grasp.

"Roberto, come back," Rachel held out her hand. "And Patricia, will you listen? Did they find your cousin?" she asked the boy.

Patricia sat back in her chair.

"Si, Señora. The n—news, he is good. M—maybe. He say—" The boy gave Patricia a glance.

"*Despaccio.* Slower, Roberto," Rachel coaxed, "And you'll not stutter. Now, what did he say?"

The boy rammed his hands into his pants, thrusting the pockets below the ragged hem. He stood straight, official. "*Mi primo*—cuzine, say gringo, uh, Americano, he in mountains. Silver there, mucho long ago. Now, only leetle."

He turned to Patricia with a smile that showed straight, strong teeth. "Is good, Señora? Perhaps is Max, *su hijo?*"

Patricia reached out and gripped the boy's shoulders. It took a great will to do it, but she smiled. "Max, the Americano, what else does your cousin say about him, Roberto? Is he okay?" She said the words slowly, quietly, and set her teeth until her jaw ached.

"He no say no more, Señora." He frowned and twisted one bare foot on top of the other, grinding pale dust into his dark skin. The movement freed him from Patricia's hold.

"I want to talk to your father, Roberto. Now. Can you bring him?" She leaned into the child's face.

"Si, Señora. Not now. He go to *zocalo*."

A breeze blew through the open door, tugging at her hair. She'd have helped the wind pull it from its roots if that could have calmed her soul. "Very well. Tell your father I want to see him the moment he comes home. No matter the time. *Comprende?* Go. Wait for him!"

The boy sauntered out of the garden and down some stairs, yelling, "Papa!"

Patricia clasped Rachel's hand. She was shaking with excitement. "This is wonderful, Rache. You've solved my problem. I can't believe you found someone who can take me there and I've got—"

"Take you?" Rachel jerked her hand back. "What do mean, 'take you'? That's not—"

"Don't you see, this is perfect. Just what I need. Someone who knows the area. If this cousin can get me to the miners, I can make a deal with them, myself." She got up from the table mid way of her speech and paced the small room.

"Oh? Good idea." Rachel leaned back in her chair. "The kidnappers. They'll love that. They'll probably make a trade. You for Max. Nothing like having the owner of the company in your clutches and a pretty woman as a bonus. A definite improvement over a lanky kid. Yep, they'll love it."

"I don't plan on that happening, Rachel. I'm going to get Max out of there and me with him. And Miguel Ramirez will know that he was not man enough to stop me." The more real her plan became the more sure she sounded of her success.

"And just how do you figure that?"

"I'm not sure yet. The first thing is to get there, and thanks to you, I may have a way."

"Please spare me the gratitude. I don't want anybody knowing I had anything to do with your hair-brain idea. Jim will have my head on a platter. A Morelos silver platter, I hope."

Silence fell between the two of them. Rachel picked at what was left of the cold dinner. Patricia busied herself with thoughts of preparations for going to Real.

"Señora, you no like *la comida*?" Marta asked, lifting the plate still full of *chile rellenos*.

Patricia held a fork full of rice in midair. It was cold and dry. She shoved it in her mouth and mumbled, "Yes, everything was delicious. Thank you, Marta."

The woman gave her a puzzled look, patted Rachel on the shoulder and finished clearing the dishes.

As soon as they were alone, Rachel started asking questions. "Patricia, I know Max needs rescuing, but who do you think you are? Jane Bond? Running off with a stranger into mountains and mines doesn't sound like the Madison Avenue, Bergdorf, 'Oh no, I broke a nail' Patricia Morelos I know."

"Thanks, Rache. Thanks for the confidence."

"Have you thought about the fact that you might make things worse?"

"Worse? You sound like Miguel. My son has been kidnapped by criminals. The police at home think he's a runaway, yet no one I sent down here could find him. Everyone down here knows he's been kidnapped, yet there is nothing in the papers about it. No one in this whole damned country is willing to do one thing about getting him released. And the one person I thought might, may have been behind it to start with!"

"Miguel? Why do you say that?"

"Two things. He knew too much about who's holding Max. And he's trying too hard to keep me from going up there. He's got something to hide."

"Haven't we all," Rachel muttered.

"Don't start, Rache. Miguel Ramirez told me in no uncertain terms that his worry is *his* people, not Max. He's afraid *they'll* get hurt. He couldn't care less if I ever see my son again." Her voice had pitched loud and high. The words hung in the air.

"He might care more if he knew Max was his son."

Rachel's voice seemed a whisper. It was the final pinprick to Patricia's bag of wind. The will went out of her and she slumped in her chair. She had been waiting for it to happen, for that sharp thorn of doubt to gouge her strength. When she had left Miguel's building, she was so sure she was right. There in the heat and stagnant air of the bathroom she had decided against telling him about his son. Had she been wrong?

She picked up a small silver bell and shook it. Marta reappeared. "Coffee, Marta. On the balcony, please."

A breeze stirred as the sun dipped into the ocean lighting the clouds in soft pinks. They said nothing more until steaming cups were placed in front of them. On a tray with the cream and sugar was a bottle of Kahlua.

"Marta's trying to tell me something," Patricia said. "She doesn't like me to raise my voice. How about some strong stuff in your coffee?" Patricia poured a good measure of liqueur in both cups.

While the hot brew raked her throat, she tried to rebuild her self-command. She began with an unalterable fact. Whatever doubts she might have now about not telling Miguel the truth, there was no doubt about why. The same clear reason confronted her. Telling him that he had a son would not be the secret key to free Max and make everything right. Miguel would hate her. He probably wouldn't want anything to do with Max even if he knew Max was his son. He would think Tomas had tainted him. If she told him why she married Tomas, it would only be the beginning. Opening that door would mean opening others. The first of all the secret doors of her life. Was she ready for that?

"Patricia, listen to me," Rachel finally spoke. "I don't want you going to Real, but I can't do much to stop you. Looks like I've helped you, as you said, but Miguel cares too. If he didn't, he'd leave you alone on your hell-bent road to disaster."

"Like the one he was running down eighteen years ago and wanted to take me along for the ride?"

"Well, Miguel was a young idealist. He wanted to save his people."

"Even if it meant jail or death? For both of us? You're forgetting how he deserted me to go protest in Mexico City. I didn't jump at the opportunity to martyr myself along with him, and he went without me. Never even cared to know what happened to me after he left. The only ones he cared about were the poor souls his mother created as idols for him. Now he has a chance to use my son to get them everything they want. The mines. The Morelos fortune. And why shouldn't he? What better way to get even with Tomas? What better way to get even with me for not going back to Mexico with him?" Her back went rigid as she contemplated the worst.

Rachel gave a little laugh, breaking the tension. "I bet you never knew how I envied you back then."

"You?"

"Well, it was before the suave and debonair Mr. Roger Davis arrived on the scene. I would think about you two, making out every night in that little Thunderbird Tomas had given you."

Patricia almost choked. "Is that what you thought?"

"Of course, why not?"

"Because it didn't happen."

"What do you mean? You got pregnant with Max. Are you saying it was immaculate conception?"

"No. Max is Miguel's all right. It just wasn't the way you imagined it." She was serious again, somber.

"Tell me about it?" Rachel's voice matched Patricia's.

"Oh, it seems rather ridiculous now. Things have changed so much. Wonder if young Mexican men feel the same today as Miguel did back then."

"How?"

"Expecting the girl to be a virgin." There. She had said it. What more should she tell Rachel? Would she understand?

Rachel laughed. "Male chauvinist pigs."

"Miguel wasn't just disappointed in my 'being ruined'. The conclusion his jealous mind jumped to was what did us in."

"He thought you had been Tomas's mistress?"

"Give the lady a star," Patricia said, reaching her hand out into the black night as if she could pluck one from the heavens.

"So that's the real reason he left that summer. Why wouldn't he believe you?"

"He tried. I think he wanted to. In the end, when I wouldn't go to Mexico with him, that was his proof, his out, and I was 'guilty as charged'."

"Did you tell him who it really was?"

"No."

"Why not?"

"Because my life before I met Miguel was none of his business."

She thought about how Rachel was always so sure that truth could turn trash into treasure, could right the wrongs of the world. Maybe Rachel didn't understand how a lie was sometimes necessary because she depended on being told how things were instead of seeing things for herself. That still didn't mean that people didn't have a right to privacy. A right to secrets. She wanted to get back to talking about Max and how to bring him home. She thought about the night he left. For once she could prove Rachel wrong. "So you think Miguel would have understood if I had bared my soul and told all?"

"Yes." Rachel's head nodded once. An exclamation point.

Patricia slapped at mosquitoes that found her arms now that the breeze had died. "Just like Max understood?"

Rachel jerked her head as if she had been struck. "What do you mean? You told him about you and Miguel?"

"No. Just some things about me. The night before he left." She sank into a chair and kept talking, trying to drown out the echo of her son's voice. "He was upset about the cave-in. Actually, he was raving. About the mines not being safe. About the poor and the rich. You'd have thought this kid who loved caviar at six and got a Corvette for his sixteenth birthday had the inside tract on poverty. Like he was the only one. When I said I also cared about these miners and their families, he had the nerve to ask me how I could, when all I'd ever known was money and power. I didn't even think it out. I just wanted him to stop accusing me. So I told him just how wrong he was."

"Exactly what did you tell him?"

"That I didn't live with you after my parents died. That my family didn't have any money and I had actually lived in a foster home. I told him about Elsie and Jeff. How poor we were. I even told him about coming to find you that day."

"I should still be angry at you for that."

"What? Coming to your house?"

"No, for *not* coming until five years after you were in D.C. I guess if you hadn't seen my engagement picture in the *Washington Post*, you wouldn't ever have come."

"Well, I had reasons," she said, quietly.

Rachel turned toward Patricia, her eyes blank, but intense, as if she wanted to see into Patricia's soul or at least into those missing five years. Patricia had tried to tell Rachel about why she left Alabama and why she didn't look her up immediately, but the words would never come. Shame had buried them too deeply.

Bats swooshed through the air feeding on mosquitos.

Patricia broke the silence with a laugh. "Do you remember how tongue-tied you were that day, trying to explain who I was to your mother?"

Rachel's cheeks dimpled with the memory. "She was so sure she had met you before. She even called you Dorothy. If you hadn't called me first, I probably wouldn't have believed it was you. I didn't know how much your looks had changed, but your voice sure had."

"And you're always kidding me about my Southern accent."

"I didn't say you had lost all of it, but as Mrs. Tomas Morelos, it didn't take much to convince Mom you were not Dorothy Tucker."

"Max had a hard time believing I ever was." Patricia drifted back into the memory of that night with her son. "He kept staring at me like I was a stranger. I thought he was listening, understanding, but he—" She cupped her hands around her knees and drew them to her chest. "He said he didn't know who I was anymore. Then he walked out. Next morning he was gone."

"I'm sorry, honey." Rachel rubbed her hand down Patricia's arm. "He's just a kid. He'll give you another chance. He'll even be proud you had it tough when he thinks about it. Max has always rooted for the underdog, the losing team."

"Ironic, isn't it?" Patricia asked.

"What?"

"Miguel and Max. Like father, like son."

Marta interrupted and asked if they wanted anything else. She took away the coffee cups when they said no, but left the Kahlua and two small glasses.

Patricia watched the stars brighten in the darkening sky. "I never told Max the truth because a child needs to know he comes from good people."

"Max isn't a child now, Patricia. He can handle it."

"Can he?" she whispered, looking from star to star, as if asking them.

"Sure, try him," Rachel said.

Patricia nodded as if Rachel could see her. Yes. That's what she'd do, she thought. Sure. Next time she saw her son, she'd tell him all about what a wonderful reunion she and her father had when she was fifteen.

CHAPTER FOURTEEN

ALABAMA 1962

Dorothy flipped the metal dividers on the jukebox selections. Rachel sat across the table. It was the first Saturday of the new year and Rachel had just come back from the holidays. All the talk was about the President being shot and how sad that he wasn't there for Christmas with his family.

"Gee, I'm sorry, Dorothy," Rachel said. "I'd forgot about your Mom and Dad." Her hand reached for Patricia's. Fingers touched and squeezed, their signal for a smile.

In the four months they had known each other, Dorothy had confessed to Rachel that Elsie and Jeff were not her mom and dad, replacing them with loving parents who died tragically when she was six. The story grew in details drawn from books she read.

Rachel had told Dorothy about being blinded in a car accident when she was fourteen. She had described how her life changed to solitude and darkness, how she was terrified leaving her parents and her home in Virginia. Dorothy consoled her friend, knowing *her* perfect parents would not have sent her away.

"What you want to hear?" Dorothy tossed her raisin-colored curls to one side, propped her hand against her cheek, covering pimples. She looked at Rachel, at peaches and cream complexion. Not with envy so much as puzzlement. Rachel couldn't even see her face. Wouldn't matter if it was covered with a million zits. Dorothy wasn't sure why she didn't feel sorry for Rachel. It had something to do with things evening out.

A loud screech interrupted her thoughts.

"That damn nickelodeon stuck again?" Elsie called out from the kitchen.

"I'll fix it, Elsie," Dorothy said and squeezed in behind the machine. She pulled the plug from the wall. An icy wind circled her, as someone entered the diner.

"Are you Elsie McFall?" A man's voice came out of the cold.

"That's me. Who's askin'?"

"Name's Cecil Tucker. Pleased to meet you."

Dorothy looked at the cord in her hand. No current flowed through it. Yet, she was electrified, paralyzed.

"Likewise. What'll you have?"

"Coffee. Black."

A cup and saucer clattered. "Anything else?"

"Yeah, I'm looking for somebody. My daughter, Dorothy."

She threw the black line away as if it had shocked her, stumbled against the machine, then moved around it, eyes flashing.

"Pa? Is that you?"

"Sure is, little 'un. How 'bout a hug for your ole man?"

Dorothy glanced at Elsie, then at Rachel, unseeing and yet knowing too much.

"Well, little Doe. Been awhile, ain't it?" Flat moss-green eyes stared at her. She didn't move. His arms folded around her. Coarse cloth scratched her cheek. The smell of mothballs and stale whiskey choked her.

"Rachel, go in the kitchen and call Jeff to fix this machine." Elsie's voice shook.

Rachel felt her way out of the booth and through the swinging doors. Cecil sat back on the stool. Dorothy stared at him, her eyes burning.

"Where you been, Pa? How long you been out?"

"I been home awhile, but—can't believe how you've growed. Spittin' image of your ma. Same dark eyes and hair." He looked back at Elsie, ran his fingers through greying, brownish-red hair. "I been tryin' to find you. Never knowed who had you. Hank and Billy joined the Army. Don't know where Jackson is. Just went off, the Bakers said." He sipped some coffee.

"What happened to the twins and . . . the baby?"

"Well, I don't rightly know, for sure. Preacher Johnny took them, but I heard tell his missus was poorly and they give the kids up to the county people."

"Couldn't you find out where they are?" Dorothy fought tears. Her nose pinched inside. She sneezed.

"Well, it ain't easy, Doe. Them folks like to keep things secret." His cheeks sunk beneath high bones and creased in waves around a smile marred by tobacco-stained teeth.

"How did you find me?"

"Oh, I knowed—well, somebody that knowed somebody." He kept his eyes on the counter, as Elsie refilled his cup.

"You want something, honey? A cherry Coke or float, maybe?" she asked Dorothy.

"Thanks, not now," she said, then mouthed the words, Where's Rache? as she nodded toward the coat and cane hanging on the coat rack. Elsie nodded back, then picked up Rachel's things and disappeared through the swinging doors.

"I got a surprise for you, Doe. I come to take you home for a late Christmas. And guess who'll be there?" His grin widened. "Hank and Billy."

"They're home? Now?"

"Sure are. On leave. Got another surprise, too."

"What?"

"See that green car, out by the curb? That's Billy's. He let me drive her here to get you. Handles like a dream."

Her breath caught. "I can't go." She looked toward the kitchen.

"You can't? Why can't you?" He leaned into her face, then glancing around, backed off. "Billy and Hank expects us. They got things all ready," he whined.

"I got a friend here, Pa. Spendin' the weekend with me, and Elsie and Jeff." How could she explain Rachel to Pa? Or Pa to Rachel? Her heart beat hard, taking her breath. Rachel would know all about her now. She wouldn't want to be friends with a girl whose Pa had been in jail. She'd never be able to face Rachel again.

With a sigh as deep as a well, she whispered, "I'll go."

* * *

Dorothy recognized the little church on Dry Valley Road as Pa turned onto a dirt lane an hour's drive from Talladega. All the way there, he had talked, about Hank and Billy, and she had thought about Rachel. Jeff and Elsie had put up an argument about Pa taking her. She had wanted to go, as long as it was just for a visit. Elsie promised to see that Rachel wasn't lonely, and Dorothy would have a few days to think of what to tell Rachel.

Barbed wire lined the road. Fence posts sprouted cedar trees. Sooner than she expected, there was the old house. Smaller than she remembered, with clapboards missing, but some new tin on the roof. The chinaberry tree was taller. Car parts and tires lay tangled in high weeds like burrs in a dog's fur.

As soon as she got out of the car, two slim men in Army fatigues rushed out of the house and grabbed her, turning her to face one, then the other.

"Well, if it ain't little Doe."

"Ain't she a beauty?"

She stared at them. One had Pa's high cheek bones and green eyes. Billy. The other one was Hank. He looked like Ma. She searched his dull, brown eyes for something familiar, but it was like looking into Choccolocco Creek after a rain: beneath the muddy water were things you knew—fish, turtles, tadpoles—but out of sight, they were mysterious and frightening. She shifted her weight and shrugged their arms from her shoulders.

"What's wrong, kiddo? Ain't you givin' out no hugs, at least? Betcha there's a lineup at your door like the kissin' booth at the fair. Ain't that right, Pa?"

The older man glared at his sons. "Aw, you two leave her be, now." He squinted at Dorothy. "Don't want you rilin' up the cook. Let's go, girl. See what you learned in that diner."

In the kitchen a wild turkey covered the table, its feathers mud-caked and bloody. The top of a cold wood stove was cluttered with yams and onions, jars of green beans and a sack of flour. It was obvious what the men expected her to do. It was also clear that not much had been cooked in this kitchen since her mom had died. It would take hours of cleaning before she could think about cooking the feast they had planned for tomorrow.

As she moved around the small space, touching the old pots and pans, the sink and table, she was overwhelmed by memories.

Ma, one hand mixing dough, the other on one of the twins hanging on her hip. Children chattering, grease frying. The feel of the soft tops of unbaked bread.

Hard work was the only way to keep back the tears. She had learned that long ago.

As the hours between plucking feathers and peeling potatoes went by, she kept the men content with beer and sandwiches. Except for an occasional question, they ignored her as long as the food and drink kept coming. When they had passed out and the fire had died, she went down the hall to the tiny bedroom where she and the twins had once slept.

Earlier she had swept the room and opened the window. Now she lowered it against the cold night air. A rusted iron bed, small trunk, and kerosene lantern furnished the room. She lit the lantern and set it on an upturned bucket. In the trunk she found two old quilts. And a glassless metal frame. She picked it up and stared in the lamplight at a picture of her family.

Jackson, Hank, Billy. Pa, straight and stern in a chair, his hands stiff against his thighs, oblivious to her, the baby on his lap. Ma, standing behind, only her head and shoulders in view. Probably she was pregnant. No one was smiling. This was her family. Not the man and woman she had described to Rachel. She was not the darling daughter of lost and mourned dead parents. She rebelled at the thought. No matter how hard she tried to imagine otherwise, with every pump of her heart, her mind chanted: this is my pa, my brothers.

She propped the picture against the lamp, blew out the light and drew herself into a ball, ghosts of the twins crowding her.

The next day was a disaster. She slept late, didn't get the turkey in the oven until noon and it took the rest of the day to cook. She didn't have enough wood and when she asked Pa to get some, he slapped her and sent her out to chop it herself. They sat down to eat after dark, the men drunk and grumbling.

It was late when she put on her gown and fell into bed. A noise woke her. Dawn was aglow through the torn curtains.

"Dorothy, you awake?" Hank was calling her.

"What?" she answered.

"Can I come in a minute?"

She pulled the quilts around her and whispered, "Yes."

The tall young man who looked so much like their mother eased quietly through the door and shut it. He was dressed in his uniform, his hat held flat in his hand, burred head tilted, as if embarrassed to look at her.

"Why're you dressed? Where're you going?" She sat up against the iron bars of the bed, dragging the quilts with her.

Hank put his finger to his lips and frowned, glancing at the door. "Me and Billy got to go back to base. Our leave's up."

"Why didn't ya'll tell me you're leaving this morning. I'll get up. I won't have a way back if I don't go with you." She swung her feet on to the cold floor, but Hank put his hand out and sat on the side of the bed.

"Pa'll take you later. He's keeping the car. Me and Billy's going overseas. Can't take the car with us, now can we?" He laughed quietly, glancing again at the door.

"But I don't want to stay if you're leaving."

"Pa won't take you now, Doe. He—he's got some things, washing and stuff, he wants you to do, then he'll take you. He promised me he'd do that, as soon as the chores are finished. You'll just have to stay another day if you work fast."

They said nothing more for minutes. A rooster's crow split the quiet. As if it were a signal, Hank said, "Gotta go, kid." He stood up, turned to leave, then came back. "One more thing, Doe." He reached in a pocket and brought out a slender box.

Dorothy jumped as he took a knife from its case.

"I want you to keep this." He squatted down and held out the knife. The smooth, milky handle touched her hand.

"Why?" She drew back like he was handing her a snake.

"Just a gift. Could come in handy some day. You might use it, say, to open a letter, or if you went fishing, to cut some bait." His words came fast and low.

"I don't understand—"

"Take it, Doe. Keep it handy. That's all." He dropped the knife on the quilt, leaned forward and pecked her cheek. "See ya next time I'm home. Take care of yourself." The door closed on his last words.

Long after the car rattled down the road, Dorothy lay in bed. She would have stayed there, but if Pa was going to take her back home, she had to get up and do the work he expected.

She took the knife from its box and looked at it more carefully in the sunlight. The white handle glimmered like the inside of muscles and periwinkles they used to gather from the mud of the creek. The blade glistened like a new dime. She was sorry she hadn't thanked Hank properly. It was a nice gift. She slid it between the picture frame and the lamp.

The pile of smelly clothes she gathered reached almost as high as the old wringer washer on the back porch. By the time they were all hanging in the sunshine, she was exhausted. She still cleaned floors and scooped ashes out of the fireplace. Pa had not returned by supper time. She ate a sandwich and sat in a willow rocker in front of the fire she had started and waited. When he got back, he would take her home. To Elsie and Jeff's. Back to school, the diner and Rachel.

His hand on her shoulder woke her.

"What you doin', girl? How 'bout something to eat? Nothin' cooked and you sleepin'? Done let the fire nearly go out." He headed out the door for wood.

Dorothy cooked biscuits, gravy and some of the leftover turkey. They ate in silence. When she started taking the dishes away, she said, "I got all the chores finished, Pa. When I'm done cleanin' up, I'll be ready for you to take me back home. Elsie'll be needin' me."

His green eyes seemed as dead as algae on the pond when he turned to her. "Home? What you mean go home? Don't you know that's where you are, girl? Why, I ain't takin' you back nowhere. You're mine. Nobody better get no ideas otherwise."

"But—but what about school?" Her hand pressed against a cold emptiness in her stomach.

"You got enough of that book learnin'. You know how to cook. That's all you need to make a man happy. Well, almost," he laughed.

The cold inside her hardened into ice. "But Elsie's depending on me. And Rache—"

"There's nobody but me, now. You best understand that. I need you here."

"But Hank said—"

His hand came across her face, twisting her head. "Don't you backtalk me, girl."

She worked at the sink until she heard him go outside. Then she went to her room and dropped to the bed, all emotion drained away. She stared at the photo of her family. Her future stared back in black and white images. No more school, no job, no life, just years of hard work that would defeat her in the end. And worse than all, she would never see the McFalls or Rachel again.

She looked at the knife Hank had given her. Perhaps she understood now why he was so mysterious this morning, and kind. He knew Pa wasn't going to take her back to Talladega. He knew she was going to live here forever.

Well, she wouldn't. She put the picture frame and knife back on the upturned bucket and paced the room. She'd leave. She'd show them. All of them. She would not let this happen. There had to be a way to get back to Elsie and Jeff. That was where she belonged. They were really her mom and dad.

Pa was yelling for her to get him a beer. When she took one to him, she tried to talk to him again. "Pa. I need my other things from the McFalls. Can you take me back to get them?"

He swigged half the bottle of beer in one swallow, then his eyes moved down her blouse and skirt. "You got better clothes and more of 'em than your ma ever had. I seen what all you brought in that fancy suitcase. You don't need nothing else of those folks. Looks like they done spent plenty on you. County paid 'em well enough I guess."

She wasn't sure she heard him right. Her hands gripped each other, her nails digging into her flesh. "What? The county paid them? What do you mean? Why?" Her legs went out from under her and she sat hard in the willow rocker.

He laughed. "Why, you don't think them people kept you and bought all these fancy clothes for nothin', do you?" He reached for her shirt sleeve, but missed. "Hell, no. They put me in jail and then pay somebody else to take care of my kids. I'd done that myself, if they'd just left me alone. Damn sheriff." He turned up the beer bottle.

Inside her a dam broke. She fought back hateful tears as she ran from the room, out of the house, to the clearing along the creek bank. The sound of his laughter rang in her ears. She flung herself on the ground and let the flood inside her flow like the swift currents at her feet. When there were no more tears, she considered his words.

All this time Elsie and Jeff had me live there because they were paid to, she thought. That's why Elsie wanted to make sure I was coming with Pa just for a visit. If I don't come back, they won't get any more money.

Her anger grew. She picked up pebbles and hurled them into the creek. Truths that denied her accusations were as obscured as the rocks that fell beneath the murky water. She never wanted to see the McFalls again. Or Rachel. But she couldn't stay here either.

A plan formed in her mind. She had some money saved. It was hidden in an old coat pocket. It wasn't much, but if she could get back to Talladega, she could go to the house while Elsie was at work, get her things, her money and take a bus. Somewhere. Rachel had told her all about Washington. It would be easy to get work in a big city. As she made her plans, her heart became as hard and cold as the December ground.

When she went back to the house, Pa was still drinking at the table. He watched her every move as she cleaned up the dishes. She gave him another beer, willing him to drink more. When he was asleep, she would leave. If she could get the keys to the car, she'd try to drive. If not, she would walk. The evening wore on, but he still sat, half-awake in the chair.

"You better get yourself to bed, girl. Don't want you thinkin' you can sleep all day like today." He slurred his words. His eyes glowered at her from under half-shut lids.

She lay on her bed, waiting for him to go to sleep. She dozed. A noise woke her. She reached for the covers and felt a hand close around her leg. The dark was all hands, pushing her down as she tried to get up. One hand lifted her skirt, the other pulled at her blouse. It ripped. Sandpaper skin rubbed her knee. She flailed the black veil of night. Fingers groped her panties. A scream, caught in her throat, strangled her. She couldn't breathe. A knee came down on her thigh. She jerked her leg to one side, raising it with force against nothing but air. A hand crushed her left breast. She shifted her weight and dumped the hand off to her side. Unpinned, he fell on top of her. Flattened against the mattress, she had no leverage to keep him from separating her legs. She felt a hard mass of flesh slap against her thigh.

He raised his shoulder and put his hand beneath her hips. She slid her right hand free and reached for the wooden bucket. She searched for something solid. Touched the lamp. Couldn't lift it. Something metal. Slender metal. She gripped the picture frame like a lifeline, digging the edge into the palm of her hand. The weapon found its mark. Only a grunt came from its victim. Then a hand gripped her throat. Her head jerked with a slap, and everything went black.

Unconsciousness was a blessing that didn't last long enough. But she pretended. She was awake, but she kept her eyes closed, her body still. Her mind contained all her energy, blocking out the torture she refused to feel.

His body shuddered and his grip on her bare hips relaxed. His breath was rhythmic. Hers had been shallow so long that she was light-headed. She tried to push out from under him. When she had almost succeeded, his hand grabbed her hair, and his body, seemingly more alert than ever, closed over her again.

He was saying terrible things to her, words that she knew only from bathroom walls and in boys' laughter. His hand was trying to unwedge her legs.

She couldn't endure it again. She wouldn't. She had to stop him. Her mind raced. She had to get the knife! She felt along the upturned bucket. The knife wasn't there. Had she heard it fall to the floor when she picked up the frame? Her right hand edged slowly down the mattress, felt the cold metal of the bed frame and the empty space between bed and floor. Spider webs pulled at her skin. Her fingertips touched the rough pine planks, pushed outward and back, slapped and stretched. Cold steel nicked her thumb. She gripped the blade and tiptoed her fingers to the handle. Purchase was slight. She raised the knife carefully onto its tip, then grabbed for a hold.

She was riveted toward her goal. The knife was in her palm, fingers closed tightly against the handle. Secure, ready. She repeated the words, not again, over and over in her mind, like a cheering chant. She lifted the knife, pushing away the knowledge that this was her father. Stab for stab, an eye for an eye, she thought, and brought her hand higher.

It was not the pain between her legs that made her drop the weapon. It was her scream. The knife clanged against the floor, louder than all other sounds.

"What th' hell?" He sat up punching at the air, fighting unseen assailants.

Dorothy scrambled from the bed. He caught her arm as it darted about. Flinging her against the wall, he lunged for the blade that glistened on the floor like a severed moonbeam. She ran from the room through the dogtrot to the kitchen, searching for a weapon. A heavy iron skillet was on the stove. She crashed it against his head as he came through the door. His body slumped, then sprawled. He didn't move.

She wrapped a quilt around her nakedness and ran through the woods to the creek. In the dark, leafless kudzu and honeysuckle vines grabbed at her like long fingers. She dropped the quilt and ran into the water. The dark depths that had frightened her as a child could not keep her from the cleansing current. She dipped her hands in the frigid water and tried to wash away her horror.

Her body shook so hard she had trouble keeping the quilt around her shoulders as she walked slowly up the path back to the house. She would leave now. He could not stop her.

She dressed in the dark, gathered her things, then remembered the car keys. His pant's pocket, she thought. Where were his pants? She felt around on the floor, hoping he may have left them there. She touched wool cloth. And keys.

When she reached the car, she threw her things in the seat and scrambled around until all the doors were locked. She didn't breathe deeply until she sat behind the wheel, staring at the house. He wasn't coming after her. No one was. She wasn't sure where she would go or what she should do, but she was leaving without a doubt, without a look back.

Jeff had let her drive his pick-up, but it was a straight shift. This car had no gears, no clutch. Her hands shook uncontrollably. When she had the right key, it turned with a click. The motor sputtered, caught, but she held the ignition down. The car screeched like a wild, wounded animal. She released the key and tried again. The motor coughed, started. She felt for the light switch. She'd never driven at night. She pulled knobs, flipped switches. The radio blared. Then, two beams shot across the yard, illuminating the house, the porch, the doorway. Pa. He was leaning against the door frame.

She screamed and threw the lever to reverse and crashed across the yard, bouncing over half-buried tires. Her eyes stayed on the naked figure until she shifted into drive and swung the wheel. The car lurched down the rough road.

Above the sounds of mud clods slinging against metal, she thought she heard Pa scream.

CHAPTER FIFTEEN

MEXICO
September 28

Slender, leafless willow branches caught her hair and it whipped around like a monstrous spider web. Her arms flailed, tangled in the willow ropes that tied, gagged her. She slipped on a moss-wet rock, stumbled against a pine tree and fell in the cold creek. Her breath heaved ragged, discordant with the murmuring sounds of the drifting water. Hands gripped her ankles and pulled her lower and lower. She screamed and the water swirled the sound.

Patricia jerked the sheet over her head to block out the cries coming from her nightmare, though it hardly seemed that, since it was so familiar. The cover was stifling. She sat up, clammy and breathless, reaching for air. Her gown clung to her body as she stepped onto the cool terrazzo.

In the shower, instead of turning the water on to the shower head, she pulled a heavy chain. Cold water poured onto her head. She silently thanked Tomas for not tearing out the old plumbing when he modernized the bath. She stood under the stream until the dream was washed away. As she dressed, the sounds of a rooster crowing, the surf pounding, and someone crying "tortillas" brought her thoughts of Max.

She sat at her dressing table, putting her hair high on her head against the inevitable heat of the day. The sun had pinked her cheeks already since she arrived, lessening the sallow, haunted look that had become her familiar image since Max's kidnapping. She dressed in a pair of linen shorts, a halter top and slipped on sandals.

She began to make plans for the day. Mario was sending over the cousin she hoped to hire to take her to Max. There was no reason why she couldn't just get into a car and drive herself to Mexico City and on to Matehuala and Real. She had maps. It wasn't as though they were in some uncharted territory with goat paths for roads. Driving there wasn't the problem. Finding Max was, and arranging payoffs. That's why she needed a guide. No sense being foolish, she thought. Head out alone and wind up going in circles on top of some mountain. Thoughts of actually moving in a vehicle in the direction of where Max was being held made her stomach contract, forcing a quick intake of breath.

The phone rang.

"Patricia, what the hell do you think you're doing, running off without seeing me before you left Mexico City?" Jim shouted at her.

She didn't answer.

"Well?"

"I didn't know you were in Mexico City, Jim, and why are you?"

"You know very well why I'm here," Jim snapped. "Elena was supposed to tell you. I came right after your meeting. Where did you go?"

Ignoring his question, she asked, "Did you get anywhere with the Juan Sanchez brothers?"

"I might have. We're meeting again in the morning."

Her spirits didn't rise a peso's worth at that news. "Jim, those men are puppets. If you don't get to who pulls their strings, you're wasting your time."

"I know what I'm doing, Patricia. You have to go about these things differently down here. You don't know how these guys operate."

"Oh, yes I do. On bribes."

Jim was silent a moment, then said, "Not everyone. I have contacts that might help."

"I'm wondering if we couldn't try again to get the police or FBI in, Jim. And the media." She dropped onto the end of the bed, defeat suddenly creeping around her.

"We've discussed this, Patricia." He raised his voice. "The police aren't going to do anything. I talked to the FBI guy again. He's going over to the Mexican consulate office. I'll let you know what comes of it. And you know you can't get the papers down here to run anything the government doesn't want printed. You push that and it'll get Max killed for sure. These people don't want any bad publicity. What can you be thinking?"

She winced at his words. She knew all the arguments. They had gone over and over them. However rational the reasons not to, she still wanted to shout from the top of the world the injustice of her son's disappearance. She wanted the FBI, CIA, and whatever other initials there were, to be swarming over the mountains with one purpose in mind—freeing Max. Despite it all, right this minute, she wanted the nightly news programs to be filled with Max's picture and the story of his coming here to help the miners. She wanted the world to cry out with her to let him go. And she wanted there to be nowhere the kidnappers could hide.

Jim interrupted her thoughts. "Can I trust you to stay put in Acapulco. I'll be there day after tomorrow. I have people to see here and leads to run down near Real."

She said nothing.

"Patricia? Can I?"

"I'll be here," she answered, remembering how Miguel had told her the same thing. She would not let either of them, for whatever reasons they had, stop her when she decided to go.

He must have sensed her insincerity. "Or better still why don't you go on home, Patricia? There's nothing else you can do down here. Let me take care of this. I want to take care of you, Sweetheart. I can call the crew; the plane can be ready by the time you get to the airport. Don't be stubborn, now. I'd never forgive myself for letting you come down here, if anything happened to you."

"You didn't let me, Jim, if I remember correctly."

"Well," he laughed. "You can't blame a fellow from trying to protect his girl."

She was touched by his words. "I know you're looking out for me, Jim. I do. But I have no intention of going home. Not without Max. Just help me find him, please."

In the silence a clock ticked.

"Okay, Sweetheart. I understand. Just so you won't be twiddling your thumbs, there is one other thing you might do. I know I didn't think it was a good idea at first, but I think you ought to try to contact Miguel."

She thought she'd heard wrong. Or he must be talking about another Miguel. There must be millions of them. "Miguel?"

"Yes. Tomas's brother."

"Why do you think I should talk to him?" It was her heart she heard, not a clock.

"Well, like you said back home, he is Max's uncle. Whatever differences he and Tomas had, that can't stand in the way of helping his nephew out of trouble. And, seeing that his sister-in-law doesn't get into any."

She let the phone line twist around her finger, capturing it, turning her skin white. "I did see him," she said. "Yesterday. After I left the office. He won't help." She released the cord, rubbed at marks left by the coils.

"He probably just told you he wouldn't to get you to leave Mexico. I'll talk to him while I'm here."

"Leave him out of it, Jim. Miguel's got his own agenda."

"His agenda? Do you mean he's still working with the miners? I did hear—"

"What did you hear?"

"Oh, probably more rumors. About his having an interest in the mines or maybe it was just the miners. I told you he's the Special Liaison to Labor. If he is involved someway, maybe that's all the more reason why he should be in a position to help find Max, don't you think?"

She couldn't think at all. *Miguel had an interest in the mines?* Was he making some legal claim as his brother's next of kin? Jim wasn't seeing the picture. If this were true, it was a good reason for Miguel to make sure Max was out of the way for good. And maybe her, too. "If you learn anything, whatever it is, leave word if I'm not here."

"What do you mean, if you're not there? I thought you just said—"

"I may be out to the market," she said to ease his suspicions. "Just talk to Rachel, okay?" She hung up and went in search of Mario.

* * *

Jim stared at the phone. Rachel. A flush of anger seized him at the thought of what she might be encouraging Patricia to do. That woman gave him the willies. It wasn't just her blind eyes that seemed to look right through you. Dammed if she didn't read your mind half the time. If she'd just stayed home, Patricia would have.

He swung his long legs onto a white leather couch in the penthouse apartment in the Morelos Building in Mexico City. Relaxing, he sipped *El Presidente* over ice. He hadn't told Patricia he was staying here. She hadn't asked. It had been his for the using while Tomas was alive and afterwards when he made trips here that Patricia wasn't privy to. No need to start asking permission now.

He looked around the room at the black and white leather furniture. The stark contrasts were softened by some of Juan Barbosa's pastel paintings. The whole was spiced by jade, onyz, malachite and gold artifacts from the hands of Aztecs, Mayans, and Olmecs.

He liked what he saw, but the thought occurred to him that Tomas Morelos had been a greedy bastard. Most of the pieces in the room belonged in a museum somewhere. Maybe he'd donate some of them eventually. Appearances. They were important. Of course, he might have to sell a few more things, if those greedier bastards in Virginia hit him up again. The biggest mistake he had made was getting up-front money from Willie Bates's "boys" as he called them. What in the hell was he supposed to do? He couldn't carry out Tomas's plan on his director's salary. Someday he knew Patricia would be proud of the way he had carried out Tomas's wishes and made the fortune that would be his and hers.

He picked up a clay figure with a large headdress and prominent Mayan nose. Ugly thing, he thought. Looks kind of like Miguel Ramirez. He laughed aloud. So Patricia had already tried to enlist his help. He had expected that she would, and now he knew for sure. Obviously Ramirez had told her nothing, if he knew anything.

A cloud drifted over his mood. He was riding a filly on the last lap of the race and he felt the reins slipping from his hands. With Max in jeopardy, he had seen his chance to win it all. He thought it'd be simple to negotiate the kid's release and get Patricia to sign over the mines in return for Max. Of course, she'd be signing them over to a dummy company and he'd have control. He needed the mines, dammit. He needed the money to finish the project in Tlantoloc.

Things were not going as planned. If he succeeded, he could make Patricia understand why he needed the mines, why he needed to finish Tomas's plan. But, he would never be able to make her understand if he wasn't able to get Max home safe. She would never forgive him. He would lose her. He would lose everything.

He poured himself another whisky. Nearby, on a table was a photo of Tomas and Patricia taken at a Mexican festival. He stared at it. His short, ugly friend looked like a Mexican caricature in wide brim hat and poncho. Patricia was a Spanish princess, dark hair piled high under a black lace *mantilla*. A fan held coyly to her chin. The contrast between the two was comical. He didn't laugh. If she could fuck Tomas, then why—He couldn't quite ask himself the question. She was just being loyal and time would take care of that. A person can be faithful to a corpse just so long. He imagined himself next to her. They would make a striking couple. With his Irish sandy hair and green eyes and her dark looks, they would make a different kind of contrast. No one would laugh at them together. No one would laugh at him ever again.

He picked up the phone. "Elena? Get me Gabriel Perez on the phone. Chase him down if you have to. I want to talk to him."

Several hours later He climbed aboard a Cessna 310 for a flight to Ixtapa. As they approached a small landing field, he could see high rise hotels and condos lining the beaches. Somebody was making a new Acapulco. And a pocketful of money. Here and there were abandoned constructions, concrete honeycombs, monuments to graft. Pockets really got lined on those jobs. "Shares" of a building would be sold while a token construction went up. Once the sales were in, the owners disappeared with the money, only to start their game over somewhere else. He knew how they got away with it. They paid off Perez. He controlled the construction industry in Mexico.

Jim had paid him plenty himself in the past year. It had cost him everything he owned and all he could borrow, but it would pay off in the end. Tomas had started this project, but it was his now. The largest construction venture any company had tried in Mexico.

Tomas had been paying officials for years, trying to set everything up. In the meantime the property he owned had been taken over by squatters. It wasn't easy getting them to leave. He didn't like remembering about the fire that cleared the land. There wasn't supposed to have been any explosion. Tomas had said you couldn't trust these guys down here to do a simple arson job right. Tlantoloc had finally been ready for the bulldozers. Permits had been bought and paid for, most of the money going to Perez, but things had gotten done.

Then Tomas died and the ball stopped rolling. Morelos Enterprises Construction was dead in the water. The suppliers, the contractors, the tenants, all disappeared. Wouldn't even return his phone calls.

Then the *pepenadores* had moved in. And the garbage trucks. Juan Catera's bunch. Good God, he called himself the "garbage czar." Took over land like he owned it. Perez had been working to free it up again for almost a year. But the dam garbage and the vermin that picked it were still on the land. His land!

Patricia knew nothing about the deal. Tomas didn't want her to, and it had been easy to keep it that way. Besides, Jim knew he had done all the work. He ought to be the one in charge, not her. It was not a business for a woman. He'd surprise her with it someday. A wedding present.

Perez had tried to contact Patricia, but another bribe had stopped him. Since then, Jim didn't know if he was paying bribes to get the land away from the garbage people or blackmail to keep Patricia from knowing about it. If he could just pull this off to get the mines.

It had been like a kick in the teeth when Juan Sanchez and his bunch had told him that the miners were only talking to Perez. How Perez wormed his way in with the miners he didn't know. It scared him. He could see the finish line up ahead, but he had a feeling Perez was trying to snatch his filly out from under him. He wasn't sure what he was going to have to do to get this project completed, but damned if he wasn't going to have a showdown with Gabriel Perez. This was going to be more than a friendly invitation down to the beach.

A young man named Raul was waiting with a car when he got off the plane. It was a twenty minute drive to his destination. The sleepy village of Zihautenejo. Nestled into a small bay, a travel brochure picture of fishing boats and native houses, pristine beaches and swaying palms.

Jim took in the perfection of the scene, then blinked in disbelief at an enormous columned structure dominating the far side of the bay. He pointed to it and Raul smiled. "*Es el Parthenon.*"

"The Parthenon? Well, either I've been transported to Athens or Señor Perez has built himself a real mansion on the hilltop. Some of it with my money." He spoke in English doubting that Raul understood him.

"*Si, es el Partenon,*" the young man repeated.

The grounds began several blocks below the mansion. Manicured lawns outlined by hibiscus hedges. Royal palms, their white trunks gleaming. And statues everywhere.

Looks like Michelangelo's discount house, Jim thought. It certainly wasn't to his tastes. Modern architecture with its sleek lines was so much cleaner, uncomplicated. All these dadoos, as his pop used to call them, reminded him of the junk his mother used to bring home at times when she'd been off with some man.

Huge wrought iron gates were slowly opened by two young men and they drove up the final stretch of driveway. Jim tried to calculate how many tons of concrete it took to cover the winding road they had traveled from the village below. He couldn't begin to estimate the cost of the marble portico where they entered the house.

A man in white coat and pants led him into a mirror-walled room of immense proportions. Dark, heavy Spanish furniture cast shadows on the marble floor. They walked out into the mid-afternoon sun to a large patio surrounding a glistening pool. Giggles came from several bikini-clad girls leaning against a mahogany bar.

"Señor Jim, over here," someone called.

On a corner of the balcony overlooking the bay sat three men dressed in swim trunks and open shirts. One was Gabriel Perez. A short man, bald and round, dressed in a green shirt and looking like an olive, Jim thought. Two of the others he knew only by sight. The man called the "garbage czar" with his hair slicked back in 1920's gangster style, another "pretty-boy Floyd." And the Chief of Police of Mexico City. The Chief rose to meet him. Large and tall for a Mexican, Carlos Guterriz, looked like a prize fighter from the projects.

"Welcome to my home, Señor Mainland," Guterriz said.

Jim was speechless. The house was not Perez's. It was the lion's den. His neck hairs bristled. He finally spoke, unable to keep the sarcasm out of his voice. "Quite a place you have here, Chief. Glad to see police work pays so well in Mexico."

Two men Jim had not seen walked up behind him. The Chief said something hastily in Spanish. They moved away.

Guterriz picked up his beer and in unison the three men said, "*Salud*! A tradition as ancient as the brew they drank. Yet, somehow, Jim felt he had just been hailed a marked man.

CHAPTER SIXTEEN

Miguel did not go to Cuernavaca after Patricia left his office. He brooded for hours. Gena was sure he was ill when she returned from siesta.

"Señor. You say you go home today. Carmina cook for you. She wait for you. Will Daniel be there? My English is better, you—, right?" She grinned, hand over mouth.

He looked at her, but said nothing. He wondered what this interest in Daniel meant. She left him, shaking her head.

A few minutes later, he called her into his office.

"I am sorry, Gena. Forgive me for being rude. I am not myself."

She gave him a look that he knew was an agreement.

"Is Señora Morelos a problem?" She asked.

He didn't see a smirking grin on her face, but one would have been an appropriate accompaniment to the question.

"What makes you think this?"

"Nada," she said.

He looked at her again, and that time, damn it, she did smirk. Patricia. He couldn't get her out of his mind for two minutes rest. He had thought seriously about having her arrested when she left his office, but he knew it would be an outrage and she would gain from it.

He had hoped, instead, that she would come to her senses and leave Mexico. Instead, she went to her villa in Acapulco. He had learned that she'd been trying to find a small plane and no one was renting her one. Had she been planning to fly to Real? That was a laugh, he thought. The only things that flew into there were birds, and maybe a helicopter, if you could find a landing place.

No matter how many strings he pulled, so far he hadn't been able to find out who was stopping her. And whoever it was, what were they up to.

He was reacting to things he found out, not acting on what he knew was right to do. He didn't like it.

"Señor, why you not help her?" Gena asked, snapping him back to the present.

He was about to ask her how she knew about Patricia when her question, which was more of an accusation, stopped him. Why? he thought, why not help her? Take her to Real, or somewhere along the way. At least then he could keep an eye on her while he worked to get Max released.

"Gena, get me Daniel on the phone," he said, his eyes on the instrument as if it would ring instantly. "Then, get me Señora Morelos's phone number in Acapulco.

* * *

Patricia paced and slammed around the house all day waiting for Mario to send his cousin they all talked about. Rachel retreated to a quiet lounge chair, put on some head phones and effectively drowned out Patricia's ravings. Finally, in the afternoon, Marta brought the phone to Patricia where she sat in the garden.

"It is a call from Mexico City," Marta said.

Patricia grabbed the phone. "Yes?" She asked.

"I hear you are looking for someone to take you to Real."

Patricia frowned at Marta as if she had something to do with the voice on the line. "Miguel? What—what do you mean?" She quickly became defensive, wondering how Miguel had heard.

"I will take you there myself."

Patricia wasn't sure she had heard his words right. "*You* will take me? You can get me to where Max is?"

"I will do my best," he answered.

"What made you change your mind? Has something else happened?"

Miguel laughed. "No. You are just a very persuasive woman. I thought about it after you left, and decided to call you. I will be there at dawn tomorrow to pick you up. Be ready."

"Miguel, wait. You may not can tell me all you know, but can you at least tell me that he is okay." She held her breath.

"I can only tell you that everything is being done to secure his release. Perhaps you want to be there when that is accomplished. Dawn, tomorrow."

The dial tone was as loud as a siren in Patricia's ear. Just like that, she thought. No more answers. She still wasn't sure she could believe Miguel, or trust him, but she certainly wasn't going to turn him down.

"Rachel!" She headed through the house with her news.

CHAPTER SEVENTEEN

September 29

Patricia had spent the evening hours arguing with Rachel who was trying to talk Patricia out of going with Miguel. They were still at it the next morning. While she dressed, Rachel sat on the edge of the bed, her hand on the phone.

"Give me one good reason why I shouldn't call someone, maybe Jim, to stop you?"

Buttoning her blouse, Patricia stared at Rachel. "I've given you a hundred reasons for what I'm doing and why you shouldn't call anyone. And I can't believe you'd even suggest calling Jim. Now, will you put down that phone and help me think if I've forgotten anything."

"How about your good sense?" When Patricia didn't retort, Rachel added, "And that probably shows in what your wearing, too. My guess is silk pants and flimsy leather shoes. Like you're going to lunch at the Willard Hotel instead of the mountains."

Patricia wove a belt through the loops of her beige raw silk pants and slipped her feet into her soft Italian slippers. "We're riding, not walking and this is comfortable for a long ride." She half-mumbled, "I swear sometimes you can see."

"You better be glad I can't or I'd be tying you to the bedpost right now."

"Or hiding in the car with your bag all packed?"

They both laughed.

"That's an idea, though," Rachel said. "Why don't I go along?"

Patricia sank onto the bed and put her hand over Rachel's. "You know I have to do this, and you know I need you here for me, don't you?"

"If you say so." Rachel turned her hand upwards and the two hands entwined.

"You've got to keep Jim off my back and be here if there is news of Max. And you'll need to keep calling Annie and making sure she's all right and hasn't gotten wind of what's happening to Max." She squeezed Rachel's hand.

"She told me to quit buggin' her. I think she's getting like Max. Too damned independent. Knew I shouldn't have let the two of them play together when they were kids."

"That's right. But you were a bad influence on me, so we're even. Tell her Aunt Pat sends her love." She got up and slipped her purse strap over her shoulder.

"Well," Rachel sighed, "Since I'm going to be relegated to telephone duty, when will I hear from you?"

"Everyday. Promise."

The two women embraced quickly. Patricia struggled to close a bulging Gucci bag, then set it alongside a large canvas pack. Roberto would carry the bags to the street.

Miguel drove up at the first light of dawn in a dirt-encrusted jeep that looked like a tank. He was dressed in plaid shirt, jeans and boots. A Mexican cowboy except for a baseball cap that he whisked from his head at the sight of Patricia and Rachel.

Although they had never met, Miguel embraced Rachel like a long lost friend, Patricia left the two of them and went to the kitchen to get the basket of food Marta had prepared for them. When she returned to the sala, Rachel and Miguel were in a heated conversation. She supposed Rachel was reading him the riot act on taking care of her.

"I'm ready," she interrupted them, giving the heavy basket to Miguel.

Rachel was quiet until all was placed in the jeep. She hugged Patricia tightly, then extended her hand to Miguel. He took it lightly in his. Then, without a word, he took her hand and placed it against his cheek. Rachel lightly touched his features, her fingers moving swiftly. When the moment was over, she withdrew her hand, nodded her head and smiled. She gave Patricia one last hug and said, "You had better call!"

Acapulco was just coming awake. Along the Costera, native fishing boats were being unloaded after a night at sea. Vendors were taking cloth coverings from their hut-like shops, which were stocked with everything from iguanas to T-shirts. A few joggers ran along the beach. The sun peaked over the cross on the mountain above Las Brisas as they turned at the statue of Diana and headed over the mountain toward Mexico City.

The jeep felt like a buckboard as they dodged potholes, bounced over concrete *topes*, and swung left to right along the road to Chilpancingo. The valleys and mountains were emerald green in their lush summer growth. Coconut palms whipped their heads in sudden gusts of air. Clouds gathered. It would rain again soon. They crossed the Papagayo River. It rode its banks high, threatening villagers hawking their wares to the few who traveled this road in September.

Between towns it was quiet. It would have been peaceful had the trip been for another reason and had she been with someone else. Neither one of them offered to make conversation. It was as though they had been ordered not to talk, as if breaking the silence would be a deed that would not go unpunished. She felt no need to talk, no need to question Miguel about what he was doing. Somehow, she was confident that he knew. She admitted to herself that she didn't. A deeply rooted quivering told her she was scared. Afraid for Max, for herself, afraid of the future, and of the past. She tried to force herself to think positive thoughts. She called up images of her son and made herself dwell on the stories each told. Lulled by steamy heat, she rested against the seat, hovering between thoughts and dreams.

It happened fast. Swirling, swishing air was the first warning, barely bringing her from the edge of sleep. Then her head whipped forward and back as if she were on a carnival ride. Miguel threw his arm across her shoulder and neck to brace her.

The road turned to dirt and brush. They bounced to a stop. The only sound, trailing horn blasts.

"You okay?" Miguel's arm still bound her to the seat.

"I think so. What happened?"

"Crazy bus drivers," he said, gradually moving his arm. "They race the road from Acapulco to Mexico. It is a game. We were lucky to have some place to go."

"He passed right on the curve," Patricia said, her voice quivering.

A silver bus rounded the next hillside, close on the bumper of a small white car.

Miguel wiped his arm across his brow. "They will play cat and mouse all the way to Chilpancingo." He put the jeep in gear and started easing forward. "Maybe you better not watch."

As if he had ordered her to do so, she looked out. Straight down. They had stopped inches from a three or four hundred foot drop. She closed her eyes and didn't breathe again until the jeep had eased back onto the road.

"Thank you," she sighed.

"De nada." He said. "I guess you never rode buses in the States. It is a great thrill to ride this one to Chilpancingo. You should do it sometime." His smile softened the sarcasm she knew lay behind his words.

"Maybe I should," she answered, and shut her eyes against his stare. She leaned her head back as if to rest. She felt dizzy, her thoughts a broken kaleidoscope. He still thought she had always lived a rich life. He knew nothing of long, tortuous bus rides. He knew so little about her. She was beset with images of a bus whirling by and of the dream she'd had the night before. She tried, but couldn't fight the memories.

CHAPTER EIGHTEEN

Alabama 1962

She drove away that January night with Pa's scream echoing in her mind. When she got to Talladega, she sat in the car down the street from where she'd lived since she was seven.

She watched Jeff and Elsie leave together in an early morning hour. It took her only a few minutes to pack her clothes in an old Army duffel bag of Jeff's, get the money she had saved, and the one possession she could not leave behind. The china doll her mother had given her.

She drove out of Talladega without looking back. When the car was almost on empty, she parked it on a street in Heflin, a town near the Georgia border, and walked to the bus station.

An hour later she was settled into a seat toward the back of a Trailways bus with a ticket marked Washington, D.C. She had no plan beyond riding the bus that far.

When a police car passed the bus, she slid down in the seat, wondering if they were looking for her. She could be put in jail for hitting her pa, and running away was like stealing from the McFalls. Her cheeks burned with the shame of knowing they had been paid to keep her. And when she thought of what her father had done, tears flowed freely.

At one of the numerous stops the bus made, a heavy set woman shoe-horned her way into the seat beside her. After a few miles, the woman spoke.

"Gracious child, if you're gonna cry all the way up the road, you're gonna need some hankies." She fluttered a large white cloth in front of Dorothy's face.

After blowing her nose soundly, Dorothy folded the soiled cloth and looked at the woman.

"Keep it," she said and smiled, face framed by gray-black strands of hair escaping a red hat.

Dorothy tried to get comfortable in her small space, leaning more against the soft shoulder of the woman than the cold wall of the bus.

"Looks like we're both traveling alone. I suppose we ought to introduce ourselves. My name's Dorsey Mayren Hicks. Just call me Dosey."

Dorothy looked into twinkling brown eyes set into what seemed a dough face, sculpted by amateur hands. "My name's—my family used to call me Doe," she said.

"Well, lordy. Don't we make a pair. Dosey-Doe." The woman howled and slapped her heavy thigh.

A man looked over his seat, frowning. The two covered their mouths and snickered until they wore down their laughs.

"That's more like it," Dosey said. "Hate to sit next to a sulk all the way home."

"Where do you live?"

"Washington, D. C." The woman said proudly.

Dorothy couldn't believe her luck. She'd have to sit and listen to this woman all the way to the end of the line.

"I've been visiting my daughter in Tallapoosa. And her daughter, my grandbaby."

The woman's voice had a little catch in it, like she was going to cry, so Dorothy didn't ask any questions. Anyway, she didn't want to hear about families. She shut her eyes and feigned sleep, hoping the woman would tire of talking.

"Looks like we're stoppin' here in Villa Rica."

Dorothy stretched and looked out the window at more unfamiliar surroundings. She thought she might find another seat and looked around for an empty one.

"May's well stay put, you know," Dosey said, seeming to read Dorothy's mind.

"Why?"

"More people'll get on. You might wind up next to some ol' boozer that'll have his hand on your leg before we get goin'."

The woman couldn't have said anything more convincing to Dorothy. Whatever her discomfort, she felt protected with the woman between her and everybody else. She snuggled back into the seat and the warmth of the red coat.

Over the hours, Dosey talked more about her family.

While she listened, Dorothy created a new family for herself. Mostly she embellished on the story she had told Rachel. The loving parents killed in an accident. Now the aunt she lived with had died. No brothers or sisters. She was on her own. She told Dosey what little she had to.

They changed buses in Atlanta and Dorothy stayed close to Dosey through the maze of the Atlanta bus terminal. She had never seen so many people in one place.

Back on the bus, which was an express and wouldn't be stopping in every little town, Dosey slept and Dorothy thought about her future. Working in a diner, cooking for someone, cleaning house. These were her choices. She knew nothing else. If she didn't finish school, she would never have any other choice, and how could she do that and work?

Over and over, her thoughts came back to Rachel. Her friend. Maybe, she would get in touch with Rachel someday. But what would she tell her? That question and the idea of being on her own were like stone walls that rose in front of her. Impenetrable, unscalable.

At the few stops the bus made, Dorothy and the woman got off for food or to walk around. After many hours it seemed that they had been traveling together forever. To get her mind off Rachel, Dorothy asked, "You've been visiting your granddaughter? How old is she?"

"She's goin' on seventeen." Dosie's voice lowered with the words, and Dorothy wondered if she should have asked about her.

"Why, she's just a year older—" she stopped herself quickly. She shouldn't tell this woman she was only fifteen. She'd probably turn her over to the law. "—than my friend Rachel," she finished, with what she hoped was only a moment's hesitancy.

Dosey looked at her, red hat bobbing.

"She must still be in school, then. Your granddaughter," she stuttered out the words.

"No," Dosey said softly. "She can't go to school anymore. She's just had a baby."

Dorothy had known girls who were forced to quit school because they got pregnant, but most of them got married. She'd see them with their husbands and the baby and envy their little family.

The woman was silent for a while. Finally, she said, brightening, "The prettiest little girl you've ever seen."

"I'll bet her and her husband's happy then," Dorothy said, wistfully.

Dosey's eyes searched the young girl's face, then looked past her to the fast moving landscape beyond the window. The dark eyes glittered like wet coals.

"She ain't married." A heavy sigh lifted and lowered the lapels of the red coat.

"I'm sorry. I just thought—"

"I know. It's shameful. I wanted Franny to have a weddin', a husband. Her mother did, too. She was heartsick till the baby came, now I guess she's all right with it."

"What happened to the father?"

"Oh, he's off in the army somewhere. He talked fast and smooth to my Franny the night before he left, promisin' all sorts of things he had no intentions doin'. Just like a man." She grunted. "Franny figured if they were goin' to be married, it was no harm in doin' what he asked. Wanted her to 'prove her love.' He sure proved his. Proved he didn't have none. Not for poor Franny." The red hat shook back and forth.

Dorothy's spine pulled up and straightened; her attention caught, riveted. "He must not've been a very good man. Did they know each other a long time?" That wasn't the question she wanted to ask. It cowered in the back of her mind and wouldn't be put to words easily.

"No, not long. He was just home on leave."

"And they only, I mean, just the night before? Just that one time?" The words tumbled out of her mouth.

"Why, honey, you know that's all it takes to get pregnant, being exposed."

Dorothy watched the fields of South Carolina go by in the bright January day. There was a mist between her and the distance creating a foggy, rain soaked landscape. Her mind and heart were as blurred as the scene beyond the window. Her face warmed with thoughts of bruising hands and foul lips. The sharp heat made her shiver. Tears cooled her burning cheeks. The seed of a thought began to grow. She clinched her teeth, pushed the idea into the pit of her stomach like it was bile rising in her throat. She denied it words, denied it birth. It couldn't be. If she refused to believe, it would not come true.

She knew Dosey was watching her, a question printed in the dough face. The woman had marked her words, her curiosity, and she did not conceal her stare. Dorothy tried to pull herself together, but no matter how hard she tried, she couldn't stop the flow of her tears.

She felt herself pulled into the soft shoulder of the red coat. With no will to resist, she cried to the crooning and rocking of the woman.

She slept for a long time. When she woke, she ached to stand, to walk. No, to run. But she was running. She looked behind her, as if to see where she had come from. She tried to clear her mind, but something pulled at it like gum on a shoe. Silent words flashed. Exposed. One Time. Shame. A word got stuck. Pregnant. PREGNANT. It echoed, bounced from ear to ear while she tried to catch the reality of it.

Once when a friend of Elsie's had died, Dorothy had tried to imagine what it would be like if she died. She had said the words, "I'm going to die. Someday, I'm going to die," over and over, until, for a fleeting moment, she could grasp the finiteness of her being. An ephemeral moment of recognition that made her heart leap, then was gone. She tried the same thing now with this new possibility. This time, the thought took form. She saw a baby in her arms with the face of her father. She fought an urge to laugh, then knew if she made a sound, it would be a scream. The baby grew and became her father. Deep inside her a core of hatred took hold that seemed evil itself. She tried to soothe it, but it hardened.

When Dosey was awake again, she began talking about the man she worked for in Washington. A "foreigner". He was a good boss, though, and he liked Dosey's cooking. "He's a little strange now and then, but the pay's good," she said more than once. Tomas Morelos was his name. He was from Mexico.

She talked about other people who also worked for Mr. Morelos, Natty, the driver, and a lady who cleaned, Carmina. Carmina was also Mexican, and Dosey said she was always on "minwanna" time, wanting to do things tomorrow.

As Dosey talked on, Dorothy realized that this aging, worn out woman was her future self. A life of menial jobs and heartache. Cooking. Cleaning. No education. Never a house like those on "silk stocking" street.

Finally, Dosey seemed to be lost in thought or drifting off to sleep again. Dorothy had many more questions to ask. She wanted to know how to go about getting a job, where to get a room, how to live in the city. She had to find another life. She missed Rachel, and Dosey and Jeff, but she would not call them, ever. Besides, they wouldn't want to hear from her anyway. She was on her own. Resolve settled over her numbness, beneath which the core of hatred glowed, galling her, guiding her.

Hours later the bus started across the Potomac River into Washington. Dorothy couldn't take it all in. Despite her bleak thoughts, she began to feel excited. Buildings, like Greek temples she'd seen in her history books. Limousines. People everywhere, walking on the snow-covered sidewalks.

Real snow.

Dosey kept laughing at her, as she pointed at one thing, then another. She didn't care. At least the fear was hiding out for a moment.

"I'll have to give Natty a ring to come for me. Would you watch my things while I call?" Dosey asked as the bus pulled into the terminal. Dorothy absently agreed.

They collected their bags with the help of a porter and walked through a sea of people to the public phones. Dorothy felt as if her head was a pinwheel moving in the wind. She didn't know which way to look.

The man sat down their bags and Dosey gave him some coins. "Keep a sharp eye on these things," Dosey said, watching her. "You're not in friendly territory anymore. People rather steal from you here than work! I'll be right back."

And she was, before Dorothy could begin to think of what she was going to do. Of where she would go.

"Carmina says Natty's already on his way. I know what he wants. He's been missin' my cookin', I guess." A deep chuckle shook the red coat like Jell-o.

Dorothy pulled Jeff's old duffel bag out of the midst of Dosey's suitcases. "Thanks for your company. You sure made the trip easier."

Dosey's laughter stopped. A frown furrowed her brow. "What are you goin' to do, child?"

"What do you mean?"

"Honey." The woman frowned like Elsie use to when she caught Dorothy lying.

"Oh, don't worry 'bout me. I can take care of myself." She straightened and lifted her shoulder under the weight of the bag.

"Dosey! Dosey Hicks, you a sight for sore eyes, woman." A short, wiry black man encircled Dosey with arms too short for her girth. He had on a uniform and a squatty hat that shaded his face. His eyes, as dark as chinquapin nuts, twinkled as he looked up at Dosey.

"Natty, you ole liar. You're just hungry." She pushed the little man away and turned to Dorothy. "This is—my goodness, I don't even know your name. Can't introduce you as Doe."

Dorothy hadn't given thought to a name. She couldn't say Tucker or Mcfall. What if people were looking for her? She thought of Rachel, and said, "Wellington." Said it aloud before she even considered what she was doing. Patricia Wellington." She let the bag drop to the floor.

"Well how—"

She read Dosey's face. "Oh, my nickname was Doe, but that was a long time ago."

"Well, Miss Wellington, it's a pleasure meetin' you." The man smiled. "This all yours, Dosey?"

"That's all." The woman stared at her, holding her gaze, for what seemed minutes. Finally, with a nod of the red hat, she turned to Natty, "Grab that bag of Patricia's, too. She's going home with us. I've been needin' a helper. So I brought me one along."

Natty looked from her to Dosey and back again, then shrugged. He motioned for a young boy to help him, and the two of them walked away with Dosey's suitcases and Jeff's duffle bag.

Dorothy Tucker gazed around the crowded terminal at a world of strangers. She took the crumbled bus ticket from her pocket and looked at it. Heflin, Alabama, to Washington, D.C.

A trash can stood nearby. She lifted her hand and tossed in the crumbled paper.

"Wait for me!" She called to Dosey.

CHAPTER NINETEEN

MEXICO

The future and the past were separated by that bus ride. Now, in the present of that future, on a winding, narrow road high above Chilpancingo, Patricia suppressed memories of that life-altering trip made twenty-five years ago. Dorothy Tucker got on a Trailways bus in Alabama, body and soul ravaged. She died somewhere along the countryside of southern Virginia. In Washington, D.C., Patricia Wellington stepped off that bus and began the life that had brought her to Mexico.

If Miguel had not been a quick thinker, the Estrella bus could have been the death of Patricia Wellington Morelos, she thought, and shivered. She drew her arms close. If they had gone over, down the mountainside, there would be no one to go after Max. Patricia looked at Miguel, intent on his driving. Doubts nagged at her about not telling him about Max. What if something did happen to her? Maybe that tangle with the bus hadn't been an accident. Jim had warned her of danger. She shook off the thought. Now, she was being paranoid. The bus driver could hardly have known who was in this jeep.

Before noon, flower fields came into view. Miles of roses heralded the outskirts of Cuernavaca, summer retreat of the rich and famous from Cortez's time. Patricia knew it well from visits she and Tomas had made to nearby spas and endless trips to Taxco in the mountains to the west where Morelos Enterprises owned several silver shops. Her mind wandered over memories like a wizened hand on the squares of an old quilt.

"Are you hungry?" Miguel asked, interrupting her daydreams.

"Not really," she said, then realized he probably was. "But, I suppose it is time we had some hot food." Miguel had snacked out of Marta's basket the entire trip. "How about *Las Mananitas?* My treat," she added quickly, knowing the prices at the restaurant.

"I need to stop at my house for something. My cook will have something ready for us. Okay?" He smiled briefly, as if he had forgotten how.

"It won't take long will it? This stop at your house?"

"No. We will be on the road soon to get through the city before the worst of Friday traffic. We have plenty of time to get to *La Mansion* before dark."

She resigned herself to the delay, determined to be thankful that she was moving in the right direction.

Miguel pulled up in front of a modest low wall with purple bougainvilla cascading over the top. She could see a flat roofed two story house beyond the wall.

"Welcome to my humble home," Miguel said as he directed her through a lovely oak door.

"Señor!" A voice called from one of the windows. "You have come in just the right time. *La comida* is ready for—"

Through the *sala* door appeared a slight woman of definite Aztec heritage. Grey streaked her short, dark curls and soft lines etched her cheeks. Her twinkling eyes and wide smile froze and faded as she stared at Patricia.

In a moment Patricia realized who the woman was. A dark fear crept out from behind a long shut door deep inside of her.

Miguel filled the silence. "I think you two have probably met before. Patricia, you remember Carmina, she used to work for Tomas. Before that she worked for my mother, and now she keeps my life straight." He gave the rigid woman a hardy hug almost toppling her like a statue.

Patricia knew she wasn't breathing, couldn't breathe.

Miguel left the two women, heading for the kitchen with some remark about food trailing behind him.

"Señora? Señora Morelos?" Carmina asked, then almost whispered, "Patricia?"

Patricia hesitated, then held out her hand. "Carmina. After all these years." She fought a rising fear. Knowing that Carmina knew too much about her as the girl Dosey took in, she wasn't sure how to react, but surely the woman would be discreet.

Carmina took Patricia's hand, but held it only briefly. Long enough for Patricia to notice how much she was shaking. Patricia didn't understand. It was she who had much to fear from the Mexican woman.

Miguel came out of the kitchen with two plates of hot tamales, beans and rice. "Carmina, bring us a couple of beers. Or would you prefer something else?" he asked Patricia, but Carmina rushed away before she could answer.

Patricia sat at the table, her plate of food untouched. Carmina had brought them two *Dos Equis*, then disappeared quickly.

Miguel looked at Patricia, then in the direction Carmina had gone. "You two did know each other at Tomas's, didn't you?"

"Well, yes, slightly," was all Patricia could say.

"I cannot imagine anyone knowing Carmina only 'slightly.' She has a way of taking charge. It is good for me. I need someone like that here in Cuernavaca. I am away too much. And, her son, Daniel, is *mi amigo*. He is still a young man, but he is trustworthy, a good man."

Patricia was remembering that Carmina had lost a son and her husband before she came to Tomas. She was silently happy for the woman that she had a family again.

As soon as Miguel had eaten and gathered some papers from a desk in the dining room, he suggested they leave. Patricia was only too happy to climb back into the jeep and be on their way. She thought no more of Carmina. Whatever threat she might be to Patricia paled in light of the trouble Max was in.

The earlier easy silence continued for the first few miles. As they wound their way up the mountain from Cuernavaca, Miguel slowed and pointed to a huge monument on the left of the road. "General Morelos," he said, as if introducing her to the granite figure on the horse that she had seen many times. "He is the ancestor of Tomas. The Moreloses have always been important."

She ignored what she thought was a hint of sarcasm in his voice. "They have at that," she said.

"Did you know the great Frenchman Napoleon said if he had five officers like this man, he would conquer the world?"

"Yes, Max used to love hearing stories of General Morelos." "It is good that your son liked the great leader of our independence. He must not be ashamed that he is Mexican."

She bristled. "He isn't ashamed. Why would he be?"

"His father certainly was."

"Tomas?" She hesitated. "I think his feelings were more complex than that. He loved the U.S. more perhaps, but that was where he found success. He certainly never brought our son up to be ashamed of his heritage. Quite the opposite." She wondered if Miguel was going to taunt her this way for the rest of the trip, but for awhile neither of them spoke.

The road peaked and Mexico City lay below them in milky smog. As they descended, the air warmed and stagnated. It took over an hour to get past snarled traffic on Insurgentes before they could turn onto the Periferico that skirted west around the city. They picked up speed for awhile, then slowed to a crawl as they passed the Museo Tecnologico.

"You have brought your son to see the old trains here before?" Miguel broke the long silence.

"Yes, many times." She smiled, not at him, but at an image in her mind. "Max loved to come here. He could spend hours climbing through one old engine after another." She could see him, face blackened by age-old coal dust, hands greased like a miniature mechanic. A smile on his face as wide as a boxcar.

"They are new, these trains, compared to Aztec history." Miguel pointed to a statue in front of the Anthropology Museum. "Tlaloc, the Aztec Rain God. Here is the place to learn. My mother brought me here many times. You speak of Max, but not of Tomas. Did he never go to these places?" he asked her as they drove through Chapultepec Park.

"Not often. He was always seeing to business when we were here. He wasn't very interested in history, the past." Her words trailed off. This conversation seemed to lead to Tomas at every turn. Why must she feel a need to defend him to Miguel? She didn't want to remember her past either and damned if she was going to apologize for that! How many times had she and Tomas agreed that what had happened to them before they knew each other did not matter? Only the present and what future they could have was important. It was a bond between them. She sighed heavily. Had Miguel felt the same way twenty years ago, her life might have been very different.

"Tomas was not interested in the present either."

"What are you saying, Miguel?"

"Only that my step-brother did not care what happened to others."

Patricia felt a prickling at the back of her neck. "You seem to have something specific in mind."

He drove slower than the snail paced traffic, and Patricia thought he was going to stop. Her nerves were drawing into a knot at the endless drive, which seemed to be turning into a cheap tour of the city. She knew it would be the next day before they headed to the mountains, but Miguel's dragging along was maddening.

Finally, he did stop and pointed to a sign at an intersection. "This is the way to Tlantaloc. I would like to show it to you. Do you mind? We have time."

The light changed, but Miguel didn't move. A horn blew.

Patricia spoke out of frustration. Another delay, she thought. "What is it?"

"It is the place where the garbage is. Where the *pepenadores* live."

Patricia had seen stories on TV of people who lived near smouldering heaps of refuse and picked through the garbage, selling the things they found. "I don't think so," she said quietly.

"It has history. I insist." He turned the car down the pot-holed road.

Patricia crossed her arms, barely containing her frustration. She had a good idea what Miguel was up to. He wanted to show her the "real" people of Mexico. He was still on the crusade that carried him away from her a lifetime ago. To him, she knew nothing of poverty, so he was about to show her what it looked like. She drew herself up inside and braced herself against images, smells, and emotions that she knew all too well. They had reached the outskirts of the suburbs, and the houses were no more than lean-to shacks. Pieces of metal or cardboard, maybe one or two walls of concrete blocks. Pigs roamed the sides of the road rooting at coconuts. An acrid burning odor drifted on the air even before a seared landscape came into view.

Patricia leaned forward and tried to take in what she saw.

"What in the world happened here?" Charred earth and blackened walls of houses stretched for acres around them. "Was it the earthquake?" She twisted around in the seat. Devastating destruction was all around them. Anger and frustration melted as if touched by the flames that had burned the very dirt beneath them. Her definition of poverty was being rewritten.

"Surely, you know about the fire." Miguel declared.

"What fire?" She hardly knew she asked the question, still enthralled by the power of flames.

"Tomas did not tell you?"

"Miguel, I told you I don't know." Her vision blurred as she watched two little boys, blackened by soot from head to toe, digging what looked like peaches out of a charred can. She hardly heard the words Miguel was saying.

"A year before the earthquake, a truck parked here in front of Pemex tanks exploded. Five hundred people were killed. Burned to death. Thousands were injured and homeless. And you did not know?"

"The Pemez fire," she gasped. "Of course I heard about it on the news. It was horrible." More terrible than words, she thought, as she tried to comprehend what he was trying to say.

"Miguel, what did Tomas know about this place?" Her voice trembled.

They had moved past the blackest of the ruins. A gray mountain of debris rose in front of them. Like disoriented ants carrying food away from their hill, people moved down the ever crumbling, ever moving mound with pieces of metal, plastic or cloth in their hands. Anything of any semblance of value. Around the base, small piles of like material grew slowly, minutely. A raw, acrid odor, so thick it was almost visible, drifted in the air.

Before Patricia could get an answer to her question, a little boy about seven, dark skin lightened by ash from head to foot, ran up to the jeep, shouting, "Miguel!" Several people looked up and hurried down the avalanching refuse. A crowd surrounded them before the vehicle stopped. Patricia shrank against the hot leather seats as if the pungent odor of garbage and the people's coarse shouts pressed her there.

A little girl held a dirty package of Chiclets up to the window and Patricia fished in her purse for a dollar. Miguel shooed the child away as he shifted the jeep into gear and they began to move on.

"I do not think I would chew those," he said as he maneuvered the vehicle past the mounds of debris. "Most likely they will taste like burned oil."

"I asked before, Miguel, what Tomas had to do with this place. Will you tell me?" She felt as if she had visited Hell.

He turned to look at her, slowing the vehicle to a crawl. "Well, if you do not know," he offered, his voice had a new edge to it. "Tomas owned this land. He wanted to build many new apartments, but the people wouldn't move away. So, there is a fire and a great explosion."

"You can't think Tomas caused this fire." Patricia slid forwards on the seat and turned to stare at him.

He shrugged. "No one could prove anything. Anyway, before Tomas could get his buildings started he died. And the people came back."

"Who owns the land now?" She asked.

"Why, you do, Señora Morelos. Morelos Enterprises still owns the land."

Patricia slid back in her seat. She could not bring herself to say a word. She knew nothing of this land or any project to build apartments here. This was news to her. What other secrets did Tomas have? And who was dealing with the problem now? As they turned out onto the main road, she turned to look back at the mountains of garbage, the people, the waste and poverty. How could she be a part of this?

CHAPTER TWENTY

Patricia was safely ensconced at *La Mansion,* and for the second time in three days, Miguel waited for the Secretary in the shadow of Diego Rivera's murals at the National Palace. On the wall behind him were the figures of the six military cadets who wrapped themselves in Mexican flags and jumped from the windows of their school rather than surrender to American invaders in the War of 1847.

Miguel had often identified with the *Ninos Heroes.* He did now. It was obvious to him that Patricia knew nothing of Tlantaloc. Her horror at the sight that afternoon could not have been feigned. So it was all the work of Tomas and his henchmen. Whoever it was, he had to be stopped. Miguel would give his life to see that happen.

When the Secretary arrived they were free to walk and talk anywhere within the grounds. It was late Friday and the Palace had closed. It had evidently been a relaxing day for the man who was Miguel's mentor. He was dressed in casual clothes, and a floppy hat covered his gray hair. Miguel had changed into durable clothes for traveling and possibly hiking in the mountains. He would not go back to Cuernavaca for a while.

"I have a report from Zihautanejo," the Secretary said. "Jim Mainland arrived there yesterday, basking in the sun at the Parthenon. Catera is also there. And our beloved chief. And Perez. Looks like they are working out their deals. Mainland seems to have taken Tomas's place. We have been able to obtain a copy of the agreement they hope to make." He handed Miguel some papers. "You might need this."

"Mainland must be loco to get involved with these vermin. I do not know which one is more dangerous." He scanned the paper. "Looks like Catera is playing to win. Strange, is it not, that in our country one who commits murder can 'hide out' in the home of the chief of police."

"Not when the chief is a murderer himself. However, he is making mistakes more each day. He can not last long. Even many of the officers are becoming disgruntled. They say the demand for bribes is more than they can collect. This 'Parthenon' he has built may be his undoing. "We must get rid of this man, Miguel. He is going to be the end of me. And maybe of Mexico." The aging face sank into a network of lines.

"Well, we have a more immediate problem at the moment. If Mainland works a deal with Catera and the Chief, it will be that much harder for our people and maybe impossible to rid ourselves of either of them. The whole Tlantaloc project must be stopped, at least if these thieves are in charge of it."

"What do you plan to do with Señora Morelos?"

Their path had taken them once again to the skull rack where they had stood only days before when Miguel first learned that Patricia was indeed in Mexico. Now it was his decision to play God with her life. He placed his hand on the fossilized bone of some long ago forgotten warrior. Death came to all, sooner or later, he thought. "I will take her to Real," he said.

"Yes. It must be." The Secretary laid a hand on Miguel's shoulder, then turned and walked away.

* * *

Patricia sat alone in a wicker chair inside a small walled garden. A lantern cast shadows on ancient stones, covered with vines and yellow *cupa de oros*. A small table was at her elbow, a glass of brandy in her hand. Behind her were glass doors leading to her room at *La Mansion*.

A small breeze swirled, filling her nostrils with the acrid, smoky fumes of Tlantaloc that still lingered in her clothes. Her stomach heaved. She placed the small glass on the table and rushed to the bathroom.

She stripped off her clothes and stepped over the low tile wall that separated the shower from the rest of the bath. She washed vigorously, but the smell seemed to come from inside her. Standing with her head beneath the faucet, as if under a waterfall, she let her thoughts run backward.

Had it been an hour, two perhaps, since she walked down the chocolate-colored terrazo hall of the hotel? The porter had carried her bag. She didn't recall checking in. She had spent so many other nights in this hotel, built from a century old hacienda, that her memory of the place could be from today or many other days.

The ride from Tlantaloc was a blur. She tried to remember if she had said anything at all to Miguel. Had she slept? No. Of that, she was sure. She had been in a daze or something when they left Tlantaloc. The idea that Tomas might somehow be mixed up in the devastation and loss of life there, and that she now owned that piece of land had sucked all the life out of her. How could she own Hell?

She threw her head back and warm water splashed into her throat, choking her. Shivering, she turned off the faucets, wrapped herself in a bathrobe, her wet hair in a towel, and went back to the garden, picking up a bottle of brandy on the way. A tray brought from the hotel kitchen sat untouched.

Two glasses of the warm liquor and her body shook less. She noticed for the first time a plank door on the outside wall of the enclosure. It was almost covered with ivy. She could hear laughter coming from the other side. The latch on the door was old and rusted. It gave under slight pressure. The gate squeaked against the stones as she opened it.

In the nearby garden under a string of lanterns between two trees someone was having a party. A birthday party. They were singing "*Feliz Cumpleaños.*" A boy about nine was swinging a stick at a *piñata*, hoping to spill the candy it contained. Several other children tried their hand. Then a man, pulled from the crowd by a young woman with dark hair that flowed around her like a *mantilla*, was given the stick. She wore a blue skirt and blouse, the top pulled down on her shoulders. He was tall, his face covered with a handkerchief. He bent over her face, kissing her through the cloth, then made half-hearted swings with the wood, obviously trying not to break the colorful paper-shaped donkey. The people sang "Happy Birthday" again. The man took off the blindfold and stepped into the light of one of the lanterns. He looked strangely familiar. It must be the lights, she thought.

A September birthday. She pushed that thought away.

She shut the door and retreated to the tiny patio, pulling the terry robe close around her. She paced the smooth stones, stopped at one wall, and plucked a length of ivy. Easing into the wicker chair, she pulled at the leaves, giving herself over to memories that linked the past with the present, as surely as the vine ripped from the wall lead back to its roots.

CHAPTER TWENTY-ONE

WASHINGTON, D. C. 1963

Many times in her life Patricia had thought of how a day could start out in an ordinary way, then have some little thing happen that she hadn't thought much of at the time, but that ended up signaling a change in her whole life. Like the day she first met Rachel. The day her Pa came to the diner. The day she first had morning sickness.

She was so overwhelmed when she first saw the Morelos house, she couldn't speak. They drove in a big silver car from the bus station, up Massachusetts Avenue out to a place called Spring Valley. There the car drove through black iron gates, up a curved drive lined with snow-covered bushes. Beyond was an expanse of snow, dotted with shrubs and what looked like Christmas trees. The three-story white house with arched windows and a red-tile roof showing in patches beneath the snow looked like something out of a fairy tale. Its massive wooden doors set in a carved, stone arch led into a hall as wide as a school corridor.

Instead of lockers there were mirrors, paintings, large wooden tables with vases of flowers, and a round brass bucket filled with umbrellas. Thick floral-patterned rugs covered much of the gleaming wood floor and a stairway curved upward and out of sight past more and more paintings.

Those first days were perfect. Mr. Morelos was in Mexico and would not return until February. The house seemed to belong to Dosey, Natty and Carmina. And Patricia shared it.

The work she was required to do was easy. She helped Carmina dust the beautiful furniture and clean the wonderful pieces of silver, china, and pottery that filled cabinets in every room. Patricia was fascinated by the Mexican woman, who not only taught her how to take care of all the fine things Mr. Morelos owned, but also told her about *piñatas* and *Feliz Navidad* and Mexico City.

Carmina also talked about life in Cuernavaca where she had lived until two years before. She worked there for Tomas's stepmother. Her husband and child had been killed in an accident and she had wanted to live somewhere with no reminders, so Tomas had brought her to the States to work for him. Now she wanted to return to her family, her sisters and *tias* and *tios* she missed. Soon, when she had saved some money, she was going home.

Then it was February and one day Mr. Morelos came home. He wanted to meet his new employee. He sent Dosey for her.

Patricia was in the bathroom throwing up when Dosey came for her. She hadn't thought much about it that morning, nor even the next day, when Dosey again made excuses for her to Mr. Morelos. The third day, she made herself go to see him despite her queasy stomach.

He had not been charmed. When they were introduced, he stared at her white face and her shaking hands. He asked her questions, but she was afraid to open her mouth. He frowned and cut his dark eyes from Dosey to her. Finally, he said she could stay, only because Dosey deserved some help. And if she was what Dosey wanted, so be it. She was no concern to him.

In the weeks ahead, he didn't seem to notice when she was around, or care that for a month, at least, she wasn't working in the mornings. Dosey shook her head and clucked her tongue when Patricia dragged into the kitchen mid-morning, but she never confronted or questioned her. She simply covered for her and did her best to alleviate her misery. Each morning when Patricia awoke she found saltines and a cup of tea on the night stand by her bed.

The sickness passed and Patricia was herself again.

By spring time she began to put on weight. Mr. Morelos kidded her about Dosey's cooking and they all laughed. Dosey gave her a knowing look, and seemed worried. Then one day, he was gone again, back to Mexico. As much as Dosey fussed about his long absences, she was in a much better mood after he left.

On June 28, Patricia's sixteenth birthday, she and Dosey took a bus to the Tidal Basin. They walked around the water, enjoying a free afternoon.

"We have to be over on Connecticut Avenue at four o'clock," Dosey said and walked on.

"I thought we were going to stay here 'til late. I wanted to ride the paddle boats. What do you have to do?" A petulant tone clipped Patricia's words.

"It ain't what I have to do. You have an appointment." Dosey stared at the waist of Patricia's skirt. She had been trying to fasten the button that morning, and after a silent tug of war and some frowns, Dosey had taken the skirt and moved the button over as far as it would go. Still tight, it had slipped above the pooch of Patricia's stomach that sought the comfort of full gathers below the band.

Patricia stopped near two young mothers with babies sitting under one of the cherry trees. Over tousled blond heads, round pink faces, and squeals, she and Dosey stared at each other.

Without a word, Dosey walked on. When Patricia caught up with her, she said, "You say you made me an appointment? What for, a new hair style for my birthday?" She threw Dosey a smile.

Dosey stopped. People moved around them. She stared into Patricia's eyes and seemed to dive in, head on. "Like you don't know. Why are you actin' ignorant? I know you ain't. You know what kind of appointment. With a doctor, that's what. Not a beauty parlor. That baby you're carrying ain't going to be ignored forever, you know. It'll be here, whether you like it or not, in another few months." She took a deep breath and shook her head. "You and that sweet-talking fellow of yours, probably just like Franny's boyfriend, could best say exactly when."

Shock etched Patricia's face. "There was no sweet-talking fellow!" she shouted. People stared. She pushed Dosey aside and marched across the rest of the bridge, then stopped on a grassy slope, eyes down, toeing the dirt beneath the green blades.

When she sensed Dosey at her side, without lifting her head, she spoke in a low, sharp voice. "I know I'm pregnant. That doesn't mean I want to go to a doctor. So you can forget what you got up your sleeve this afternoon."

"Well, now we got that fact out in the open, for everybody to hear," Dosey looked around and huffed, "Maybe you'll just listen to some reason." She touched Patricia's arm, then gripped it firmly and steered her to a bench that some tourists had vacated. After a tense pause, Dosey folded her arms beneath her breasts and started her speech.

"The good Lord provided women with all they need to have a baby, but it's just plain dumb not to see a doctor to make sure everything is okay. That way your baby has the best chance of being—"

"I don't care. I hate it! I wish it'd die!" Patricia kicked her foot against worn grass beneath the bench. Her movements felt like those of a sulking child, but she was old and wise. How many hours had she thought about IT? Her entire life seemed concentrated into the past few months and into the region beneath her swollen belly. IT seemed to be devouring her. SHE was getting smaller, insignificant. IT was growing, taking over. She'd thought about the words she'd spoken. She DID want it to die. No doctor could help, because she couldn't have a healthy baby.

Everybody knew babies were deformed if the parents were related, especially close kin, she reminded herself. Every night when she moved her china doll from its special place on her pillow, instead of rocking it in her arms for a moment as she had done since her ma had given it to her, she would run her fingers along the small rosy cheeks, examine the tiny hands and arms, and see in her mind some of the legless, armless dolls she had played with as a child. As she touched the perfect little features of the doll, a sadness gripped her like a stomach cramp. Her baby could never be perfect. Within this acknowledgment lay a question like an illusive beam of light in the distance; hadn't she still loved the ragged dolls?

Sometimes she went to sleep remembering how it had felt to hold the twins when they were born. Ma would tend one while she cradled the other in the big willow rocker. She may have been a child herself, the baby, her doll, but she knew the touch of downy hair in the crook of her arm. Not to love a baby was foreign to everything she'd ever known.

Dosey patted the girl's leg. "Oh, you don't want your baby to die, Patricia. I know better. You just wait. You'll see. You'll be just like Franny is about her baby."

Patricia turned shimmering eyes on Dosey. "I don't want it. When it's born, I still don't want it. I wish I could stop it from being born. And I won't *never* change my mind." Her voice dripped cold, like water from an icicle.

"I know you've been wronged, honey. I see that, but you can't feel hate toward a innocent child. I know you can't."

Dosey sounded convinced, but Patricia wasn't listening. She refused to go to the doctor that day or any other day. She accepted her increasing girth and Dosey's remade uniforms without comment. She felt good, laughed and worked, and went for walks on her day off like a teenager without a care in the world.

August heated Washington like a well-stoked furnace and September brought no relief. People prayed for rain on Sunday and cursed the heat the rest of the week. Even behind the usually cool masonry walls of the Morelos house, the air was stifling. Seemed as though everyone who could had left the city. Mr. Morelos had spent the summer in Cuernavaca.

Patricia lay one hot, still night in a pool of water. She enjoyed the coolness against her body and dreamed of swimming in Choccolocco Creek. A pain wrenched her awake. She pressed her hands against her stomach, and with her eyes closed moved in sync with the rise and fall of her thin-stretched skin. Through the breaking of dawn and early hot light of morning, she lay quiet, waiting. The pain came again, like dull scissors rending cloth. Then it subsided. The scissors gaped open, waiting.

Dosey called softly as she opened the door about nine o'clock. Patricia felt a cloth wipe sweat from her brow as she writhed with another contraction, twisting on the water-soaked bed. Soon Carmina was bathing her forehead. First, Dosey and then Carmina came into her view and her consciousness.

Patricia heard Dosey say she was going to tell Natty to stay near, just in case they needed a doctor. Carmina held Patricia down when she tried to stop Dosey.

When Dosey returned, Carmina was sitting in the rocking chair near Patricia's bed, holding the china doll. It was naked. Its little dress and panties, tiny shoes and stockings lay in a crumpled heap in the corner of the room. One arm had popped from its shoulder socket and was hanging awkwardly by a cord.

"Lordy, what happened?" Dosey took the slender doll from Carmina and bent to pick up its rumpled clothes.

"I do not know. She take the clothes away. Why she do this to *la muneca*? She love it." She stood by the bed and fingered the little dress hanging from Dosey's hand. "She must be crazy with the pain, *si*?"

"Leave it alone," Patricia pleaded.

The two women stared as Patricia started a low groan that gained in volume and ascended in pitch. Her face twisted in pain.

Dosey pushed the doll's arm back into the shoulder and gave it to Carmina. "Put its clothes back on." She took a wet cloth from the night stand and patted Patricia's forehead.

"You should have called me when you first started this, honey. You didn't have to go through this by yourself. And what'd you do to that doll? Pretending it's your baby?" Dosey smiled. "It'd be a funny lookin' thing, come here grown up like that doll."

Patricia's eyes opened wider and wider. Beyond surprise and pain to terror that was like another skin that trapped the sweat covering her body. Dosey was bathing her face faster, pushing against her hair as if she saw the fear. "Don't you worry now," she crooned. "This baby's gonna be fine. It'll be prettier than any doll baby you've ever seen."

Patricia stared at the doll as Carmina held it out to her. She reached out, flailed and struck the doll, hurling it into the rocking chair where it slumped like a puppet whose strings had been cut. Carmina and Dosey looked as if they shared the hurt meant for the doll.

Patricia didn't turn her head to see where it landed. She didn't care. The pains came harder, faster, ripping her, punishing her. For what? For getting pregnant? For hating the baby? *Maybe it wouldn't live.* The words were a prayer. A pain gripped her and she was almost sorry for the thought. She heard screams. Were they hers? She stared into the round globe of the overhead light. She could see the farmhouse. She was sitting in the yard and sunbeams were glancing off the tin roof. She heard screams again and saw one of the boys running. Was it Billy? He was yelling something. Something about it was two. Two babies, that's what he was saying. "No, no," she cried aloud. "I don't want two, I don't—"

Dosey's voice came to her out of the light. "You might not want to, but you have to push to get that baby out. Now when I say push, do it!"

She had to tell Dosey she didn't want the baby. Or was it babies? Billy had said two. Two dolls to play with. She could give one to Rachel. The one that wouldn't have eyes. Dosey was telling her to push. Why? Wouldn't it come out by itself? She'd watched some kittens being born at Elsie's. Five of them. They came out by themselves.

Dosey's face was blocking the light. Carmina was yelling, "*Adelante!*" What did they want her to do? Carmina was holding her down, but Dosey kept wanting her to push. How could she move with Carmina holding her arms?

"It's crownin'. Just a little more, honey, and we'll have ourselves a baby."

Patricia squinched her eyes. She tore her hands free of Carmina and put them to her ears. She heard only the word "No" coming from her mind and mouth, but she screamed pleas to Dosey, begging her to take care of it. She didn't want to see it. IT. IT would be deformed, or retarded.

It would look like Pa.

The heat enveloped her, like a dark, hot oven. She couldn't get her breath before the searing pains came again. One last push reeled her in and out of consciousness. Voices buzzed around her. Carmina's. Dosey's. Did she hear a baby's cry? She forced the sounds back; she didn't want to hear.

"It's better this way."

"*Pobrecita.* Is what she want."

"She can start over."

"I take care of him. She thank me if she know."

Him. Patricia moved under the word. It was a heavy rock sliding down a hill. She was beneath it, struggling. If she could just get it over the top, but the hill kept getting higher, higher. She was exhausted.

When she struggled into consciousness, Dosey looked away and quickly whispered that the baby was dead. "Poor, little th—"

"No." Patricia whimpered.

"I know you—"

"No. Don't say it. Please, Dosey. Don't ever say anything. I don't want to know." Tears bathed her cheeks. Suddenly, you was wracked by deep, shuddering sobs. "I'm so sorry," she cried. "I didn't really want it to die."

Dosey held her until she quieted. "Well, it, it's better child. It's really better this way. You'll see. You can forget all about it. Go on with your life."

"I'll never forget, Dosey. I'm the reason it died. I said I wanted it to," she said quietly, resigned.

"Nothing you said caused anything. You don't worry your head about that. Things happen. That's all." Dosey smoothed her hair and held her so close she could hardly move.

Through a blurry mist she searched the overhead light for the distant farmhouse she had seen in her pain. "It's over then, isn't it, Dosey? Really over?"

"Yes. It's over." Dosey rubbed a cool cloth across her head, then kissed her on the cheek. "Get some sleep, honey."

Patricia heard the door close and knew she was alone. She lifted the heavy rock she had been under, shifted and struggled with it, until it was out of sight and mind, buried somewhere with Dorothy and Pa. Then, she cried until unconsciousness claimed her.

She slept in a feverish state for days. She knew at times that Dosey was bathing her, changing her milk-stained gown, watching her, giving her a soothing tea.

A cool breeze blew the curtain from the window one morning. Her hand slid from her breasts over her slightly swollen stomach. She opened her eyes and gazed around the small room. Everything looked the same. The closet door with her poster of Elvis that Natty had given her for her birthday. The dresser, its mirror circled with magazine clippings. The rocker. In it sat the china doll, fully dressed.

Slowly, Patricia slid from under the sheet and sat on the bedside. She lifted the doll, turned it and straightened the clothes. She brought it closer and started to fold her arms around it, but stopped. She looked at her pillow, placed the doll in its special place, then went to the closet. From behind her shoes, she dragged Jeff's old duffel bag into the room and placed it onto the bed. She opened it and without hesitation, picked up the doll and slid it head first into the dark circle of canvas. She retied the cords, knelt, and slipped the bag and doll gently into the corner of the closet.

Even though she knew all that Dosey said was true, guilt smothered her. But, no matter how she felt, she gradually came to understand that nothing could change things. She would just store away the memory of the child, like the china doll, where she wouldn't have to see it.

For a long time, she sat in her chair, rocking and looking out the window, listening to the wind and breathing in the fresh, sweet scent of rain.

CHAPTER TWENTY-TWO

MEXICO
September 30

Children squealed in the courtyard. It was past midnight and the fiesta was still going on. *Feliz Compleaños.* Happy Birthday.

Patricia didn't want to be reminded that babies were born in September.

She had come in from the little terrace outside her room at La Mansion and now lay on the hard mattress, watching the ceiling fan circle slowly. The blades became bats held by children circling a *piñata*. She felt dizzy and closed her eyes. She was moving round and round.

It was her sixteenth birthday. Carmina twisted cereal boxes into cone shapes and attached them to a clay pot. Covered with crepe paper, it all looked like a star, with tassels streaming from each point. Dosey blindfolded her and spun her in a circle. She swung a broken broom handle at air until she felt drunk. Natty pulled the rope up and down, keeping the prize out of her reach. He tired before she did and allowed her to whack it several times. One last sound hit and the pot fell into pieces on the driveway, spilling its load of candy and surprises.

She opened her eyes and watched the fan whirl. Birthdays begat birthdays and she shifted her thoughts to Max. He had been born on February fourteenth. They had always had a heart shaped *piñata* for him.

"Max," she whispered the name. Would they find him tomorrow? Was he all right? She tightened her arms around her body and felt their emptiness. She'd tried to tell him there was nothing that he could do here in Mexico. Why hadn't he listened to her? She clutched her hands into fists.

He had called the people of Real "his people." He had always looked to the past for someone to identify with, but the past is nothing, she thought. Ancestors aren't important. It's who we are today, who we've become that matters.

She should never have told him about her impoverished childhood. Even the little she did tell. She had only wanted him to understand. She'd only lied to protect him. So many lies. The hollowness she had felt after that September her unwanted baby was born was filled by Max. She always felt that she didn't deserve him, making every ounce of love from him more precious. Now that he was missing, she wondered if her punishment had finally come. She wrestled with that thought until her whole body ached. All she could do was shut her eyes and pray for another chance.

In the few, hot restless hours she slept, the children moved inside her head with their games, but she was up at dawn, dressed and ready to leave. While she waited for Miguel she stretched out across the bed. She jumped at a noise and sat up, unaware that she had fallen back asleep.

Miguel sat in a leather strap chair, his feet propped on the end of the bed. He was staring at the tossed covers she had so recently left.

"Miguel," she said quietly. She picked up the spread from where it had fallen to the floor and straightened it across the sheets. She knew how meaningless her action was, but it gave her distance and time. "Why didn't you wake me?" she finally asked, walking away from the bed and him.

"I thought maybe you needed to sleep."

"I've been up since dawn. I just fell back asleep waiting for you." Her words were sharper than she meant for them to be, but she didn't stop there. "You know how important it is for me to get there soon." She tried to calm herself. "Let's go. I'm obviously ready." She pushed by him on the way to the door. His hand caught her arm.

"It is still early. Here," he picked up a shoebox. "Some boots for you to wear. Pants and shirt are hanging in the closet. I will wait for you at the desk. As soon as you are ready we will leave."

He started to walk past her, but she caught his arm.

"I'm ready now. See?" She held her arms out to her sides, as if presenting herself to him.

"You can go no farther in what you are wearing," he said like some over-bearing father. His eyes took in her floral silk blouse, tan silk-blend pants and thin slippers. He opened the closet and brought out a new pair of chino pants and a denim shirt, and held them out to her.

She stood with her arms to her sides, staring at him.

"Put these and the boots on. There are socks inside," he said with force.

"Where do you think we're going, the Alps?"

She didn't take the clothes, so he dropped them in a heap on the floor.

"The mountains are rugged and cold at night."

"Well, I don't plan to climb them. That's what vehicles are for. And I certainly don't plan to spend the night outside."

The words "especially with you" hung in the air between them and they stared at each other.

"We will go when you change. I will meet you by the desk." He slammed the door.

She stared at the heavy, metal-banded wood. Her anger was revved, like a race car engine. She couldn't let it go, and since Miguel was no longer a target, it turned inward. Why was she turning on the one person she hoped would help her? Why did she care what clothes she wore? Naked or in a space suit, what difference did it make? She hurried into the thick, hot clothes. Miguel was offering to get her to Max. Bottom line.

She thought what a kick Rachel would have at this turn of events, but even that idea didn't put her in a better mood. Then she remembered she needed to call Rachel.

"So, you are at *La Mansion*. Separate bedrooms?"

"Don't get cute," Patricia answered. "Jim will be calling today, I'm sure. I want you to tell him now where I'm going. Have him bring some men and meet us in Real tomorrow. They may have to finesse their way in, but I want them there in case there's trouble with getting Max free."

"You got it. He'll probably yell at me, but I can handle him. You just be careful and stay in touch. Promise?"

Miguel was not at the desk, but in a corner of the restaurant when she was finally ready to go. She sat down across from him, as a waiter placed two huge plates of pancakes on the table with a pot of coffee. She pushed the pancakes away and asked for a glass of water. It was too hot to eat.

"You will be glad of the clothes. The mountains are cool."

"I don't think I'll ever be cool again," she wiped perspiration from her neck.

He shrugged and motioned the waiter for more coffee. "I have learned some more of Max."

"What?" She came half out of her chair.

"I sent Daniel to Potrero yesterday. He talked to the people, to some of the miners. They had not seen Max, but the word is, he is being treated well."

It was all she could do not to jump up and hug him. The thought made her stare at him, as if seeing him for the first time. Her tenuous hold on eighteen-year-old indignation tightened, and she pushed her chair back, stood up and walked to a window. Through tears she saw fragments of *piñatas* that still littered the ground from last night's fiesta. He was alive. Max was alive.

She composed herself and returned to her seat. Suddenly, she was hungry. Fresh pancakes were brought and she ate greedily. Over a last cup of coffee, she remembered something. "Wait a minute. You told me in your office that it wasn't the miners who were holding Max, but some renegade bunch that didn't like the name 'Morelos'. Or was that just a story you made up to keep me away from there?"

His eyes dropped. "It was no story. Most of the people in Real hated Tomas Morelos."

She bit her lip. "And because they disliked him, for whatever reason, some of them took my child?"

His eyes squinted, as if assessing whether to answer her. "They asked the government for help before the cave-in, but no one did anything. They might have thought they would keep your son until something is done for them."

"Do you mean Max may be caught up in some political mess?"

He shook his head, dark strands falling on his brow, and stared at her. He seemed to be expecting her to read between the lines. To figure out what he meant by looking into his eyes, as if they were crystal balls. "That we will have to find out. Maybe we should stay here for more word."

"No way," she said. "We go, or at least I'm going. Today. Now." It was only a little disturbing that arranging for Max's release might not be as easy as she'd thought. Paying a ransom, bargaining with gold-thirsty thieves was one thing. She did that in the business world every day. Dealing with ideal-crazed political movers and old grudges was something else. An uneasy thought entered her mind. Max had come down here in a fervor to help "his people." What was he mixed up in, and how much was he to blame? How much was Tomas to blame?

"What do you know about the miners, Miguel? What did they want from the government?"

He looked at her hard, as if to see what she meant.

"I would think that as the owner of the Morelos mines you would know better than anyone, Patricia." He raised his dark brows.

She felt her face redden. "I have someone who is in charge of the mining division. You may know him, Marco Cortina. I can't personally see after every detail of Morelos Enterprises. It is too vast." She hated the haughty sound of her voice. First, she knew nothing of Tlantaloc and now she had to admit to more ignorance. For a fleeting moment, she was sure she saw a look of disgust on Miguel's face. A look so like the one-sided, half-smile, half-smirk Max often wore that she turned her head.

"Do you not know the story of Real?" He waited, but when she didn't say anything, went on. "Silver was found there by accident in the late 1700's. Spaniards came in and mined it. Thousands of them lived in grande haciendas all around the mountains and in Real. It was a beautiful *ciudad*, but in this century, Revolution came and the wealthy left. The poor stayed behind. The mines had almost played out anyway. Real de Catorce became a, how-do-you-say, a town of *espiritus*. Fewer people every year. Houses falling in.

"Then about thirty years ago, my greedy step-brother and some of his amigos bought the land and reopened some of the mines. Machines could locate silver that was unseen a hundred years ago, but workers were still needed to get it to the top."

"Why was that bad? Didn't the people need work?"

"The machines that made the work easier also made it dangerous. The mines are old and fall in. Over a hundred people have been killed since they were opened. "The men want a safer place to work, maybe a better way to take silver from Real. You can see, I am sure, why they want help."

"Well, why hasn't the government done something?"

He gave her the little half-smile, half-smirk again. "Why has Morelos Enterprises not done anything?"

Or why haven't *you*, he seemed to be saying. She owned the mines, she was responsible. A scathing retort sat on her lips, but something in his expression stopped her, a combination of innocence and hostility.

Guilt worked its way under her skin like a splinter, as she remembered her argument with Max, his conviction that they must do something. His people had been hurt and he had only wanted to help them, out of compassion, not out of responsibility. And what had she done?

She felt her anger slip away like a shadow.

"Why hold my son?" she asked Miguel, tears brimming. "I didn't know all of this." Her eyes pleaded for an answer. She felt as if she invited him to look through them, down a tunnel into her soul. Look, she was saying, and understand how I feel.

Miguel watched her fight a flood of emotions, and he felt his heart give, as if it had experienced the slip of a brake.

"We will go to Cedral now. Perhaps some friends there will know something." He held his hand out and smiled.

They drove north to Matehuala where they turned west toward the Sierra Catorce Mountains. They passed small rancheros surrounded by fields of nopal cactus. He told Patricia how the fiber from the cactus was used to make carpets and bags. She made no comment. Perhaps she could find no sympathy with the hard, grueling work, he thought.

He pointed out the twin peaks of Friar Mountain rising out of the desolate plain. She stared at them a moment, then looked away. He told her he thought the ridged slopes, sparsely covered with cactus and scrubs, looked like the bony back of a mange-infested dog, and she smiled.

He watched her pull at her shirt, as if to dislodge herself from a cocoon of clothes, dust, and helplessness. He knew her world was generally ordered by her commands, but here, where she must feel the most need to do something, she was forced to ride along, at the mercy of someone else.

Cedral spread out from the road in hopscotch squares. Miguel swerved around ankle- and knee-deep holes, like a drunk. Old men stared at them from under sombreros; women carrying baskets of fruit or pans of watermelon slices on their heads turned cautiously. Children waved or gave chase.

He drew up alongside a stone wall covered in yellow *cupa de oros*. Pig sty and garbage odors hovered over the road. He saw Patricia wrinkle her nose. She said nothing.

Inside the wall, three men waited on the porch of a tile-roofed stone house. The day had already grown hot, and what breeze there might have been was kept out by close walls. The only shade was on the porch, and Miguel told Patricia to stay there while he talked to the men.

They greeted him with enthusiasm and tipped their worn sombreros at her. When they stood far enough away from Patricia, they told him Carlos Randel and his wife, Rita, had everything ready at La Paloma. Longtime friends, they had rebuilt one of the old ruins for their retirement home in the hills above Potrero. The place was a mecca for expatriate Americans.

Once Miguel and Patricia reached Potrero, they would be "abducted" and taken to Carlos and Rita's at "gunpoint". After Miguel left for Real, Patricia would be watched at all times. When her boy was released, Miguel would bring him back.

When they finished making their plans, one of the men disappeared into the house and returned with four bottles of *Dos Equis* beer. A young girl was coming with a cola for la Señora, but Patricia stalked right over to where the men stood and took Miguel's beer from his hand. She turned it up, drained half the short bottle, handed it back to him. The men looked at each other and laughed, raising their bottles in the air. "*Salud!*" they shouted in unison. The one closest to Miguel whispered in Spanish, "La Señora may be too much for my friend, eh?"

Outside Cedral they turned onto a blue-gray cobblestone road. It was a seventeen mile long, teeth-chattering expanse that glistened in the sun and seemed to disappear into a mountain. He thought it was beautiful. She probably hated it.

"See the road? There." He pointed to a winding ribbon of dirt that circled the cliff to their right. "We will stop at Potrero, the little town in the distance. After we get some more supplies, we will go to the other side and to Real."

Well, I will, he thought. He would be leaving her, well—cared for and guarded at the hacienda of his friends.

"How did Max ever find this place?" she asked.

"Many people come to Real de Catorce, to the old town or mines. Now many will come to worship St. Francis."

"I thought St. Francis was in Assisi, Italy."

"He is here in Real, too. His statue is. See the people there camping on the side of the road? Thousands more will be traveling here in this week. Coming to worship, bringing *milagros*, silver and gold, to say prayers because of sickness, death. Or to give thanks for miracles. Perhaps you will take a *milagro* of a child to St. Francis."

He was driving across a cattle guard in the road, when he turned to smile at her. Instead, he watched in horror, and what seemed slow motion, as her head hit the ceiling of the Bronco. He felt a jolt to his neck, as he realized he too was flying through the air. He heard gunshots at the same time.

When he opened his eyes the front of the vehicle was buried in a muddy creek bed. The grates across the road had fallen beneath them. It was no accident. Gunshots rang out again.

"Down!" He shouted at her as she tried to climb through her door. He pulled her arm, pushed her head down, grabbed their packs from behind the seat and slid out of the vehicle on his side. She followed him into the gully. Water swirled around their ankles. They stumbled and fell and crawled and ran. Bullets whizzed over their heads, exploded into dirt behind them. The banks of the arroyo lowered, giving them little protection. They crouched in the water and waited.

The only thought in Miguel's mind was this sure as hell was not what he had planned.

CHAPTER TWENTY-THREE

Jim sipped his third beer. The afternoon sun slanted across the bay and under the umbrella. The light glanced off the pool like a thousand watt bulb. The heat and glare suited the feeling that he was sitting in a hot seat waiting to be interrogated.

Being ignored by the three Mexican "*bribóns*" didn't help. Except for the cute gal who kept bringing him beers, no one had spoken to him since the initial greeting. Catera, Perez and the Chief talked and laughed without looking across the table at him, as if they were playing some silly child's game of "ignore."

He knew enough of the lingo to follow what they said, but he didn't let on. They weren't saying anything of importance anyway. Their chatter reminded him of a bunch of old hens.

In the middle of a conversation about the local brothel, the Chief started talking about some deal and how the profits were going to be divided. Perez and Catera reacted with hostile looks, but the Chief didn't notice. He was watching Jim.

Jim had been catching droplets of water meandering down the green *Dos Equis* bottle. His hand had jerked at the shift in subject and his head came up, but he just threw it on back, brought the bottle to his lips and pretended he had heard nothing. He wanted to look at the Chief to satisfy himself that the man had been fooled, but he motioned instead for the girl with the beers.

A heated argument followed. Jim listened. Whatever the usual split of the spoils, it seemed the Chief was pulling rank and a fast one on Perez and Catera. Jim thought so, at least, until he heard what they were casting lots for. They were talking about the Morelos mines.

It was all he could do to stay in his seat. If he confronted them, questioned them, he'd give away that he'd been pretending not to understand. Did he want to do that? It might be the only advantage he had being here in this den of thieves.

Finally, he decided to let them know he was still there. Maybe they would start talking in English, and he could throw out some questions without giving away his secret. "Hey fellows, let's don't waste this spectacular sunset." He pointed across the bay where the sun looked like a hot air balloon at the ocean's edge, and waited for one of them to react to his statement.

The Chief looked at Jim and stood up. "We'll continue our discussion later, Señors. Mr. Mainland is right, it is getting late." He turned, never having glanced toward the light show off the balcony, and headed into the house.

Catera jumped up and followed. Perez stood up. Jim reached his hand out and caught his arm.

"I wasn't invited to come all this way to listen to a soap opera in Spanish. We have some things to talk about, my friend."

Perez looked toward the house, as if wanting to join the others, then he sat back down. He was what Jim would call a "refined" man. Spoke with more of an Italian accent than Mexican. Ought to be Perillo, not Perez, Jim thought.

"You are right, of course," the little man said. "I did ask you here. At the Chief's request."

"Yeh, I figured that since it's his shack."

Perez winced. "I would not make remarks like that to Carlos, if I were you. He is rather proud of *El Partenon*."

"Well, I don't work for *Architectural Digest*, so let's get to why I am here."

"I, we wished to talk to you about the problem at the mines."

"And I want to talk to you about the problem with the construction project. And Mr. Garbage himself in there, who's holding up the works."

"That is good, because the two are entwined, shall we say."

Perez motioned to a young man who was lighting torches around the edges of the balcony. "What time is dinner, George?"

"Soon, Señors," was the answer.

"Let us find our rooms and make ourselves fresh for dinner, Jim. We will discuss this more with the others over some food."

Without looking back, Perez went to the young man, said something to him, and disappeared into the shadows of the garden.

Jim thought about pinning Perez to the ground until he got some answers. However, he was outnumbered here, and had no doubt Perez would scream like a fighting cock at *palenque*.

George had reappeared and was holding his hand out in the direction of the house. "This way, Mr. Mainland."

No one at dinner broached the subject that Jim wanted to discuss. It was hard for him to eat. Time was tight and all this socializing was shrinking what he had. Thoughts of Patricia, Max, the mines, and Morelos Enterprises, not to mention his debts, made his food sour as he swallowed it. When coffee and Kahlua had been poured, Jim could stand it no longer.

"I came down here to see if we can come to an agreement on the construction project, Chief. Tomas made sure you knew how important this work was before he died." In other words, Jim thought, he paid you enough. "Tomas trusted me," he continued. "You know you can too. So what's holding us up?"

The Chief stared at him, and Jim felt sweat trickle down his sides. Somehow facing the worst barbarians in prison when he was a teenager didn't compare to what he knew this man could do to him. And had done to others. Tales of the cruelties carried out by his office would be too much for Vincent Price.

"The question is not trust, Señor Mainland. It is timing. This last year our need has been to rebuild from the earthquake. We have had few resources to start new projects." He took a Havana cigar from an elaborately carved box and lit it.

Jim had to bite his tongue not to say, "Bullshit!" Instead, he said, "I realize the earthquake is a problem for the government, but our project doesn't require any funds or assistance. We just need the permits to build. And the use of our land."

Catera sipped his coffee and eyed Jim above the rim of the cup. His long eyelashes and girlish features made it look like he was flirting. Jim winced.

"Mr. Mainland," Catera said, in a lilting voice. "If you build on that property, what will happen to the poor people who work there now? Have you thought about them?"

"That's not my problem, is it Catera? You can move your garbage piles somewhere else. The people will find them. What right—"

"Jim, my friend," Perez interrupted. "Let's discuss this matter calmly. It seems we have a legitimate problem. Mr. Catera has many people employed in his salvaging operation. He cannot very well turn them into the streets."

The food Jim had swallowed seemed to lurch into his throat at the delicate way Perez was describing Catera's garbage business. The last thing Juan considered were his "employees."

"Seems to me we could solve this problem if we had another place for the workers to go," the Chief said without taking the cigar from his mouth.

"That is where the Morelos mines come in," Perez said. He smiled as if he had just solved the puzzle.

"What the hell do the mines have to do with a garbage dump?" Jim almost shouted.

"Well, if you knew more of Mexican history, Jim, you would know that many of the people who work for Mr. Catera are actually displaced miners. Their ancestors are of the Indian tribes who use to work the mines when silver was plentiful. As the mines have played out, the people have come to Mexico City, but they could find no work. Luckily, Mr. Catera has employed them."

The little man nodded to his cohort as if honoring him. Jim's rage was like ants under his skin chewing their way out. "I ask you again, what in the hell does that have to do with the Morelos mines?"

"Don't you see, that is the beauty of the plan. You want to build on this land. Mr. Catera needs somewhere for his workers to go. The workers are miners at heart. The Morelos mine has no workers since the cave-in. You have arranged for the miners to detain Señora Morelos's son to force her to give them the mines in return for the child."

"What th'—" Jim shouted as he pushed his chair back to stand. Perez grabbed his arm and forced him back down.

"Of course," the Chief continued, "She does not know that you will be the holder of the mines. If we intervene and secure the mines for Mr. Catera instead, well, then she never has to know that you were behind the, uh, detaining of her son. You get to build on your land, and no one is the wiser. Don't you see everybody would be happy."

The ants were out and crawling over Jim's body like warriors on a march. He was unable to think. Of all the convoluted nonsense. But only to him, he began to realize. It made perfect sense to these three thieves. They'd get the Morelos mines and he'd get the promise, again, that his land would be cleared. He could kiss his job and Patricia goodbye, and he'd have no money to pay off Willie Bates and the "boys" back in Virginia. He could almost feel the cold steel of Bates's gun in his ribs. He tried to make his mind work. He got up from the table and paced the room.

"How do you propose to "intervene" and get the mines?" he asked.

"That, my friend, is your job," Perez said.

"Patricia Morelos is the only one that can sign them over and the only person she's going to deal with is the one that has Max," Jim snapped.

"WE have the *muchacho*," Catera said, smiled and winked.

Jim propped his fists on the table and leaned into Catera's face. "I don't believe you. The miners would never give him to you."

Catera's smile widened, his teeth bared like an animal. "Believe it, Señor." He stuck his face so close to Jim's they almost touched.

"Why you—" Jim reached for Catera's throat, but missed when Juan jerked his head back. "You'll never get her to sign those mines over to you," Jim growled, lunging again.

"You must hope she does, Señor Jim," the Chief said. His chair scrapped the terrazo floor as he stood and grabbed Jim's arm in a vise grip. "She is already making her way to Real. We will see that she arrives at the right time and is ready for you to convince her. Then you can try to get whatever you can from her for yourself, as I am sure you have already done many times."

Guterriz threw his head back and laughed. He released Jim, shoving him backwards as he did.

Catera and Perez joined in, guffawing with exaggeration. Jim stood, rubbing his wrist, watching as the three slapped each other on the back and made their way toward the garden.

He walked alone toward his room, glancing through the arches of the *sala* at the great iron gates to the driveway. A padlock and chain reflected the light of torches mounted on flanking posts.

Surely that wasn't the only way out of this hell he was in.

CHAPTER TWENTY-FOUR

Sounds of a ricocheting bullet echoed through the arroyo canyon. Miguel and Patricia crouched below the desert floor in a soft pocket of dirt where recent rains had caused a minor landslide. They sat motionless, their ragged breath in discordant harmony. They had run as far as they could go. The gully ended here.

Patricia's mind raced with images of gun-toting bandidos just out of sight, crawling toward them, blasting around the last curve of the crevasse or catapulting over the rim of their refuge. She could smell her own fear. Every nerve in her body screamed for her to run while there was still time. She had not come this far only to sit and await her fate. She made a move as if to rise and Miguel's arm stopped her. She stared at him.

His eyes said no.

Minutes passed. No more gunshots. Buzzards circled in the clear sky. Flies buzzed over a tiny bird carcass. A lizard nosed its way into the shade of a rock. The desert was coming back to life. She wasn't sure how long they had, but the sense of danger had lessened.

"It's been quiet a long time," she said, sitting up.

"Do not talk." Miguel spoke into her hair as he pulled her back onto the ground.

She lay rigid. Her muscles began to ache. She rolled onto her side and mud seeped in around her waist like an invasive hand. She bit down on sand and grit. Splatters of mud on her face dried, pulling at her skin. She was exhausted and the heat made her drowsy.

She watched Miguel through a haze. He sat on his haunches, his face hard, sun-creased and handsome. The layer of dust that had settled on him softened the darkness of his hair, his skin, making him seem indistinct. It wasn't hard to let her mind play with that image and see him as he was eighteen years ago. She hated herself for the thought.

She lay for what seemed like hours. The sun sliced itself away on a ridge and bled down the valley. When the mountain threw a protective shadow over them, Miguel rose slowly.

"Stay close to me," he ordered, scrambling up the embankment.

Patricia listened for gunfire. Miguel's dark outline looked like a target, and she wanted to pull him back. To keep him safe. Fear touched some dormant emotion.

"*Venga.* Come," he whispered.

His outstretched hand was too far away to grasp. She struggled up from the scooped-out seat. Like the rabbit and the Tar-baby, her hands sunk up to her wrists, and her boots sucked grossly at the mud as she pulled them behind her. She struggled up the slope, grabbing at rocks and brush. Too late she felt the cactus hiding in a tangle of weeds. She screamed and slid back into the deep ditch.

Miguel created an avalanche of rocks and dirt as he settled down beside her. "Well, perhaps the gunmen are gone. If not, your banshee cry scared them away, I am sure. Let me see."

He held her hand at an angle to catch the fading light. She winced as he pulled thorns from her palm and fingers. He mumbled in Spanish.

"If you're going to cuss at me, at least do it so I can understand," she said through clinched teeth.

"Why do you not speak Spanish? *Mi Dios*, you were married to a Mexican for years," he hissed.

"Because HE never spoke Spanish," she almost shouted as he pulled out one of the needles. Her palm oozed blood.

"That is no excuse for your ignorance."

"I am not ignorant." The higher pitch of her voice was due more to pain than caring what he thought.

He put his hand over her mouth as her voice rose. His breath moved a lock of her hair. She thought he must have heard something, but he held her too long. She tasted dirt and sweat and fought the realization that she wanted to taste his skin against her lips.

"You talk too much. Be still and be quiet." He pulled at another thorn.

She jerked her hand away. "I don't need you to do acupuncture on me. You're twisting those things." She pressed her bruised hand against her stomach, closed her eyes and tried to breathe. Miguel disappeared over the rim of the arroyo.

Good, she thought. Leave me here by myself, wounded and hunted by some maniacs. I don't need you anyway, Miguel Ramirez. I didn't need you years ago and I don't need you now.

"Hold still." Miguel had reappeared holding a long, spiny stem of a plant.

"Do I need more holes in my skin?"

"Aloe," he said. "It will make you heal."

"Sure it's not poison?"

He ignored her, pulled her up to the desert floor, then darted quickly behind a Joshua tree, motioning for her to follow. The meager protection it provided was comical, but no other shelter was in sight. He put his arm around her waist and held her tight, making their profile as narrow as the tree. His belt buckle cut into her back.

They darted from tree to tree, resting behind clumps of maguey cactus, always moving away from the arroyo toward the mountains. Road Runner cartoons she used to watch with Max came to mind, and she hoped they were smart enough to outwit whatever wily coyote was after them. When they had walked at least a mile, Miguel announced that no one was following them, and stepped into the open, near a low, crumbling wall.

Patricia joined him, searching the shadows of the dim landscape they had crossed. The upstretched arms of Joshua trees looked like an army of giants marching toward them in mock surrender. She wasn't sure they didn't move as she turned away.

Miguel led her around the wall into the ruins of a large hacienda. Columns rose up to meet the darkening sky where the roof of a long veranda had once shaded a tiled patio. Shadows of bright paint framed paneless windows. A huge doorway loomed dark in the wall. Carved panels of rotting wood hung on rusty hinges.

"What is this place?" she asked.

"Just one of many homes abandoned by the Spanish long ago," Miguel said, as he pushed against the door. It squeaked, and scurries in dried palm fronds answered back. Geckos and night birds fell silent.

Inside the walls of the great house it was dim, lit only by stars that speckled the sky. The cool breeze that had made her clothes feel cold and clammy out on the desert was shut out. The dark carried a deeper chill. She shivered.

Miguel took a flashlight out of his pack and shined the beam around the room. Along one wall was a large stone fireplace.

"Oh, we can build a fire," she said through chattering teeth.

"No. Someone might see the smoke."

"Of course," she murmured, and hugged her arms across her chest. She willed herself to stop shaking.

Miguel glared at her clothes.

His smile made her angry. "What do you want?" she asked. "For me to say that you were right? That it is cold in the mountains? Had I known I'd be half-drowned in some drainage ditch on the way to Real, I'd have worn a fur coat. You'll notice these clod-hopper boots didn't keep me dry." She stomped her feet, making sounds like a squeegie mop. She grabbed the light from his hand, picked up her pack, and stalked through a doorway.

"Where are you going?"

"To find the powder room." She blinked back tears. Cold, wet and miserable, she would be dammed before letting him know. He made her feel so inadequate, a child, incompetent. Her, of all people. Miss Self-Sufficient. She thought of how he had held her as they ran and hid. The comfort of his arms surprised her. She didn't want the complication of thinking about it.

The narrow beam of light bobbed before her. With the dark pressing in, she didn't feel so defiant. She eased through rooms filled with debris until she found a small, almost clear area behind a wall. She kicked some broken plaster to scare away its inhabitants, propped the light on a ledge and opened her pack for some clean, dry clothes.

Linen and silk caught at her mud-caked, bloody hands. She searched until she found a package of moist paper wipes and a tiny bar of French soap, then stripped to the waist and started scrubbing. It was an impossible task, like cleaning a muddy pig with spit and a Kleenex.

She shivered with every touch of the wet towel, then washed harder to warm herself. Anger rose in her at the delay once more in rescuing Max. An image of her son looking through bars in a dungeon prison leaped into her mind. Other images flashed by like frames in a horror movie. Stop it! She silently screamed at her imagination. I can't think of him like that. He's okay. I have to keep thinking good thoughts.

She redrew the picture. He was peeking through the bars of his baby bed. A dark-haired toddler holding his fuzzy blanket that he called "Boo." She held the image as if it were a photograph, remembering every detail of his round face and dark, laughing eyes.

The wipes were gone, but she still smelled like mud. Her hair hung in strands of dirty dampness. She tried to button her shirt, then groaned at her injured fingers. An answering sound made her jump.

"I am sorry. I did not mean to scare you." Miguel held out a clay pot. "I found this and a well in the courtyard. It is not good to drink, but is okay for washing." His hair was wet, glistening with caught moonlight. He smelled of earth and rain.

"Thanks," she mumbled, reaching for the water. The shirt she had been holding together fell open, and the slim beam of the flashlight focused on her breasts.

She grasped the pot and they stood, holding the water vessel between them. Miguel's eyes moved from one half-revealed breast to the other. His gaze lifted.

She felt the movement of his eyes as if he moved his fingers across the rise and fall of her cleavage, up the flat plane toward her neck, lingering there in the shallow dip between her collar bones, then riding her pulse to her lips. The wedge of light stopped at her cheek and her eyes hid in the darkness like a voyeur.

The weight of the earthen jug filled her hands. He was gone.

Miguel could still feel the softness of the dust-covered clay pot in his palms. He imagined it was Patricia's touch. A vision of her half-draped bare breasts danced before him like a sprite. He made his way back to the *sala* of the hacienda, putting distance between himself and the sounds of water splashing. Or maybe he imagined the sounds, too. He kicked some brush out of his way, realized too late that plaster lay beneath it. A pain shot up his leg. It felt good.

He hobbled onto the veranda, into the courtyard and beyond the walls. Scouting. Thinking. Whoever had been shooting at them had not intended to kill them. He and Patricia would be sprawled in the arroyo not ten feet from the jeep, if that was what had been ordered. No. Someone had just wanted to delay them. The "why" would come later. They were almost within site of La Paloma, but he couldn't risk leading someone there to Carlos and Rita's. No, he would have to wait until it was light when it would be easier to see if someone were following him. He shook his head at how far his plan to be "forced" to a hacienda had gone awry. He would have to get word to his men in Cedral and Potrero tomorrow.

He sensed Patricia behind him. "Do you always go about so softly?"

"Wouldn't want our enemies to hear us."

"Oh, I do not think we need to worry about them tonight."

"What are those?" Patricia asked, pointing to distant wisps of smoke.

"The people we saw today on their way to Real de Catorce, camping for the night." He began to gather sticks and scraps of wood. "We will build a fire and be just one of the many pilgrims. It will be safe." Besides, he thought, if there was warmth in the room, he would not be tempted to hold her against the cold. When the fire was ready, he opened a can of beans and warmed them, then divided a hard *bolillo* and the beans onto tin plates.

Patricia ate greedily. He smiled as she sopped up the last of the bean juice with her bread. She licked each finger hungrily. She caught him watching her, and for a moment their eyes held. He took the plates, wiped them with a cloth and stuck them back into his pack.

Busy work. Woman's work. It did not matter what, as long as he kept occupied and his eyes away from hers. After gathering more wood and stoking the fire until it warmed the corners of the room, he settled down on his blanket. It overlapped the edge of hers.

He lay back on his pack and watched her as she watched the fire. He could only see the right side of her face. It was all shadow and glow. The flames seemed to dance on her cheek, her perfectly formed nose and the curving corner of her lips. She had washed her hair, and it hung loose in dark, wet waves.

He took a lock and tucked it behind her ear. She turned. The firelight fell on the other side of her face. And what had been like the dark side of the moon was beautiful in the light.

Twisting another long, dark curl between his fingers, he tugged at it lightly, playfully. No response. He dropped his hand.

He was quiet and still, listening for her breath. The fragrance of the soap she had bathed with seemed the only tangible thing in the room. Crisper than the acrid smoke of the fire, stronger than the hard floor beneath him, more real than the stars in the blue-black canvas overhead. It was as if the only sense he had was that of smell. He took a deep, filling breath of her.

Her touch made him jump. She had placed her hand on top of his. Still, soft and warm. A light blanket covering his skin. He turned his hand and clasped her fingers, splaying them with a tight clinch. She stiffened.

He knew he was hurting her, but he had to struggle to release her. He wanted to grab her, pull her beneath him and make her pay for eighteen years of loss and loneliness. He wanted to caress her, soothe and love her with eighteen years of longing.

A log fell, and sparks burst like fireworks. Patricia jumped. She let go of Miguel's hand and was immediately sorry. Confused as to why she had even dared touch him, she had no doubt that it had felt right, had felt good. If she tried to sort out her reasons, she knew she wouldn't be able to do it again. Then she wasn't sure she wanted to.

Civil war waged within her. Self against self, teenager against adult, love against loyalty. She feared even more the battle Miguel seemed to be waging. One moment he was gentle, and his touch dissolved time and treachery. Then he would stiffen as if he were struggling against some hidden enemy.

She sensed his shoulder near her back. He leaned forward, bracing her. She held her position. His arm circled her, drew her tight. It was at once a loving gesture and a relentless vise.

Words bombarded her mind. Questions. Accusations. A thundering NO. Her mouth refused to give form to a single thought.

He rocked her. A soft, soothing movement. With each tilt, she was drawn closer to him. How clever to lull her into his embrace, she thought, ignoring her own desire to press against him.

The rocking stopped abruptly. Miguel's arm tightened like a wet rope that had dried in the warmth of the fire, cutting off her circulation. She struggled, half-heartedly, then made her decision.

As she pulled away, he captured her hand in the quick smooth movement of a dancer catching his partner to twirl her. Her stomach lurched as she turned with a snap and fell into his arms. His hands braced her fall. Before she could regain control, her head was pinned between the frond-covered floor and Miguel's lips.

Soothing softness and hateful hardness. She wasn't sure which was beneath her and which above. And the fire. It was no longer between the great stones of the fireplace. With every kiss, on her lips, her neck, her cheeks, kindling sparked within her, and the blaze spread rapidly. It consumed the combatants of her war and drew all attention to itself.

The pain in her hands was forgotten as she kneaded his back, pressing him closer. His fingers slid slyly beyond the bands at her waist. Her hands met his. Fingers unused to joint efforts fumbled with the buttons of her blouse, his shirt, her jeans, his trousers.

"Patricia," Miguel sighed as he kissed her. His tongue traced the outline of her mouth, then guided her lower lip between his teeth where he tugged it until she moaned. His fingers lingered across her breasts torturing her nipples with sensations too complex to name.

She dug her nails into his back, lifting her body closer to the power of his assault. When she could no longer stand being a separate entity, she arched her back.

He accepted the invitation.

* * *

Exhausted, battle-worn, they entwined in a truce.

Like a sculptor reunited with an early, forgotten work, Patricia's fingers traced over Miguel's body, comparing it to her memories. The deep "v" along his spine, the dimples just below his waist. She smiled, content in recognition.

"A peso for your thoughts," he said, pushing her wild, damp hair back from her face.

"A peso?"

He smiled and lay by her side, his arm a pillow for her head.

Patricia stared up at the night canopy. "Lousy hotel," she said. "But, nice ceiling work." She tucked her thoughts away where they wouldn't attract attention.

He pulled his blanket around her shoulder and followed her gaze to the stars. "Do you make a wish?" he asked.

"Yes," she whispered,

"Tell it to me."

"Can't. It won't come true."

"Perhaps if you tell me, I will make it come true."

"Okay," she smiled. "You first."

In the distance a dog howled. The fire popped and sizzled. In a corner of the room plaster rustled.

Miguel pulled her closer.

"I wish," he said softly, "I want, very much, Patricia, to know what happened eighteen years ago."

CHAPTER TWENTY-FIVE

Miguel's question hung above his head like the blade of a guillotine. Answered, it could descend and cleave him and Patricia apart as surely as the relentless interrogation he had made of her so long ago.

Patricia was silent, settled into his arms. Was she contemplating her answer? Remembering as he was?

He had come to Washington right before Christmas. The first few days he had spent arguing with Tomas about the reasons for the student demonstrations at the University, in his room sulking, or out with his friends drinking.

He had not yet met Patricia, but he had heard a great deal about her. Tomas praised her constantly. She was an independent thinker, a rebel in many ways. An astute businesswoman, a born leader. Miguel tried to contain his jealousy.

There was to be a party Christmas Eve. Even though Tomas had hardly listened to Miguel's arguments, the optimism of youth made him hope that this was a celebration for him. If Tomas admired the traits he did in Patricia, he must see the same and more in Miguel. Even if Tomas didn't agree with Miguel's politics, surely family pride would bring Miguel support.

He imagined Tomas introducing him as a leader of young patriots who would restore rights to Mexico's downtrodden. The son of the famous Maria Ramirez who helped women get the right to vote. Funds would be raised and he would be sent back to their homeland a hero, suitcases bulging with contributions to the cause.

Patricia had stood at the top of the grand staircase that night. A vision in green velvet. Tall. Slender. Hair the color of rich coffee swept up into a cascade of curls. Brown eyes, like Mexican topaz.

Shyness tilted her head and confidence made her look straight at him. He was filled with passion for her. He might have claimed that he fell in love at that moment, except for what happened as she descended the stairs.

Tomas called for everyone's attention. A hush fell over the room. All eyes were on Patricia as Tomas took her hand.

"This is a special occasion tonight," he said. "This fantastic young woman has just finished her college degree." Mild applause interrupted him. "No. That's not the best of it. She's not been just studying books. She's also been working for Morelos Enterprises for these three years. Now a reward is due." Murmurs of agreement came from the crowd.

"May I present the new director of our Morelos Gallery." Soccer match cheers filled the room.

"And," Tomas raised his hand. "I have a special gift to show my appreciation for her loyalty and hard work." He took from his pocket an emerald set in an intricate silver design, dangling from a long chain. Patricia's eyes grew large as she allowed Tomas to fasten the clip. She picked up the enormous jewel and caressed it. Her eyes glistened.

Miguel thought he was going to be sick. Humiliation washed through him like a purgative. He and Tomas stared at each other. A sneer turned up the corner of Tomas's mouth.

Miguel's passion turned to hate as he stared at the emerald. He was very familiar with it. Maxmillian had given it to his mother for a wedding present. She had worn it almost every day before he died. Tomas had evidently taken it away from Maria. And now he hung it around the neck of his lover.

It was weeks before Miguel considered that he was wrong about Patricia.

Poverty and jail awaited him in Mexico, so he stayed on in D.C., working for Tomas. He found a certain justice taking money from his hated half-brother and sending it to his friends, or in stashing it for his own return. It didn't matter that he worked hard to earn it.

He started out as a janitor in the Gallery, riding to work each day with Patricia. The trip always started in silence, but she would eventually break it. Every day she would question him about his life in Mexico, but he refused to answer, thinking she was probably reporting everything he said back to Tomas. Then he decided what better way to get Tomas to see things his way. The fervor of his convictions found a new audience.

To his surprise, Patricia showed interest and understanding of the students's movement. He poured out his ambitions, his disappointments, his history. Except for Dosey, she seemed to have no friends. She never volunteered anything about herself, but he was too self-centered, to immature, at the time to care.

His friends accepted her as one of them. Laughter and his growing love for her softened the drudgery of living in his stepbrother's world. He repented of his earlier thoughts about her and Tomas. She was shy, virginal. Tomas was exploiting her in the same way that Maximillion Morelos had Miguel's mother. It was his duty, he told himself, to free her. He longed to make her his, only his.

He began to look at Tomas without hate. His love for Patricia overshadowed all other thoughts, all other feelings. Except one: his allegiance to the cause in Mexico. It grew stronger, as if his desire for right in his homeland was at one with his desire for Patricia.

He wanted to return to Mexico City, with her. He knew she loved him too. He was sure of it. For many nights they had parked on a hill above Great Falls, kissed and caressed each other. He could tell she was afraid. He wanted her to trust him, to want him.

He had planned a special evening. It was time. To propose. To plan. To make love.

The night took an ugly turn. His expectations were shattered. Not because she was not a virgin, no, not that, but what that revelation meant to him. For he now knew without a doubt that Tomas had been her lover after all. He was convinced. Her relationship with Tomas mocked him. He questioned her, demanded she tell him who her lover or lovers had been. She was silent, refusing to talk to him. Their turbulent affair lasted another month. She gave him her love time and again, asking often was that not enough, but he was tortured with visions of her and Tomas. He could not get her to tell him what he longed to know. Who had her lover been, if not Tomas?

All his plans were shattered. Maximillion Morelos had stolen his mother from him and from her cause, had made Miguel a beggar in his own home, and now Tomas Morelos, the bastard's son, had usurped him with Patricia.

When she would not return with him to Mexico, he was convinced of her great guilt. In a blind rage he had deserted her.

He was in prison when he learned Patricia married Tomas. He wanted to kill him. When he was released, it no longer seemed important. He was not even bothered that a simple, easy death, a heart attack, had at last taken Tomas. The thorn that did prick him was the knowledge that Tomas had been the winner. He had been married to Patricia all these years and she had had Tomas's son. Nothing she could say now would change that.

His muscles tightened around Patricia until he knew he must be hurting her. She said nothing, as if accepting some form of punishment. Is that what she thought he wanted, to punish her? Was that why he asked the question? It was he who deserved to be punished. And he had been for eighteen years. He no longer wanted to know the answers he had sought then. What purpose would they serve?

If he was to have anything from her, it had to be in the future, not the past. He would not let Tomas take that from him, too, by dredging up those days and reliving them.

He relaxed his muscles and Patricia felt herself go limp in his arms as if he had been holding her together.

"Where shall I begin?" she asked, and snuggled into his shoulders, searching for answers in the stars overhead.

"I changed my mind," he said. "It does not matter. Not after all these years. You are in my arms now. That is enough."

"No," she whispered. "It isn't. I owe you the truth." The story lay before her like the long cobblestone road outside Cedral. The end was beyond the horizon, but she was ready to start the journey.

She took Miguel's hand in hers, clasped his fingers as if to say, "Hang on."

She started at the beginning. Told him about her childhood, her mother's death and going to live with the McFalls. When she got to her father and his awful deed, Miguel stiffened beneath her, but did not interrupt. She recalled her friendship with Dosey and the Mexican woman Carmina who worked for Tomas. Finally, she told him about the baby, her father's child, and how Dosey and Carmina had delivered the baby boy who died.

She braced herself for his reaction. He had alternately tightened his grip and caressed her as she had spoken. Now his silence filled the room and loomed up into the dark sky.

"Why did you not tell me then?" he said finally, his voice flat. "You could have told me. I would have understood."

She held her breath. She couldn't read his thoughts or anticipate his feelings.

His arms laced around her, holding her to him. *"Pobrecita, mi carino,"* he said in a rush of pent-up breath. "What a terrible thing to happen to you. If, if I had only known."

He shifted her head so that his cheek touched hers. It was damp. She reached up and brushed her hand across his face.

He cleared his throat. "It is all over now. You must think about the future. That was all finished there with the baby. You must forget about it."

She had forgotten. Memories of that child were lodged so deep in her subconscious that telling the story was like reading a book about someone else's life.

Miguel pulled her closer. "Now your thoughts must only be for getting your son Max home again. I will pledge my help to do this. A son needs his family. I can not imagine how terrible it is to lose a child since I have none."

His words were like the wind, so soft, yet with the power to bore deep into her soul. Max was his son, his family. How could she hold this truth from him? How could she tell him?

CHAPTER TWENTY-SIX

October 1

The sun had not yet topped the twin peaks of Friar Mountain, but rays shot upward from the "v" like so many arrows warning of its approach. A spiny green iguana swished its tail and stayed its place. A rat scurried into a cool, dark corner, shuffling dried palm fronds and stone shavings.

Patricia stirred in her sleep.

She was standing at the foot of an ancient Mayan pyramid. A boy was being carried up the high stone steps by a figure covered in silver scales. Indians dressed in brilliant feathers, blue jeans and miners' hats danced on the steps. The boy turned his head, and she saw the face of her son Max. She watched the procession climb into the burning rays of the sun. The silver began to melt, run down, then fall away in drop-like coins. The dancers slowed their rhythmic movements, catching the drops of silver. The one that held her son moved on, carrying the sacrifice to the gods. Out of the midst of the dancers, scattered in their search for coins, she ran up the steps, stretching to reach Max. The silver figure turned. It was Miguel who held her son. Max pointed a finger at her and screamed, "I don't know who you are!" She tried to tell him she would save him, but the heat drove against her face like a wind of fire, silencing her. Miguel continued up the stairs, Max lying motionless in his arms.

Patricia stretched her stiff limbs, scrapping dirt against the terrazzo. Her nightmare leapt full and threatening into daylight. Thoughts of where she was and why she was there crushed her. It was as if she had crawled beneath the stone slab floor.

She had not even the luxury of a moment's peace. At times in her life when she had gone to bed with things unsettled, she would awake with a vague knowledge of a problem. Just a gnawing realization. For a moment the forgotten worry would have no name. But not now. She wished she could stay huddled on the floor and not face the day, the truth, or Miguel.

She had taken the coward's way out the night before. Cuddled in Miguel's arms, she had feigned sleep as she hosted the war within. When she had heard Miguel's soft snores, she breathed a sigh of relief and gave herself up to the refuge of sleep. Now, she must face her turmoil again.

The bed roll next to her was empty. She pushed herself up, holding the blanket against her naked body and grabbed her clothes where she had thrown them the night before. Dust mushroomed around her. She coughed and spat grit.

Looking around for Miguel, she remembered that he had planned to go for help and another vehicle, something to take them on to Real.

On the ledge of a window cased with ornately carved stone, a piece of paper reflected the sunlight. A small capped container of water weighted it against a nonexistent wind.

"*Buenos dias*, Sleepyhead. Left early. Sun will heat water. Coffee in pack. Return soon. Love, Miguel." She read the words aloud to the iguanas and scorpions. Memories of the night before staggered her and tears flowed unheeded. "Miguel, Miguel," she whispered. "I am so sorry."

Shame heated her face and dried her eyes as she recalled telling Miguel of her father and what he had done. She trembled at flashes of Miguel's anger, and shivered at the thought of Miguel meeting Max. She wasn't sure what he would do to her if he learned about his son. What chance did she have of keeping the two of them apart in Real? The only hope might be that Miguel was so blinded by his hatred of Tomas he wouldn't pay attention to his brother's son. Father and son meeting was frightening her, but something more had nagged and plagued her sleep. And made her have that awful nightmare.

It was something Miguel had said. Something that she barely registered. The words stuck in her subconscious like the thorns that had pierced her hands.

She prowled through the hacienda trying to remember. They had talked about so much. Max. Tomas. She stared through a window at the mountain looming in the distance. She could hear Miguel's laughter. No, the memory of his laugh. He was saying something about Tomas and Max. If Tomas had known. Had known his son would love *ejitos*. One who would give peasants and miners everything he owned.

Had he really talked about Max inheriting Tomas's company? Max and something happening to her? Or had he simply laughed at how Tomas would kick his way out of his grave if he knew? She felt broken inside, in a place unseen, unreachable.

The truth glared at her: if she and Max were out of the way, Miguel could conceivably become the owner of Morelos. Which he, too, would quickly give away, she reassured herself. He certainly wouldn't do anything to get Tomas's money for himself. She tried to shake off these crazy thoughts.

Miguel had once loved her, said he did now. She put her fist to her abdomen, as if to stop the fluttering that took over her stomach at every thought of Miguel. Could it really be? She asked herself over and over.

Miguel was taking too long. Even if he had had to walk all the way to Cedral, he should have returned by midday. She began to pack up their things to be ready when he arrived. Maybe they could still get to Real tonight.

She stowed her things, then gathered their bedrolls. She was stuffing a dirty shirt and trousers into Miguel's pack when the sores on her hand caught on something. "Damn!" she swore and jerked some papers out of the pack.

Her name jumped out at her. And the company. Morelos Enterprises. A legal document. "Damn!" she said again, frustrated because she couldn't read it. She searched for words she knew. "Legalese in Spanish," she groaned.

It seemed to be some kind of agreement involving Morelos Enterprises and someone named Juan Catera. Official seals and stamps made it look like a "done-deal." But there was no signature page. Who was Juan Catera? If she didn't know him, the papers couldn't be legal. She looked at the date, 04 October. It was only October 1st, so how could it be a legally executed document? Maybe Catera was one of the miners and Miguel was anticipating an agreement she might make with them.

The questions grew like monsters. Proliferating, evil monsters. *If she and Max were dead.* The thought became an endless chant.

Had she been a fool to trust Miguel? He had always hated his brother and everything he stood for. This agreement probably assured the miners that they had no reason to negotiate anymore. If they thought they had won, Max was in mortal danger.

The very marrow of her bones cried out to her to go to him. To protect her son. Where was Miguel? What was taking him so long?

Almost the same moment that she decided something must be terribly wrong, she heard a noise in the distance. She was sure it was a small explosion. Then shots. Not just gun play, but the sounds of war. She looked out around the wall at the end of the veranda and saw smoke rising not too far away.

Trying to still her breathing, she looked back at their belongings. Should she try to carry their packs and make a run for it? Where would she go?

Shots continued to echo around her. She might not know where she was going, but she liked the idea of staying put less. She quickly took what supplies she thought she could carry, gathered her pack and hurried from the ruins.

Using the maguey plants and Joshua trees for cover as they had done the day before, she half-ran, half-crawled across the desert landscape. Whoever had shot at them yesterday could be watching. Or had they followed Miguel when he left? Her heart lurched at the thought. Her eyes burned and she wiped them roughly with the back of her hand. If she could just make it back to the road they had been on, maybe she could find help. She might see Jim and his men on their way to Real.

She would not allow herself to dwell on how different things might have turned out, or on the loss of Miguel for a second time in her life. She had to think of Max. She looked in the opposite direction from Cedral, toward the mountains and Real, and hurried on.

The road lay glimmering in the distance like a shiny snake. She could hear the rumble of an occasional vehicle. She skirted the foothills, weary, alert. On an upward curve, a group of people walked slowly, no doubt heading for the festival in Real. The women were dressed in long, flowing skirts and shawls. Some carried baskets delicately balanced on their heads.

How could she know if they would help her, if she asked? Without knowing who had shot at them, who wanted them dead, she could take no chance in approaching these people. Her clothes made her stick out like a stalk of corn in a wheat field. Her legs were wobbling from running in a crouched stance. She needed rest and a disguise. She walked on more slowly until the distance between the road and the mountain narrowed. Climb or walk in the open. Finally, those were her choices.

She leaned against a gnarled tree and watched the sky darken. It was going to rain. A small adobe structure lay nestled into the near hillside. It looked deserted. She ran along an arroyo, up a bank and into the tiny one room building. Soon the rain beat and swirled on the roof like some god washing clothes on a washboard.

A three-legged table was propped against one wall. A broken lantern and some pans lay under it. Hammock strings clung to a peg like a macrame hanging. A basket with a torn bottom dangled from a nail. On the floor was a pile of rags. She pushed at them with her foot. Something scurried away.

She took the basket down from its nail and examined it. The bottom was frayed. She tore lengths of thread from the hammock and pushed the string and frail straw back and forth until she had rewoven and secured the hole.

The basket finished and set aside, she dumped the contents of her bag into a scrap of cloth, added her watch and tied it into a bundle. She took what she needed from the backpack and threw the rest into a corner. She lined the basket with her blanket, putting the bundles on top, shook the dirt out of one of the cloths and put it around her shoulders like a shawl. Then, she wrapped a longer cloth over her pants, tucking it under her belt, and cuffed the trousers until they no longer showed beneath the makeshift skirt.

Her pale ankles glowed above dirty brown socks and muddy mountain boots. She slipped off the socks, the boots, then took a pair of shoes from her pack. Scraping a stone across the soft leather slippers, she defaced them, taking color and hide away, then rubbed them with mud. She wiped her hands on the top of her feet and ankles.

Everything was ready. She picked up the basket and stared down at the dirty shawl and shirt, the rag of a skirt, her mud-brown ankles and feet, the worn shoes. A soft whimper escaped her throat. Time took a giant step back and she was Dorothy again. Back in that corner of her mind which still held the memories, images, and shame.

    She whispered the words Max had spoken in her nightmare, "I don't know who you are."

CHAPTER TWENTY-SEVEN

Patricia waited until almost dark to leave the little adobe shack. When she reached the road to Potrero, she squatted by the shell of an abandoned car until a group of people disappeared around a curve. Then, basket balanced on her head, bending forward under its weight, she stepped out into the open and headed up the mountain.

Not daring to look around to see if anyone was watching, she forced herself to think of Max and breathe deeply as if she were in labor and needed to calm her pains. In minutes her heart pounded less. After an hour of steady uphill walking, her leg muscles cramped and her shoulders drooped. Her pace slowed. She fell farther behind.

She listened for the sounds of vehicles, jeeps. Surely, she would see Jim as he passed by. But, she realized, that would probably not be until tomorrow at the earliest. She had to keep going on her own.

Sounds of music, hands clapping and laughter reached her long before she could see people settled around a campfire. Without drawing attention to herself, she moved along the outer rim of the circle and sat down behind several darkly clothed women. They were not dressed so differently from herself.

A slight-faced Mexican plucked at the strings of a guitar. His deep baritone voice, too big for his small form, filled the smoke-smudged sky with the strains of "La Paloma." His sombrero, held by a string around his neck, framed his face like a halo.

Sizzling sounds seemed an odd accompaniment to the music until Patricia caught a breath of meat frying. Since morning she had eaten only part of a *bolillo*. The aroma of tortillas, onions and garlic made a mixture of smells that played on her senses along with the music.

She didn't dare move forward as others did to hold out a hand for one of the meat filled tortillas. Her teased stomach grumbled angrily. Finally, she inched into the circle to one of the platters. She took two tortillas and slipped back into the dark.

She ate slowly, prolonging the satisfaction of filling her empty stomach. She sipped from her canteen. Others swigged from bottles of *El Presidente* or tequila that bounced from hand to hand.

Mariachi music and off-key voices grew louder with every note and every new bottle as the food ran out. The women around Patricia began to move their baskets and packs to make room for dancing. They plucked their heavy *rebosas* from their head and shoulders and began to twirl in place with the rhythm of the song.

Feet trampled near her. Dust rose. Patricia was forced to stand.

Men in sombreros and *jorongos*, or *sarapes* parted the swishing skirts of the women, stomped their booted feet in hard flamingo steps, and spun their partners like tops.

Some of the women were dressed in colorful costumes. Reds, yellows, vivid blues flashed in the twinkling lights of the many two and three foot tall *velas* that dripped wax and filled the air with the fragrance of burning wicks.

A tall figure, head tipped so that the wide sombrero hid his face, mingled through the crowd. Hands behind his back, he strutted first with one señorita, then another. He stood only a few feet away, dancing for a time with a long-haired girl regaled in an Azeteca costume.

As Patricia watched, he tilted his head and looked straight into her eyes.

He looked like the young man at the fiesta at *La Mansion*.

His rhythm never broke as he bowed to the one he had been dancing with and stepped in front of Patricia. He brought his mouth to the side of her face. "I will take you to safety." When she backed away, he took her by the arm in a vise grip. "Dance," he said. His voice was soft, but the word was spoken so close and with such strength, it stung.

She moved her body. Her feet were like stones. Her motion was arrhythmic. She didn't want to dance, tried to pull away. His arms tightened with her least resistance. "Do you know Miguel Ramirez?" she ventured.

The young man leaned into her face again. "*No habla*," he whispered. Lifting his free arm above his head, he threw his shoulders back and took up the rhythm of the music.

As the song faded into loud talk, he spoke to one of the men and nodded toward Patricia. The man howled like a night animal, grabbed a bottle of tequila and threw it to the young man. A spray of liquid shot up and splattered Patricia. The men's laughter rang in her ears as she was steered toward the rim of the crowd. They hesitated just long enough for her to grab her basket of belongings. Then he took it from her and rushed them out of the lights of the candles.

When they had blended with the shadows of the mountains, she cried out in a hissing voice, "Where are we going?" She tried to jerk her hand out of his. He tightened his grip, and whispered, "*Quieto.*"

They made their way over outcroppings of rock, around brush and cactus. With no light except a sliver of moon and twinkling stars in a black sky, Patricia couldn't imagine how he knew where he was or where he was going.

Thoughts tumbled through her mind like the pebbles and clods of dirt that rolled under her sliding feet. The little scene back at the camp. He must have said something about taking her off somewhere. That's why the men were laughing and giving him tequila—to get his whore drunk. She winced. They had all laughed at the young man taking the old, dirty woman to his bed. The thought, the implication made her sick. She staggered, but he pulled her on. In the dark it was impossible to make out his features, to comfort herself with the idea that he must know Miguel or why would he be there.

She shivered in the mountain air that crept in around them. Her lungs filled and burned with every step. She stumbled and sat down hard.

"We can rest now," he said as if her stopping had been his idea. He sat down beside her and turned up the tequila bottle he had stashed in her basket. "We have to reach the other side of the hill before we find camp and the others."

"What camp? What others? Is Miguel with you?" She slid off her shoes and shook out debris and dirt that had been gouging her toes and the bottoms of her feet. A few places were bleeding. She slipped the shoes back on before her feet began to swell.

For an answer, he offered her the bottle of tequila.

She grabbed it, tilted it and swallowed. Tears burned as if the alcohol coursed her body and pooled in her eyes. She coughed, choking.

"*Quieto.*" He reached for the bottle.

When she had her voice again, she asked, "Why?" whispering more because of her throat than to please him. "Who's going to hear us? And who are you anyway?"

"I am an amigo of Señor Miguel."

"Is Miguel okay? Did he send you? Why didn't . . ."

"You made a bad choice to join the group below, Señora," he interrupted, ignoring her questions. They would not be so kind to learn you are a gringo. Especially, to learn you are Morelos. Be glad no other came to take you away before me."

"I've made a number of bad choices in my life," she said. "Would you just please tell me where we are going and who's waiting for us?"

His silence chilled her. He was so still he seemed to be soaking in all sounds and snuffing them out. If only she could see his face, but his profile was like a woodcut against the night sky. She strained to hear anything other that the festivities below. Then, a twig snapped.

He stood soundlessly, bringing his finger toward his face, telling her to be quiet. He motioned for her to get up and pointed toward the summit of the rise above them. Without a word he climbed.

Distant music and laughter floated on the air. Below them the *velas* and campfire threw a soft glow against the sky. Where was the danger she sensed, below or above? Stones rolled behind her. She made her decision quickly and rose to follow this friend of Miguel's.

She didn't have a chance to turn around. Empty space was her first sensation. She was falling, plummeting feet over face. Gravel scrapped her skin, dirt filled her mouth. Rocks slowed her, and brush caught at her clothes. A final jolt. Darkness.

CHAPTER TWENTY-EIGHT

Beneath her hand was a rough board. She moved her fingers slightly. A splinter pricked her skin. She drew back and tried to lift her arm but found that she couldn't. Her eyes fluttered and opened to darkness. Slowly they focused. A light flickered somewhere to her left. A fire, maybe, Patricia thought.

She was lying on hard, lumpy bedding. Above her, shadows contrasted until she could make out slats of wood, the underside of another bed. Bunks? Where was she? How did she get here?

She didn't know if it was the memory of tumbling down the mountain that made her start hurting all over, or the fact that she was now fully awake, fully aware. Her senses filled. Dampness, mold and smoke. Sizzles and soft pops of burning wood. Murmuring voices. Soft snores.

Turning her head, she could just make out the close walls of a room, a fireplace, and some figures sitting at a table.

She tried to sit up and moaned.

"You awake?" someone whispered.

Patricia shook her head at the voice, denying she heard it. Her brain throbbed when she moved, and she shut her eyes against the pain.

"You got yourself in a hell of a mess this time." The soft voice returned.

"Rachel?" Patricia felt strong hands push her back.

"Easy kid," Rachel murmured.

"Where are we? What—"

"Shhh. Don't want to wake up the *gendarmes* over there." She gestured toward the room behind her.

"How did you get here?" Patricia whispered.

"I should stay put while you're having fun playing Dolores Del Rio and the Mexican Bandits?"

Patricia groaned. She tried to raise her right arm again, but still couldn't. Something was wrapped around it. She turned over on her side to prove she could and winced.

"Lie still," Rachel said, pushing Patricia back on the bed. "Going head over ass down a mountainside is not good for somebody your age, you know."

"How long have I been out?" Patricia asked. The windows were so heavily curtained, it was hard to say if it was day or night outside.

"Daniel, one of Miguel's men, carried you in like a rag doll an hour ago. He wasn't sure he'd picked up all the pieces until they looked you over good. Don't think anything's broken, but they put your arm in a splint anyway. And you've got scratches and bruises. Carmina cleaned you up. She seems to know what she's doing."

"Carmina. She's here? How did you two get here?"

Miguel thought it was best to get me out of Acapulco, and I wasn't going anywhere unless you were there. I won. He sent this nice young man to bring me here. We stopped and picked up Carmina, presumably to take care of me. Then we were coming to Real, I thought, when—"

"Simple as that."

"Well, almost."

Before either could ask more questions, a door creaked on its hinges in the far side of the cabin. A man stepped into the room carrying an armful of wood. It was the one who had whisked her away from the campsite and up the mountain.

He whistled a low sound, and a grunted greeting in Spanish came from the shadowy figures. A dark, older man dressed in slacks and a white *guayabera* shirt followed into the doorway. Patricia thought he looked like the government officials she had met with in Mexico City. He stopped the young man with a hand on his shoulders.

"*Tiene problemas,* amigo?"

As if the man had said nothing, the other one walked into the room, threw the wood onto the floor and bent to stoke the dying embers of the fire.

While the two talked in low, fast Spanish, Patricia and Rachel sat quietly. The growing fire illuminated the room. It was movie-set pioneer with two women and two men sitting at a wooden table. Patricia stared into dark faces that stared back.

One of the women poured some water and coffee into a tin pot and placed it on a grate in the fireplace.

Rachel leaned closely and cupped her hand against her cheek. "I hear Daniel's voice. Was he one of the ones who came in?"

"If he's the one who kidnapped me from the camp below, yes." Patricia stared at the young man whose face was shadowed in the firelight. She couldn't make out his features clearly, but he was obviously the same man.

She wanted to sit up, to call out to him and say—what? So much was happening that she didn't understand. Rachel was a complication. Why did everyone keep throwing stumbling blocks in her way to Max? God, her head hurt. It was hard to think. She closed her eyes and tried to sort her thoughts.

"*Cafe?*" One of the women gave Patricia a mug of coffee, then took Rachel's hand and brought it gently to the other cup she carried. Her gaze lingered on Rachel, as she went back to the others.

Patricia sat up and sipped the hot liquid and watched Daniel and the short man. The others sat quietly, eyes watching each other, occasionally glancing at her.

She heard her name spoken.

"Can you make out what they're saying?" she asked Rachel.

"Daniel's telling how he "rescued" you. Evidently, there are some unsavory characters looking for you."

"More so than this bunch?" Patricia gave a little laugh. What did I do to win such attention?"

"I don't know. This character isn't supposed to be here. Daniel's trying to get him to leave, but he doesn't seem to be in a position to run him off. Either that or he wants something out of the guy."

The young woman who had given them coffee stood next to Daniel. Not touching him, just leaning into him possessively. Her smooth brown face glowed in the soft flicker of a candle that sat atop the mantle, and her eyes twinkled as if they had captured a thousand fireflies when she looked up at Daniel. She wore a tight black skirt and a white peasant blouse that stretched down over her shoulders. Patricia recognized her as Miguel's secretary. She was also the girl and he the young man that had been dancing the night of the birthday party.

She stared at the three other people who sat at the table. One woman dressed in costume. Two men in shirts and pants, their *sarapes* and *jorongos* that could transform them in seconds piled in a chair. Pilgrims headed for Real to place a silver *milagro* at the feet of St. Francis? Unlikely, Patricia thought. So who were they? And where was Carmina?

Perhaps Miguel had brought Rachel and herself here to be held hostage for the miners. Extra leverage. Maybe he had no intentions of aiding her in getting Max released. Maybe he wanted her and Max out of the way. And Rachel. Whatever was going on, it was time she found out.

She swung her legs off the bed and sat up before Rachel could protest. The movement released a herd of donkeys in her head, kicking and jumping against their skull corral. Rachel's arm came out to stop her, but Patricia was on her feet with her last tiny burst of energy.

"Daniel." She pushed her way into the circle of firelight and leaned against him, her head swirling. "Is that your name? I, I don't know what you'—" He took her arm and held it tight, keeping her upright, making her arm throb worse. Her head was numb with pain. She gritted her teeth against the dark that swirled around her and tried to focus.

The man who had been talking to Daniel let his eyes roam like a slow moving fly over her bandaged arm, her dirty, scratched face, her peasant's garb. She realized how ridiculous she must look. Well, she wouldn't be intimidated. A fire kindled in some shadowy corner of her spirit.

She shrugged the shawl-like cloth from her shoulders, untied the skirt with her good hand, then brushed at her pants to roll them down. She saw where blood had dried on her feet from blisters and cuts. Her shoes felt glued on.

She pulled the rag from her head and twirled her hair into a bun. She didn't look like she just came out of a salon and the dirty chinos and shirt weren't a Chanel suit, but just looking more like herself made a difference. One she felt and the others seemed to acknowledge. She could read the men's surprise and she pushed on.

"Miguel was taking me to Max. Where is he? Where's my son?" She stared at Daniel's face where the flames of the fire danced along lean lines and lightened his eyes. She was struck by his unexpected Caucasian features. Her knees threatened to buckle. She stiffened her legs. "Take me to him. Now! Tonight!" Her voice bounced back at her from the walls of the shack. She clutched her arms to stop herself from shaking.

Rachel's hand settled on her shoulder like a soothing balm.

"*Dice la Señora*, Daniel. Tell her, amigo." The man's eyes glowed like the coals in the fire.

Daniel's jaw clinched. He turned his back to the room, spinning the girl from his side. He took his cup from the mantle and tossed down the coffee like a shot of tequila.

"Tell me what, Daniel?" Patricia scanned the faces watching her. They looked away.

"You stay here," Daniel said. He moved to the fireplace, kicked a log with the toe of his boot, sending sparks flying.

Patricia swayed and Rachel steadied her. Daniel grabbed a chair and practically pushed Patricia into it.

"What do you mean, stay?" Rachel asked, she hovered over Patricia, hands on her shoulders. "Is this some plush mountain resort you brought us to and I just can't appreciate the view? You said you would take me to Real, too."

"I said I would take you to Señora Morelos."

"One in the same, since that's what Miguel told her. Besides, I heard St. Francis could work miracles. Does that mean you're going to deny me a chance to see again?"

Murmurs came from the ones sitting around the table.

"You have to wait here, that is all," Daniel said in a low voice.

"No, that's not all." Patricia stood on a strength gathered from some unknown place. "What about Max? Is Miguel going to bring my son here?" Her voice cracked like a china cup. She felt her shoulder squeezed again. It was not Rachel.

"Señora Morelos, perhaps you need to sit down." He held his hand out to Patricia like a *maître d'*. His head tilted. "Please. You have walked a long way today. Surely you are tired. Put your shoes off and Gena will bring water to wash the Mexican dirt from your feet. It will make you feel better." Crooked teeth slid from the cover of his lips as he grinned. The contempt in his voice was as palpable as the sound of water splashing in some corner of the room.

Patricia stood on hollow reeds, but she refused to sit again. Someone placed a pan of water near her feet. She ignored it and stared at Daniel's back. "Miguel never was taking me to Max, was he? He lied to me from the beginning." She rubbed her hands against tear soaked dust that caked her face. "Why?"

Daniel grabbed her by the hands and pulled her down into the chair. Squatting, he stared her into place; his gaze, steel bands that bound her arms. "There are things you do not know. Lives at stake," he said through his teeth. "Max is all right. If you want to see him again, you must do as you are told."

He took a handkerchief from his pocket, stuck it into the basin of water, squeezed it and placed it in her hand. His eyes pleaded with her. His tone and the words he spoke threatened.

The man jerked Daniel by his shoulder. Daniel's fist clamped shut, but he said nothing.

"Señora Morelos, we are not unreasonable people." The man turned his attention to Patricia. "But what you want is for us to kill ourselves in your mines, so you can steal our silver and add to the Morelos empire." He stood still, his legs almost touching her knees. "Your husband stole from his country with no shame, and now you, who never come to Real to see the conditions in the mines, ask for silver to be taken from them at the cost of many lives."

He pounded his open palm with his fist. Patricia braced herself for it to shoot out at her. While he ranted about the thievery of Americans and the poor people of Mexico, she watched Daniel's back. The muscles beneath his shirt flexed as if readying for a fight. Maybe he was the one who would end up striking her. Every word the man said was in sympathy to Miguel's views. She had learned that at Tlantaloc. Daniel worked for him. Surely she, and probably Rachel, would be the victim of one of these two.

She withdrew into the chair until the uneven slats imprinted her legs. She looked at the others and wondered if they would help. She thought that they had not liked the idea that Rachel was being kept from going to St. Francis. Would their beliefs outweigh their politics?

Garlic-tainted breath brought her attention back to the man. He was leaning into her face. "Tomas Morelos fought who he was. The poor people of Mexico remember."

As he bent over her, a heavy gold medallion slipped out of its hiding place inside his shirt and almost hit Patricia in the face. The incongruity of the wealth the man wore and his words did hit Patricia, like a bucket of cold water.

The sight of the gold steeled her and heated her blood. How dare this hypocrite attack her like this? She seemed to come out of some kind of shock.

"That's a nice piece you have on Señor—I don't think we were ever properly introduced." She nodded toward the shiny form that the man held clutched in his hands. "The god king Xipe Totec, a replica of the gold mask, I believe?"

"It is no replica," the man growled.

Patricia acted as if she didn't hear his confession to thievery. "It seems you have a lot of information about me, false though it is. Yet, I don't even know your name or why you're here." Her words at first were fragile, like pieces of new pottery, but a fire blazed within her. The words came out harder and harder. She raised up from the chair until she was barely sitting on the edge.

The man was caught off guard. His eyes darted to the others in the room, quieting their whispers. "Well, the Señora can speak without crying, I see." He walked to one of the windows.

"I am a Mexican." He pulled aside a curtain and spoke to the dark outside the little house. "My name is Jorge Morelos."

Patricia turned in her chair and stared at the back of the man who began to take on another dimension.

"A familiar name, wouldn't you say, Señora? My ancestor was a very famous Mexican general. The same ancestor of your husband. I am only a poor *primo*, a cousin. But still a Morelos. There are many of us who did not shame our ancestor by moving to a foreign land and raping his mother country. It is a famous name." He squared his shoulders.

Patricia stood up, flinched when her weight pushed her swollen, bloody feet against the mud-stiffened shoes. "We all have black sheep in our families, Señor Morelos. These's no need for you to excuse yourself to me. Whatever has been your history, you need only apologize to me for keeping me from my son. I assure you, Señor, I know men who are today's generals. And if you don't release me and allow my son to return to the States with me, there will be people to answer to who will make your name infamous."

Jorge Morelos glared at her. His eyes narrowed and the crooked tooth glistened beneath his moustache like a weapon loosed from its sheath. Then, in a blink, he wiped the expression away and smiled.

"We will see who is the most powerful here in Mexico, Señora, when our most illustrious cousin comes and celebrates with the people when they take their silver back from the one who steals it. I think you are acquainted with Señor Miguel Ramirez." The man threw his head back and laughed.

CHAPTER TWENTY-NINE

Patricia placed her hand on the back of the chair. The floor beneath her felt like quicksand dragging her under. So Miguel was coming back after all. But not to rescue Max. He was on the side of the miners. Wasn't that what Cousin Jorge was saying? She slid into the chair and leaned her side against the railed back. She slipped her tortured feet free from her shoes and rubbed one atop the other.

Jorge barked orders to the men and woman who sat as silent as sleeping cats. The men slipped *sarapes* over their heads. The woman swathed herself in a long scarf completing her *teguana*. Daniel waited at the door a moment, they were gone.

As Jorge followed them, Patricia swallowed her anger and pride and reached out to catch his arm. He stopped just short of her hand.

"Maybe you have reason to hate Tomas and since I was his wife, to hate me too. But my son has nothing to do with the Morelos mine. Do you know who is holding him?"

Jorge looked at her without pity.

"I am asking as a mother, not as Tomas's wife."

The man's tense muscles settled onto his frame. His eyes clouded and for a moment she had hope.

"Perhaps, Señora, you should go to the women who lost their sons, and their husbands in the Morelos mines. See what sympathy they have for you."

She dropped her hand and lowered her head. "I know that they would understand my sorrow, and my need to find my son."

Jorge moved away quickly to the door. Without looking back, he said, "The miners do not have your son." He turned and faced her, jaws slacked, bravado gone. "It is true, your son was to stay with us until we got the mines from you."

Patricia bristled but held her tongue.

"We no longer have him, Señora, so your mines are safe from us."

"You—then where is he? Who has him?" Patricia bore down over him.

He looked up into her face, his eyes tight, as if trying not to see her. "The army have taken your son from us, Señora. Men in the service of General Ruiz," he said and opened the door, but she moved between him and the dark.

"Please," she said. "What will happen to him now?"

He sighed and looked beyond her as if searching for words. "They say he will be released at the festival. These heroes who 'rescued' your son, beware Señora. There are those you think are friends who would kill your son and take your mines."

Before she could recover from his words, he pushed past her into the night.

She stepped through the doorway and was immediately flanked by the two men who had been sitting at the table. One had a rifle cradled lightly across his forearm. She stared into intent dark eyes, then turned and went back into the cabin. Where could she go barefoot and without Rachel?

How could she hope to escape from the men outside? The pressure in her mind that pushed her toward Real grew more intense with the thoughts of Jorge's words. Friends who would want to kill Max? Who could it be but Miguel? How could she protect Max? She didn't know, but if the best happened and the people who held Max were planning to release him, she knew she had to be there when it happened.

She wasn't sure she should even believe Jorge, but if he were an example of the fervor and hate these people felt, Max was also still in danger from the miners, no matter who held him.

Despair fell over her like a dark, heavy blanket.

Rachel. What was she going to do about her? She groaned at the picture of the two of them stumbling up the road to Real. One blind, one wounded. What choice did they have? Going back now was out of the question, for her and for Rachel.

Rachel had jokingly called her "Jane Bond." Nothing could be further from the truth, so how was she going to help Max? How would she protect him from some crazy miner or sympathizer? She had to hope that an answer would come. The thing she knew she couldn't do was *nothing*.

She sagged into the rickety cane chair, as if she were becoming a part of it. Gena was putting a kettle of water on the grate in the fireplace.

"Where did Daniel go?" Patricia asked her. The girl shrugged.

Patricia sat alone staring into the fireplace. Rachel leaned against the window, as if she stood watch. With the others gone, the girl might be the only one to stop them from leaving, Patricia thought.

"You're Miguel's secretary, aren't you?" she asked the girl.

"*Si*," Gena smiled.

Patricia realized the girl was quite pretty in an exotic way. "Do you know where he is?"

"The Señora see him last." With that the girl walked over to the table and began to play a game with match sticks.

How had this trip to Real splintered into such strange events? And where was Miguel? It had only been twenty four hours since she had been snuggled into a happy moment of past and present with him. A brief respite from days of torment that threatened now to lead to even greater heartache. Suddenly, she was more tired than she had ever thought possible. Leaning her head against the back of the chair, she shut her eyes, but her mind did not relax. Rest had no place in her thoughts.

"Rachel," she whispered. Rachel moved slowly away from the window. Without speaking, she clasped Patricia's outstretched hand. Patricia drew Rachel's face close. "I'm so sorry I didn't listen to you."

"What do you mean?" Rachel asked.

"I should not have trusted Miguel. If I had called Jim earlier like you said—"

Rachel squatted down by Patricia's side. "Well, as much as I like being right, I don't know that that would have helped. Jim seems to have disappeared, absconded. No one knows where. I called Elena, Bonnie in D. C., and even that idiot Luis. No one has seen or heard from him since Thursday. I left messages everywhere, just in case he returns from his 'vacation'."

Patricia felt the blood drain from her face. "That means no one will be in Real to help us," she whispered. Neither one of them spoke as they thought about this truth.

Finally, Patricia spoke, "We have to get out of here. I'll watch for a chance. Okay?" Rachel nodded. "In the meantime maybe you should try to rest some."

"Me? What about you?"

"I'm going to indulge in some foot washing first. I need to take care of these blisters, then I'll sleep. We'll take turns. I don't think either one of us wants to try to sleep on that top bunk." She squeezed Rachel's hand to stop her protests. Slowly, Rachel made her way to the small bed.

Moments later, above Rachel's soft snores, Patricia heard the door open quietly behind her. A woman swathed in cloths came into the room, bringing the smell of the cold night air with her. Then she moved to the fireplace, slowly unwrapped and removed a dark shawl from her head while keeping her back to the room. When she turned and poured steaming water from the kettle into a basin on the floor, Patricia caught her breath.

She had known it was Carmina before she saw her face. Inside Patricia was shrinking, but her hand reached out and lifted the woman's chin. Dark eyes met hers. Patricia thought she saw anger, then realized it was the deep sadness in Carmina's eyes that held her fast. A sadness she had seen there many years ago and had forgotten. So much could be said. Where would she begin? She said nothing.

Carmina lowered her face, carefully lifted Patricia's bloody and mud caked feet and eased them into the warm water.

"Too hot, Señora?"

Patricia would not have felt the water if it had been scalding. "It—it's okay," she winced. She stared at the top of Carmina's head. The light from the fire highlighted gray streaks in the once ebony crown.

She moaned. The wounds on her feet stung and itched. She focused on the sensations, bringing her thoughts to the less painful present. When she bent to rub the broken skin, Carmina pushed her hand away.

"I am a nurse, Señora. I will see to the blisters." She submersed her hands and rubbed gently.

"Some of it is more than blisters. The rocks were cutting into me when that young man was dragging me up the mountain."

"You do not wear the boots Señor Miguel buy for you. Walking to Real is no place for tiny *zapatos*."

"I think somebody intended for me to die with those boots on."

Carmina's hands stilled. The water that slipped around Patricia's ankles felt charged.

"Señor Miguel would never harm anyone." Carmina's words were chiseled.

Gena had brought a towel to Carmina and held it out for her. When Carmina reached for it, Gena held on. The girl stood immobile, staring at something.

The water had cooled and Patricia rested her ankle on her thigh to see the damage close up. The light of the fireplace fell full on her bare foot.

Gena leaned over and traced her finger along Patricia's toes. "*El dedos del pie de la Señora son palmeando*," she whispered, raising her brows and looking at Carmina. "*Que piensa?*"

Patricia knew what the girl said. Gena could have been speaking Swahili and Patricia would have understood. She stuck her foot into the pail, sloshing water, then sat back in her chair and tried to shrug off the women's reactions to the webbing between her toes. A gift from her father. When she was a child, her brothers taunted her, calling her "quack-quack," until Pa would take off his big brogan boots and proudly display his own webbed toes. He would brag about how they helped him swim the marshes when he was a boy in south Georgia. Patricia didn't brag. She had always worn slippers when her friends wore sandals or went barefoot. Still there were the inevitable moments when someone saw her feet and laughed. She wasn't about to tolerate that ridicule now.

She lifted her foot out of the water, braced it against the edge of the chair and rested her chin on her knee. Splaying her toes apart, she defied them to stare again.

Gena's eyes sparkled as she looked at Patricia. "Daniel—"

"*Quieto!*" Carmina clamped her hand around Gena's arm and pushed her toward the table.

Patricia saw a twisted mask of emotions in Carmina's face and thought for a moment that the woman would strike the girl. She was relieved when Carmina turned back to her and began sprinkling her wounds with a white powder from a small bottle.

"This will heal *las ulceras*, she said, rubbing in the medicine, pulling at the red, raw wounds dotting Patricia's skin.

She winced, but did not withdraw her foot.

"The pain will stop soon," Carmina said, keeping her eyes on Patricia's feet as if she were healing them by her sight.

The door opened with a loud creak. It was Daniel. Rachel stirred at the sound, but stayed on the bed. Playing possum, Patricia thought, and rose to join her.

"No, Señora. We must put more medicine." Carmina took Patricia's hand and pulled her back into the chair, quickly draping the towel across Patricia's knees.

Gena hurried to Daniel's side, put her arms up to embrace him, and sent Carmina a side glance of defiance.

Daniel gave her a quick hug, then went to Carmina. He placed his hand on the woman's shoulder. The touch looked like a blessing. Carmina smiled up at him.

A pain started in the pit of Patricia's stomach. Her hands moved without her willing them from her knees to her foot which she drew out from under the towel.

Her movement caught Daniel's attention. "Better?" he asked, and bent to see for himself.

"I have something to tell you, Cariño." Gena was at Daniel's side, smiling into his face.

"Gena. "*Callate!*" Carmina hissed.

"*Pasar en silencio!*" Daniel said as he held Gena behind him. He tilted his head sideways. "*Que pasa?*" Getting no answer from either woman, once again he reached toward Patricia.

Carmina spoke quickly, as she pulled Daniel away. The words sounded harsh, but her lips parted in a curiously coy smile. Her hands were shaking as she tried to make Daniel stand.

Patricia was not sure what game the two were playing. She watched as he took Carmina's hands from his arm, disengaging himself from her. Then he stooped in front of Patricia, and like a doctor examined the sores and her splayed, webbed toes. The chiseled contours of his face relaxed, then contorted, his eyes wide with a kaleidoscope of questions.

Then Patricia thought she saw amusement. After all, he was looking at her feet. She pushed up from the chair. Instead of the smile or sneer that she expected, Daniel only stared at her. His eyes moved over her face.

Without a word, he grabbed his coat and tossed it at Carmina. "*Venga!*" he ordered and went out the door. Carmina quickly followed. The silence left behind was solid, preventing movement.

"What was that all about?" Patricia asked Gena, bringing the girl's attention away from the door.

Gena smiled. "Oh, the mother of Daniel is *siempre mal.*"

Daniel's light eyes and pale skin danced before Patricia's face like a ghost. "Carmina's s-son?" A deep cold so stiffened her that she felt she might shatter if she breathed. "How could that be?" She finally asked of no one.

"Si," Gena was saying, "And she is, how you say, a tiger to hold him."

"But, he, he's not Mexican," Patricia stammered.

"Si, he has American father. She live in America one time, you know."

Questions tumbled through Patricia's mind, like shiny, hot marbles, painful, yet intriguing. Which one to pick up? Which one meant less hurt? Which might hold a particular beauty? Or horror? She pulled at a thread on her shirt, unraveling a button stitch by stitch. She concentrated on the lengthening thread and tried not to listen to Gena talking to Rachel, telling her about the Festival at Real. She was trying to hold on to other words. When they appeared more clearly in her mind, she pushed them away. Her eyes changed their focus from the string to her feet. The words she was trying to forget hid under others coming from Gena. The girl kept talking, talking.

Time lifted to another plane while she remembered Daniel and Carmina and how they had smiled at each other. The beatific smile on Carmina's lined face was worthy of Michelangelo. The muscles in Daniel's face had been set firm as a marble bust. In her mind the outlines of bone and muscle shadowed by the soft lights aged and hardened him. The fullness of youth on his cheeks faded into deep creases like elongated dimples.

Her father's face swam before her eyes, and she shuddered.

She tossed the button into the fire, watched tiny flames leap up the chimney and vanish. "Gena, what did you want to tell me about Daniel?" The words came out in a whisper. The air in the room seemed to have vanished.

Gena stood between her and the fire. Her silhouette quivered as she made a soft, giggling sound, her hands covering her mouth. She moved one hand and bit her bottom lip. "Daniel would be angry for telling," she whispered.

Patricia knew the answer; she waited for the words.

"The toes of your feet, Señora, you know." She pointed down. "Daniel's are the same."

The light from the fire sputtered and died and all was dark.

CHAPTER THIRTY

Patricia opened her eyes slowly and realized she was huddled into the bunk bed. She wondered briefly if she had been dreaming the scene in the cabin that assaulted her mind at first thought. Surely she had, she reasoned. Reasoned, because no other reality could be true. Before she could give more time to the turmoil within her, Rachel touched her face.

"You okay?"

Patricia nodded and whispered, "Yes."

"You gave us a scare there. I didn't know if someone had clobbered you or if you'd taken a dive. What happened?"

Patricia felt for plain, non-revealing words. "I, I just felt faint."

"Well, that's certainly understandable." Rachel shifted position to lean against the wall. "Anything else you—?"

"Señora, you are awake?" Gena interrupted, moving closer and putting her hand on Patricia's forehead. Patricia recoiled from the touch.

Gena stood back, fists on hips.

"Why you take bandage from arm, Señora? You must have it, you know."

Patricia flexed her arm, which hurt like hell. "It is not broken, Gena. I don't need to be hobbled."

"Hobbled, Señora?"

"Nevermind."

"Okay, Señora. You take these *medicina*."

"I don't need them."

Gena ignored her and placed a small white pill in Rachel's hand and reached to put another one in Patricia's mouth.

Patrica pushed her hand away.

"You must. Take *medicina*. Pronto."

Gena stood over them, her demeanor changed from menace to pleading. She haltingly explained that Carmina had sent them something to make them sleep, to keep them quiet. "You must, Señoras. If not, you know, I must say to Carmina." The girl looked toward the door with a flicker of fear.

"Are you afraid of Carmina, Gena? Do you think she'd hurt you?" Rachel asked.

"Afraid? No hit and bite, no. But, she can hurt." The girl's features pinched as if she tasted something unpalatable.

"What do you mean?" Patricia whispered.

"With Daniel. She hurt me with him."

Patricia looked toward the window. She could hear voices outside the cabin and knew the time to learn anything was short.

"Hurt you with Daniel?" Rachel asked.

Gena's brow rose, and she smiled at Rachel. "*Si*, she with him *siempre*. She say he go and to do. He go Tlantoloc and help *pepenadores*, even when he work and have money. His *madre* want, you know, how you say—control him." She talked rapidly, watching Rachel's eyes. "She not like me, Daniel not." She swung her arms out, as if to shove away the thought.

"When he works, is it for Jorge Morelos?"

Gena stared at Patricia, her eyes wide. "No, Señora. Daniel no work for him." Her face pursed in anger.

Patricia knew she had made a mistake. Before she could think of what to say, Rachel put her hand out toward Gena. She smiled. "Are you in love with Daniel, Gena?"

Gena's face softened. "I say *mi te amo*," she said. "Daniel no say, only two time."

"He loves you. I can't see how he looks at you, but I can hear it in his voice. You're a lucky girl," Rachel said.

"Señora, you not look like you not see." Her eyes brightened. "You think he love me?"

"Yes. A man has a way of speaking to a woman when he is in love and others understand."

Rachel sounded as if she were reading the words out of some romance novel. Patricia hoped Gena believed them. She held her arms, forcing herself to be still.

"Is true, Señora. Si, I know this. Daniel, he never say to his *madre*, but he love her. She no want a woman for him. She keep him home."

Patricia reached out for Gena's arm and drew the girl near her. "Gena, I know you love Daniel. I know you don't want him hurt. I don't want that either. But, I think Daniel is mixed up in the kidnapping of my son. Do you know anything about Max?"

Gena stared at Patricia. She tensed her arm and jerked away. "I not know *su hijo*. Daniel not take him. He help you, you know. How you say bad things? Daniel love Señor Miguel; he love you. Senior Miguel say to Daniel go down the mountain for you, he go."

"Miguel? When did he talk to Miguel?" Patricia asked more sharply than she should have. She watched the girl stiffen, wary of the quickly spoken question, the muscles of her face telling a story of doubt and fear.

Gena lowered her head, but her eyes stayed in link with Patricia's. "Daniel only help you, Señora, to find *su hijo*. He know a mother love her *hijo*."

Mother. Son. Miguel. Max. Daniel. All the unthinkable possibilities of life's twists of fate slammed into her and she couldn't breathe. She tucked her hands under her arms to still their trembling.

She bent over, rolled her trouser legs down, and eased herself onto her sore feet. "Please, Gena," she stared into the girl's eyes. "When my son is free, I want to do everything to be sure that Daniel isn't blamed. Can you help us? We must get out of here."

Sounds of a vehicle silenced her.

"It is maybe Señor Jorge come back," Gena whispered as she ran to the window.

Patricia rushed to her side, leaving white powder prints on the cold plank floor.

"Señor Jorge is not always a nice man." Gena hesitated. "Daniel not happy that he come here. He say Daniel does not do his job."

"What job?"

Gena looked wary. "*La medicina*, Señoras," she ordered, tossing the pills on the bed. Throwing a glance back at Rachel, she slipped outside.

Patricia looked at the door, willing herself on the other side. She could hear rising voices. All she could see were shadows.

"Sounds like an argument," Rachel said. She too stood at the window. "Daniel and Jorge, I think."

Patricia wanted to storm out there and demand to be taken to Real, but she had already faced Jorge Morelos and knew that wasn't going to get her anywhere. Besides, she also had to think of Rachel. What if they separated them?

Other voices joined in and sounds of a scuffle erupted. As the din increased, Patricia's heart seemed an accompanying drum beat. Rachel clasped her upper arm and the pressure of her fingers felt like a tourniquet.

The door opened and shut quickly. It was Gena. Her eyes were wide with fright, her dark skin, pale.

"Hurry, Señoras," she whispered. "*Su zapatos.*" She pointed at Patricia's feet, reached for the mud-stained shoes still drying before the fire and thrust them into Patricia's hands.

While Patricia winced at her efforts to cram her swollen, bruised feet into the stiff shoes, Gena rolled up a blanket and put it in Rachel's arms. Then she hurried to the single window on the far side of the cabin.

"*Aqui, ayuda!*" she called, pushing on the wooden sash.

"What's happening?" Patricia asked in a gush of breath as the window gave and slammed upwards. Cold air wedged around them.

Gena seemed paralyzed, hands clasping her mouth as they waited to see if the noise had been heard outside the front of the cabin.

When no one came rushing in, she pushed Rachel toward the window. "Hurry, Señora Rachel. You climb. Hide in rocks."

"Why? What's going on?" Rachel hissed the words.

"Señor Jorge mucho mad. He say Daniel made deal for mines. Angry miners come."

"What are you talking about? What deal?" Patricia held the girl by her shoulders.

"Go. Now. No time." Gena shoved Patricia away. The two women stared at each other for only a second.

"Let's get out of here, Rachel," Patricia said, still staring at Gena. "I'm going out first. Wait until Gena tells you, then follow me." She took the blanket roll from Rachel and tossed it outside. With one leg over the window sill, she grabbed Gena and gave her a quick hug. "Thanks," she whispered into the girl's hair.

Once Rachel was out, Patricia glanced back into the cabin and saw Gena bunching pillows and clothes under blankets to make it look like the two women were bedded down for the night.

"Gena," she called as loud as she dared. The girl ran back to the window. "My basket, over there by the bed."

"No time, Señora."

"Yes! Give it to me!" If she had to, she'd crawl back in for it. She and Rachel were not coming back.

Gena thrust the basket through the window, pulled the sash down and snapped the curtains closed. Patricia took Rachel's arm and they stumbled up the hill that rose behind the cabin. She steered them toward the road that edged the mountain. They would need to stay in the scant brush for cover, but she must keep her bearings or they would be lost. They both kept slipping on the dew covered rocks, but never slowed their pace. When they had reached a small plateau a good distance from the cabin, they stopped to catch their breath in the thin mountain air.

"Who do you suppose was our hero down there, besides Gena?" Rachel asked, her voice unsteady, breathy.

"Maybe she just felt sorry for us and acted on her own. I can't imagine any of the other—"

"Listen! What's that?"

In the direction of the cabin below the crack of gunshots rang out. Crouching behind a rock, Patricia searched the dark night for someone on their trail.

"Do you see anything?" Rachel asked.

"Nothing."

The night was quiet. No bats swooping above them, no dogs baying in the distance. An unreal silence.

"What do you suppose that was all about?" Rachel whispered.

"I don't know. I just hope to God they didn't find we were gone and take it out on Gena." Patricia shivered.

"It's probably just Jorge letting off steam. We better get farther away while we can. If you're okay." Rachel stood in place, waiting for guidance.

Patricia took her hand and led her back into the brush. "My feet are better. I should have put some of that white pow—"

An explosion cracked the air. Light flared around them. When Patricia whirled to look in the direction of the cabin, she saw splinters of wood streaming through the sky in an arc of fireworks. Words began to form in her mind to describe the sight to Rachel, but her murmurs were drowned by screams that split the night like sharp knives thrown on swift winds.

"Oh, my God," Rachel whispered.

CHAPTER THIRTY-ONE

Light swirled, igniting the dark night. Timbers crackled. Patricia stood motionless, her hand caught viselike in Rachel's.

"I can smell smoke," Rachel whispered. "What do you see?"

"Just flames. The cabin. It exploded."

"You don't see any people? No one running?"

"Not up the mountain. I think I'd see movement. Can't see the road." The cool mountain air crawled beneath her clothes. She shivered and wondered why she didn't feel the heat of the inferno. She drew closer to Rachel, seeking warmth for the chill in her soul.

"What should we do?" Rachel asked.

"Go back."

"Don't you think that'd be dangerous?"

"We can't leave. What if he's—they're hurt?"

"And what if the men Gena told us about set that fire and are just waiting for us to come back?"

Patricia couldn't argue with the fact that if the cabin had been blown up by someone who thought she and Rachel were asleep in it, they might have lingered, waiting to make sure. And if it was Daniel, she didn't want to know.

Neither of them spoke for awhile. Patricia listened for voices in the popping of the flames.

"If someone had been hurt, we would have heard shouts and calls for help," Rachel offered at last. "Sounds carry pretty far out here in the night air."

"What about the screams?" Patricia asked, her voice irritated.

"It was before the explosion. Maybe Gena was trying to protect us. To make them think we were inside."

"Unless they're all hurt. Or dead. What if . . .," her voice ceased, choked off by an invisible noose.

"Go then. You have to see, don't you?"

Patricia put her hand on Rachel's arm. "I do. I can't just leave."

Rachel felt around for somewhere to sit. Easing down onto a smooth stone, she said, "I'll wait here. Just be careful."

"I can't leave you out here at night by yourself."

"And why not?"

Patricia flinched at the truth. It probably made no difference to Rachel if she were left on the mountain at midnight or midday.

"I'll be okay. I'll sit here and listen for you. If the lizards get too loud, I'll sing. Go on now."

The path Patricia took was a straighter, quicker one than that coming up. She still skirted around jagged rock ledges and slippery slopes, trying not to send noisy pebbles and dirt avalanching before her.

Large rocks lay at the edge of the clearing. She climbed until she could see all around, stretched out, and tried to breathe. The air seared her eyes, nostrils and throat. Her arm and feet throbbed. Her hands, still raw from thorns and falling down the mountain, burned as if she held them in the fire she watched.

Suddenly, a motor roared above the crackle of flames. A jeep.

She hid in the shadows. Voices, muffled and speaking Spanish, drifted in and out as two figures appeared. Three men silhouetted by the light of the burning embers. She changed positions to keep them in sight. They walked all around the cabin.

One of the men bent and picked up a piece of wood. It flamed like a torch, lighting their faces.

Miguel. Daniel. Jorge.

While they stood there, two other men moved out of dark shadows into glowing light.

Patricia clamped her hand over her mouth. A cruel mixture of relief, anxiety, love and hate forced tears onto her cheeks. Her muscles warred with her mind. She wanted to tear over the rocks to them. She wanted to hide forever.

She muffled her sobs with her hand, trying desperately to hear their words. She heard only the pounding of her blood. What her eyes saw spoke like thunder.

Daniel gave the torch a heave into a pile of glowing timbers. He said something to Miguel. Miguel laughed loud and long and clapped Daniel on the back. A congratulatory gesture. Two men celebrating a victory. A job well done.

They were a blur to Patricia as the men all piled into the jeep and drove away. She leaned against the rocks and swallowed a scream. Her thoughts raced and darted like sand fleas, each one a minute creature, but collectively capable of causing great misery.

Miguel and Daniel. Together with the miners. Celebrating her death. And Rachel's. She had no doubt Max would be next.

A short while later she limped back into the clearing where Rachel waited. The light that guided her back down the mountain had burned itself and she struggled beneath a softly moonlit sky, stumbling, disoriented and afraid that she would not find Rachel again. When she did, she sank exhausted on the ground.

Catching her breath, she took a blackened water bottle from a cloth pouch she carried and handed it to Rachel. "I found some water," she said.

When they had quenched their thirst, she wet a square of cloth and began to remove black smudges from her face and hands as best she could.

"You've carried the smoke back with you," Rachel said.

Patricia tasted the smoke and the soot. The flames themselves seemed to smoulder within her.

"There was no one there," she said. "No one in the cabin. I stirred around in the ashes, but I didn't see any signs." How could she say aloud what she had seen?

"Good. They must have left after the explosion. I thought I heard a jeep go by."

Patricia started, but said nothing.

They sat quietly for a time, then Rachel suggested they might sleep for awhile. "Don't guess anybody'll be looking for us now," she said. "They probably thought we were sound asleep when the cabin blew. Maybe we've seen the last of all of them." She stretched out on the blanket that Patricia placed on the ground, and curled up against the cold. "If I ever get back to my own bed, you can have Mexico. When I think how it was my idea to have that young hoodlum, Daniel, bring me up here, I faint at my own stupidity. Tell me, Patricia, does he look like the devil incarnate, too, or does he just take his orders from him?"

Patricia sat stiffly at the edge of the blanket. A face appeared in her mind. She wasn't sure if she were seeing Daniel or her father in her imagination. Until the image was joined by Miguel, and she could see his hand clapping Daniel's back. She had often thought of her father as being the devil himself, and now she may have seen Daniel in that role. Or did Miguel wear the horns?

"Oh, well," Rachel continued when Patricia didn't say anything. "We'll just hope he doesn't do anything else to keep us from getting to Max. I feel like we've almost forgotten why we're here."

Patricia flinched as if Rachel's words were a slap. Her focus on Max had been blurred. She had forgotten, at least for a while. It shocked her. Her mind had a new torment. For the first time in hours, her thoughts began to clear, and she considered the impossible.

"Tell me, Patricia," Rachel said.

Drawn abruptly from her musing, Patricia didn't answer.

"Tell me what you're fretting about."

"Fretting?" Patricia repeated. She sat with her arms encircling her legs, knees to her chin.

"You're just stalling. You know what I'm talking about. I usually can figure out what's happening around me, but I'm more in the dark than usual here. What exactly is going on?" Rachel rose to brace herself on her elbow and faced Patricia as she spoke.

Patricia stared at her faint dark outline and knew that those sightless eyes were directed straight into her. She started to argue, to say there was nothing to tell. She was exhausted, had no strength to talk, but her mouth seemed to move of its own need.

"There is something," she finally said.

"Oh no. From the tone of your voice, I think I'm going to regret asking, aren't I? I am not going to go back without you and Max. You can forget it."

"That's not it. It's Daniel."

Rachel sat up quickly. "Did you find him down there?"

"No. He wasn't—in the cabin." She whispered, "Thank God."

"Thank God? Now you really have me worried. What do you mean by that?"

"It means, I'm glad he wasn't hurt, wasn't in the cabin."

"Well, of course, you're glad. I am too, I guess. Hey, there's more to this, isn't there?"

Rachel's voice slid off into the night as Patricia's mind drifted far away. It seemed hours before she spoke.

"Remember the baby? My baby?"

"Max?" Rachel's voice spoke more than a one word question.

"No. The baby I would never talk about. The one I was pregnant with when I left Alabama. You knew about it."

Rachel nodded. "Yes. Dosey slipped one day when I came to visit you. You were sick, the flu, I think. She said something about you hadn't been 'laid up' since the baby came. You and Tomas hadn't been married long and no one knew you were pregnant with Max, so, yes," she smiled.

Patricia smiled back at her. "Dosey thought I would be angry, but I was glad she told you."

"Well, that was all I knew. You never told me anything. I knew it died, so I understood why. When I left that day, I asked Dosey what happened to your baby. She muttered something about "poor child" and said I wasn't ever to ask such questions again. I was never to mention it to you. She sounded terribly grave and threatening. I didn't pay Dosey much mind in those days, but she got through to me then." She cleared her throat. With a half-laugh she asked, "Why are you dredging up that ole soap opera?"

"Because it didn't . . . he didn't . . . he didn't die."

Rachel's hand reached out with a jerk in Patricia's direction, missing her. Her pale arm glowed in the moonlight. Patricia looked at it. The two sat motionless, like the stones around them. For a moment their breathing could not be heard and sounds of cicadas brushing their spiny legs filled the air.

Patricia relived in a moment the night her baby was born. Felt intensely the finality of the birth, the relief at Dosey's words. Those words. What had Dosey actually said? Her pain-tortured mind had thought Dosey said the baby was dead. Or was it just that he was gone? Had she really heard a baby cry? She thought it was in her dream.

She could remember something about Carmina was going to take care of it. She'd thought they meant the burial. Dosey had said it was for the best. Patricia knew she remembered that right. What exactly had Dosey meant? Days had gone by before she had been herself after the birth. By that time, Carmina had left for Mexico.

Why had she never questioned Dosey, Patricia chastised. It was an easy answer. She never had wanted the baby. She had been so afraid to have it, afraid of what it would be. Her father's child, a reminder of her horror. At sixteen it had been easy enough to wish it away. Dosey and Carmina had made it possible.

So much had become clear tonight. Carmina's fear of her. Her attempt at keeping Daniel from seeing the deformity of Patricia's feet. And above all, Daniel had her father's face. With a sigh of acceptance, Patricia knew. There was no other explanation.

"He?" Rachel finally said.

"Carmina worked for Tomas at that time," Patricia continued as if the monumental revelation she had just made were only a footnote to her tale. "She and Dosey must have decided it would be better for me if I thought the baby died. They also decided that Carmina would bring him to Mexico to raise."

"Carmina! Did she tell you this? How do you know that?"

"I know. Because I know Daniel is my son." Tears filled her eyes and sobs dammed her throat.

"Daniel?" Rachel said the name with a mixture of reverence and disbelief. Then she shifted abruptly, rose up on her knees and slapped her thighs. "His feet. It had something to do with his feet. And yours. That's what you and Gena were talking about, what Carmina didn't want Daniel to see, wasn't it?"

"Yes. I'm afraid he inherited a peculiarity of my family. Webbed toes."

Patricia waited for the laughter, but all animation drained from Rachel's face and she bit her lower lip, then slid over until they faced each other, knees touching. She seemed to be looking straight into Patricia's eyes.

"My God," Rachel whispered on expelled breath. She put her hands out and brought them together gently, catching Patricia's face between her palms. She moved her thumbs slowly, spreading lines of tears until Patricia's cheeks glowed with a wet sheen.

Leaning over, Rachel rested her forehead against Patricia's. "My little friend," she said softly, and then pulled Patricia's face down to her shoulder.

When her body had given up the last wracking sob, Patricia lay with her head in Rachel's lap. Her face ached, her eyes felt twice too large for their sockets. Memories had clashed ruthlessly against reality and slowly numbed her thoughts.

She seemed on the verge of sleep when she realized there was one more thing to tell. It wouldn't take strength to do so, quite the contrary, if she had any, she would use it to keep from telling. Rachel would want to know, and she couldn't stand the thought of Rachel kidding her about some beau doing her wrong, or worse, ask if Daniel was Tomas's son. So she began to tell the whole story.

When she had finished, the first hint of dawn scrolled across the sky. "I'll need you when I have to tell Max. Maybe when I talk to Daniel."

"I'll be there. You know," Rachel said. She stroked Patricia's hair.

"Yes. I know," Patricia answered. "Of course I do."

"Then we can get some rest. Nobody will be looking for us now. They won't be looking for ghosts."

As they huddled beneath the blanket Gena had given them, a breeze found its way around the boulders and swirled dried leaves and the lingering scent of smoke around them.

The question now, Patricia knew, was what would she do, that is, if she got the chance to do anything. Was Daniel really responsible for trying to kill them in the cabin? Did he know who she was and hate her for it? How could she blame him. Whether he was good or bad, she was now pulled two ways. Like a mother of two sons would be, should be?

Daniel. Max. If they all lived through this, there would be a time of reckoning. Max might hate her. Daniel would for sure. She argued with herself about which son had more cause.

Ghosts. The word echoed in Patricia's mind and she prayed that she and Rachel would be invisible to Miguel and Daniel until she could get to Max. Then she would find the strength to confront whatever reality the two of them represented.

CHAPTER THIRTY-TWO

October 2

Miguel pulled the jeep up to the railed gate at La Paloma hacienda in Potrero and honked the horn loud. A young boy, barefoot and sleepy, ran out of a small shack, quickly loosened a chain, and swung the gate open. Miguel sped across the cattle guard and up the drive to the home of his friends, the Randels.

He bounded out of the jeep through rising dust, Daniel in his wake. By the time they reached the front door, it was open.

"What in the world are you two doing out so early?" Rita Randel, still dressed in her nightclothes, red hair waving like a flag, was clear-eyed and enthusiastic to see them. "I'll get some coffee and tell Carlos you're here."

"No need." Randel stood in a doorway, pulling his shirt on, his belt hanging loose at his waist. A wiry little man, he moved with grace, even half-asleep.

"Sorry to wake you, mi amigo," Miguel said.

"It's okay. Been wondering what happened to you. Where's the woman we were supposed to keep for you? We got word that the situation had changed." He sat in a chair and laced on boots.

"It is a story much too long to tell now. But, I need your help. Again."

"You know you have it. What can I do?"

Rita returned with steaming coffee. The men drank guietly.

"We had some trouble up at the cabin. Some of Jorge's men."

"That the same bunch shooting up the town yesterday?" Carlos asked.

"Probably," Miguel agreed. "I think they were looking for me and Mrs. Morelos. Maybe they were the ones who shot at us on the road. Maybe not."

"Did they bring the boy?" Rita interrupted.

Miguel looked at Daniel, and sighed. "No. The miners do not have Max."

"They let him go?" Carlos asked.

"The truth is, they only had Max for a few days. The army took him. We have not told anyone because the officials have not said when he will be released. You understand."

"Well, that's good, isn't it? That means you can tell Mrs. Morelos that Max is safe."

"Rita," Carlos smiled at his wife, "We're not in the U.S. The army is not always on the right side down here. Does that explain your sad face, Miguel?"

"You are too smart, mi amigo."

"Well, what happened at the cabin?"

"Jorge must have told his men that Señora Morelos was hiding there. A couple of the hotheads blew the place up."

Shock elongated the man's face. "Was anybody hurt?"

"No. Thank God. And Daniel and Gena. They got Señora Morelos and her friend out the back window, but Jorge doesn't know it. He and his men won't be looking for her now."

"Where are they?"

Daniel and Miguel looked at each other.

"On the way to Real, no doubt about it," Miguel said. "And that is why we need help. We had to leave with Jorge to keep him from being suspicious. When we went back, there was no tracing them in the dark. Too much area to cover. Now I have to get into Real. They are two resourceful women, that is for sure, but we need eyes. Can you get some of the men and women and station them outside the tunnel? I have some photographs of Patricia you can distribute. The other woman should not be hard to spot; she is blind."

"A blind woman?" Rita's eyes widened. "How did she—"

Miguel gave Daniel a quick look.

"I brought her here," Daniel said, sharply. She was going to call the FBI if I did not. If they found out the army had Max, he would have to disappear to quiet the story."

"I told Daniel to bring her when he could not persuade her to wait. We thought we would be able to keep her safe here with you and Patricia. After the problem last night, I told Daniel to take the blind woman on to the cabin and to find Patricia and keep them both there. Now they are gone."

Carlos laughed heartily and poured himself more coffee. "Well, Rita, my dear, looks like we would have had our hands full with this little lady." He stared at Miguel. "Noticed you called her 'Patricia.' When do I get to hear more?"

Miguel walked to the fireplace and pretended to warm his hands. "We must find them," he said, turning to face the others. "I am afraid she is still in danger. There are others, besides the distraught miners, or the army, who have reason to harm her. Patricia was traveling alone, disguised like a peasant, when Daniel found her. The hope is that the two ladies will continue on to Real. They will be safer moving with the peasants. That is, as long as we watch over them. The festival is in two days. We don't have much time."

The Randels moved closer to each other.

"That sounds ominous," Carlos said, reaching up to pat Rita's hand that rested on his shoulder. "We'll get the people together. Where will you be if they spot her and what do you want them to do?"

Miguel and Carlos outlined a plan. When everything was settled, Daniel was to stay in Potrero and help bring the people to the tunnel, then he would meet Miguel in Real.

As they walked out to a breaking dawn, Carlos clapped a hand on Miguel's back. "Some day soon, my friend, I have to hear the rest of the story about how you two guys were outfoxed by this little ol' American businesswoman and her blind friend. In the meantime, we'll all do our best to keep them safe. I look forward to meeting the woman that lights up your face like this."

Miguel's only answer was a grunt.

* * *

Jim Mainland paced his room like a caged animal. He ticked off the days in his mind and found it difficult to accept that it was Monday morning. He thought he would be headed back to Mexico City or D. C. by now, his weekend at the beach in Zihuatenajo over.

What he had not counted on was being thrown to the sharks.

He rubbed the back of his head where a lump the size of an egg still throbbed. His attempt to get out off the grounds Sunday night had left him unconscious for hours.

He had suspected that he wouldn't be allowed to leave as he had planned, but he'd played out the weekend as if nothing was wrong. Swimming, flirting with the bikini-clad girls.

Mealtimes were not much different from that first afternoon. The Chief, Catera and Perez chatted away in Spanish, ignoring him. He had learned little, but he was glad they didn't know he understood them. He had heard them say they were still looking for Patricia. She had given them the slip, evidently, but they still expected her to show up in Real, where they would be waiting for her. After his attempt to barge his way out, he'd been confined to his room.

The idea of these crooks taking over the mines made Jim's legs weak. He sat down on the end of the bed. In the United States a maneuver such as this, disguised as a legal agreement, wouldn't last in court long enough for the judge to don a robe. Mexicans lived by a different set of rules.

If he lost the mines, he had no doubt he'd lose the construction project, too. These three racketeers had no intentions of letting him succeed with Tomas's plans. They'd just take the idea, the plans, the land, and get rich themselves.

Thoughts of all the money he owed set off a jackhammer against his skull. One thing about crooks in Mexico, they openly dealt with their enemies. The "boys" in Virginia would be waiting for him in some dark alley when he least expected it. The hammer sank into his brain.

After awhile, he walked to the window and looked out at the brightening day. A movement on the hill above the house caught his eye. At first he thought he imagined it, but as he watched, a shadow came and went. Someone was walking down a path.

A man stood on the other side of the iron fence surrounding the property. He hesitated for a moment, bent down, came up on the inside of the barrier. It looked like George, the gardener.

Jim pondered what he had seen. It was a way out. If he could get out of the room. The windows were covered with wooden louvers. He examined them carefully for the first time. They had not seemed important before, because he knew he couldn't get through the gate. He had tried that last night. His hand automatically went to the lump on his skull.

He found a butter knife left on a tray that had been brought to him yesterday. The screws holding the louvers were rusted. Some of them broke off with just a little pressure, some he had to dig out. He laid the loose boards quietly on the floor. When there was enough room for him to squeeze through, he grabbed a jacket and a flashlight he had seen in a drawer. Even though he was on the second floor, it was only a short drop to the ground because the land rose on this side of the house.

He was across the garden and at the fence before the first shot rang out.

"Going somewhere Mainland?" George asked.

Jim staggered back to the house, his head felt shattered by the relentless jackhammer. He sagged into a chair in the *sala*.

"Never knew someone to dislike my hospitality so much," the Chief said. Jim had not seen him sitting on a couch at the far end of the long room.

Jim just glared.

"I am sure you will be glad to hear that the time has come for you to leave. Juan will be around this morning. He will take you to where the Morelos boy is. That is where you would like to go, is it not?"

Shaking his head to clear it, Jim measured carefully what he should say. Finally, he spoke. "I never like to overstay my welcome."

"Si. While you are still in my care then, we will have breakfast." He made a motion to George, who brought coffee within seconds.

Catera arrived while they were eating, and Jim was escorted back to his room for his belongings. By midmorning they were in a plane to Mexico City.

Jim made two more attempts to get away. The first time he was tied up and thrown into the back of a van, the second he was given a shot of some kind of sedative.

He awakened slumped against a curved wall. Cold, dark, and wet invaded his nostrils, his throat, his face. All but his eyes, which were warm beneath a coarse cloth blindfold. He put his hands out and pushed himself to his feet. A round bore of metal poked him in the back. He assumed it was a gun, so when it prodded him again, he started walking. He had to hold onto the walls on each side to stay upright. They were slippery and cold. He gagged at the piercing odor of mold and decay and the stench of urine.

He didn't talk. Opening his mouth meant tasting what he was smelling. Besides, he had already exhausted himself asking questions. He'd get even with Catera. There would be a way.

His arm was jerked back, and he stopped walking. Sensing the area around him was larger, he cautiously extended his arms. Fingers grazed his forehead and snatched the blindfold from his face. Expecting any light to blind him, he squinted, then realized it was almost as dark without the blindfold.

He was deep in a mine. He recalled the grade of his long walk, the increased cold, the odors. Above him the ceiling was high, a dark hole in the center. A shaft. He could feel a stir of air pressing downward from an unseen source. Looking around, he couldn't resist staring at the walls as if a vein of silver might pop out at him.

A chair, table and cot. Bars cut off passages in two directions. Between Jim and the way he had come were two beefy men, one armed with a .357 magnum, the other, a rifle. The rifle pointed toward the chair.

"Such wonderful accommodations. I think I like *El Partenon* better after all," Jim muttered as he sat down. "*Quantas tiempo aqui?*"

Both men acted as though they heard nothing.

"You fuckin' bastards. Don't even know your own language, huh? Don't know English either. *Stupido. Stupido.* Your mothers worked in *la huerta.*" He watched for a reaction and was pleased to see a flicker in the eyes of the one with the rifle. He smiled. "Your sisters fuck 50 men a night and only pay you 50 pesos." Another flicker. "Your padre is not your padre."

The rifle swung out at Jim and he caught it midair. He jabbed the butt back into the ample stomach of the Mexican. The man managed to keep his grip on the gun and shoved at Jim with the barrel. The two were rolling on the floor of the room when a loud crack split the air.

Jim saw a flash of black. Then he felt the thrash of leather across his back. He was stunned by the pain that one lash of the thin material had delivered.

"Handy instrument in a mine," Catera said, rolling the riding crop. "A bullet might ricochet."

Jim knew the time to fight was over. He sat in the chair and rubbed his arm. "When the Chief said you were bringing me to where the Morelos kid was, I didn't know he just meant to the same mountain."

Catera laughed. The sound echoed off the walls.

"Glad you get such a charge out of my pain and ignorance," Jim said, wincing at the stab in his chest where the tip of the rawhide had cut him deeply.

"Mainland, you disappoint me. I thought I could count on you to make this deal work out. It is the best one you will get."

"Why should the Moreloses have to give up their mines to get you to stop trespassing on my land." Jim tried to take the edge out of his voice when he saw Catera flex the hand holding the whip. "You know I'm going to marry Patricia Morelos soon. Then I'll have control of the mines and other deals, better deals can be made," he continued, buying time.

"You've been playing Romeo too long, amigo. I don't think she wants to be Juliet." He smiled.

"My God, man," Jim rose from the chair, "Her son's been kidnapped! You expect her to be off on her honeymoon now?"

"I am sorry to be the one to tell you this, Mainland. When Señora Patricia goes on a honeymoon, it is more likely to be with Miguel Ramirez."

"What th' hell do you mean?" Jim took a step toward Juan.

"Maybe you can say better what it means when two people spend the night making love?"

Jim flinched, then turned away. "That's your story, Catera. Patricia probably has a different one."

"Perhaps. In the meantime, we will see that she signs the papers, or she will be lost forever in the Sierra Catorce Mountains. She and her son. Pity, wouldn't you say?"

Jim sank back in the chair. "What do you want me to do, Catera?"

CHAPTER THIRTY-THREE

Patricia shook a large square of faded cloth. Dirt and lint gathered in a small cloud.

"What in the world is that?" Rachel asked, coughing and pinching her nose.

"Some rags and stuff I found in an old house yesterday." Patricia emptied out the basket.

"I'm almost afraid to ask what you wanted them for in the first place. I know I don't want to know what you're going to do with them now." Rachel wrinkled her nose and folded her arms.

"Wearing these was the only way I got as far as I did. I think I still have enough to disguise you. We'll be peasants going to Real to see St. Francis."

"Do you really think that'll help? How hard can it be to spot two women, one blind and the other all scratched up?"

"Well, I can cover my scrapes, and you, my dear, don't look blind to most people, and you know it. We'll manage if we're careful and I keep you alerted to things. So, you game?"

"Sure. Just so I'm a pretty peasant," she said, as Patricia took the cloth and wound it around her tiny waist, tucking and pulling at the ends until the swath of material passed for a skirt.

"Does the color suit me?" Rachel turned in a tight circle when Patricia had finished.

"Yes, you look great in chartreuse," Patricia teased. "Here, tie this over your head." Patricia knew how much pride Rachel took in being able to dress herself and she watched as Rachel fashioned a scarf out of a ragged cloth.

"Let me look at you," Patricia backed up a few feet and appraised the changes. "Need to roll up your pants legs and you're all set."

"Good thing Annie and her friends can't see me. They'd copy my outfit and claim it as a new fad."

"Well, it would beat those jeans your daughter wears with the knees that look like ragged windows."

They both laughed aloud.

"God, that felt great. I don't think I've laughed in a century," Patricia said. She felt giddy.

Rachel reached out and embraced Patricia. "You'll be okay, you know. It'll all be okay. You have to have faith."

"Oh, Rachel. How can you always be so positive? I've made so many mistakes. I don't know how to make it all right anymore."

"Maybe it isn't always your job to make right."

Before Patricia could respond, Rachel rubbed her hands down past Patricia's waist to her legs.

"What are you doing?"

"Well, you seem to be having so much fun a minute ago, I wondered if you had me dressed in this `git-up' while you were wearing your own clothes." Rachel smiled. "Just checkin'."

They both laughed. Patricia wiped away her tears.

"Rest assured that I look as ridiculous, no, as impoverished as you. Now, we better head up this mountain before it gets any later." She took Rachel by the hand and guided her carefully over some rocks and between some scrub brush until they saw the road. The road to Real de Catorce.

The lightness of their laughter left Patricia. She had been on and off this road to Max so many times, it was as though she were the pawn in some cruel game the gods were playing. Throw the dice and go back two spaces, three miles, get shot at, go through the desert, meet some crooks. At that thought, memories of Miguel and Daniel and the cabin surged up and she fought them back.

Patricia helped Rachel down an incline to the edges of the dirt road leading up from Potrero. Indian women cooking over a small fire watched them with interest. Aromas from a sizzling pan stopped Patricia like a wall.

"Heaven. I smell heaven," Rachel whispered reverently.

Patricia turned her back to the women to keep them from hearing. "It's *chorizo*," she said.

"Ummm. On corn tortillas? Food of the gods. Buy some or I'll start begging."

"You ask. You speak better Spanish. Remember? Here's some pesos. And keep your head down like you're looking at the food." She placed some coins in Rachel's hand, then steered her to the makeshift kitchen.

"Tortillas, *por favor*," Rachel said.

One woman stood and stared at Patricia, then looked away. Patricia thought she saw the woman smile.

Another one slapped a generous pile of steaming meat onto hot, flat bread. Patricia reached out for the food while the woman took several small coins from Rachel. "*Vayas con Dios*, Señoras," she said as they walked away.

Patricia moved them up the road, breathing deeply. They had passed their first test, for surely the woman had thought they were just two more poor pilgrims heading for Real to ask a miracle of St. Francis. And weren't they?

Despite the delicious taste of fresh food, Patricia ate slowly. Hunger was a necessary urge she didn't care to acknowledge. As they paced themselves up the ever inclining mountain road, they passed more low fires. Around some, people still slept in rolled blankets. At others, women had set up stands offering coffee, tamales, tortillas and meats for sale.

They rounded a curve in the road and Patricia stopped.

"What is it?" Rachel whispered.

"The tunnel," was all Patricia could say. The mountain curved around a cul-de-sac of a courtyard. A dead end except for the dark, gaping hole. The entrance to Real de Catorce.

"What does "*ogarrio*" mean?" she asked.

"Ogre what?"

"It's written above the tunnel. O-G-A-R-R-I-O."

"Maybe it is 'ogre.' Rachel smiled. "For the monster that waits for us in the cave," she said, using a Lon Chaney voice.

"I doubt it." Actually, Patricia thought, "Ogre" was a good name for the looming arch that seemed to take on a life of its own. She wasn't afraid. The tunnel was beautiful. It was the passage to Max. She smiled and lifted her face to the morning sun as if in adoration of the day.

"Sounds like a market place," Rachel said.

Patricia drew her attention back from the tunnel to the courtyard in front of it. People milled around an old hacienda. Food stands covered with striped shades ringed its crumbling walls. Vendors were putting out their trinkets. Dogs barked and chased each other through the stalls. Small children toddled around, rubbing their eyes in the hushed movements of morning.

Guards stopped those carrying goods, pushing carts or leading burros laden with supplies. Sometimes they gave a cursory glance at what was carried, sometimes they poked their rifle butts into mounds of fruits, bruising bananas and toppling mangoes. Often they took a handful of fruit or a bottle of beer and laughed if the merchant held out his hand. One guard looked almost official in a dusty army jacket. The others had only their rifles to give them authority. No one defied them.

What were they doing here, Patricia wondered. Miguel had told her that day in his office that no one but vendors were allowed through the tunnel before the festival began. She had lost track of the days. Figuring it up, she realized it was the second day of October. Just two days to the Saint's day.

She watched people disappear into the mountain. Some of them were not carrying any goods to sell. Maybe the soldiers stayed to keep order.

Maybe they were there to watch for her. Tensions over the cave-in and the kidnapping of Max might be the reason. Either way, she would get by them.

One sentry no older than Max took several bottles of *Dos Equis* from a cart and hid them under his coat. Veiled by dust curling up from the pilgrims' feet, he sneaked drinks, downing two beers. A cart pulled up. In the back rode several women dressed in black and carrying small bunches of white flowers. The young man waved them through with an unsure swing of his hand. Other women came in small groups, all carrying flowers. Each time it was the same. The women were waved on into the tunnel. The guards hardly gave them a second look.

"Come on. I know how we can get in," Patricia whispered to Rachel. Cramped from squatting so long, she stretched and groaned. Brushing her palms against her skirt, she cried out. One of the wounds where Miguel had removed the thorns was infected. It was red, angry-looking. For a moment she allowed herself to remember how gently he had cleansed each puncture that night in the hacienda. The thought became an emptiness, filling her, crowding out her breath.

"I wish you wouldn't do that," Rachel said.

"What?"

"Make dying noises. Unless you're going to tell me what's wrong, don't grunt and groan. What's your plan?"

Patricia swallowed a retort along with her pain. She helped Rachel over a low wall and led the way to a flower vendor's stand, explaining what she'd seen as they walked.

Rachel sniffed the fragrant blossoms while Patricia paid for them. "Now what?" she asked, her nose buried in the tiny *nubes*. "When some other people come along, we walk right by this kid that I've been watching. Hopefully he's drunk by now. You keep looking down, smelling the flowers."

Soon a burro-pulled wagon passed, followed by a group of men and women. Herding Rachel along, Patricia stepped into the midst of the women, who chattered on as if not seeing them. She clutched Rachel's hand until she heard a stifled moan. The arch of the tunnel rose ahead of them. Each step took forever.

Suddenly everybody stopped. The official looking guard was questioning the man leading the burro. With the end of his rifle he lifted the tarp on the wagon bed, revealing yellow and green mangoes. He took several, pitched one to the kid who had been drinking. It hit the ground.

Patricia dropped her head as the older man stomped by her. He was yelling at the young soldier. Empty beer bottles crashed and broke in a garbage heap. Patricia wanted to dart into the tunnel, but didn't want to attract attention. Why didn't the others move on? Why did they have to stand and gawk at the silly battle? She turned and drew up inside as she saw everyone in the street crowding around to see what was happening. She could almost feel someone's eyes on her, not on the quarreling men. Her breath was shallow, filled with the musky odor of the rags she wore. She pulled Rachel in the direction of the mountain. They had come so far. Nothing was going to keep her from getting through that tunnel. She scanned the crowd as secretively as possible, looking for anyone that might recognize them.

Several women ahead of them moved a few steps. Patricia tried to urge them on by pressing closer and closer, her eyes on the inscription OGARRIO that now loomed directly above her.

CHAPTER THIRTY-FOUR

As they entered the darkness of the tunnel, the hair on Patricia's neck rose as if detecting a breath of movement. As if a hand were reaching for her. She wished she could run.

"I can feel the dark," Rachel said and tightened her fingers around Patricia's arm.

"I know, but there are some lights along the ceiling." She looked up at the few dull bulbs spaced far apart. Eyes straight ahead, she disciplined herself. Don't look back. Don't watch the shadows.

A group of people shuffled along ahead, disappearing at times in the cloud of dust they created. The air was cold, stale and gritty. Rachel coughed several times. Patricia slowed their pace to let the dust settle more.

"How long did you say this tunnel is?" Rachel asked.

"Mile and a half."

"Feels like we've already been that far. Wonder how long it took them to carve this out of the mountain." Rachel stretched her hand and let her fingers trail along the rough hewn rocks. "Smells like death. Must be people buried in these walls. 'The Catacombs of Real'."

"Shh," Patricia whispered. There was no one near enough to hear them speaking English, and she knew Rachel was trying to get her mind on other things, but she equated everything in this place to Max. Especially the possibility of death. She didn't need Rachel's macabre suggestions.

Suddenly, those up ahead stopped. A crescendo of voices echoed around them.

"What's happening?" Rachel asked.

"We must have reached the chapel."

"And you said there weren't any people buried down here."

It's not a grave. It's a little altar. Miguel told me about it. Our Lady of Sorrows, they call it. People stop to pray for those who died in the mines." Her voice trailed away.

"And where do you think their graves are?"

Patricia squeezed Rachel's hand, shushing her again.

People standing outside an arched portal leading into the mountainside waited their turn to enter. Some carried small sprays of white flowers like the ones they had bought; others, candles. Patricia studied the stone columns and decorative swirls and patterns of fresco that surrounded the doorway. A dedicated soul had spent many hours here in darkness and dust to create this way station for prayer. She tried to store the details to describe the chapel to Rachel later, who would no doubt want to know who did the work and why. The why was all Patricia could think about. Death. A memorial. When she looked into the faces of the women around her, she saw the pain of memories and wondered if her face had taken on the same look.

Rachel tugged her arm. She was being pushed toward the niche. Not wanting to draw attention, Patricia moved with her and the flow of those who circled clockwise through the door along the wall to the end of the room. Over the scarfed heads of some women, Patricia saw a small houselike structure with a gabled roof. A tiny arched walkway rose up below and on each side of it. And slender, delicate columns. They framed a painting of the Virgin Mary. Below was a table filled with candles. The odor of burning wax mixed with the fragrance of flowers that lay all around. The hand that had seemed to follow her in the tunnel seemed now to grip her heart. She placed her broken blossoms among the others.

She watched the women cross themselves, mumbling prayers for the dead. If they knew that it was in her own silver mine that the last deaths occurred, what would they do to her? She recalled Jorge's words and shrank inside her ragged garments as if warding off anticipated blows.

The space around her closed. The air seemed as heavy as the stones so close above her head. A pressure, the weight of the mountain, sagged her shoulders. She imagined the terror of beams splintering, rocks grinding, dust filling the air. Her lungs felt empty.

These women around her knew real cave-ins. They had felt the mountain shake, heard the news, waited for the names of the dead. And many considered themselves lucky if the mines gave something back to them to be mourned and returned to the earth.

She looked at the altar and stared at the figure in the painting as if it would lift an accusing finger and expose her. She saw only the face of a mother who had also lost a son.

If she ever needed prayer it was now. Not being Catholic, she wasn't sure of the ritual. She didn't hesitate. She picked up a candle that was unlit, held the wick to a flame, then placed it on a wooden holder. The words, "Let me find my son," seemed to come from outside herself. Then she heard herself whisper, "Daniel," but did not know what words to pray.

She had no sense of movement in the room, as if they had all become part of the stone carvings that surrounded them. In the silence of her mind she lived again through the days since this place had dragged her world down with its cave-in.

She took a deep breath and marked the filling of her lungs. She was only in a tunnel. There would be the proverbial light at the end. The light of Real and Max. Someone near her sobbed. Patricia straightened her shoulders. These mountains would give her back her son, if she had to tear him away with her hands.

"¿*Milagros*, Señoras?" A wizened man brushed his hand over a small tray that he held in front of them. Fingering pieces of silver, he held up a small donkey and a miniature house. Patricia shook her head and tried to push past. He set his dark sharp eyes on Rachel and thrust a charm into her hand, then slid his fingers through the pile of shiny silver and handed Patricia a tiny figure. "*Cinco pesos*, Señora," he whispered. He blocked their way, so she paid him. Clutching the thin talisman in her hand, she pushed their way through the crowd.

"Well, what trinket did you buy me? Something silver?" Rachel asked when they were away from the others.

Patricia took the *milagro* the man had given Rachel and examined it beneath a dim light, then pressed it back into Rachel's palm. "It's a little face. With closed eyes. Guess we're not fooling everybody."

Rachel nodded and smiled. "Oh yes, these are like charms. *Milagro* means 'miracle.' The pilgrims place them at St. Francis's feet and he sees to it their prayers are answered. Did you get one?"

"Yes." Her fingers shook as she slid them around the delicate edges of silver. "A little boy."

CHAPTER THIRTY-FIVE

Patricia felt as if she were shoveling the mountain passage with each step, makeshift skirt catching against her pants, tripping her. Rachel coughed more deeply as the air became more stale. The roof of the tunnel lowered. The walls moved inward. The lights ahead were gone, but they walked in the darkness.

The tunnel made a slight turn. In the distance, light silhouetted those who moved in front of them. At the tunnel's end, sunbeams shot through a veil of dust, creating a gossamer gate. On the other side wavered the ghost of a once thriving city of stone houses, mountains, steep paths and throngs of people. Patricia wanted to describe the magical scene to Rachel, but all she could say in a whisper was, "Max is here!"

Once out of the tunnel they were in a valley towered over by barren rocky peaks. Up the main street a background of pink and gray stone was splashed with brilliant colors. Bright *charro* costumes of pilgrims. Striped awnings lending shade to stalls. Tables spread with hundreds of things for sale. Patricia wondered how anything so wrong as a kidnapping and all the pain it had caused could take place here.

At some distance up the street she turned back to stare at the tunnel. To confront at last whoever or whatever she had felt was following her. There was only the dark empty hole.

Rachel pulled on her arm. "You know, a seeing eye dog would let me know more about where I'm heading. If you don't tell me what's up and why you're so quiet, I may get me one."

Patricia tried to shake off the chill in her flesh. "I don't believe what I'm seeing. Don't know if I can describe it." Reluctantly, she turned away from the tunnel. "The streets, they're cobblestone," she began.

"No joke. I can feel those crazy things. Like walking on boiled dinosaur eggs. You'd better hang tight to me. Don't want you to fall. What do you see?"

"Stone buildings. All attached. Holding each other together. Only way to tell one from another is the stage of decline. Looks like some of them are being restored. New buildings being built on top of the old." She was panting. The air was thin, as if they had ascended thousands of feet since they entered the tunnel.

When they reached the first makeshift stalls, voices of vendors told more. Fruits and vegetables, hats and shawls, leather and silver. A dog barked at a burro tied in a doorway. Smells of sweet mangos and frying tortillas mingled with offal and rotting fruits. Rachel drew her scarf closer to her nose as they passed yellow chickens trussed by their feet.

Patricia wanted to look into the buildings as they passed by, wanted to search people's faces, but she kept her head lowered, the scarf drifting over her cheeks. She watched the uneven path for both of them. Steep steps. Potholes. Dung and trash.

She yearned to be free to move quickly. Now that they were through the tunnel, she wanted to turn the town inside out and find Max herself, but she knew how unrealistic that was and resigned herself to finding out more about the festival and when Max might be released. As soon as she could, she had to leave Rachel somewhere. She wouldn't like it, but she'd understand.

"We need to find somewhere you can stay, so I can look through the town." Patricia said.

"And just what do you plan to do? A house to house search? First time you open your mouth, you'll give yourself away."

"I can still have a look around, keep my ears open. There must be plans for a finale, a big celebration. I'd think that would be when the Army would release Max."

"I hate to say this, Patricia. But do you really think Jorge told the truth, and that's what is going to happen?"

"I have to believe it." Patricia answered without hesitation. "And I have to hope Jim will get your message and come barreling into town tomorrow and rescue us all. In the meantime, it's up to us to learn what we can. So while I'm looking around town, you ask questions of anyone you meet. Be subtle and stay put."

Rachel sighed. "See any first class hotels?"

"I don't even see fourth class. Let's sit here and rest a minute." They climbed some steps of an old mansion and sat under its portal, leaning against the door.

Patricia looked down over the town below and tried to paint a picture for Rachel of the once wealthy Spanish mining town. She scarcely heard her own words as she repeated what Miguel had told her of the old city. Great houses. A municipal band. A natural scientific club. A visit by President Diaz.

Instead, her mind took in the story of time told in different shaped windows, color changes in stone, odd angles and roof lines. No architect had planned these changes. This town was a patchwork of necessity. Almost as much as her own life. No best laid plans for her. Only the twists of fate had led her here, searching for her son, running from Miguel and Daniel, watching for the evil she felt close at her heels.

With her back to a crumbling house and the city where Max was hidden before her, the fear that had gripped her in the tunnel began to take a shape. It was not a man's breath she felt on her neck. It was her past catching up with her. *Oh Daniel*, she thought, *how could I have known I would be so wrong.*

"Must have been a really different place at the turn of the century when silver was king and forty thousand people lived here." Rachel said.

"There could still be that many here behind these walls and you couldn't see them. Max could be hidden three feet behind us." She looked around at the door they leaned against. "It's beautiful, Rache. This portal. Must have been the entrance to a grand old house. The lintel is one massive stone carved with what looks like angels."

Rachel pushed at Patricia. "Well, I don't want to become one. So, let's get out from under it. From what you've been saying, every stone around could come plunging down any minute."

"This one has been here since the Spanish laid it."

"Well, it's time is up, then. Please move."

"We have to find a place to stay."

"I don't care where you desert me, but I need something to eat first. Anything but chicken." She wrinkled her nose.

"Okay. A tortilla stand is across the street. You order."

"Oh boy. The blind leading the dumb again. St. Francis has his work cut out for him. Come on. I'm starved."

"Maybe they'll know where we can stay. Ask."

"Is there a man or woman selling?"

"A man."

"Good. We'll charm him."

They crossed the street to a faded red awning stretched between a wall and two wooden stakes. A dusty *serape* almost hid a small man standing behind a metal table. He was rolling steaming tortillas around pieces of chicken, scoops of beans, chopped onions and chiles.

"*Señor, su olor del tortillas delicioso. ¿Cuanto por cuatro con frijoles? No tenemos mucho dinero.*"

The man absorbed Rachel's smile. He wiped his hands on his pants and shifted his gaze to Patricia. She dropped her head. Rachel held out her palm. "*Tres pesos,*" she offered.

"No, no, Señora. *Diez pesos.*" His eyes asked Patricia's help. She stared at him blankly.

Rachel reached out with radar-like precision and found the man's hand, pressing the coins in his palm. "Gracias, Señor. *St. Francis para del pendecir del habia Ud.*"

Patricia reached for the tortillas, but the man grabbed her wrist. "Señoras!" The man crossed his beefy arms across his chest.

A large woman carrying a pan with a great lump of maize eased through the doorway behind the man just in time to see the foiled purchase. Putting down her burden, she questioned her *esposo*, berating him that he was chancing the wrath of St. Francis by overcharging the poor women. Patricia felt sorry for the woman's husband, clearly no match for the three of them.

The woman directed them to a table and scowled at the man as he reached for a bottle of *Dos Equis* he had left there. In a moment, he reappeared from the building with two cold drinks. Pausing between bites, Rachel asked the woman if she knew where they might find lodging. As the woman's eyes lifted to the window above her, the man had had enough. He took his sombrero from a peg on the wall and strode off up the street, mumbling something about saints.

Patricia listened intently as the woman talked about the festival, the planned parade, the dignitaries that would speak. A commotion from the lower end of the street abruptly ended their talk. A truck rumbled up the narrow passage, and vendors were quickly taking in their awnings to let the vehicle pass. Patricia got up just before the woman moved her poles letting the red cloth collapse over their heads. As the truck neared, Patricia peered out, hiding behind the drooping fabric.

The windshield of the truck was veiled in dust. The figures behind it obscured. Men in military clothes standing up in the back lunged forward as the vehicle screeched to a halt on the cobblestones in front of the great house where she and Rachel had rested earlier.

The woman reset the stakes of her canopy, shouting Spanish epithets at the men who were piling out of the truck. The cover lifted from Patricia's head.

She froze. Miguel was climbing out of the cab. He mingled with the men as they waited for the weathered wood doors to open. Quickly, she whispered to Rachel.

"Señora? Rachel called to the woman. "*¿Tiene un cuarto por nosotros, por favor?*"

"*Si, si, Señora. Venie.*" The woman led them through the door into a corridor and beyond to a large courtyard. She made apologies as they went along for everything in the house, which must have been a glorious hotel in another time. They wound up a stairway, past several ornate doors, then entered a small room on the front of the building. What had once no doubt been a storage room was clean with two small cots, a wash basin, three crooked hangers on a peg, and a lamp. It looked as wonderful as the Willard to Patricia. The woman told them where the bathroom was and left with no demand for money.

"Think St. Francis rewards this kind of hospitality?" Rachel asked, sitting cautiously on the hard bed.

Patricia stood at the open window, holding the dusty lace to one side. She looked down on the table where they had eaten. Then up the street to the truck. The men were gone. Inside, she supposed. As she started to turn away, the door of the *casa* opened. She jerked the curtain almost pulling it from the rod.

"What? What is it?" Rachel asked.

"Down below. The truck. Men in uniform. And Miguel."

"What are they doing?"

Patricia pulled the lace away from the window again. She watched as a small boy ran up with three beers. Miguel gave the child money, handed a beer to a man in a brown, freshly ironed uniform of an army officer. The sound of glass clinking accompanied their *"Salud."*

"They're drinking." Patricia felt her face getting hot.

She stared hard and puzzled at the broad shouldered, dark haired man she had made love to three nights before in the ruins of the ancient hacienda. Just as she released the curtain, she saw him lift his eyes to the window.

CHAPTER THIRTY-SIX

A distant, but distinct cry, snatched Miguel's attention. He turned and looked at a building behind him. Stared at the cracked and weathered door panels as if the figures carved there had just reacted to the woodcutter's knife.

The building had once housed the royal mint. Easy to believe that ghosts haunted it. Ghosts of the workers who had inhabited its dungeons stamping out millions of gold and silver coins. The deserted fortress-like structure was the closest thing in town to a government office. The Secretary had suggested he use it. The army also had offices here, but no one was supposed to be here now.

Another sound from beyond the doors. Miguel exchanged glances with Daniel who had just arrived. They cautiously climbed the stairs. As they reached the entrance, Miguel looked back at the window he had been watching. For years Patricia had haunted his dreams, now he saw her in the face of every Mexican peasant. He turned and hit his fist hard against the dry wood of the door, as if to warn away the sound that had interrupted his thoughts.

Daniel more effectively leaned his shoulder into one of the panels and the door opened. As he stepped into the hall, Miguel grabbed his arm.

"Stay here and watch," he ordered, directing Daniel back outside. "Keep your eye out for the women. Have someone check to see if they are in that hotel across the street. Just make sure our people find them and someone has them in sight. Damn them both for the trouble they have caused," he growled.

The young man pushed against Miguel as if he would force his way into the building, but he said nothing. After a moment, he went back down the steps. The great door squealed a protest of its own as it swung shut again.

Daniel is in enough danger, Miguel thought, after what happened with Jorge's men. Better to keep him in the open. The kid had a stubborn streak as wide as the Rio Grande.

The dark narrow entrance way was suddenly alive with staccato shouts and cries. Miguel looked back, expecting the door to open and Daniel to rush in, but the thick walls had contained the sounds.

The stale, oil-tainted air seemed as impenetrable as the stones that had over the years absorbed the odors of stamping machines. Miguel followed the phantom voices until he saw light spilling on to the floor at the end of the corridor.

"*¿Que?*" he asked the ghosts.

Stepping cautiously into a room, he saw two soldiers, their backs to the door. Between them a man's legs splayed outward, the toes of his boots pointing at the ceiling. He was slumped in a chair, the only piece of furniture in the room. Beams from an oil lantern sitting on the floor chased dim shadows into the corners. The late afternoon sun squeezed between boards that covered the only window, making bar-like stripes on the far wall.

Miguel tapped one of the soldiers on his arm. The man spun around, hands up, ready to strike. Miguel could see that the man in the chair had not been able to do the same for himself. Ropes across his chest pinned his arms and held him upright and helpless. Blood streamed from both sides of his mouth. A cut on his left cheek gaped. The glare in his eyes was bright and threatening. Jeff Winn was obviously tougher than Miguel had ever given him credit for being.

"*Que pasa?*" Miguel asked the men with ease and a grin. He had a healthy respect for the lack of allegiance some of the underpaid, unpatriotic soldiers felt. They knew he was in a position of authority, or he would have joined Winn on the chair. They didn't know for sure if they had to answer to him, and before they had a chance to question anyone, he needed to know what was going on.

The elder soldier, a sergeant, explained that they had caught the prisoner inside one of the mine shafts. One that opened near the entrance of the tunnel and connected through passageways to this side of the mountain. They had been ordered to learn why he was there.

Before Miguel could ask who had given the order, Jeff cried out again as the other soldier slapped him, yelling, "Who sent you?"

Miguel did not have much time. Taking a chance, he held his hand out. The soldiers glanced at each other, hesitated, then moved back slowly like two cats reluctant to give up their catch. Miguel leaned into Jeff's face, their noses almost touching, the scent of fear and blood mingling. Searching his eyes for cooperation, Miguel asked who he was, what he was doing in Real. And no matter how urgent the question, the prisoner did not respond.

"What has he told you?" Miguel asked the soldiers.

"He has told us nothing; however, we will know everything yet," the sergeant said. "He is obviously not one of the miners. His weapon . . ." He pointed to an expensive high-powered rifle propped against a wall.

The younger soldier took over the interrogation. Miguel put his hand out and deflected a punch headed for Winn's face.

"I think I recognize him," Miguel almost whispered, uncertain what he should say. "He works for Juan Catera. Isn't this true?" Miguel stared at the bleeding face. Jeff's own mother wouldn't recognize him now. His eyes were mere creases between dark shades of blue and purple.

"Yes, I think he does," the sergeant agreed.

If their prisoner really worked for Catera, Miguel thought, he would deserve worse than he had received from these two brutes. Thinking he was a henchmen of the "garbage czar" would make them think twice before roughing him up further. Catera was known to exact extreme vengeance.

Jeff glanced toward the rifle. Miguel sent a torrent of questions rushing at the prisoner while he circled the chair and assessed his chances of freeing him. As annoyed as he was at the newsman sometime, Miguel considered Jeff a friend. When he had told Manuel to take care of him, he figured some false charges would keep him out of sight in jail for a few days. Guess something went wrong. Now, he had to get Winn out of here. The Army officials had made it clear that no one was to know they had Max. If they knew Winn was a newsman, he would not live to print the story, or at the least, he would disappear until they had used Max for their purpose.

Miguel was only a few feet from the weapon. His hand reached toward it. Scurried movements of the soldiers stopped him. He expected an attack, but turned to see them snap to attention and stand at full alert, saluting. General Martine Ruiz stepped in from the shadows and gave the soldiers a half-hearted salute as he brushed past them.

Miguel moved away from the rifle and breathed deeply. At least Ruiz was not a known enemy. They always had to wait until the last bribe was made to know where the General stood.

Ruiz's eyes held a questioning look. Muscles in Miguel's face, arms and torso tightened. He forced himself to relax, to uncoil the springs that wanted so much to snap. He hated Ruiz with a passion that bordered on obsession, but now was not the time to show it.

The General looked at the slumped form tied to the chair. The wounded man stared at this new oppressor with eyes still defiant, if less bright.

Without saying a word, Miguel kicked Jeff's shin, knocking his leg back under the chair. His shoulders came forward so sharply he almost toppled over. As he did, Miguel sent his head backward with a fist well placed on the man's jaw. It was a smooth, almost choreographed movement. One Miguel had used before.

"Meet Esteban Cervantes." Miguel ran his fingers through Winn's disarrayed hair, lifted his head and let it fall. "He works for Catera."

"What is he doing here?" Martine asked. "You must have all the answers, since you have made sure he is incapable of saying anything more." He stared at Miguel.

"I know that Catera is in Real. Although I do not know why. Do you?"

General Ruiz smirked. Miguel wondered what pleased him. Had he set some kind of trap for Catera? The General and the Chief of Police were old enemies, and nothing would please Ruiz more than finally getting his hands on the allusive Catera.

Miguel cursed under his breath. He felt as if he were walking in socks made of cactus needles, trying not to step the wrong way. If he got in the way of Ruiz's plan, he would be out of Real in handcuffs.

Ruiz gave the soldiers an order to remove the prisoner to another room. "Keep him tied, but do not touch him." When they had left, he went to the boarded window and jerked one of the planks free. Dust fogged the room. Light struggled through cracked glass and a sea of motes.

"Juan Catera is a fool, a dangerous one. We can not know what he might do. Fools are unpredictable, do you not think?"

Miguel didn't want to say what he thought. Instead he parroted the question, "He is after the mines, and he needs the boy to get them, do you not think?"

"We have men everywhere. If Catera wants the boy, there is no way for him to get to him. Not where we have him. If Catera makes a move, we will deal with him." Martine looked up and down the street as if searching for someone.

Deal? Or make a deal? Miguel thought. He suddenly understood the General's plan. He was using Max. He was holding the boy out as bait. Catera would need the boy and Patricia out of the way if he were taking over the mines. The papers the Secretary had would just be for show, after the fact.

When Juan made his move, Ruiz would do one of two things. Kill Catera, exposing the plot and embarrassing the Chief, or cut himself into the deal. It was a toss of the coin as to which it would be.

An uneven silence settled like dust over the room. Miguel thought about the woman he had seen in the window and wondered again if it were Patricia. He had thought she was safer wandering around in her disguise, as long as they kept her in sight. Keeping her captive as they had in the cabin had almost been a disaster. Now he had an uneasy feeling about his plan.

CHAPTER THIRTY-SEVEN

October 3

Rachel licked her fingers and hummed. "Aren't these sweet tamales wonderful?"

Patricia tried to make a similar sound, but her share of the raisin and honey flavored sweets was soaking through the paper wrapping and soiling the bed cover.

Rachel stopped eating. "You just think you're fooling me with that beehive roar. I know you haven't eaten a thing. Haven't even unrolled one of them. No paper sounds, Patricia. Come on. How do you think you can keep this up?"

"I'm not hungry, Rache. Want mine? You're welcome to them." She crossed the tiny room in three steps and looked out the window again, which she had done for most of the night. The bed had been comfortable enough, especially compared to the ground she had tried to sleep on the past two nights, but how could she rest knowing Max had to be within a mile of her, no, maybe blocks. Or maybe even inside that imposing old building across the way that she knew Miguel had disappeared into.

Although the light was still a rosy haze, it was long past dawn. Real de Catorce sat in a valley amid mountains that cheated the town on each end of the day. Fooled by the lack of light, Rachel had still been asleep when Patricia answered a soft knock on their door earlier. The landlady had sent a girl with a tray of tamales, papaya and strong coffee.

Now Patricia was eager for Rachel to eat her fill so that they could leave. She didn't feel safe in this room anymore. They were better off on the move.

She looked up and down the street. There had been no sign of Jim or anyone else except the people setting up their stands. In the past few minutes she had watched a group of priests walking up the hill toward the church. Maybe she and Rachel would go there, too. After all, they did have silver *milagros* to offer to St. Francis.

She checked the time. Already after ten, time they went out. She returned her watch to its hiding place and straightened her shabby clothes. Even though she and Rachel had been able to bathe, they had swathed themselves once again in rags.

The need to be disguised was greater than ever. She still had the feeling Miguel had seen her at the window the afternoon before. And even though it had not happened, every noise during the night gave her visions of him breaking down the door.

"I wish we could get out of this garb," Rachel said. "I'll never kid you again about being a clothes horse. If I ever get to wear my own things, I'm going to become one myself." She tied the scarf around her hair.

When they were ready, they made their way out of the old hotel and into the street. Tomorrow was the feast day of St. Francis and the streets were crowded with makeshift shops. They walked up a narrow street in the cool shade of two and three story buildings that stair-stepped up the steep incline.

Patricia tugged her scarf close to her face as they passed the building she had watched Miguel disappear into the afternoon before. For all she knew he could be inside now, looking out the windows, watching her.

They circled around the building and back to the street the church was on. An iron rail fence surrounded the grounds of La Parroquia de la Purisima Conception that soared above them. Statues of saints lined its front roof.

"Well, we've found where St. Francis lives," she told Rachel. "Reminds me of the old place I used to call the chocolate chip house that was down the street from the McFalls. Mixture of light and dark bricks. Strange looking on a church."

"Does it have a *campenario*?"

That was one Spanish word Patricia knew, since it was the name of her favorite restaurant in Acapulco. "Yes, a bell tower and a dome."

Across from the church was a collection of the best restored buildings Patricia had seen in the town. Most of them had cafes on the ground floor and rooms to rent on the upper ones. Wooden tables and metal chairs covered that side of the courtyard. Men and women sat drinking and eating. This was obviously the heart of town. Colorful banners swung across the street from building to building. Festival preparations occupied groups of workers all along side streets. Music blared from a roof top speaker setting a festive mood.

Patricia leaned toward Rachel. "We're going to sit at a table, have coffee." She took some coins from her pants pocket through an opening in her skirt.

They sat down at a table near the center of activity and ordered. Patricia watched Rachel. Since the conversations that floated in the air around them were in Spanish, she waited for a sign on Rachel's face that she heard something interesting.

Two men sat close behind them, talking and arguing. When they left, making their way through the maze of tables, Patricia asked her what they had said.

"Do you see a police station?" Rachel asked. "And `barandales`? Not sure what that is."

At the upper end of the street was a large yellow sign over a one story building. Palacio Municipal. "Is that it?" Patricia asked, after telling Rachel what she saw.

"They were talking about the jail," Rachel said. "This place doesn't have problems with its citizens. They never use it. The walls are like `crumbling paper`, one of them said. They're worried about possible arrests. Something about the miners. Wouldn't you know Max'd be mixed up in their first crime wave of the century?"

Patricia squeezed Rachel's hand.

"If that's the police station up there, why don't we just walk in and tell them who we are and why we're here and demand they do their sworn duty to uphold the law?" Rachel asked.

"Whose law? That's the question. Who do you think they would side with in this place? The Moreloses or the miners?"

"You have a point, I guess. What's that hammering?"

"On the other side of the church, near the fountain. I can just see it through the fence."

"*Barandales*. A fence. That must be the place they were talking about. They're building something close to it, a platform, I think. Probably to do with the festival."

"Yes. I can see a plaza up there. And a fountain."

"So, if we can't go to the police, what do we do?"

Patricia had been watching groups of men and women enter the little street from all directions and go into La Parroquia. "We'll go to church," she said. "Come on."

Two enormous metal doors had been propped open, inviting the pilgrims in. An arched ceiling covered the nave. Clerestory windows filtered the bright sunshine, spilling a sheen of light over the pews that marched toward the altar in two single files.

"What is this?" Rachel whispered, as she almost tripped.

Patricia looked down for the first time. Uneven planks formed rectangles. As far as she could see the floor was covered with them. "Coffin lids," she murmured.

"What?"

"The floor is wood. We're walking on graves," Patricia whispered.

"My grandmother would have a fit. She taught me that was disrespectful. Not to speak of bad luck. No other path, huh?"

Patricia didn't answer. She was too busy taking in the silver candelabras, gold gilded statues and wonderful mosaics along the walls. The church was certainly the most prosperous place in town.

The heady fragrance of incense barely camouflaged the musty odor of old cloth, dust and death. Murmurs and clicks of rosary beads, like the sound of summer insects, rose and fell as they passed small groups of people standing before glass encased saints. At the far end of the nave, at the apse of the church, stood a tall bearded figure. Its red cloak was faded. Plaster showed beneath pealing paint. An aged St. Francis. His hands stretched out to the mass of people at his feet.

They moved at a snail's pace from left to right. Each person held a gold or silver *milagro*. At some right moment the symbol of prayerful request was laid reverently on top of a multitude of shiny pieces. Men and women alike looked up into the chalk face of the Saint as hope replaced helplessness. Patricia watched the transformation again and again.

Rachel reached out and touched the talismans. In her hand she held the silver face that Patricia had bought from the man in the tunnel. Her head lifted and her sightless eyes seemed to rest on the face of the saint. A smile dimpled her cheek. She dropped the *milagro*.

Patricia quickly retrieved it from the table and stepped back from the crowd. Her *milagro*, the figure of the little boy, was clasped tightly in her other hand. A ledge jutted from the wall near the opening of the apse. Patricia placed the little silver boy and the face with no eyes on its dusty surface.

She looked back at the ever growing pile of hopes laid before the saint. If nothing else, she thought, perhaps some priest surveying the bounty of the day might be touched by the two misplaced pieces and say a special prayer for their offerers.

"Let's sit over here," Patricia said quietly. At the end of the transept was a small chapel with a short wooden pew against the wall.

"Now what?" Rachel asked.

"What I'd like to do is go out there and stand on that platform they're building and scream until someone tells me where he is."

"Any sane suggestions?"

"Shh," she whispered. "A priest is coming this way."

"*Buenos dias, Señoras.*" A thin, dark-cloaked man, a bright twist of cloth around his waist and a rosary around his neck, bowed to them. "*Bienvenidos a La Parroquia de la Purisima Conception.*" He moved nearer until the coarse fabric of his skirt rubbed against Patricia's hand. He glanced over his shoulder at those gathered behind him, then bent closer to her. She could smell garlic on his breath. And whiskey.

"*¿Tiene alguna cosa especialle para San. Francis?*"

Rachel answered him in Spanish. Patricia listened. The man was strange for a priest, she thought. He had rough skin, leathered by the sun. A gardener for the parish, perhaps, but his dark eyes held no benevolence, no compassion.

"*Si, si.*" He nodded, then turned to Patricia. "*¿E Usted, Señora?*" Patricia shook her head, at what she didn't know.

"Perhaps you look for your son?" The man spoke low, in heavily accented English.

Patricia and Rachel came off the pew. Stood only a breath away from the man.

"What?" Patricia whispered. "My son?" She struggled with the words. Afraid not to take a chance.

"*Si*, Max."

Patricia's body went rigid, holding her still against the tide within her. She wanted to rush the man and demand all he knew.

"*Venie.* Come. *Rapido.*" The man turned and walked toward a door at the far end of the transept. Only when he had opened it did he look back.

Patricia whispered to Rachel to stay. To wait for her here in the church.

Rachel held firmly to Patricia's arm. "I'm going. You're not leaving me here alone with a basement of dead people beneath my feet."

The priest was going through the door as if he didn't care if they followed or not. Hesitating only a moment, Patricia grabbed Rachel's hand and headed after him.

CHAPTER THIRTY EIGHT

Patricia ran her fingers along the rough, cold wall to keep her balance as they descended the dark, narrow stairwell. Rachel's hand gripped her shoulder as she followed one step behind. The priest plunged ahead of them, heedless of the treacherous passage. By the time they stepped into a small dirt room, Patricia calculated they had dropped below street level. The air was damp, earthy.

A lantern sat on the floor. Shadows danced on the walls as the man discarded his vestments. Beneath them he wore a pair of dark pants and shirt. He picked up the light and headed for what seemed the entrance to a tunnel.

"Wait a minute," Patricia called to him. "We're not going any further until you answer some questions. You're obviously not a priest. Who are you? Where are you taking us?"

The man backed out from the dark and turned to Patricia. He held the lantern up to his face. Coal eyes shone as if with a light of their own. Gold teeth glittered. "If you want to see your son, Señora, you will follow, and do it quickly. The people who wish him dead are tired of waiting." With those ominous words the eyes and teeth disappeared into the hole.

Patricia grabbed Rachel's hand and they followed in the dim light of the swinging lantern. The roof of the shaft was low. She told Rachel to keep her head down.

Thin air and the acrid odor of damp earth made breathing difficult. Bending over and looking up at the same time soon made Patricia's shoulders ache and her calves throb. They were also on an incline. She tried to visualize the topography of the town. Walking upward, but still underground, would mean they were going farther up the mountain, above Real.

After it seemed they had walked a mile, she turned to Rachel. "You okay?"

"If you call feeling like a hunchback earthworm, okay, I guess so. How 'bout you?"

Patricia looked forward again. The light was gone. "Hey, wait!" she shouted and scrambled on, knees almost striking her chin. Blindly, her hands groped the way. Suddenly, a rectangle of light appeared. A door. Open.

"Where are we?" Rachel asked.

"Some kind of a basement. Small, high windows. Looks like gravestones outside. Must be a church."

"Not again," Rachel groaned.

"Stairs. Come on." At the top, Patricia cautiously opened a wood door.

"It was a church," she said to Rachel. "But the saints all moved out. It's deserted."

They went out an open side door. The sun struck like a blow. Patricia's eyes adjusted to the scene of a small graveyard of ancient stones. Then she looked past the church. They were above the town. She could barely make out the square tower and dome of La Parroquia in the distance. The air was cooler. A mist was rolling up the valley erasing everything in its path.

A rustling sound came from behind her. The man was standing by a crumbling wall, holding back some hibiscus bushes. Beyond them were shadows. She looked again toward the town. No one was in sight. No one knew where they were. This could be a trap.

The man's words about Max were beacons in the mist. Her only hope. Her only choice. She gave him one last sharp look. "Duck down, Rachel," she said and led her under the bushes.

Before she could straighten her back on the other side, an arm circled her in a tight embrace and lifted her off the ground. She lost her grip on Rachel. She struggled, slapping wildly with her hands. Then she saw who held her.

"Jim! Oh, Jim!" You got our message!" She cried out in relief and embraced him as tightly as he did her. She sobbed against his shoulder.

"My god. We went through that tunnel to find you on the other end?" Rachel laughed.

Jim scowled at her over Patricia's shoulder, but said nothing. He gave Patricia's cheek a quick kiss.

"Have you got Max already?" She looked past him. Searching. Women milled around an open fire where large pots hung on spits. Several men sat on the edge of a porch on the front of a large hacienda. She didn't see Max anywhere. She strained against Jim's hold. His grip hardened.

"Where is he? You've found him, haven't you? Tell me you have." She beat her fists against his chest. He held her tightly, making the blows ineffectual.

"Listen to me, Patricia." He took her hands in his and held them. She struggled to get free. "Listen, I said." His voice was quiet, edgy. "I'm working on a deal. There's papers to sign. You'll see Max . . . after. After you sign them." He hugged her close to his chest.

"I'll do anything. You know that." She struggled to raise her head. Why was he holding her? Then she saw the man that had led them here. Jim had put his back to him, trying to keep him from overhearing what they said. She shivered and wiped at tears, smearing her face with dirt.

"I've got to see Max first, Jim," she said into his chest. A ramrod of fear as hard as flint shot though her. She had to know Max was safe. Or no deals, no papers. "Where is he? Did you bring some men to help us? Where—"

"The papers first, Patricia. They won't negotiate."

She stared at the man and then at Jim. The flint rod within her had become daggers aiming out of her eyes. "What is going on here? Who are these people? Why did he bring us here? What do you mean 'negotiate'? I thought the army had Max. What would they want from me?"

"I've got everything under control. Promise. Just do as I ask." He pulled a handkerchief from his pocket and wiped her cheeks.

It seemed Jorge had lied to her after all. What had she expected? With resignation she said, "Let me see the papers, Jim." She jerked the cloth out of his hand.

"It's not that easy. They aren't here yet." He glanced back at the man who stood only a few feet away, watching them.

"Not here?" she asked.

"The men with the papers."

"B-but when?" She felt herself crumble. Her calves were weak from their trek in the tunnel. The adrenaline that had kept her going for days was depleted. She swayed. Jim caught her, steadied her.

"You need rest. We have a room ready for you. You can wash up. Sleep. I'll get you something to eat. Some clean clothes. No one knows you're here. Let's keep it that way. For our safety and Max's. Will you do that, Patricia? Just trust me?"

"Everything but the trusting part sounds great, Jim." Rachel folded her arms, as if challenging him. "Lead the way."

He kept his arm around Patricia as they walked toward the house. She held Rachel's hand. They were shown to a sparsely furnished room. Twin beds, a couple of chairs, a table, dresser and bath. It smelled clean, fresh. A young, dark skinned girl was putting towels in the bath. She frowned at Patricia and Rachel as she left the room. The priest man stood in the open doorway.

"Jim, the clothes. Don't forget," Rachel said as she felt along the wall for the bathroom. As soon as she had shut the door, Jim tried to put his arms around Patricia. She would not allow herself to be hugged, but pushed away and sat on the edge of the bed.

"I'm tired. So much has happened. I'm so disappointed." The effort to speak drained the last of her strength.

Jim bent down and slipped the scarf from her head. "You'll feel better. I'll be back later. Remember, don't go out of the room or talk to anyone. Okay?"

Patricia wasn't aware that he was leaving. Didn't hear the door close. Her head snapped up at a sharp click. It was the tumbling of the lock.

* * *

Jim put his hand out for the key. The man who had found the women only grinned, looking beyond Jim.

"*Gracias*, Fernando," Juan Catera said, sliding the key into his pocket.

The three men walked across the porch and entered another part of the house. Catera ordered a young man to bring them *cervasas*.

"Good job, Poncho." Catera slapped Fernando on the back. "Now go clean up. You smell like a *pepenadore*." They both laughed.

Jim drank the cold beer and watched Catera go to a basin of water and wash his long slender hands and arms all the way to his elbows before he picked up his own beer. A clean freak who made his money off people who collected garbage. The "garbage czar", what a joke, Jim thought.

"What about clothes for them?" Jim asked, the beer giving him a little courage. After the incident in the mine, that had turned out to be a passage to this hacienda, Jim had been more cautious in his words to Catera.

"I have sent for something better than the rags they wear. Maybe they will get the clothes, maybe not. Perhaps the way to keep them in their rooms is to keep them naked." He threw back his head and laughed.

"What about Max? When are you bringing him here?" Jim hated the belly-aching sound of his voice. He wanted to ask him about Patricia's claim that the Army had Max. Oh God, what had he done? He reached over to a tin bucket filled with ice and beer and took another one.

"Is the Señora going to sign the papers?"

"I told her they weren't here yet. I wanted to give her a little time. The more anxious she is about Max, the easier it will be to convince her." Patricia's words that she would do anything swirled through Jim's mind. Catera couldn't know she would need no coaxing once she saw her son. When her name was on those documents, Catera wouldn't have any need to keep any of them alive. The thought made Jim sweat.

"What will you tell her is in the papers?

"She trusts me. I'll tell her what she wants to hear." He wondered what that would be, as he got up and looked out the window.

The scene outside was straight out of a John Wayne western. Women in pioneer long skirts, cooking over a fire, a wagon and two horses under the shade of a lean-to shack. If he didn't know there was a helicopter pad and a couple of jeeps on the other side of the house, he might expect the calvary to ride through the gate to save the day. Only he'd probably be the one swinging from a tree.

"What if she wants to read them?" Catera broke into Jim's thoughts.

"I told you. She doesn't speak or read Spanish. And unless you have them in braille, that bitch Rachel's no threat." He felt his anger rise as it always did at the thought of Patricia's blind friend. How in the hell did she get to Real with Patricia? For that matter how had Patricia gotten here? Jim wasn't sure he believed Catera's story about Miguel helping Patricia, much less that they spent the night together. If that was the case, where was Miguel now? She had obviously asked Jim for help in a message she had left and he didn't get. Now, she thought he had come through for her. He had to keep her thinking that.

He turned to Catera. "She may not sign until she can see Max. What will I do about that?" Jim got another beer.

"Well, you have two choices, Mainland. You can convince her to sign, and she can take her nosy kid back to the States. Or, you can join the two of them at the bottom of a mine shaft."

CHAPTER THIRTY NINE

Patricia had been dreaming. Of home. She tried to hold onto the veil of sleep. Her body was exhausted. Her eyelids weighted. She wished that when she opened her eyes, she would see the mint green drapes hanging from the arched windows of her bedroom. The ornate armoire Tomas had shipped back from Madrid. Her collection of cats on the dresser, catching the morning light. And she wished with all her might that Max was asleep down the hall in his room.

One lid fluttered, then the other. Brightly striped curtains hung at a window. Sunlight emphasized the coarse weave. A simple wooden table and a heavy chair stood in shadows. A narrow bed. Rachel. Mexico.

Her nightmare lived. She shut her eyes.

"You up?" Rachel asked.

Patricia did not think she had moved. "Yes," she answered and sat on the side of the bed. "I dreamed I was at home. In my bedroom. Then I opened my eyes and saw this place."

"Looks the same as home to me," Rachel said.

Patricia grabbed her pillow and threw it onto Rachel's legs.

"Hey! You deserved that remark. Wallowing in self-pity is not allowed, remember?"

"You're right, but wallowing sounds pretty good right now," Patricia smiled. She hadn't thought she would go to sleep when she and Rachel laid down, and felt guilty that she had. "God, I wish I knew what was going on. If Jim doesn't come back soon, I'm going to break my way out of here."

"Do we have any clothes?"

"No. Not yet. Guess we can wear sheets."

"How good are you at playing Scarlett O'Hara? Or don't we have any drapes?" Rachel laughed. "I sure need more than a sheet. This wafer of a blanket did little to keep out the ole mountain chill during my siesta."

A knock at the door sent Rachel back under the covers.

"The sheet will have to do," Patricia said, jerking it from the bed and wrapping it around herself.

The lock clicked and the door opened slowly. "Señoras?" a female voice called.

"Yes?" Patricia answered from behind the door.

The same girl who brought them towels and food earlier came in, arms full of clothes. Patricia pointed to the bed. The girl placed them there and left. A hand held the door open a crack.

"Patricia?" It was Jim.

She clutched the sheet to her and leaned into the opening.

"Hope the clothes fit." He smiled. Stared at her wrap.

"As soon as I'm dressed, Jim, we need to talk," she moved to close the door. He stopped her.

"I have the papers," he said.

She almost dropped the sheet as she reached for the folder in his hand.

"I'll hold them for you." He placed a page on top and held out a pen.

She hesitated and he glanced, almost imperceptibly, to his left. In her peripheral vision she caught sight of the priest man on the porch. She leaned out of the room and stared at the man watching them. He turned his back. She studied Jim. Her friend. Her husband's friend. One of the directors of her company. Something was wrong.

"Jim, why have we been locked in?"

"For your safety," he answered. "And so no one would disturb you." His eyes did not meet hers.

"If I needed to be safe, why wouldn't I have the key?"

"Just sign the papers, Patricia." His voice had that edginess again.

"Where's Max? I won't sign anything until I see him."

"But you said—" He turned quickly toward the left again. Off his guard, he could not react before Patricia grabbed the folder. He reached for it, but she had shut the door.

"Patricia, sign the papers." His voice came from the wood panels. "Max will be here tomorrow. Just sign them. Now."

"If Max won't be here until tomorrow, then I'll sign them tomorrow." She waited, hardly breathing. Nothing. Then the key and the tumbling of the lock.

She sat on the bed. Stared at the papers. She recognized the document. It was just like the one she had found in Miguel's pack at the hacienda.

"Guess it doesn't matter that I don't know what it says. I've seen it before," she said, as if Rachel knew what she was doing and thinking.

"What do you mean?"

Patricia told her about finding the paper in Miguel's pack.

"Was it a copy of this? You said there were no signatures."

"Jim's job, I guess. To get me to sign. Doesn't mean Miguel's not in on it. They could be in cahoots." Patricia locked her arms across herself.

"Miguel didn't try to get you to sign anything, did he?" Rachel asked.

"No," she had to admit.

"Well, you're smart to hold out until Max is here. Jorge said the army had him, so who do you believe now?"

"Jim said he would be here." The words were like froth, no substance. Patricia dropped down on her bed. "Oh Rachel, something is wrong, terribly wrong, and you know it. You're just not saying anything, for once. What is it?"

"Jim Mainland. In a word."

"Of course, you'd think that. You've always hated him. Why, I don't know."

"Being blind gives one an advantage sometimes. I'm not moved by looks. Voice. Words—they say more than people with sight hear. But, you're wrong, I don't hate Jim. I fear him."

Patricia stared at her friend. "Fear. That's it! That's what's wrong with Jim." She stood and paced the room. "I've never known him to be afraid of anything, but I saw it in his eyes. He kept watching that man, the one that brought us here. He's afraid of something. Or someone."

"If that's true, the answer may be in those papers," Rachel said. "I'm surprised he let you keep them."

Patricia thought about that for a minute. "It can mean only one thing, Rache. They don't care if I know what it says, only that I sign them." That was a chilling thought because it also meant that they were holding all the cards.

"Tell you what, you pick out my wardrobe and let's get dressed. Then you read me the document. Spell the words if you have to. We'll figure it out between the two of us."

The clothes were a considerable improvement over what they had been wearing, which Rachel said should be burned. They each had a long skirt, off the shoulder blouse and sandals.

"I feel like I'm going to a Mexican costume party," Rachel said.

"Probably the standard dress for the festival. At least it's clean. Let's sit at the table where I can get more light." By the time the sun had gone down, they knew what the document said.

"Do you think we really have it right?" Patricia asked. "It's hard enough to read these things in English, much less decipher legalize in a foreign language."

"We've got it, Patricia. Face it. Jim Mainland has sold you and the Morelos mines, not to speak of Max, down the river. Or rather the mine shaft."

"Who do you think Catera is? What if it's a name for the union of miners or something?"

"Patricia, it says 'Juan Catera'. Now do you really think that's an anagram for some organization?"

"No." Patricia paced the room. She must have walked two miles in the last hour, sixteen steps at a time. "I do think that Jim is being made to do this. He has to be."

The door rattled, then opened.

"It's about time they fed us," Rachel said. "Smells good."

Patricia watched the door, looking for Jim. She paid no attention to the girl who slipped in carrying a tray.

A voice whispered, "Señora Rachel."

Patricia looked around in time to see the girl give Rachel a quick hug and move away.

"Gena," Rachel said in a hushed voice.

Patricia shut the door and leaned against it. Gena put a finger to her lips. She lifted one of the plates filled with chicken and rice. A piece of paper lay under it.

Someone knocked on the door then pushed it into Patricia's back. She moved. The priest man stepped in and motioned for Gena. She ducked her head and hurried out. The man stared at Rachel, then Patricia.

"The papers, Señora." The man held out his hand.

Patricia's heart tripped. For a moment she thought he meant the note Gena had left. Then realizing what he wanted, she snatched up the legal document and shoved it at him.

He smiled, closed the door and locked it.

Patricia leaned against it and waited. When she didn't think he was coming back, she grabbed the paper from under the plate, scanning it. "Spanish, damn it!"

"Well, if we can figure out something a lawyer wrote, something Gena wrote won't be a problem. I'm so glad she's okay. The shack. She might have been in it." Rachel's voice quivered. "I know," Patricia said and hugged her.

Patricia read the note, spelling a couple of the words. Gena would be back some time before daybreak. As they waited, Patricia expected someone to come barging in with those papers again. What had happened when they saw she had not signed them? It was maddening not to know what was going on, they agreed. How had Gena found them? They speculated about everything and were more confounded by the little they knew. They finally stretched out on the bed with their clothes on.

"I couldn't sleep if we weren't waiting for Gena," Rachel said. "I'm freezing."

"I know. Me too." Patricia didn't want to talk. She wanted to listen. As if the silence would bring Gena sooner. Despite the cold, Rachel slept, snored softly. Hours passed. Patricia wished she had Rachel's braille watch. Not that time mattered, she thought.

Gena. Gena. Her name was like a mantra, calling for her. She thought of Daniel. Was he behind Gena's coming here? Did she know where Max was? If she wanted them to go with her to Daniel, what would they do? She didn't trust Jim. She faced that. For whatever reason, he was on the wrong side now. Did she trust Daniel? Just the thought of his name put her mind in a circle of thorns.

She jumped out of bed like a jack in a box at the sound of a key in the lock. She must have gone to sleep. The door creaked. Gena.

They sat on Rachel's bed, as far from the door as possible and talked in whispers.

"Señor Miguel, Daniel look everywhere for you," Gena said.

"How did you find us?" Rachel asked.

"In market, a man named Fernando buy clothes. He say it not matter the color." She dropped her head. "It is bad Señora Rachel. He laugh and say you are blind." She became animated again. "When I hear, I catch up and say to the man I bring clothes to him and he say yes. He not know I still here. I look for Daniel before I come. No time. I go now and tell him," she said, proudly, and got up to leave. She held a key up to them. "You want? Or I put back?"

"Wait, Gena." Patricia put her hand on the girl's arm, taking the key as she did. "Do they have Max? Is that the reason Daniel and Miguel are searching for us?"

"No, but—"

"No buts," Patricia expelled her pent-up breath. "Why should I trust them? They've both let me down. God, I don't know what to believe." She hugged herself, shaking from cold. And fear.

"She has to go and tell them, Patricia," Rachel whispered.

"Not yet." Patricia tried to pull herself together. "First, Gena, you must tell me everything you know. If Miguel and Daniel don't have Max, what do they want with us? And what happened at the cabin?"

"Daniel was to make you safe in cabin. Jorge, the *problema*. Some miners, they have family in cave-in, they know you there. They follow Jorge. Daniel not stop one when he make blow the cabin."

"How did you get away?" Patricia asked.

"Señor Miguel and others come. The miners run away."

"We thank you for our lives, Gena." Rachel reached her hand out, found Gena's and held it. "If you had not helped us—"

"Oh, Daniel tell me help you out window. I so afraid, you know."

"No, you were very brave," Patricia said, taking her other hand.

The girl looked at their entwined hands. Her eyes shone brightly in the moonlight streaming through the window.

"Gena, what do you know about Max?" Patricia tightened her grip on the girl's slender fingers.

"Señor Miguel say Army release him *mañana*."

"The Army?" Patricia bounced off the bed. "Then they do have Max?" She twisted around in a circle as if to unwind her swirling thoughts. "That must mean he's safe. They wouldn't harm him. And they'll give him up to me, if they know I'm here." She could hardly contain her excitement. Then, she looked at Rachel. "That also means Jim has been lying to me, doesn't it?"

Rachel's hand went out and Patricia clung to it.

"Sorry, Señora. Not so easy. Some miners not want boy to go. Say that `reyes de pepenadores', very bad man, he have mines now. Some say you sell mines to him."

"Does that mean 'garbage king'?" Rachel asked.

"Who the hell is that?" Patricia quickly put her hand over her mouth to muffle her rising anger.

"His name Juan Catera."

Rachel took in an audible breath. "The papers."

Patricia understood what it all meant. "I have not sold the mines, Gena. To anyone!" she yelled in a whisper.

"Señor Miguel say you not. That is why he need you. He have many people watch you. You go in church and you not come out, you know. He is, how you say, go in circle? You must tell people you not sell mines. If not, . . ."

"What?"

"The boy. Maybe miners stop Army and not let him go." Gena dropped her eyes.

"Gena," Patricia took both the girl's hands in hers. "We will all go. You show us the way. It's not safe for us here."

"Señora, is not possible. Guards see you. Maybe in morning, when people come to sell *cosas*."

"Then how were you going to leave?"

"Tunnel. Under church."

Rachel groaned. "The one we took to get here?"

Patricia released Gena and paced the floor.

"What are you thinking?" Rachel asked.

Patricia looked at her friend and frowned. She wasn't sure about her plan. She just knew she had to find Daniel and Miguel quickly.

"I'll go through the tunnel," she announced. "Gena, you hide Rachel. As soon as it's safe, bring her to the church in town."

"Can't we go back through the graveyard together and get to the street around the guards?" Rachel asked Gena.

"Someone see you. Army men in streets at night, and you not know who to trust."

Patricia sighed. She certainly didn't. She thought of the dark, smelly tunnel. Would she be able to find her way even through the hibiscus bushes?

As if reading her mind, Gena said, "You want, I lead you to *Panteon*, graves. You go in old church, how you come. In town ask for Casa Moneda. Señor Miguel there. Señora Rachel and I hide at edge of *Panteon*. In day and people come to sell, we go." She went to the window and looked out. "Light come from sun soon. We go now."

"Rachel, you okay with this?"

Rachel was still sitting on the bed. "I think this is one time that you would be better off without me. I'll stay with Gena. Meet you in front of St. Francis."

Gena put her arm around Rachel. There had been a bond between the two of them since they were in the shack. Patricia hated the thought of leaving Rachel, but she knew Gena would take care of her. She pulled Rachel to her feet and hugged her tightly. "Don't get into trouble. Promise?"

"Promise."

Patricia picked up a candle and matches from the table, put them in her skirt pocket. She took the blanket from Rachel's bed and draped it around her like a shawl, then did the same with hers.

Gena looked outside, motioned for them. They shut the door, locked it and pocketed the key. Gena led the way across the dirt courtyard to the break in the hibiscus.

"*Buena suete, Señora*," Gena said.

"Take care of Rachel," Patricia answered back. The bushes closed around her.

CHAPTER FORTY

October 4

The old church shone like a beacon where soft shades of dawn lit its whitewashed walls. Patricia crouched in the shadows of the hibiscus hedge surrounding the cemetery. She tried not to think about where she was, alone in the dark. When she heard a scratching sound, she ran. Her skirt caught on the uneven edges of a gravestone, pulling her to the ground. Righting herself with the help of a marble angel's wing, she brushed gravel from her palms and shut out the macabre image of hands reaching out of graves.

Once inside the church she took deep breaths and slowed her pounding pulse. She looked back across the cemetery. Nothing moved. No one was following. There were only stone shapes that she was sure would dance as soon as she turned her back.

She made her way down the steps to the room beneath the sanctuary. The high windows allowed enough light for her to see the opening of the tunnel. She wished she had the lantern the priest man had carried. At least she had the candle. The match flared. A tiny light flickered. Went out. She tried again, then gave up. Better to wait until she really needed it.

She took a deep breath, and held it, as if she would not find air again until she came out the other side. Darkness surrounded her like black water. She inched forward, her hands seeking, head lowered, stroking the walls for balance. She took shallow sips of rank, earthy air.

They had climbed up the mountain through this passage on the way to the hacienda. Now she descended. Down, deeper, as if into the bowels of the earth.

She worked her legs hard, crouching, back bent, arms flailing until they touched surfaces. Sometimes damp, slick walls. Sometimes jagged cold rocks that scrapped her skin. When she straightened her knees and stood too tall, spider webs caught her hair. She pulled the blanket over her head. The dirt-tinged air filtered through musty wool.

The first heavy clod of earth was just a thump. Then waves of vibration circuited her body from her feet to her teeth. Muffled booms like crashing surf rebounded from the dark. Dirt and rocks rained on her. She put her hands over her head and screamed. The echo hurt her ears. In terror she ran through a gauntlet of missiles. When the earth shook, she braced against the walls, as if to hold them in place, and absorbed trembles through her hands.

She stopped running. Only a spray of dirt fell against her outstretched arms. She stood still, not breathing. The word "cave-in" struck her in its full horror. Thoughts of the tragedy that had brought Max here, of the altar in the tunnel, of the families who had lost loved ones in the mines flashed around her like psychedelic lights. Urgency beyond her control made her move. Without allowing herself to think if the passage was blocked behind her or ahead, or even whether she was still going in the right direction, she kicked and dug through fallen dirt and climbed through narrow holes like a single minded mole.

Stepping over a fallen beam, she shut her ears to the sound of creaking above her. Debris on the floor lessened and she walked on a smoother earthen floor. La Parroquia had to be near. Some light should be coming through the opening. The room beneath the church where the priest had shed his robes had not been totally dark, even without the lantern. High windows must have let in sunlight.

She walked more slowly, expecting any moment to step out of the tunnel. Sensing something in front of her, she reached out, touched wood. Her hands patted the entire surface. There was no knob, no latch. She pushed with all her weight, but it didn't move. The tunnel had been sealed.

She took the candle and matches from her pocket. Three tries and the flame stayed. In the faint edge of sight, she noticed something above her, sticking out from the wall. She held the light high and saw part of a wooden box. Then, she remembered the floor of the church. Coffin lids. When they dug this tunnel, the floor must have given way beneath one of them. It hung from the earth precariously.

Maybe she could reach the end and pull it down. Wouldn't that bring down the whole casket, lid and all? Leaving a gaping hole in the floor? It might just rip open and dump a rotting corpse at her feet. She shuddered.

If the top of this coffin was the floor above, why had she not heard people walking? It was still early, maybe no one was in the church. She tried to visualize what part of the floor this would be. The pew at the far end of the transept where she and Rachel had encountered the priest was near the door. To their left had been where the people came to leave their *milagros* for St. Francis.

She stared up at the protruding coffin and knew what she had to do. The only place to find what she needed was where the tunnel had caved in. In the glow of the candle she found it. A rock she could climb up on. She rolled it over on her blanket and tugged and pulled it down the incline.

Once she had it in place, she stepped up closer to the casket, examining it in the feeble light. The lower edge was rimmed with a board two inches wide. Her fingers dug in. She lifted herself almost off the makeshift step. A shower of clods fell from where the box was lodged in the wall.

She tried again. A creak. More dirt. Encouraged, she grabbed the boards, her back to the wall, and swung her weight up and out, landing on the floor beyond the stone step. She cried out as her nails caught in the wood, ripping them into the quick.

Ignoring the pain in her fingers, she reached higher the next time and caught hold of the boards placed in an elongated "x" on the side of the coffin. This time a crash reverberated above her. She ducked, shielded her head, expecting bones, or ashes, or wood to cover her.

Something jingled. She opened her eyes. Light glittered above her in a shower of silver. *Milagros!* Falling through the floor. Hundreds of them.

She scooped some from the dirt and laughed.

Footsteps thundered and she heard voices. She called out, "Help! *Ayuda*! Help!"

Through grunts and groans, sounds of something heavy scraped the floor. Light spilled though and wide-eyed faces stared at her. A babel of Spanish filled the small space. Several men came into the tunnel. She stumbled past them toward the stairs and set down hard on one of the steps.

From somewhere she heard the name "Morelos." She looked up into dark eyes staring at her. Without thinking whether she trusted any of them, she whispered, "Miguel Ramirez. I have to find him."

The room was silent as a tomb. Then a man bent over her and tried to help her to her feet. She hesitated. "Come," he said, "We go to Casa Moneda."

She remembered the name. Gena had told her that was where she would find Miguel. She stood, her legs like willow branches, bending under her weight. The man placed his arm around her and half-carried her into the church.

A great commotion was going on inside. The table in front of the statue of St. Francis was tilted. The pile of silver offerings was falling to the floor in an avalanche of tinkling sounds. Some had already found their way into a hole surrounding the table leg.

Patricia only glanced at the people scurrying around on the floor trying to pick up the tiny charms. She leaned heavily on the man who was taking her to Miguel.

* * *

The old woman was almost incoherent. Something had happened in the church. The *milagros* were disappearing. Maybe someone was trying to steal them, Miguel thought. He had other worries.

He was returning to Casa Moneda from the police station, when the woman had grabbed his arm in hysterics. He was about to ask if she wanted him to do something, but she took off up the street, calling out "*milagro*."

He needed a miracle, he thought, as he entered the old mint. "Any word?" Daniel asked. He was waiting on the stairs. Dark circles intensified the young man's green eyes. Lack of sleep had aged him.

"Yes, Winn will live. It will be some time before he is poking his head around again. He had been following Catera and Jim Mainland, he said. When they disappeared into the mountainside, he fell into the hands of the soldiers. He was lucky the General did not keep him better guarded. The men got him out. He is on his way home."

He shook his head, and sank into a chair. "We should have been better guards of the women. I have been to every part of this town. No one has seen Señora Morelos or Señora Davis." He looked at Daniel. "Or Gena."

"They have to be somewhere in Real."

"I know. And we must find them soon, or it may be too late. From what Winn said, Catera and Mainland are working together, and they are here, somewhere. General Ruiz will give Max to the miners to parade through town, to dangle in front of Catera, hoping to draw him out. He won't care what happens to the boy."

"You do not really think they will release Max back to Jorge and his people, do you? Not after the beating they gave him. It is a miracle he survived."

Only the young, the innocent, can doubt the cruelty of men, Miguel thought. "The act of sacrifice is ancient, mi amigo. Think of Pontius Pilate. The Indians have a great tradition of it. When men have greed or power behind them, sacrifice becomes an accepted ritual. Even today."

"What would the Army gain?"

"Not the Army. General Ruiz. He'll go anything to bring Catera down. And Chief Guterriz. An evil, vain man, Catera. Whatever deal he has made with Jim Mainland, he knows it will not stand. Unless he is rid of Max and his mother. He will let Jorge and his men do his dirty work. He is just here to see it done. I am sure his men are posing as some of the miners, telling them what to do. It was his men that whipped Max." He looked again out the window. "If Ruiz brings Max into the open today, he will be the sacrifice."

From this vantage point, he could see the platform that was now completed. An image of a young man being carried up the stairs to a sacrificial altar burned his eyes. Not that they would see such a gruesome sight. A cleaner, modern lynching would be more likely. He turned away.

"If they would just let me see Max. Talk to him." Miguel sighed. "There must be a way he could convince the people that his mother has not sold the mines to Catera."

A shout came from downstairs.

"*Si!*" Miguel answered, and went to the landing.

"Señor Miguel!" A man stood in the doorway, half-supporting a woman covered with a dirty blanket. In his uplifted hand was a picture of Patricia. One that Miguel had given the people of Carlos Randel.

Miguel's heart pounded, as if a fist squeezed it. He took the steps two at a time. When he reached them, he slipped an arm around the woman and pulled back the blanket. The fist strangled his heart at the sight before him.

"*Gracias Dios!*"

He helped Patricia up the stairs and onto the mat he used for a bed. The man told all he knew. Miguel remembered the old woman in the street. Now he knew what had upset her.

Daniel brought a basin of water and a cloth. Miguel gently washed Patricia's face and her blood encrusted hands.

She cried out in pain as one of her torn fingers caught in the cloth. She tried to sit up, but Miguel pushed her back and said, "Lie still."

"Max?" she asked, biting her lower lip.

"He is safe." It was the truth, for the moment. She gave out a deep breath as if she had held it for days.

"Why were you in the tunnel beneath the church? Where have you been hiding?" He tried to keep his voice tender to match her need, but he wanted to yell at her, to scream outrage at her foolishness. If Daniel and the man were not in the room, he would take her in his arms and kiss away all her pain. He combed her hair with his fingers while she talked.

"We've been in the house above the old church. A man told Rachel and me that he would take me to Max. We went . . . through the tunnel, but Max wasn't there. Jim was. He tried to make me sign some papers. I think the man . . . Catera. I think he must have been there. When I came back, someone had closed the tunnel and, I don't know, maybe tried to cause it to cave-in." She sat up. "Rachel. Gena. They were going to the church. It might collapse."

Miguel would have had to hurt her to make her lie back down. Instead, he cradled her in his arms. "We will send someone for them and make sure it is okay," he said.

Daniel moved closer to her. "Gena? She found you?"

"Yes," Patricia whispered against Miguel's shoulder.

"They will be okay," Daniel said. "Señora Davis has a special power. And Gena, she is smart." He smiled.

Voices filtered through from below the windows. Loud, angry voices. All morning there had been processions of the faithful coming to the church, loud music and singing, but this was different. Miguel nodded. Daniel looked out.

"Miners. Many of them," he reported.

Miguel left Patricia on the mat and joined Daniel.

Men marched up the hill, carrying picks and shovels. Shouting. They cried out, "Morelos. Morelos. *Muerta á* Morelos."

Miguel felt a hand on his shoulder. He turned to look at a portrait of pain. How she stood, he did not know. To his amazement, she straightened her back and set her jaw.

"They will not kill my son," she said.

CHAPTER FORTY-ONE

Miguel turned Patricia toward Daniel. "Keep her here," he ordered, and headed for the door.

"Wait!" She tore loose from Daniel and pulled at Miguel's arm. "I'm going with you."

"No." His dark eyes were like bullets shooting at her, staying her.

"You can't stop me, Miguel. Haven't you learned that?"

His hands went around her upper arms, squeezing the flesh until she cried out.

"You'll have to do worse than that," she said through clenched teeth. "To keep me here."

"Can I reason with you? Will you be so stubborn?" He walked her backward, hands still on her arms. They moved like two stiff forms in a strange dance. He pushed her down into a chair. Knelt in front of her, his hands holding both of hers.

"These men who shout *"Muerta á* Morelos" do not care if it is death to señora or señor. They have heard so many lies, from Catera, Mainland, from Tomas. They have been told lies for so long. They will not believe you. A Morelos. A woman. You go out there, tell them who you are, and you will say no more. No one will listen."

"I can tell them I didn't sign over the mines. If Catera is caught, I can prove I didn't. I will give *them* the mines. They have to believe me." She struggled to free herself, but his eyes bound her to the chair as firmly as the pressure of his hands.

"They *have* to?" he asked.

Tears stung her eyes. She was so tired, so spent. His sarcasm cut her. The dark eyes that had once sparked with love, now bored into her like cold flint. Her drained body, slumped. She was defeated. If Miguel could free Max, nothing else mattered. She lifted her head to him. "That night, in the hacienda, you promised to find my son and bring him out of here. You said you would take care of my son. Have you forgotten?"

"No. I have not." His eyes left hers. He looked at Daniel. She held her breath, frowned at him. He looked back at her. Her stare pleaded. Inhaling deeply, he turned toward the window, then back again to her. She thought a tear glimmered in his eye.

"Max is safe for the moment. And you must stay here. I will try to quiet these people. Then I will go to General Ruiz. He wants Catera. We know now where he is. I will use him to bargain for Max."

She leaned forward as if falling slowly. He caught her head on his shoulder and held her. After a moment, he pushed her back into the chair and went to the window.

"I made a promise to you. I will keep it. And see my brother's son safely out of Real." He turned on a heel and was out the door before she could recover from the blow of his words.

She pulled herself away from the chair as if she had become rooted to it and looked out the window. Miguel was shouting something at the men. Several of them came forward and argued with him. Finally, they turned away and the voices died down. Miguel disappeared up the street. The men were quieter now. Mingling with the festival crowd around the fountain.

"Why do you want to hurt my child?" She cried out, pounding her fist against the wooden frame, welcoming the pain that edged her hand. Daniel grabbed her arm and held it still.

"That will do no good, Señora."

"Then you answer my question," she shot at him. "You've been in on this from the start. You must know why these people want to harm Max."

Daniel flinched at her words. She looked into his eyes and whispered, "I'm sorry. I just need help, please. Someone must have answers. If I knew why this was happening, maybe I would know what I can do."

Daniel looked at her with a compassion that softened his features. "Do you still not know it is because of Tomas Morelos, your husband? It is the hatred built by years of oppression, death, of cave-ins and Tlantoloc, of promises and betrayals."

"But Tomas is dead, why blame him now for this cave-in?"

"Señor Jim Mainland worked with Señor Tomas."

"But—"

"He is still alive. He works with Catera now to get the mines and to build the buildings at Tlantaloc. If Catera owns the mines, more die. The people know their fate at his hands and they rebel."

"But I, I didn't—," she stopped herself. "I should have known. I should have made it my business to find out. She shook her head in disbelief at the betrayal she felt.

"The people of Real de Catorce have always been kind, good." Daniel went on. "Now there is hate. You must not blame them."

"Even if they kill my son?" She stared, daring him to answer. "An eye for an eye. Is that your philosophy, Daniel?"

"No, Señora. But a man who lost his eye does not see the world as he did. He makes mistakes." He shifted his feet and looked out the window.

His words swelled in her mind, crushing all other thoughts. Mistakes. God, she had made so many. Tears fell on her cheeks and she shivered deep inside.

Daniel stood close enough for her to touch him. His presence filled the room as if it had shrunk. She had been so engrossed looking for Max that she had tried to push Daniel from her mind. Logic fought with her. He was just a stranger. A young Mexican who had been caught up in this hated drama of her son's kidnapping. She thought she had accepted the impossible, but could it really be?

Daniel's hand hung by his side, inches from her face. She hunted for familiarity along the lines of his fingers. The nails, curve of the joints, raised veins. She looked down at her own and saw no resemblance. Then she lifted her head and studied his face. The evidence was there. The lines of his cheek, cut of his chin, shape of his nose. They were her father's and hers. She thought of the little silver boy she had placed in the church. Would St. Francis have the last laugh? Give her the miracle of finding the son she didn't know she had, while losing the one she sought?

She stared at the grains in the wood floor as if studying a map of her life. The roads led here. Ended here. These people wanted to end the Morelos line here. They would take their revenge for Tomas's evil deeds out on his son, Miguel had said. So many lies had been told. Jim. Catera. Tomas. But she was the greatest liar of them all. Her eyes followed the elliptical pattern of a tree's growth rings on one of the boards. She began to visualize the tree itself. In its leafy glory of spring. Its shivering skeleton of winter. It was so clear. This tree had good years and bad years. Now they were all laid open for everyone to see.

Like the tree, her own life began to take shape. Her life had no true ring. No one knew her. Not really. She had taken the events that had made up her days and done whatever she wanted. They had been manipulated, changed, forgotten, lied about. She had shrouded her whole being in disguises. Even Max had told her, "I don't know who you are."

How simple it seemed. She would just lay it all out in the open. Then she would be able to save her son.

"Tomas is not Max's father," she said aloud. They were just words, but she doubled over at the pain of voicing them. The saw had made its first cut.

"What did you say?" Daniel asked.

Her eyes met his. She turned away. There were many other cuts to come. But not now.

"Max is not Tomas's child." She tried this different way of saying it. She felt no additional hurt.

Daniel moved closer to her. A frown drew his brows together. "Is this true?"

Would she be doubted even when she told the truth?

"Who is his father?" Daniel asked.

One name. One more word. This secret out in the open would call for all others. She felt no fear, only hope. She would face the consequences of her actions and her father's. It was the only way. As determined as she was, she could barely breathe the name.

"Miguel," she whispered.

"Miguel is the father of Max?" Daniel whirled around as if propelled by the force of his statement. "Yes." He hit a fist into his palm. "It is true. Max is like him. His hair and eyes, and chin." He scratched his head as if trying to think of other similarities.

"You've seen him?" Patricia was on her feet, pulling at Daniel's arm. "When? Was he hurt? Why didn't you tell me?" She struck his arm with her fist. He turned and held her hands.

"*Mi Dios!*" he exclaimed. "Miguel does not know this! He has never seen Max. Never seen the mirror of his face. This is why you wanted to find him, so Miguel would not see him. But why? Why keep him from his son?"

She pulled free of his grasp. Turned her back. She was not willing to say more. Not until she talked to Miguel. The gravity of the plan she had put in motion began to pull her down.

"We must tell them, Señora. I did see Max. Yesterday, they let me. He is okay. I promise. There are only a few men who want to harm him. The others will listen to them. You must tell the leaders." He started for the door.

"Wait!" She turned away when he stopped. "I want—."

"What? Why do you wait?" In the dark rims of his green eyes she saw her father and trembled.

"You don't understand," she almost shouted. She could not say his name. She could not think of Daniel. It was more than her heart could take. She sobbed once from her depths.

"*Verdad*! I do not. Do you want to save Max or not? The decision is yours, Señora," Daniel spoke calmly.

She looked out toward the church trying to compose herself. Suddenly there was movement in the crowd. Arms raised, pointed toward the street above the church. The commotion drew Daniel to join her at the window. Patricia had no idea what was happening, but her heart swelled in her chest.

Several blue-coated men hurried down the steps of the Palacio Municipal. They held their arms high and confronted the first men leading about fifty or sixty others down the hill. A cloud of dust floated above them. Voices filled the air. Men from the back of the group came around the flanks and mingled with those near the fountain.

A skirmish broke out. The blue coats, evidently policeman, were pushed aside. Two of them ran back into the building. For reinforcements? Weapons? The crowd drew together, like a spring wound tighter and tighter. Their attention was drawn to something in their midst. Three men struggled. A fight? No. Two were holding one. He struggled. They thrust him forward. He was taller than the others. His feet dragged the ground as they lifted him by his arms, carried him toward the platform. His black hair flopped across his forehead. A red cloth hid his dark eyes.

A keening came from Patricia before she knew what she was seeing. She placed her palms against the dusty window pane. The glass reverberated with the force of her cry. She screamed Max's name loud enough for the men to hear, but no one looked her way. It was as if she were watching a movie.

The door opened with a jerk. "Come," Miguel motioned for Daniel. "You stay," he pointed at her.

Daniel's eyes met hers. His mouth opened just slightly, as if wanting to say something. Her head ached with the echo of her scream. No time to think, to consider. Her mind was fixed on the scene out the window. Still looking at Daniel, she spoke. "I have to go with you, Miguel. What I can say to them will save Max's life."

CHAPTER FORTY-TWO

Miguel stared at Patricia. She was calm, determined. He had no time to deal with her. He had reached General Ruiz too late. The boy had been turned over to Jorge Morelos and his miners. The General had made a show of standing up to them, at least he said he had, but since his main interest was in apprehending Catera, it was to his advantage to let the miners create a diversion. Max Morelos was only a pawn in the game.

The best Miguel was able to get from Ruiz was a promise to come to their aid in return for the whereabouts of Catera and Mainland, but only after he had arrested them. Miguel had shown Jorge the illegal document that Mainland had drawn with Catera, but Jorge would not listen. The paper only angered the miners more. He hoped Daniel could help convince them.

"You can not go, Patricia. I have said all you could say. These men are not interested in anything but letting the blood of Tomas Morelos fertilize their soil. And they are trying to bend that mob to their desire. Daniel knows some of the men. Maybe they will listen if he is with me." He grabbed at Daniel, but she stood between them.

"Daniel will agree, Miguel." Her voice was a calm in the storm.

"*¿Que dice la Señora*, Daniel?" He asked, even though it did not matter what she would say.

"*Ella salvará a su hijo. Créala. Es la única manera.*"

Miguel fought with logic and fear. Daniel would not interfere unless he knew something. But how could he know Patricia would be able to save her son? Why believe her or him? The moment was desperate. The police were too few. They had sent for more. God help them, but it may be too late. If he could talk to the crowd, there may be enough who knew him and Daniel to listen to reason, even if their leaders would not. Perhaps it was only fair to let Patricia do whatever she could. It was the life of her son at stake. His heart melted with the agony in her eyes. He grabbed her and pulled her into his arms. "Are you sure? I do not know what they will do when they learn who you are."

"I'm sure." Her lips quivered.

He crushed his mouth against hers for a moment, then took her hand and pulled her down the hall. They had to shove and push to make way through the growing crowd. Patricia stumbled on the cobblestones and Miguel held her close to keep her upright.

As they reached the fountain, Miguel looked up to see a young man on the wooden platform in the plaza. He was blindfolded and gagged with his hands tied behind his back, his shirt torn and bloody. He was standing to one side of the raised structure, guards at his elbows. One of the men had a rope in his hands. Miguel didn't have the heart to look at Patricia to see her reaction. He pushed on to the edge of the steps.

A policeman caught up with him and yelled that help was on its way. Miguel was not sure who or what he meant. It did not matter. By the time reinforcements of any kind made it through this crowd, it would be too late. It was up to him.

A chant came from the people, filling the streets. "¡*Justica*! ¡*Justica*!" They stabbed their fists into the air. A shudder went through Patricia to Miguel's arm where he embraced her. A man in black pants and shirt and what seemed silver paint on his face shouted in Spanish from the platform and forced the boy toward the crowd. His head dropped as if in shame. He looked small, childlike, despite his height.

The son of Tomas, Miguel thought. His teeth clamped hard, his jaw ached with the pressure. The hatred he had once felt for Tomas had no place here. This boy belonged to Patricia. He would do this for her. As he watched this child that should have been his, his heart cracked.

The man was listing the injustices the people of Real de Catorce had suffered. According to him, Tomas was the cause of everything from babies born deformed to silver veins playing out. The crowd captured phrases of his speech and chanted them back to him. Someone handed him a bullhorn, and he pranced the stage like a Mayan warrior clutching the head of his victim.

Miguel was glad Patricia did not understand what the man said. She trembled anyway at the sound of his demanding cries and the echoes that rippled around them. He could not let them know who she was.

When the moment seemed right, Miguel shoved Patricia back and ran for the stairs. The crowd moved in around her, preventing her from following him. He bounded up the steps, taking the man by surprise, relieving him of the bullhorn.

A cry went up of "Ramirez! Ramirez!"

Patricia's blood rushed through her body like air-thinned water. Her heart pounded to keep up with the flow of people. She struggled against the press of bright shawls and armpits, as fists struck at the sky. When Miguel pushed her away, she had been swallowed by the crowd, like a tiny raindrop sucked into a puddle. She kicked and elbowed her way back toward the platform. Prying her body out of the mass, she gained the bottom step.

She could see over the heads of the people now. They were shouting "Ramirez!" and clapping. They were happy to see Miguel. Why? Suddenly there was no blood, only air in her veins and she was collapsing.

He was one of them, she thought. They were glad to see him because he was their ally. Had she not known that earlier with all his efforts to keep her away? She couldn't think, couldn't make out his words. An arm came around her and she felt herself eased to the steps. She raised her head and saw Daniel. Behind him was Gena. And Rachel.

Patricia began to cry. Through her tears she saw several policemen making their way through the crowd. They were coming to help Miguel. To keep her away. To kill Max. They were not even trying to arrest these people. She looked back at Daniel and he was smiling at her. God! He was against her, too. She turned and stumbled up the steps.

She barely glanced at Max before grabbing the bullhorn from Miguel. Let them kill her. She didn't care. Maybe that would satisfy them and Max would be allowed to go.

"Wait!" she shouted and clawed through her brain for Spanish words she knew. "*¡Espara! ¡Espara!*" she yelled into the mouthpiece. Her fist beat against her chest. "I am Señora Morelos! ¡*Soy es Señora* Morelos! ¡*Espousa* Tomas Morelos!"

Miguel's hand tightened on her shoulder. "What are you doing?" he shouted.

"Saving our son!" she cried out, her voice breaking. Her knees almost buckled with the words. And, the look on Miguel's face. She caught a glimpse of Max struggling against the men who held him. He moaned "Mother" around the gag in his mouth.

The crowd began to hush, as if a magic fog rolled down the valley muffling their speech and paralyzing their movement. Someone near the platform pointed to the stairs. Daniel was helping Rachel up the last step. Rachel waved her arms out as she came across the platform. No one would doubt her blindness. "No!" Patricia cried out. "She'll get hurt."

Rachel reached out for Patricia, catching her arm. "And you might tell them to go jump in a mine with your terrible Spanish. Now what were you saying?" She ran her hand down Patricia's arm until she felt the bullhorn. Taking it gently, she raised it to her mouth and told the people her name was Rachel. She was a friend of the Señora and would translate the Señora's words.

The appearance of the blind woman mesmerized the crowd. People looked to each other, but only a few voices were heard. Some were crossing themselves.

Miguel stepped close to Patricia, but Daniel held his arm. "No. Let her speak." When Miguel backed away, Daniel turned to Patricia and smiled. She knew she had wronged him again.

As Patricia spoke loud and clear, Rachel translated every word into Spanish. The people looked at whichever one was speaking, as if they needed to hear the strange story twice.

"I am sorry for your problems," Patricia said. "Very sorry. But my son Max is not responsible. I know Tomas Morelos was a bad man and did much harm to you." A single shout cried out in agreement. Tears trickled down her face. She went on quickly before they recovered from their shock and carried out their plans. "And I know you want revenge on him or his son. But Tomas Morelos is not the father of Max!"

Murmurs came from pockets in the crowd. Someone cried out "*¿Quien es el padre?*"

Patricia looked at Max. Her fingers ached to touch his face, her arms to hold him. "Forgive me, son," she whispered. She looked at Miguel and said his name, then turned back to the people.

"Miguel Ramirez is the father of my son Max!" she said in an even tone, then dropped her head, stiffened her legs. "God give me strength," she prayed.

Enough people in the crowd knew English that a general buzz almost drowned out Rachel's translation. Then everyone talked.

Max had struggled with his guards until he had maneuvered all three of them to within a few feet of Patricia. Miguel stepped between them and reached toward Max. The guards, miners that knew Miguel, seemed not to know what to do anymore. They made no move to stop him when he pulled away Max's blindfold.

Max squinted and shook his head in the bright light. His black hair scattering across his forehead. Miguel again reached out and with both hands behind the boy's head, untied the strip of cloth that had bound his mouth.

Cold stare met cold stare.

The resemblance between them was overwhelming evidence for the crowd. Someone jeered at Miguel that his brother had stolen his son. Miguel turned to Patricia. She saw the hurt in his eyes and, hate, she thought.

Suddenly, he reached behind Max, pushing away the two men who guarded him. He took a knife from his pocket and cut the bonds. His hand on the young man's shoulder, he steered him to face the crowd.

"*¡San. Francis me ha dado un milagro! ¡El me ha dado un hijo!*"

Some people shouted. Others laughed. The few jeers that were yelled went ignored.

Miguel turned to Max. "I hope you are not ashamed to call me your father. When we have time to know each other."

Patricia stood apart from the two, waiting to be cursed by her son and by Miguel. Suddenly, there were shouts. A fight had broken out on the fringe of the crowd. She saw Daniel hurrying toward her only seconds before the sun glinted off the rifle barrel.

People screamed, scattered, ran. On the platform everything seemed to move in silent, slow motion. Daniel pushed against Max. Max stumbled, but was righted by Miguel. Then Daniel leaped in front of Max to push him again.

The air cracked. Daniel's back bowed like an acrobat. He folded and fell on top of Max.

Patricia clasped her hands to her face and screamed. Miguel was saying something to her, but the only thing she heard was a sound tearing through her throat and ripping at her fingers.

Miguel felt a hand on his shoulder. Carmina. He stood and let her through, then watched as she and Patricia bent face to face over Daniel.

The crowd was crazy. He looked out over the pandemonium to see if he could spot the one with the rifle. He saw some of his men moving cautiously along the street that led up the hill. He was sure the man who shot Daniel worked for Catera. No doubt he would be escaping to the house above the old church. He looked back at the crowd around Daniel. There was nothing he could do.

He signaled some other men at the police station and they worked their way up back streets trying to intercept the fugitive. They caught up with other men at *Puente de Jesus,* the bridge across from the old church.

"He has gone through the graves and escaped." One man reported.

"There is a house on the other side of that wall," Miguel told them. He directed some of the men to go up through the cemetery, and led another group himself farther along the road to a hill above the house. As they neared the upper walls, a barrage of gunfire filled the air. Then a loud roar.

"Helicopter," Miguel said, and threw himself over the wall.

General Ruiz and some of his men were pouring out of the house, headed toward the helipad. Whoever they were chasing, probably Catera, had beat them there.

The blades created a dust storm as the machine came off the ground. It made a half-turn and hesitated. Something dropped out of it, then it lifted into the air. A figure rose from the ground and began running. Someone had either jumped or been pushed out.

Miguel and several others set out in a chase. General Ruiz and his men were gathered on the bridge, shooting at the helicopter. Ruiz was stomping his feet and cussing. Catera had gotten away.

Miguel and his men fanned out around the house and church, but the man Catera had ditched had alluded them. Then Miguel remembered the tunnel Patricia had come through.

He opened the door of the church cautiously. No one was there. The stairway and the room below were empty. He peered into the black hole and thought he heard a noise.

Moving as quietly as possible, almost bent double he made his way through the dark. A scraping sound filtered through the heavy air. When he seemed on top of the sound, he lit a match.

Jim Mainland was on his knees shoveling dirt with his hands.

"You have some answering to do, Mainland. Come back out with me. This tunnel is not safe."

Jim whirled and threw a clod of dirt in Miguel's face. The match fell as Miguel covered his eyes. Before he could try to clear them, Mainland tackled him. They tumbled and rolled in the narrow space, throwing punches and kicking indiscriminately. They were equally blind in the dark, but Miguel's eyes hurt like hell. Memories of the earthquake made him want to forget Mainland and get above ground as quickly as possible.

He threw a hard punch that connected with some part of Jim. Then, with all his strength he crawled on all fours in the direction he hoped would lead back to the church. He thought he felt a vibration in the ground.

Suddenly, Jim knocked him down and tried to climb over him. Miguel grabbed for his leg and Jim plunged to the floor of the tunnel with a crash. Before Miguel could get back on his feet, a loud crack sounded all around him. Dirt and rocks followed.

Miguel was not sure where he was. He just knew he was blind and covered with something heavy. Then he remembered. It took some time, but he struggled until his right hand was free. He felt above his face and realized he had a space between his head and a wooden beam. He was afraid to move.

"Mainland," he whispered. There was no answer.

He worked his other hand free and began to push his way out of the debris that covered his legs. He seemed to be at the edge of the cave-in. The other man may have gotten out. As he inched his way out of his partial grave he heard a groan.

"Mainland?" he called.

Another sound.

Miguel clawed through the dirt he could not see. He found a beam and when he shifted it, a cry of pain pierced the dark. By patting around the surfaces, he found Jim's head and his right shoulder. It was the only part of him not covered. Miguel dug until he had freed Jim to the waist. Another beam rested against his hips. Miguel could not move it.

"Stay still. I will go for help," he said softly.

"Wait." Jim's voice was weak. "Don't . . . I don't think I'll make it."

"You will if I get help."

"No. Tell Patr—" He coughed and cried out in pain. A gurgling sound came from his chest. "Tell her I'm sorry. About Max."

"Max is okay."

"No. Sorry about me . . . taking Max."

"What do you mean?" Miguel cradled the wounded man's head.

"Needed the mines . . . money. If I could—," he coughed and gagged.

Miguel thought for a minute that he was unconscious. "You are not making sense, Mainland. Stop trying to talk."

Jim's hand found Miguel's chest, and he held onto his shirt. "Don't want her to know my part. Just I'm sorry. Don't want to hurt her."

Miguel thought he understood. Whatever Mainland had done, it would not do Patricia any good to know. "Well, at least we agree on one thing. Patricia has had enough pain. She does not need more."

He thought of Daniel and his anger rose. "Now I am going for help. Do not try to move." He was not sure Jim heard him.

He crawled for several minutes before he felt another vibration coming through his hands. A cloud of dust rushed up behind him as he sprinted toward the opening.

CHAPTER FORTY THREE

The hotel room was sparsely furnished. A single bed covered with colorful striped blankets. A table and lamp. A picture of Madonna and child on the wall. A straight backed chair beneath the window.

Patricia sat on the hard seat, holding back dusty gauze curtains and staring out at the stars. She had bathed and changed into a clean skirt and blouse. They were on the bed when she came to the room.

She had watched the shadows of the sunset creep along the mountain peaks until they disappeared. The night breeze was cool, but she didn't feel it.

Sounds of revelry had filled the air for hours. The festival had begun in earnest once the tension broke after the shooting. Then, it was almost as if all the pent-up hatred and problems of this little town were blasted away in the fireworks that lit up the sky. Now there was silence.

She waited for someone. Who would be first to come and condemn her?

Max? She had held him for only a moment before he jerked free of her and disappeared. Later, she had seen him with Rachel, walking away, talking. She had been told about the beating he had suffered, but the doctor had said he was a brave young man and would be fine.

Miguel? He wasn't there when they carried Daniel away. She'd probably never see him again.

Daniel had been brought here. To a hotel across from the church. She didn't know if he was alive. They wouldn't let her in to see him. So she had come to the room they said was hers to wait.

Her self-exile seemed endless, but they all needed time, especially Max. She could not bring herself to seek him out, but prayed that he would come to her. She didn't care if he came to bombard her with questions. Or came only to stare at her in disbelief. Or to curse her. She needed to know that he felt something, even if it was hate. That she could work against. She could ask forgiveness. Ignoring her, he gave no hope.

Rachel would come. But first she would work to heal everyone's wounds in her own way.

Of course, there was still one more cut of the saw. One more admission of sin. If Daniel lived, what would she tell him? She had told no one else. Rachel was the only one who knew. She would never have the chance to tell Miguel, but that didn't matter.

The door creaked and she jumped from her chair. The room was dark and a figure was outlined by the light in the hall.

"Max?"

"I guess in this light, you might mistake us." Miguel moved toward the lamp beside the bed and clicked it on.

She turned back to the window, not wanting to look at him. The memory of the hurt on his face when she told him about Max made her muscles harden, as if waiting for a blow.

He sat on the narrow bed. Springs squeaked under his weight. A scent of dust floated on the air.

She could not bear the silence.

"Daniel?" Her voiced quivered. She hugged herself against a sudden chill and sat back down on the little chair.

"The doctor is with him. He must remove the bullet before Daniel is moved. It did not come through his body and may be near his heart. There is a surgeon in Cedral. At the clinic. He is coming. We can only wait."

"Is Daniel awake?"

"He was conscious, I was told, when they brought him in, but he is not now."

She stared at the stars, wishing Miguel would leave. There was nothing more she wanted to hear.

"Patricia, I have to tell you something."

She was silent.

"Jim Mainland is dead."

She jumped. "Jim? Dead? How? What happened?" She turned in shock to face him and only saw his silhouette against the lamplight like some shadowy messenger of bad news.

"A cave-in. In the tunnel under the church. He, he asked me to tell you he was sorry."

"Sorry?"

"For not being able to find Max, I think."

She wiped tears away from her cheeks and chin. Clearing her throat, she said, "Thank you for telling me."

"Patricia, I . . ."

"I'm okay. Really. Please, go." She went to the door and held her hand on the knob. He turned to face her and the light showed her his face clearly for the first time. "My God, Miguel, what happened?" Her hands covered her own face. She wanted to reach out to his, but she wouldn't know where to touch him and not reopen a cut or disturb a bandage.

"I was in the tunnel with Mainland. I tried to get him out, but a beam had caught him. When I went for help, there was another cave-in."

"You, you're okay?" she whispered.

Neither of them moved or spoke. Silence seemed to suck the air out of the room, the walls collapsing in the vacuum.

"Why, Patricia?" Miguel spoke and the room breathed.

She returned to the window, held the curtain back and studied the dim outline of the bell tower against the night sky. She had known the question was coming. An answer seemed as impossible to reach as the stars.

"Why did you not tell me about Max? About my son?"

"I was going to, that night at the hacienda," she whispered. The words were her only defense. They were not enough, and he waited for more.

"I was afraid," she said.

"Of what?"

She turned to him, her vision blurred by tears. It was as if she were talking to herself. "I was afraid that—I didn't want you to hate me because of Max. Because you didn't have your son."

He covered the short distance to where she stood in one stride. His hand clasped hers that held the curtain with enough force to rattle the window. "I would NOT have hated you."

She nodded, but it didn't matter now. "I'm sorry. I should have told you that night," she said calmly. His face was inches away. Even with the bandages and cuts, the lamplight honed his features into sharp angles and planes. He looked hard.

"No. You should not have told me then. You should have told me eighteen years ago!"

She pulled free from his grasp and walked as far away as the little room allowed. Not to escape. No. There was no reason to. She felt at peace, as if a balm flowed over her. Maybe that's what happens, she thought, when one cuts deep enough. Her voice was distant, as if coming from far away. "That last night we were together in Virginia. We had a fight. When I left from where we met at Rock Creek Park, I knew you were going back to Mexico and I'd never see you again. I didn't make it home. I—"

"I know," he interrupted. "I waited for you until early morning. To say goodbye. I thought you stayed away because you did not want to see me, so I left."

She shut her eyes and shook her head. "I drove away, crying. I didn't see a truck that had stalled on the road. I swerved to miss it. And went down an embankment. It was the next afternoon before someone spotted the car. I, I was in the hospital for a while."

She heard him take in a deep breath, but she kept talking, afraid to stop now that she had begun. "Later, Tomas told me you had gone back to Mexico. He said you had died in the student riots before the Olympics. He was there when the doctor told me I was pregnant. He offered to marry me. Give my child his name, his home. For all his sins, I can truly say he treated Max as his own."

The window sash dropped like a guillotine. Miguel slammed his palm against the frame a second time. "Bastard! He knew I was in prison. He could have had me released. I spent three years in that hell, hating him. And you." He kept his back to her.

She sat down on the bed and crossed her breasts with her arms as if holding in the sadness that filled her. Over the years after she had learned Miguel was alive, she hadn't considered that he had suffered, too.

She cried for everybody she knew. Loud, suffering wails. They had all been wronged. Life wasn't just unfair, it was mean. And she had deserved the worst of it.

Her breath was crushed out of her. She didn't know for a moment that it was Miguel's arms holding hers tightly to her chest.

"Damn Tomas, and Jim, and my father. And me!" She sobbed against his shoulder. "I've messed everything up. Everything." Her body heaved. When she had quieted down to hiccups, Miguel kissed her forehead.

"I do not ever want to hear you say that again. Not as long as we live. Understand?" He drew away from her and held his hands to her cheeks, smoothing tears away with his thumbs. He scanned her face, as if reading every curve, every line. "*Te amo, cariña.* Perhaps I have loved you without ceasing. How else could my heart still know how to beat?"

"Can you ever forgive me?"

"Only if I know I am forgiven," he smiled. His eyes twinkled in the lamplight.

"And Max? Will he forgive either of us?"

"Yes. Max will be fine. Your *amiga* Rachel has been talking to him. You must have her do your negotiations for you always. She could tell the miners that rocks have *cervaza,* and they would attack the mountain with their pick in one hand and a glass in the other."

Her laugh caught on one forgotten sob. "She has always tried to get me to let my secrets go."

"This Rachel is a very intelligent woman," he smiled.

"But what will I be without them? They've always held me together."

"They do not hold you together. They hold others out."

She barely heard the knock. While she wiped her face, Miguel opened the door.

A young boy stood in the hallway. "*El doctor de Cedral es aqui,* Señor."

"Come," Miguel said to her. "The doctor is here. We will hear about Daniel."

They went down a flight of stairs half-blocked with flower pots and crossed a patio to a ground floor room. Outside stood a man with a stethoscope around his neck. A woman in white marked with blotches of blood stood in the doorway.

Miguel knew them both. They talked in low tones, then he turned to Patricia. "Dr. Cabrera has removed the bullet."

"Is Daniel going to be okay?" Patricia held her breath.

"San. Francis smiles on him," Dr. Cabrera said, nodding.

"Can I see him?" she asked. She had no idea what she would say to Daniel, except to thank him. That was a beginning. She knew that was one more thing she had not told Miguel, but Daniel's true identity was not just her secret to share.

Two bright lamps that had obviously served as operating lights were dimmed now by red cloths drooped over their shades. The eerie glow cast a bloody shadow across Daniel's still form.

Patricia touched his hand. His eyes opened. He looked at her, then past her. His lips quivered in a half-smile. She turned to face Rachel and Max who had come in behind her. She ached to go to her young son and cradle him, but Max was watching Daniel as if she were not there. Carmina stood on the other side of the bed, in the shadows.

Daniel's hand moved beneath Patricia's. Their eyes met. She studied his face. Not looking for her father's image, but learning the features that she knew she loved and always would. "How can I ever thank you," she whispered.

"Max has." He was weak and his voice trembled. His eyes found Carmina and she took a step forward and placed a hand on his shoulder.

He turned back to Patricia. "You must thank San. Francis."

"Yes, he is a miracle worker," she whispered.

His hand gripped hers. She felt the sharp cold press of metal against her skin and looked down. In his palm lay a little silver boy, a *milagro*.

"Give this to San. Francis," he said.

She hesitated, then drew her finger across the tiny amulet. "I left one in the church. And he did give me back my son." She smiled at Max, then looked back at Daniel.

He raised his hand and dropped the silver piece in her palm. "You owe him one more."

EPILOGUE

Six Weeks Later

A rose-spiced breeze blew cool across a hammock outside an adobe house in Cuernavaca. The ropes tying the woven net to concrete pillars groaned in protest. Miguel pushed his toes against the terrazo floor and launched himself into a high arc. His dark hair blew back and forth. He had just been swimming and the air cooled his wet bathing suit and bare chest.

"Mind if I join you?" Patricia slipped off her sandals and worked her way into the narrow space beside him. Her white shorts and tank top showed off the beginnings of a Mexican tan. It was cooler in Cuernavaca than it was in Acapulco or Mexico City. So here, at least, she could wear her hair down and not be miserable. As she settled onto Miguel's arm, he twirled his fingers through the long, dark strands.

"Guess we need a matrimonial size hammock now," he said and kissed the top of her head.

She made a soft sound of agreement.

"Where were you?" he asked.

"More telephone conferences. The agreement with the miners is ready to sign. The corporation we set up to pay for the safety measures and to start the handover is operational. They want us to come to Real for a celebration, but that might be hard to do."

"Why?"

"Memories."

"You do not have to give up the mines, you know." He tightened his arm around her.

"Oh yes, it is the right thing to do."

It had taken weeks to come up with a workable plan to give the town of Real de Catorce the mines. With no money to operate them,

Patricia had to go one step farther to make it all work. She had to come up with the funding herself. Morelos Enterprises employed too many people to shut it down or bankrupt it, so prudent measures had to be mixed with righting the wrongs.

More important to her than giving up the mines was taking on the Morelos construction project in Tlantaloc. Catera was out of the picture. His helicopter had crashed just miles from Real. The shots General Ruiz fired had hit their mark. Miguel's friend, the Secretary of Commerce, had finally spoken out publicly against Catera and was working to get rid of the Chief of Police and some of the other corrupt officials. In a time of the devalued peso, the government was trying hard to boost the economy, and Morelos Construction was being hailed as a godsend.

Things were slowly beginning to happen. Some of the pepenadores were moving back to Real to help in the mines. The garbage dumps would be moved to a site farther away from the city and low cost housing would be built in Tlantoloc. Miguel was taking charge, and Patricia felt nothing but relief.

Morelos Enterprises still demanded more of her than she wanted to give, so she had made Marco Cortina the new Director of Operations. When her thoughts went to Jim, she felt sad. Somehow she feared that the debt he was in and the secrecy of the Tlantoloc project went hand-in-hand with Max's kidnapping. Whatever Jim's responsibility, she knew he had tried to save Max at the end and had paid the ultimate price for his betrayal. She couldn't be angry at him. What good would it do?

Patricia shifted to find a more comfortable place at Miguel's side. "Where do you buy a matrimonial size hammock?" she asked.

"They are made in the Yucatan. Good place to go for a honeymoon," he smiled.

She leaned back and studied his face. His dark eyes danced. "Are you sure?"

"Just try to change my mind," he whispered, and kissed her so hard she thought she would melt through the spaces in the netting. Reluctantly, he released her at the sound of voices and laughter drifting over them.

Max was the loudest, splashes of water punctuating his voice. Gena squealed and screamed something in Spanish. Daniel, a calm voice in the mix, refereed. He still wasn't well enough to join the others in the pool, but he was doing much better than the doctors had predicted.

"You have made things right with Daniel, no?" Miguel asked.

Patricia thought for a moment of the long talks she and her son had had. "I don't know that things will ever be *right*. How do I make up for all the lost years? But, he is a forgiving person. He's trying to understand. That's enough for me now. More than I could ask of him."

"Carmina was a good mother to him. She still has his heart. That is good."

"I could never blame her. Oh, I guess I did at first, but I was just trying to absolve myself of guilt. She will always be his mother."

"In a way, yes, but he has a new family now." Miguel shifted and turned Patricia to face him. The hammock slowed, but neither seemed to notice. "Max seems happy."

"I had a harder time with him than with Daniel. Hard-headed teenager. But, he loves Daniel. Saving his life got them off to a good start. And, now Max feels more secure with who he is, now that he knows where his liberal views come from."

"It'll take me awhile to work Tomas's influence completely out of my son, but he shows promise. I think he is even a little proud of his scars," he smiled and pulled Patricia to his side once more.

After a few minutes of silence, Patricia added, "Of course, Rachel helped me with both of them. She called today, fussing about Annie's friends wanting her to tell 'the story' over again. Of course, Rachel's loving it." She sighed. "I miss her."

"We all do," Miguel said. "Is she coming for a visit?"

"Only if we take her places to wear all the new clothes she's bought," she laughed and settled deeper into Miguel's arms.

He smiled and held her tight.

"And what about you. Are you happy, *mi cariña?*"

"Oh, just about," she said slowly.

He raised up on his elbow and stared at her, a frown furrowing his brow. "Something is wrong?" he asked.

"Yes. Come on. I'll show you," she said, slipping out of the hammock. She took him by the hand and led him through the cool house to a back room, Miguel's bedroom. Beautifully decorated, thanks to Carmina, with fine hand carved mahogany furniture. Chests, a desk, a dresser. And twin beds.

Patricia stood in the doorway, arms folded and nodded toward them. "Do they have matrimonial beds in Yucatan?"

BVG